THE LAST QUINN STANDING

THE LAST QUINN STANDING

THE QUINN SAGA

THOMAS E. SIMMONS

OPEN ROAD

INTEGRATED MEDIA

NEW YORK

Copyright © 2016 by Thomas E. Simmons

ISBN: 978-1-5040-7929-7

This edition published in 2022 by Open Road Integrated Media, Inc.
180 Maiden Lane
New York, NY 10038
www.openroadmedia.com

THE LAST QUINN STANDING

CHAPTER ONE

At 2:10 on the bright clear afternoon of May 7, 1915, twelve miles off Old Head of Kinsale on the southern coast of Ireland, the fastest ocean liner afloat was dancing across the sparkling sea at twenty-two knots when, with no warning, a single torpedo struck her to starboard just forward of the bridge. The torpedo, followed by a mysterious internal explosion, opened her to the sea. Driven bow-down by 76,000 horsepower turning four screws, Cunard Lines RMS *Lusitania* disappeared into the shimmering waters of the Irish Channel in just eighteen horrifying minutes. Of her forty-eight lifeboats, only six could be seen bobbing on a lonely sea strewn with debris amongst floundering survivors clinging to floating bits of wreckage, empty life jackets freed from deck lockers and bodies floating face down. Of the 1,959 passengers and crew aboard, 1,201 souls were lost.

It was 8:10 that night before the trawler *Stormcock* arrived with the first survivors to reach Queenstown, County Cork, Ireland. She was followed by *Brock, Indian Empire, Flying Fish* and other trawlers bringing in survivors and bodies all through the night and into the morning. One of the last to dock, *Bluebell*, had found the ship's captain, William Turner, with several survivors he had shepherded to the inverted floating wreckage of a splintered lifeboat. All told, only 764 persons were rescued.

Of the 1,201 passengers and crew lost in the sinking, just 154 bodies were fished from the sea. As they arrived at the docks, they were taken by truck and wagon to temporary morgues set up in the Cunard Lines sheds and at Queenstown City Hall. Photographs of the faces of the dead were taken for use later in identifying the bodies. Because the embalming process was not practiced by locals in Queenstown, caskets were immediately needed. Carpenters in Queenstown and Cork could not make enough so coffins were rushed in by train from Kildare and Dublin.

Within an hour of the sinking, the news was confirmed by Admiralty headquarters in London. Not until early evening was a report of the sinking relayed from Maritime Nationale (French Navy headquarters) to the intelligence section at the French War Ministry in Paris where American Lieutenant Ansel Quinn was assigned as a neutral observer. As a result of the delay, Quinn did not learn of the ship's loss until he read of it in the evening newspaper. There was, at the time, no word on survivors.

Three weeks before, Ansel had received a cablegram from Bethany telling him that she would be sailing from New York aboard *Lusitania* to finish "*the last of the old Quinn business*" at the Liverpool docks, and planned to cross the channel and visit him in Paris. "*See if you can't arrange a few days leave. Business was just the excuse I needed for the trip. I can't wait to see you and Paris again. What fun we will have despite the new wretched war. Europeans must be mad to engage in another war. I pray America will stay out of this one. We Americans don't understand it, can't afford it and don't want our boys, you included, involved in the fighting.*"

French Army Headquarters as well as Major Crosby, Ansel Quinn's direct commander and the military attaché at the American Embassy, were very understanding. He was granted immediate emergency leave. French Headquarters even arranged cross-channel transport via a dawn courier flight aboard a Voisin type 5 airplane. It was the first time Ansel had flown, but he was too troubled to be either frightened or exhilarated by the experience. His mind was on Bethany.

After landing at Royal Flying Corps Southend Airfield near London, Ansel crossed England and Wales by train to the port at Milford Haven. From there he traveled by special boat to Wexford, Ireland with other anxious friends and relatives of *Lusitania's* passengers and crew, and then by train to Queenstown, arriving the evening of May 8th.

Late in the afternoon of May 10th, Lieutenant Ansel Quinn fell in amongst thousands of grieving mourners, curious onlookers, military and public officials, and an army of reporters to attend the mass burial of *Lusitania's* victims. The funeral procession composed of carriages, motorcars and foot traffic wound its way slowly along the serpentine road to the Old Church Cemetery situated two miles from town. Ansel stood out in the crowd as a rarity, a soldier in the uniform of neutral America.

Upon arrival, the funeral cortege filed four abreast through an ancient stone gateway stained by 200 years of accumulated grime. The sad, the shocked and the curious filed past cedar and fir trees, ancient tombstones, statuary and tall Celtic crosses silently announcing their age with downy coats of greenish moss or black mold. The only sound was the marchers' footfalls crunching in the graveled path. The crowd's destination was marked by huge mounds of dirt piled beside two large, rectangular excavations hurriedly and laboriously dug by soldiers from the Connaught Rangers and the Royal Dublin Fusiliers. One hundred coffins, placed in twenty rows, five abreast, lay in the larger mass grave. In the lesser trench, fifty-four coffins lay in similar order. Each black-painted coffin was marked with a white number. In addition, the coffins which contained the bodies of victims that had been identified had their names painted on the lids.

The 154 bodies laid to rest at Old Church Cemetery were the total that had been recovered in three days of searching by a fleet of fishing boats. (In the following weeks a small number of other remains would wash ashore as far west as the Aran Islands at the mouth of Galway Bay, and as far east as Barry, Wales, all deteriorated beyond recognition.)

Ansel did not join the long line of mourners filing past the coffin-filled pits. He knew she was not there. He had searched the lists of survivors and spent two horribly grim days and nights apprehensively searching the temporary morgues hastily set up in Queenstown. He insisted on examining the face of every female corpse, even those that had already been placed in crude, hastily made wooden coffins. He pored over the gruesome photographs of the dead. At the docks he met the boat that brought in the last body recovered from the sea.

Ansel did not hear the somber words spoken by half a dozen clergy in turn during the long ceremony. An agonizing sense of guilt increased the burden of grief that closed around him like a shroud. His beautiful Aunt Bethany, who had always been like a second mother to him, had died crossing the Atlantic for the sole purpose of visiting him. She had begged him to leave the army to help her manage the Quinn land in Mississippi and Cuba. He always told her there would be time enough for that. He had been wrong.

As he turned to leave, he thought of another mourner who carried the most unbearable burden of all, a mourner criticized by some for surviving. Ansel had been brought up in the household of a sea captain and knew the responsibility his father, Captain Jonathan Quinn, always felt for ship and crew. He asked a Cunard representative at grave-side to point out *Lusitania*'s captain.

Wearing a dark suit and holding a bowler hat in his hands, Captain Turner stood apart from the crowd, his eyes moist, his once proud shoulders bent. Ansel introduced himself. "My father was a sea captain, sir. I know you carry a deep sorrow."

"Quinn? There was a lovely lady named Quinn in First Class, a lovely lady. Was she your mother?" he asked timidly.

"She was my aunt," Ansel replied.

"She had lunch at my table that last day." He looked away toward the sea. "I saw her just before . . . before we were struck," Turner said almost in a whisper. "She was forward on the boat deck below the bridge." The tough, weathered captain spoke with trembling lips, "She waved and blew me a kiss."

Ansel watched him walk away, a lonely man carrying a self-imposed guilt no board of inquiry could ever lift from his heart.

Ansel had his hired driver take him up a winding road that ended at the Old Head of Kinsale, a high rocky point of land thrusting into the Atlantic from the south coast of Ireland. He got out of the car and walked to the lighthouse. It stood within sight of *Lusitania* when she went down. A stiff breeze blowing from the sea seemed to agitate the herring gulls wheeling overhead. Standing there in the gloom of dusk, he stared far out at the rolling waves. *Lusitania* was there, he knew, more than sixty fathoms down in eternal darkness.

She is not there, he told himself. *No watery grave for Bethany. She is in some other place, still bright and beautiful with laughter on her lips and a sparkle in her eyes.* He turned and walked away feeling more alone than ever in his life.

I am the last Quinn.

1st Lieutenant Quinn would get little time for grieving.

Beginning with the sinking of *Lusitania,* and the continued German policy of unrestricted U-boat sinking of merchant ships, American Ambassador William G. Sharp knew that President Wilson was under increasing pressure to not only aid England and France with more material goods, but to send an American Army to fight in Europe. The phrase, 'Remember the *Lusitania*,' was circulating in newspapers the same way 'Remember the *Maine*' had splashed across headlines seventeen years before and led to public support for the Spanish American War.

Ambassador Sharp was painfully aware of the cost in young lives that would result if America joined in what was being called "The Great War." Over two million French, English and German men had taken part in the first battle of the Marne in September 1914. The German offensive was stopped just thirty miles from Paris, and then only by using hundreds of Paris taxi cabs to rush more than 6,000 reserves to the front. The battle casualties were rumored to be high but the official figures had not been published by either side.

In the coming election of 1916, Democrat President Wilson was in a tough race for re-election against the Republican candidate, Supreme Court Justice Charles Evans Hughes. Wilson had built his campaign around the slogan, "He kept us out of the war." The president desperately wanted news on the war he could use to support his stance against America's involvement while Hughes criticized Wilson's failure to make "necessary preparations" should America have to face conflict. The most comprehensive firsthand reports Ambassador Sharp sent to President Wilson had come from assistant attaché Fisher Wood who used America's neutrality to gain access to both French and German lines in 1914, but Wood was now back in the United States.

Sharp was intensely aware of the United States' need for current intelligence on the war. As regards his efforts to gain such intelligence from the French Government, he wrote the following in his personal journal:

"The French are keen on censorship. They have shut down two newspapers for violation of censorship laws pertaining to war news. Perhaps they are right . . . the Germans read newspapers, too. The French army has just launched a new offensive known as the Second Battle of Artois. No reporters are allowed to the front, though that did not stop some from writing fictitious articles of glorious frontline adventures and outrageous tales of German atrocities.

"After a month of negotiations with Alexandre Millerand, Minister of War, I have finally obtained permission for a small American party, to be appointed by me and approved by Millerand, to be escorted to the front, or as near thereto as possible, for observation. The French insist on the right to review, meaning to censor, any reports members of the neutral American party might submit. They are very sensitive to any intelligence which I might transmit to President Wilson and especially to the American press. I could have told them the truth, that what I send to the President via diplomatic pouch was none of their business, but then they know that just as they know any hoped for American support will not be based on false propaganda. The games diplomats play never cease, especially during crises and certainly during war."

Ambassador Sharp issued instructions to his Military Attaché, Major Spencer Crosby, to conduct the tour. The Major called in Lieutenant Ansel Quinn, the U.S. Army liaison assigned to French War Ministry on Rue St. Dominique.

"Lieutenant, you are going to visit the front, but it is not the result of the many requests you have placed on my desk."

Ansel opened his mouth to speak, but the Major was faster.

"Don't say a word. You are not being turned loose on your own to cause mischief. Ambassador Sharp finally got approval as outlined in this."

He gave Ansel a copy of Ambassador Sharp's "Special and Confidential" instructions for the trip which outlined the mission, instructed each member to keep a daily journal independent of each other to be turned in upon their return; to be especially careful not to discuss the United States other than its stated position of neutrality, and certainly not its preparedness for war or more importantly, its lack of same; emphasized that no member was to venture into a situation where they could become a casualty, or worse, a prisoner, and that all were prohibited from discussing the mission before, during or after under penalty of court-martial.

In addition, Major Crosby handed Ansel a copy of the French government document permitting the visit to the front. "You, Lieutenant, will use this document to coordinate all necessary travel arrangements for the neutral American party consisting of me," the Major smiled, "yourself and Andrew Hampton, assistant second secretary to the Ambassador. You will notice that the permit says we will be escorted to the front, or as near thereto as possible, for observation. Please note the words 'escorted,' 'observation' and 'as near thereto as possible.' The last thing the ambassador and President Wilson want is for a neutral American, especially one in uniform, to be captured or found dead by the Germans at the front with the French."

"We could dress in civilian clothes the same as Mister Hampton."

"Not too bright, Lieutenant. If you and I were captured in civilian clothes the Germans would shoot us as spies. For that matter, French troops might decide we were German spies and shoot us before we could straighten things out."

"Well we could wear French uniforms. Get to the trenches that way. Really see what's what."

"American field uniform with boots, Lieutenant. I'm told if it rains we could be up to our knees in mud. And we are not going so far as the trenches. Is that clear?"

"Yes, sir."

"Good! Now get on with it."

Lieutenant Quinn knew his way around French Headquarters having been assigned there as liaison to the American Embassy since March of 1915. The assignment might have gone to a higher ranking officer except for one or two things in Quinn's favor. Following a tour of hazardous duty in 1913 as a leader of a detachment of scouts fighting Moslem Moros in the jungles of the Philippines under the overall Philippine commander, General John J. Pershing, Quinn had asked for the Paris assignment. It had taken two years, but he got it. It didn't hurt that Pershing liked the young second lieutenant, told him he had spent a little time in Paris himself in 1908 assigned as a neutral observer should the Balkans flare up in another war. Then there was Quinn's personnel file. It reflected an excellent record at West Point, a letter of commendation for his Philippine service, and the fact that Lieutenant Quinn spoke fluent French.

Still, in his new assignment, Quinn was at the bottom of the totem pole. As the lowest ranking American army officer in Paris, he was used to getting all the "grudge" assignments.

Ansel began his newly assigned task by working through piles of French Army red tape to obtain written permits addressed to various French Army units manning check points along the route to be traveled by the Major and party. In addition, he obtained a letter of introduction for the party addressed to the French 10th Army headquarters under the command of General Victor d'Urbal. The paper work complete, he contacted Commandant de Montravel who was in charge of the French Army motorcar service in Paris. Montravel promised a motorcar, driver, and a certain Capitaine Paquet as escort who, he said, had first-hand knowledge of the section of battle line the American party was to be allowed to observe "from a safe distance," Commandant de Montravel emphasized.

Quinn had been told to plan for a trip of up to five days, the purpose of which was to study the battlefield for lessons, strategy, tactics, weapons and the resulting success or failure of same. Capitaine Paquet, under orders from Commandant de Montravel, assisted Quinn in making preparations for the mission. In fact, it was Paquet who made a list of supplies needed and procured them for the journey. He presented the bill to Lieutenant Quinn. As per the agreement with French Headquarters, the lot was to be paid for, Paquet reminded Quinn, by the American Embassy.

"All this stuff better be on that motorcar when we pull out."

"But of course, *mon ami*, everything with the small exception of one case of wine. Alas it was broken by the clumsy poilu loading the motorcar."

"I am shocked that you would pull such an old army trick."

"You are not shocked, but if you insist I will pay for it out of my poor soldier's allowance even if it means my family will go without supper this week."

"You have no wife and no children. I checked."

"If you insist, but I must report such a breach in trust between the Americans and French Army to Commandant de Montravel."

"Give me the bill, Paquet."

"Don't be insubordinate, Lieutenant. It is Capitaine Paquet to you, but since we are to travel together on this adventure you may call me simply Paquet provided the bill is acceptable as presented. After all, we French and you Americans are such good allies, no?"

"We Americans and you French are not allies. We Americans are neutral."

"We shall see, *mon ami*, we shall see."

Quinn presented the French requisition form to the supply clerk at the American Chancellery. He carefully scrutinized the list, looked up at Lieutenant Quinn, rolled his eyes, shook his head in resignation and stamped it "APPROVED," as per Ambassador Sharp's instructions.

CHAPTER TWO

Paris, May 1915

On the 6th of May, with all arrangements complete, the party of four met at the American Chancellery at Number 5 Rue de Chaillot in the 16th Arrondissement of Paris. Ambassador Sharp had arranged for the four to breakfast at the chancellery to talk over the plans for the trip. Lieutenant Quinn and Major Crosby were dressed in army field uniforms and boots. Andrew Hampton was outfitted in hunting jacket, boots and cap. "Not the usual diplomat's attire," he smiled when the Major introduced him to Quinn. "I'm looking forward to getting out in the country. We have been rather busy arranging credit and passage for the last of the Americans wanting to go home and seeing what we could do for non-citizens wanting to immigrate. There has been no letup following the outbreak of war. I welcome a reprieve from all that."

Capitaine Paquet, who walked with the aid of a cane, was the last to arrive. Ansel introduced him to Major Crosby and Andrew Hampton. The French captain saluted smartly.

It was quickly determined that Paquet spoke almost no English and Major Crosby but little French. Assistant Second Secretary Hampton, who did speak French, and Lieutenant Quinn would act as interpreters. Capitaine Paquet explained what the party could expect. For the benefit of the Major, Paquet spoke a sentence or two and paused while Ansel translated for the Major. He and Andrew Hampton would take turns in the process that would laboriously continue for the duration of the trip.

At nine o'clock, a clerk entered the dining room to announce that their car and driver had arrived. The Americans picked up their gear and followed Paquet out of the Chancellery and stared wordlessly at the black Renault touring car parked at the curb. It was a large machine decorated with an American flag attached to one side of the front bumper while a white flag was attached to the other. The Renault's boot and running boards were loaded with cartons of canned goods, tins of biscuits, a sack of potatoes, a number of five gallon tins of gasoline and of water, blankets wrapped in waterproof sheets, a first aid kit and two cases of wine. A sack of flour protected by canvas was lashed to one front fender. Two spare tires were lashed to each side.

The men, allowed only a small kit bag apiece for a change of clothes and personal items stowed their gear under their feet on the floor board, the only space available. As part of their kits, cartons of cigarettes and boxes of matches were included, items they had been told were in much demand at the front. No arms were allowed. Ansel wondered if the overloaded Renault would make it out of the city, much less the hundred or so miles to the county of Artois where the French, as of May 3rd, had commenced artillery bombardment of the German lines in preparation for their spring offensive.

The driver was introduced as Corporal Mott. He and Capitaine Paquet sat in the front while Major Crosby, Assistant Second Secretary Hampton and Quinn crowded into the back seat. Lieutenant Quinn was given the privilege of sitting in the middle. They motored through the streets and boulevards of Paris garnering the attention of Parisians who stared open-mouthed at the ridiculously outfitted motorcar It was just as amazing to the travelers on their way to the front to observe life in Paris carried on as if there was no war. Shops were open; the sidewalk cafes crowded, Taxi horns screeched ceaselessly, party boats plied the Seine. And why not? The German 1914 offensive of the Marne had failed. The very real threat of German boots marching down L'Avenue des Champs-Elysées had faded. The only threat since was, courtesy of Die Fliegertruppen des Deutschen Kaiserreiches (German Imperial Flying Corps) in the form of an almost daily sortie by a German Albatross reconnaissance plane. It was painted yellow and white and decorated with Maltese crosses. The observer usually dropped one or two bombs over the side resulting in little damage. Parisians found it entertaining. They would turn out in the streets and watch for its arrival, usually around five or six in the afternoon. They seemed disappointed if it failed to come into view. When it was rumored to have been shot down and no longer appeared, many Parisians missed "their little piece of excitement" with their late afternoon aperitif. Observing the hustle and bustle of Paris as they drove through the streets, it seemed to Ansel that except for those whose loved ones were at the front, in hospital or dead, no one in the city wanted to think about the war.

On the outskirts they came to the city's fortifications composed of two great arcs of parallel earthen ramparts interspersed with forts. It had all been constructed toward the end of the last century after the Franco-Prussian war of 1870-71, a war that ended with the newly unified Germany occupying Paris for several months and annexing Alsace-Lorraine on their way home. The fortifications were built at great expense and no small amount of controversy as tens of thousands of houses and shops of mostly lower income Parisians were leveled to make way. West Point had taught Quinn that the dated fortifications of Paris and other fixed defensive works of the nineteenth century provided little protection in the age of modern artillery. Regardless, the untried Paris fortifications gave a measure of comfort to the uninformed citizenry.

The car was casually flagged through the first gate and, ten miles further, through the gate of the outer ring of fortifications without so much as having to show a permit. Paquet explained that was not the case last year when the Germans were only thirty miles from the city. He said that half the population had fled Paris, including the government, in fear for their lives. The roads leading from the Belgian and French borders were clogged with refugees and interfered with the military traffic rushing supplies and reserves to the front.

Once outside the ten mile ring of Paris defenses, they had to stop occasionally and show their permits at check points consisting of small fortifications built of whatever was handy—trees, paving stones, sandbags, boxes and barrels filled with rocks and dirt, all with loopholes for rifles and manned by two dozen or so soldiers and an occasional French 75 artillery piece. These check points would do nothing to stop an army, Paquet said, but were there to stop any enemy scouting vehicles or cavalry patrols and to keep civilians from clogging the roads.

For some miles, they passed trees freshly dressed in spring's greenery, orchards in bloom, farmers working lush fields, cows grazing, barns and houses undisturbed, all as if there had been no German offensive last September. Then, as the early miles fell behind, they began to see the footprints of war. At one point Corporal Mott had to pull to the side of the road to allow a convoy of trucks, empty of their loads of ammunition and rations, returning from the front with cargos of a different nature . . . wounded *poilus*, the sobriquet the French had fondly given their soldiers. Some were dressed in outdated uniforms consisting of red trousers and dark blue jackets. Others wore the newer horizon-blue uniforms, harder to see, and therefore less a target than the flaming red trousers. There were also dark skinned men in khaki uniforms. Paquet said they were Moroccans. All the wounded were filthy, covered in mud, dust and blood; their white bandages in stark contrast.

The group watched in silence. Some of the wounded sat with blood-soaked bandages covering arms, faces, heads, legs, and stumps from missing limbs. Many smoked cigarettes. The more seriously wounded lay flat, crowded shoulder to shoulder and head to foot on the truck beds. All were painfully jostled as the solid-rubber-tired trucks negotiated the rutted, muddied, potholed road. Those not too dazed with pain to notice looked longingly at the store of rations lashed to the Renault.

Once the bloody convoy, some sixty trucks and twenty ambulances in all, cleared the road, Corporal Mott once again got underway. A few miles distant the car, grinding in low gear, topped a steep hill to reveal a small village below, or what was left of one. There was no longer a hint of the idyllic French farmland they had driven through upon leaving Paris. The fields were pockmarked with shell holes. Many buildings were nothing but rubble; shattered sections of walls and huge portions of roofs spilled into themselves or out into roadways. No house was undamaged. Shards of window glass littered the streets. Piles of soot-stained rubble had been pushed aside to clear the main road. Not a person was to be seen.

"Paquet, where does a whole village go after such destruction?"

"As far from battle as they can get. The fighting here involved units in movement, patrols in force, cavalry in flanking attacks supported by artillery. This village, like many, changed hands several times. That is the way military minds envisioned modern war. We were trained for that at Saint Cyr; a war of maneuver. It is what happened here, and evidence of the same that you will see up ahead for a while, but the *mitrailleuse* (the French word for machinegun) has changed that. From the very beginning, the Germans recognized the power of the *mitrailleuse*. We did not. They had thousands to our hundreds. They used a very effective tactic repeatedly to push us back through La Fère, Guise, and Laon and every village in between on the road toward Paris. They would mass their artillery to their right and place hundreds of *mitrailleuses;* so many their crews were pressed for room, to protect their flank. Time and time again, supported by their artillery and *mitrailleuses,* they overran our left. It was a very effective tactic. Once our left was flanked we had to fall back."

"But you stopped them before Paris."

Paquet thought a long moment before answering. "Yes, because we had to at any cost, and the cost was very high both for us and for the Germans. What I tell you will not get beyond the censors, but I know you are here to learn the truth. You will not say that I am your source, yes?"

Upon translation, the Major nodded agreement. "Tell Capitaine Paquet that whatever he may tell us we will not reveal him as the source. I speak for us all."

Paquet nodded and continued. "It is estimated that the losses in killed, wounded or captured counting both sides totaled nearly 250,000."

"My God," the Major remarked when the figure was interpreted for him, "There weren't 160,000, counting men on both sides, at Gettysburg and less than 200,000 at Waterloo."

Paquet continued, "When the great German offensive reached the outskirts of Paris their supply line was stretched too far. They ran out of steam. We counterattacked and pushed them back, but far to their rear they had been busy preparing a defensive line of trenches to hold the parts of Belgium and France they had taken. That is what we ran into, what you will see. We tried to break through. After a terrific barrage, we fired over 200,000 shells in preparation for the assault; my unit overran one of their trenches. We found theirs are better than ours, well planned, and built on high, well-draining land with concrete machinegun emplacements and concrete bunkers, some thirty feet below ground with electric lights and pumps to remove water. That is why they survived our artillery bombardment and were ready for us when we attacked. We get through their wire and drive them from the first trench to the second trench, but their reserves in the third trench counterattack. They are very good at counterattack. The German soldier is fearless and they outnumber us. My unit had suffered over fifty percent casualties in the attack and could not hold. Unlike the Germans, our general had placed our reserves too far to the rear to reinforce us in time. Those of us who were left retreated back toward our lines. That is when I got this," He tapped his hip. "They say I was lucky I didn't lose my leg. Like so many, I got hit with shrapnel. Our *soixante-quinze* (French 75 cannon) is a good accurate field piece, but the German guns are larger than ours and have longer range. Our counter-battery fire could not reach them."

"What, in your opinion, happens now?" The Major asked.

"I think the war of maneuver is over, at least for now. Neither side seems able to gain more than two hundred yards, maybe a mile at most, and the cost is high. This resulted in a race to the sea, each side trying to flank the trenches of the other. Now the opposing trenches zigzag their way from neutral Switzerland to the English Channel; over four hundred fifty miles. The ground between opposing trenches is a killing field, no, a slaughter field, even at night. It is going to be a long war."

There was absolute silence as the Americans mulled all they had just heard, tried to fathom the ramifications. Not quite a year into the conflict and the "great modern war of maneuver" taught at West Point had been stagnated, forced into trench warfare by the machinegun, artillery and barbed wire. They were stunned at the fact that the French had fired 200,000 thousand artillery shells in preparation for one attack along a line less than twelve miles in length.

Lieutenant Quinn broke the silence. "That's more than 16,000 rounds per mile of front. And the attack failed!"

Paquet nodded.

A few miles later, near what was left of the village of Soizy-aux-Bois, they passed a strange, low, flat mound of bare earth covering the better part of a pasture. Patches of new grass were valiantly trying to reclaim the table-like, rain-eroded soil. Paquet said it was a mass grave containing the bodies of some 900 soldiers, French and German.

Good God! Quinn thought, *Three years ago I learned what it is like to be shot at and see men die, Americans and Moros, but that was during small jungle actions on Jolo and Zamboanga in the Southern Philippines; nothing compared to what is occurring here. This is slaughter on a scale never before seen.*

As they drove, more signs of the hard fighting of September 1914 were evidenced by shell holed farm houses and barns, splintered groves of trees and fields pockmarked by artillery. Scraps of hide clung to bones of cavalry and artillery horses, the carcasses of which had been dragged aside to clear the roadway. Here and there they motored past huge storage dumps of artillery shells just off the road, more shells than the Americans had ever dreamed existed. Scattered along the way were camps of reserve forces, their tents spread like mushrooms across pastures and among stands of trees. The men were doing what men do in camp; cooking, washing, cleaning equipment or just idling the time away playing cards, smoking, chatting, sleeping.

Paquet offered, "We have found that life in the trenches is stressful beyond long term endurance so units are rotated nearly every week or two to provide rest and relief. A unit is relieved and moved to reserve trenches. If all is well, they are then moved further to the rear like the troops you see encamped here. After a week, the process is reversed, unless the Germans stage an assault, in which case the reserve troops will be rushed back to the front."

At dusk, Corporal Mott drove into a town that had been the scene of fierce fighting. Every house and shop was damaged, walls pocked by bullets and shrapnel, many blown out completely to reveal rooms with shattered furniture and scattered personal belongings, roofs holed or burned away; hardly a window unbroken. The streets were barely passable. The corporal steered the Renault around shell craters or over ones that had been filled with dirt and rubble. Here they had their first flat tire. It seems the Germans had raided every wine cellar in town and left the streets strewn with thousands of broken bottles. Mott had a few uncivil things to say about the Boche as he recovered the car jack and tire tools from the boot.

The town was occupied by French troops. Trucks loaded with ammunition and supplies were parked down every side street. Paquet found the army command post on the main street housed in a dwelling that had most of its roof intact. After inquiring if any quarters were available for overnight, the French major in charge said the entire village had been requisitioned by his battalion. He directed Paquet and party to the mayor's office. The Major told them, "The mayor refused to flee during the fighting. He stayed, taking refuge in his wine cellar. He felt it his duty to watch over the town. For his trouble he and eleven others were held as hostages by the Germans to ensure no interference or hostile acts were committed against the occupying forces. In the event of any occurrence, they would all be shot."

"And would they have been shot?" Hampton asked.

"Absolutely," the officer replied. "They have done so in many villages. In one town someone took a shot at a German officer. Forty villagers, men and women, were lined up and shot and the remaining males in the town marched off as laborers to dig trenches. Then the Boche burned the whole village. Napoleon said, 'Prussia was hatched from a cannonball.' Make no mistake *monsieur*, they are barbarians."

While the tire was being repaired Paquet led the party to the mayor's office. He was a short, stocky fellow with a goatee and mustache who looked them over with a rather stern countenance. Quinn and Andrew Hampton had to bite their tongues to keep from laughing when Capitaine Paquet explained that he was guiding a party of American tourists who had come to observe the French army beat the hell out of the fatherless Boche bastards. Ansel did not interpret for Major Crosby the part about their being tourists.

The demeanor of the little mayor changed immediately upon hearing that the party was American. He shook everyone's hand effusively and stated that all of France was waiting for America to join the battle. Major Crosby avoided comment.

The little mayor continued, "Our French *Poilus* are the finest soldiers in the world, you will see that, but nonetheless they would be proud to welcome the Americans by their side just as America welcomed Lafayette."

To change the subject, Andrew Hampton told him that Lieutenant Quinn had just lost his aunt on the *Lusitania*. The mayor grabbed Quinn and kissed him on both cheeks, expressing his sympathy and cursing the Germans.

Young Quinn told him he'd driven all day across the destruction and suffering the French had endured under German aggression since August a year ago.

The mayor took a list off his desk, ran his finger down the column and looked up to announce, "For our *Américain* guests, I give you to Doctor Arceneau and his wife. They will be honored." He quickly filled out a requisition for quarters and gave it to the Major.

Back at the Renault, Paquet gave Corporal Mott the mayor's directions to the good doctor's house. Quinn volunteered to walk in front to scout for broken bottles and window glass in their path. Corporal Mott thanked the lieutenant and let loose a purple string of derogatory adjectives describing the Boche.

Capitaine Paquet, met at the door by Doctor Arceneau, explained that his party of Americans needed shelter for the night. The doctor called his wife shouting, "Américain! Américain!" The couple rushed past Paquet to the curbside and warmly greeted the party. They could not help staring at the larder lashed to the car before inviting the group into their home.

The doctor and his wife were more than a little curious about the two uniformed 'soldats Américain,' but were polite enough not to ask questions. They did express the hope that it was a sign that America was preparing to join the fight.

To change the subject, Secretary Hampton, speaking for Major Crosby, asked the doctor if it would be possible for the doctor's cook to prepare supper if he would supply the food. The doctor's wife, having observed the rations piled on the Renault, clapped her hands together in joy.

"Oh Commandant," she said, "I will be happy to cook for you. We have not seen such a wonderful cache of food since the war arrived at our doorstep."

The Major let Madame Arceneau pick the items she wanted before dismissing Corporal Mott and the car. Capitaine Paquet had arranged for him to bunk at headquarters where the Renault and its precious supplies would be guarded overnight. That way the supplies, less a tin of this or a bottle or two of that, would be safe until morning.

The guests learned that the doctor's cook, maid and gardener and their families had fled before the Germans as had most of the town's citizens, and were afraid to return because of the frequent, if distant sound of artillery. Dr. Arceneau had stayed to tend to the wounded of both sides. For his efforts, the Germans did not ransack and loot what was left of his home like they did the others.

Madame Arceneau was a wonderful cook. She made fresh bread and worked miracles with the tinned beef, potatoes, and canned peas. Once seated for dinner with wine glasses full, doctor Arceneau and his wife could no longer repress their curiosity about the guests seated around the table.

The doctor began. "You speak French very well, Lieutenant Quinn."

"That is because my mother was French," he replied.

"French!" Madame Arceneau cried. "You must tell us the story."

Ansel looked first at Andrew Hampton who shrugged his shoulders, then at Major Crosby. The party had been cautioned not to give out information about their mission. The Major nodded, "Just don't talk politics or a word about the purpose of our mission."

Ansel turned toward their hosts. "It is a long story," he warned.

"We have wine and are happy to have company. It has been so long," Madame Arceneau replied.

Quinn took a sip of wine and began. "As a young man my father was a midshipman on the Confederate ship *Alabama* during the American Civil War. He was gravely wounded when *Alabama* was sunk in battle with *Kearsarge* off Cherbourg."

"Oh! Monsieur, that battle is very famous in France."

"Well, Midshipman Quinn was pulled from the water and taken to a hospital in Cherbourg. He had a terrible head wound—had a cracked skull and lost an eye and most of an ear. They sent him by train to Paris where he was treated by a famous surgeon, Doctor Paul Courbet I believe his name was."

"I know of him!" the doctor replied. "When I was a medical student, Doctor Courbet was mentioned in lectures on surgery."

"My father never forgot him. After the Civil War, my family was in danger of losing their land in Mississippi. There was no money you see—just debt and taxes. My father was able to go to sea as a captain and later had his own shipping company in the Caribbean. He made a lot of money; some of it, I admit, from running guns and medicine to the Cubans during their rebellions against Spain. Anyway, as the last man in the family left alive, he raised his niece, my Aunt Bethany. When she was eighteen or so he took her to Paris to a young ladies' school. He would not send her to a Yankee school, don't you see? To him that would be like you sending a daughter to a German school. I think the name of the place was Ecole d' Ecouen."

"Ecole d' Ecouen! I myself went there!" Madame Arceneau cried. "Go on! Go on!"

"Well, while my father was there in Paris, he went to the Hotel Dieu to thank Dr. Courbet for saving his life. He had been a handsome young man before the war. By the time he returned to Paris his head scar had faded, he wore an eye patch and his hair covered his torn ear. I was told by my Aunt Bethany that women were attracted to him even with his battle scars or perhaps, she said, because of them. Anyway, he was sad to discover that the doctor had passed away. He asked if the doctor had any family in Paris and was told that his daughter, a young widow, Madame Louisette Buisson, still lived there. He went to see her to express his gratitude to her father. She was beautiful, still in mourning, lonely I guess. Anyway, each time he came to visit Bethany, he would visit Louisette. One thing led to another and they fell in love. They married and he took her to Cuba where he bought her a lovely house in Havana. I was raised there learning French from my mother, Spanish from the Cubans, and speaking English with the Southern accent of my father, my Aunt Bethany and military school in Alabama where they sent me when fighting crept near Havana. Later they all had to leave when America declared war on Spain. Not only did I learn French from my mama, but she kept her house in Paris. Over the years she insisted that my father take her home to visit from time to time, which they did until their deaths. My Aunt Bethany kept it after that. She loved Paris and returned here at least once a year. I guess when the estate is settled I will have to decide what to do with it. Sell it, I suppose, after my duty in Paris is up."

"A wonderful story!" Madame Arceneau clapped her hands. Turning to Major Crosby, "We are so glad, Major, that your party stopped here with us tonight."

Andrew Hampton interpreted the exchange.

"It is entirely our good fortune, Madame," the Major replied, "but could you and the good doctor tell us about the battle for your village, if it is not too painful? We are on a fact finding mission."

Madame Arceneau's eyes fell. She looked at her husband. The doctor touched her hand and nodded his head. After refreshing the wine glasses, he began.

"The *poilus* first marched through very proudly. We cheered. Then they came back with the Germans not far behind. That is when the people began to flee in panic. The German artillery rained shells down on the town. Many *poilus* and villagers were killed. We took shelter in our basement and were lucky. As the artillery fire lifted there was heavy street fighting. The Germans drove our men out. When the French army retreated the mayor marched out waving a torn bed sheet tied to a broom handle and surrendered the village to stop the killing. He was very brave and very formal. The Germans took the mayor and eleven others as hostages. They said if any citizen shoots or otherwise harms a German, the hostages would be shot and the village burned to the ground. Except for a rear guard, the Germans moved out pressing hard after our retreating soldiers.

"There were dead and wounded in the shelled buildings and lying everywhere in the streets—French, German and civilians. The Boche left only one doctor behind, and he asked if I would join him to treat the injured. We moved all the pews out of the church and laid straw and blankets over the floor. It was the best we could do. We laid the wounded head to foot. There was hardly room to maneuver among them. We ran out of blankets and sheets. There were so many seriously wounded that the lesser injured had to sit on the church pews set out on the lawn. The German pharmacist put his supplies on the altar and our chemist recovered what he could from his wrecked shop. The bodies of the wounded were filthy. The few women and men left in the village brought well water for the patients to drink and to use to clean the wounds, but not enough to bathe their bodies. A little bread and tinned biscuits were all we had to feed them. We set up a surgery in an alcove. Many of the wounds were horrible. We did the best we could with the German doctor, twelve German soldiers acting as nurses and myself. We took the patients as we got to them, the most serious first, whether French or German." The doctor dropped his eyes. "There were so many we could not save.

"Then, when the Germans could not reach Paris, they came back through. Their commanding officer kept them from the mayor's house and ours, but could not control all the troops. They were angry at not taking Paris and looted the wine cellars and got drunk. They ransacked what was left of almost every house, took what they wanted and senselessly destroyed the rest—furniture, paintings, chinaware, everything. Then the French artillery began to rain down, and we took to the cellar again. The *poilus* fought their way in and finally drove the Germans out. You are soldiers, so I do not have to remind you how terrible things were. By the time the fighting moved out, the temporary hospital in the church was again full. The odor was terrible as many of the wounded had developed gangrene by the time they were brought to us. We had so little left to treat them. To clear the way for the French Army, dead men and horses along the road were pushed to the sides and left there ripening. The smell was unbearable. The French officers said they could do nothing at the moment; could not spare men to help; needed all the *poilus* to continue driving the Germans back. There was no labor force to bury the dead. A day or two later a small detachment of reserves coming up cleared the road side. They said they did not have time to dig graves. They dragged dead horses and human bodies into fields and pastures and piled them all together in big mounds, then poured petrol on them and set them on fire. It was awful and, I believe immoral. A priest blessed the flames. It was all he could do. After setting the fires, the soldiers moved on. All the bodies did not burn completely. It was a terrible sight. We finally got a unit passing through to bury what was left. I tell you I don't know if I—" he looked as his wife, "if we could go through that again."

The visitors were silent for a long while. Then Madame Arceneau rose from the table. The men all stood. She returned with a bottle of brandy and a tray of snifters and filled one for each man. Doctor Arceneau raised his glass. "To our honored guests, the Américains. We pray your country will see the way to help freedom survive in France. I believe this war will change the world forever."

"I can only say, at this time," Major Crosby stated, "our prayers are with France." It was time to retire.

Doctor Arceneau directed the visitors to the basement stairs. "Please wait here a moment. He and Madame Arceneau disappeared to return with arms full of quilts. The doctor explained, "I apologize that all we can offer you is the basement. All the rooms at the back of the house were damaged and have no roof. Please use these quilts as pallets." He handed bedding to each man.

By candlelight, Quinn added to his journal all that had taken place or was observed that day, and what the doctor had told them, all of it whether of military or personal interest, whether a subject of importance or simply mundane details. It was what the three Americans had been ordered to do. The value of such information would be judged by others.

Bedding down in the basement, the Major asked Ansel if his father was really a gun runner. "He was indeed, but please understand that the guns and supplies he sold went to the Cuban people fighting for their freedom from Spain. He risked his life to help them. He was a good and courageous man."

Hampton had evidently translated much of what was said during dinner. The Major added, "I've heard about your house in Paris."

"It's an old house, not large, and the neighborhood is not what it used to be."

"I heard about both you and the house from a young lady with the American Ambulance Field Service, a Miss Gibson. She said you had a wonderful party there."

"Yes. Well it's been a long day. I can use a little sleep," Ansel said, avoiding the subject.

By candlelight the men spread their blankets on the floor, thankful for a roof over their heads and a soft pallet to sleep on. Major Crosby asked Ansel to pose a question to Paquet, a question that was core to the mission.

"Paquet," Ansel interpreted the Major's question, "since we will not be allowed to go to the frontlines, the Major has asked if you would tell us what life in the trenches is really like? You and others have alluded to the stress of living daily under shell fire and threat of enemy attack, or of participating in an attack against the enemy, but no one has detailed the reality of daily life there for us. We need to record such details if we are, that is, in the event America should need to prepare its men to fight over here. That is the very reason we are making this tour. Without such knowledge our journals will be of little real value to the American military's understanding of this war and the planning, training and logistics that will be required should any decision be made to participate as an ally of your country. To send American troops over here without such knowledge would end in disaster."

The three Americans retrieved their pencils and journals in anticipation of recording the French captain's words.

Paquet was silent for a while. His face, reflected in the candlelight, held an expression of deep, worried concern marked by wrinkles on his brow and a flexing of the muscles of his jaw.

"I am not sure I can do that. My hip is healing, but my mind is still struggling. I accepted this assignment to see if, by visiting the front again, I could find my courage, which I seem to have left behind in the shell hole from which I was carried. You see, I survived while half of my men, boys really, did not."

No one said a word. Paquet lit a Gitanes cigarette and lay back on his blanket, the pungent smoke curling up through the arc of candlelight to disappear into the darkness above.

After a while he spoke. "All right. Since you are tourists, I will be your tour guide. You will have to see through my eyes. Perhaps if I take you back there with me I can let it all go by giving it to you." He paused. "But I think it will haunt you when you return home to prepare American boys to be shipped to hell."

He took a long drag from his cigarette, letting the smoke drift slowly from his mouth and nose. "The Germans built a fallback defensive line. As I told you before, they picked mostly the high ground that drains well. They stopped us at their line. We dropped back a few hundred yards into the fields and trees. Under sporadic artillery fire, ours to keep them in their trench and theirs to harass our work, we began to dig, first our forward trench and a second, reserve trench paralleling the enemy's. We dig communication trenches perpendicular to the main trenches. They are narrow and serve to feed men and supplies to the trenches from the rear.

"The Germans have the better terrain. Ours is not so good, does not drain so well. When it rains, the best of our trenches are ankle deep in mud. When we dug in some places along the line, we reached water three feet down. In such places we had to build up walls of earth and sandbags above ground. Then we riveted the walls with wood planks or, when we could get it, iron roofing. In the trenches you make a shelf, a firing step, where men can stand and fire over the lip. Dugouts are made for officers, communications, and so forth. They are covered with corrugated iron supported by logs or timber and covered over with earth that provides protection from shrapnel, but not from a direct hit. The soldiers dig cubby holes into the wall of the trench just big enough to wiggle into for sleep and protection from shelling. The field kitchens try to send up hot food, soup or stew, but it is always cold by the time it is carried up the communication trenches to the front line. The bread is always stale. Sometimes there are vegetables, potatoes. Soup is carried in old, open petrol cans and is often contaminated on the way by dirt and dust thrown up by shells. Coffee comes in tablets in small tin boxes. The men cherish the boxes more than the ersatz coffee. They use them to keep matches dry. Mostly the men eat cold canned meat and biscuits so hard you can hardly break them. You sometimes have to soak them in water to eat them. Besides rain, there is the constant shelling, mostly from trench mortars unless an attack is coming. Field artillery shells always hit at some degree of slant. You can usually hear them coming and have split seconds to seek cover. After a while you learn to judge from their scream what type they are and how close they will hit. Except for a direct hit, the trench affords some protection. Trench mortars are different. The German mortars are of larger caliber than ours. They are fired from down in the trench or from mortar pits. From as near as two hundred yards, they throw their shells high in the air. When they run out of energy they fall making no sound. There is no warning unless you happen to look up and see one falling. If they land directly in the trench, there is no protection for the men nearby. A large mortar round fell straight through the roof of a dugout just down the line from me where four men were sitting at a table going over maps. I ran to the site. When I got there we dug out two bodies that were recognizable as such. The other two, what could be found of them, were put into empty sand bags. There was no way to tell which parts belonged to which officer. I saw some sort of bloody joint stuffed into a bag filled with other unrecognizable pieces of bone and flesh and entrails. Each bag was tagged with a man's name and carried along with the recognizable bodies for burial in a new graveyard several hundred yards behind the lines. The graves were marked with wooden crosses with names painted on them.

"After weeks of this, shelling day and night, some men, officers or enlisted, begin to tremble all the time, some stop speaking, others develop a faraway stare. Some sit quietly for hours and suddenly scream, scaring the hell out of those around them. Such men have to be taken away, sent to the rear. I hear some recover and some never do.

"Then there are the rats. I haven't told you about the rats have I? They are so well fed on the corpses of the dead out in 'no man's land' that they grow as big as rabbits. In fact we call them trench bunnies. You wake up to them running over you, or trying to pull a biscuit from your pocket while you sleep. The trenches are filthy. The men throw empty food cans over the side of the trench, and at night you can hear a constant rattling from the rats searching the tins for the last bits of food left in them. I have seen them try to eat a wounded man who was unconscious, mistaking him for dead. For recreation, we hold trench bunny hunts using clubs, entrenching tools and bayonets and give prizes of extra cigarettes to the men who collect the most.

"The communication trenches that feed into the reserve and main trenches are just wide enough for a man to pass. I have seen them waist deep in muddy water. The main trenches are four to eight feet wide. We put wooden duckboards down to walk on so when it rains you won't sink up to your knees in mud. The mud is filthy because the rain overflows the deep holes used as latrines.

"When the trenches were being dug, sometimes under fire, the dead were buried where they fell, sometimes in the bottom of the trench and sometimes in the trench walls. There have been rains so heavy that some of those decayed dead are washed out of the walls or float up from the mud in the trench bottom.

"Whether it rains or not, there is the constant smell of the decaying dead out in 'no man's land' between the trenches. The very earth smells of rotting corpses because artillery barrages have blown men to pieces and the pieces into the soil. It takes a while before one learns to eat without retching.

"Stretcher bearers try to collect our wounded during an advance by day. Many die trying. At night we send out search patrols to try to collect the wounded and the dead in 'no man's land,' but you cannot always find them among the shell holes in the dark. It is maddening to hear the cries of a wounded comrade and not be able to find him out there. One time, we sent out search parties for three nights looking for a wounded man who kept crying for help. Finally, he grew silent. We never found him. Usually when one of our patrols stumbles on a German patrol there is sharp fighting, but sometimes when patrols carrying the dead and wounded meet, they just pass each other with their burdens.

"Night patrols for reconnaissance or to capture and bring back prisoners are bad enough, but the most hated job is putting up barbed wire or repairing wire that has been torn up by artillery or cut by enemy sappers or patrols. It is one thing to go out on patrol moving from shell hole to shell hole where there is some cover. The men on wire detail have to silently carry six-foot metal or wooden posts and rolls of barbed wire out in front of the trench under cover of darkness and work fully exposed. I lost several of my men sending them out to such duty. We construct and maintain belts of wire strung in rows six-to-ten yards deep in front of the trench as does the enemy. The posts are driven into the ground with padded mallets to deaden the sound, and the wire strung between them is three-to-four feet high. The enemy will fire machineguns in the direction of any noise they hear. Most nights, aerial flares are fired intermittently by both sides. If you are caught in the open by the stark, unnatural light you must freeze with head down so you face does not show. Such light temporarily blinds both sides. The enemy cannot see you unless you move. To move is to die.

"Neither does one show oneself in daylight. Any movement in daylight attracts the attention of the ever watchful enemy snipers. They are very good. They fire from behind steel plates with small shooting holes cut in them. Firing behind the steel armor is the only way a rifleman can survive for more than a few seconds in daylight. Of course, if the enemy is attacking your whole line, those who survive the artillery barrage, stand on the shooting step and fire for all they are worth. If the enemy gets close they throw grenades into the trench. If they get into the trench with you, the bayonet, trench knife or entrenching tool become the weapons most employed. I have seen a head lopped off with the swing of an entrenching tool.

"So, my friends, that's day-to-day living in the trench. Now for the attack. That is the solitary French doctrine for war—attack, attack, attack. Our generals, don't quote me here, gentlemen, our *Chateau Generals* like to look at their maps and plan and order attacks all without ever visiting the terrain for themselves, without seeing what a week's rain can do to that terrain. Once they set a time and date, never mind the weather. The attack will go religiously as scheduled. It is the poor *poilu* with his bayonet who must charge across 'no man's land' through artillery and into the teeth of machineguns. My men made it into the enemy trench, yes, only to be driven back by overwhelming numbers of Germans in counter attack. As I led what was left of my company in retreat, what I remember most is the wall of bodies hung like laundry on the German wire. That's the last scene I remember before I was knocked into a shell hole by shrapnel that nearly took my leg.

"It is the same for the Germans when they come at us. That is what this war has settled down to; a contest to see which side can out-bleed the other. There will come a time when you Americans must decide if a free France is worth your entry into this war. From what I have seen I believe that both sides will exhaust themselves, will run out of troops, and that only with America's help can this horror be ended. But what do I know, a mere captain, and a crippled one at that?

"I have told you all I know. Now if you will excuse me, I will chase after sleep. Sometimes I catch her, sometimes I don't. I'm told on occasion I may scream in my sleep. Should I do that, please forgive me. Goodnight gentlemen."

The room was dead silent. Not a word was spoken for several minutes. Then Ansel, anticipating the Major's request, whispered to him that he and Andrew would translate their notes for him tomorrow. The Major, satisfied, rolled up in his blanket and went to sleep. Just as for Paquet, sleep did not come easily for Ansel and Andrew as they lay pondering all they had just heard, their thoughts punctuated by the faint sound of sporadic artillery fire along the front.

The next morning, before they left, they made sure that Madame Arceneau's pantry was supplied with canned goods, potatoes, flour, cigarettes and matches. The Arceneaus tried to refuse the gift out of pride, but the Americans knew they needed it.

It began to rain mid-morning and continued off and on into the afternoon turning the road into a barely passable quagmire. Corporal Mott did an admirable job keeping the heavily loaded Renault moving in low gear. Twice they bogged down, but were lucky enough to do so along a line of *poilus* plodding toward the front. For cigarettes and scarce matches, they agreed to haul the Renault out.

The rain stopped around four o'clock but the thunder did not. Where nature left off, artillery continued the rumble in the distance. As the ceiling lifted a little, three airplanes flew overhead.

"Those are French," Paquet said. "The larger one is an *avion de reconnaissance.* The observer will sketch the enemy layout on his map or maybe he has one of the new cameras to take photomaps. Often they direct artillery fire. The two smaller ones are *chasseurs* whose job it is to protect the first one. We will see German planes when we get a little closer. 1915 is proving a very bad year for our airmen."

While Mott fought the Renault as it sloshed and slid along the muddy road, Paquet continued his lecture on flying machines. "For both sides the *avions* are the scouts, the eyes of the battle field, much more so than the balloons. With trench warfare and machineguns, cavalry no longer performs reconnaissance very well. Without *avions* the generals are blind, can't see the layout of the opposing trenches or artillery positions or troops gathering for an attack. The *avions* are learning to direct artillery fire by dropping messages or using flares. I am told that soon we will equip *avions de reconnaissance* with wireless radios that can send Morse Code signals. As you may guess, such flying duty is dangerous. Both sides try hard to shoot down the *avions de reconnaissance.*"

As if on cue, they passed a field containing the wreckage of an airplane. It sat nose crushed into the ground, wings twisted, tail toward the sky, much of its fabric covering hanging in tatters where souvenir hunters had cut away the roundels painted on the wings and fuselage, exposing the wooden bones of its structure.

"One of ours," Paquet remarked. "They were lucky not to burn. Many do." The Americans looked in silence as Corporal Mott drove on.

The party required permission from Tenth Army Headquarters to proceed further. Questioning a sergeant at the next check point, they were directed down an estate drive off the main road a distance of two kilometers where again they were stopped and papers checked before being allowed through a gate guarded by two sandbagged machinegun emplacements. A curved gravel drive led them to the front of a grand chateau that must have been beautiful before the war. In common with so many structures they had seen, the chateau had been substantially damaged during the advance and retreat of the Germans in their failed offensive. Great holes in the roof left parts of the interior open to weather while lesser damage had been temporarily repaired with timber and canvas. The outside wall of one large room was blown out entirely. The exposed interior reminded one of the open back of a dollhouse. Many windows were shattered and much of the exterior structure and the garden walls were pock-marked from rifle and machinegun fire. Still, in size and architectural design, the mansion was stately. Several motorcars and trucks were parked in the drive, all in military livery and markings. Soldiers manned sandbagged revetments surrounding the chateau, sentries could be seen patrolling the grounds and a pair of guards stood at a great, ironclad oak door marred by bullet holes.

After presenting their papers, the Americans were ushered into the former library of the chateau, now the office of General d'Urbal, commander of the 10th Army. A free-standing screen set against a wall at one end of the room was plastered with a montage of maps.

The General moved from behind a great rosewood desk to greet them. Introductions were made all around after which the General cleared the room of all clerks, staff officers, and surprisingly, Capitaine Paquet. He then gestured for the three Americans to be seated at what must have been the library's reading table.

"Gentlemen," he said speaking French, "I received word of your mission and I must say I am very glad to entertain America's interest in this war. We hope and pray that the United States will join the Entente to help defeat the Kaiser's attempt to enslave all Europe."

The General's comments, interpreted by Hampton for Major Crosby, brought a slight nod of his head but no comment.

After a pause, d'Urbal continued, "I have been ordered to use my discretion as to what information I may give to you. I do not care for my staff nor Army Headquarters in Paris to question that discretion. Therefore what is said here is between you gentlemen and me. I must ask that each of you give me your word on that."

With Andrew Hampton, assistant second secretary to the American Embassy acting as interpreter, Major Crosby stated that his orders, as a neutral observer, were to gather as much information as France would allow concerning the logistics, weapons and tactics being employed by the French and Germans. He thanked the General for taking his valuable time to meet with the Americans and stated that the United States, in order to make an informed decision concerning the war, would appreciate any and all pertinent information the General was able to give. He assured the General that information so gathered by the party would be purged of source names, reviewed with careful and critical attention and organized by subject categories into a final document classified as secret, and transferred to the United States War Department via diplomatic pouch by courier.

General d'Urbal nodded. "Gentlemen, please understand that what I tell you, if carelessly leaked, could end my career at best, or the facts twisted in such a fashion as to get me shot for treason if certain self-serving politicians thought it useful to their careers. I also inform you that what I am going to tell you about an operation that will take place in the immediate future could get you shot . . . by me, should you divulge what I tell you prior to the execution of said operation. The Germans attempt raiding parties almost nightly. Therefore, I will give orders to Capitaine Paquet and Corporal Mott, who are not privy to the information I am about to give you, that should your group stumble into a situation where your capture is imminent, they are to shoot you rather than allow you and the information you carry to fall into the hands of the enemy. Now, shall I continue?"

Without consulting those with him, Major Crosby nodded in the affirmative. Andrew Hampton interpreted the Major's words. "The Major understands General. He asks that you please pause between statements so that I may interpret your words for him."

The General nodded and began, pausing every few sentences for Hampton to translate his statements to the Major.

"Very well. Now if you will step over to the map board."

The General picked up a pointer, moving it from point-to-point as he talked.

"Tenth Army is responsible for a sector of approximately ten kilometers from here to here." He tapped the map. "General Jaffre, commander of the French Army, has ordered that Tenth Army take Vimy Ridge." The General moved his pointer along the ridge. "To do so successfully Tenth Army will have to simultaneously take the fortified villages of Souchez, here, Neuville-St. Vaast here, and this maze of fortified trenches here we call the Labyrinth." The General tapped the map at each position. If we successfully capture and hold Vimy Ridge we can advance onto the Douai Plain beyond, cut key German railway lines and threaten the entire German salient. Any questions?"

Major Crosby, looking at the map, was silent.

"Good. Now, you asked about logistics. It takes a thousand or more men and as many as four thousand horses, hundreds of wagons and all the trucks I can requisition to supply the daily food and ammunition requirements of the troops and artillery units in my sector. Just finding enough feed for the horses is a constant problem. We use the motor trucks we have and newly laid railroads as much as possible, but for the most part, an army—French, English or German—depends mostly upon horses, tens of thousands of them, to move supplies and artillery. By the way, we are buying many horses and mules from America."

Again pointing at the map he indicated a line four kilometers behind, and parallel to the front. "We have placed 293 heavy artillery pieces along this line. Our 75 caliber gun is a good field piece, easy to move with a good rate of fire, good against infantry in the open, but not as effective on fortifications as are the larger guns. Therefore we have placed over 700 French 75 field guns much closer along this line and some less than one kilometer behind our trenches. For the preparation of our attack we have accumulated over 300,000 shells for our heavy guns and more than 1,000,000 rounds for our lighter field pieces. I am sure you have heard the constant barrage we are laying on the German lines. Tomorrow will total six continuous days of bombardment of the objectives I have outlined to you. The Germans, of course, are returning counter fire in an attempt to knock out our batteries, but due to careful planning, they are having a hard time locating them. We are diverting some of our fire in an attempt to do the same to their artillery, but some of their larger caliber guns have greater range than ours; those we cannot reach. They will constitute a problem to our troops. We intend to attack day after tomorrow as soon as there is enough light for the troops to see their way over the difficult terrain of 'no man's land.' We will not lift our supporting artillery fire until the first wave of troops is within seventy-five yards of the enemy line. When the artillery lifts, our first wave should be at the enemy trench before they recover. We expect to suffer some casualties from such close artillery support. It cannot be helped.

"We expect our artillery to have softened up the enemy, blown holes in their wire, seriously damaged their fortifications and driven them to ground until our troops reach their trenches. Our main objective is to capture and hold Vimy Ridge." The General again used his pointer to indicate the ridge. "The Germans are well invested all along the ridge which controls the entire front sector of our line. We learned from the first battle of Artois to move our reserves closer to the front to defend our initial successes against German counter attacks.

"During the night before the attack, we will open lanes through our wire to allow our troops to rapidly pass through to attack on a wide front. We will assemble them before daylight. They will move out at first light. Once we reach the enemy's forward trench we will direct our artillery fire deeper to disrupt their secondary trenches and the movement of their reserves. Our observation aircraft will help direct that fire, weather permitting. You understand that I cannot allow you as far forward as our trenches. You gentlemen will be directed to a relatively safe artillery observation post from which you can observe the attack up Vimy Ridge."

Major Crosby asked, "General, how do you handle casualties?"

"Yes, the casualties, of course . . . Each company has stretcher bearers. They will collect the wounded and carry them to regimental aid posts where wounds will receive initial dressing. From there casualties will be moved to regimental aid stations back at the reserve trenches where wounds will be assessed again and some emergency essential surgery can be performed. From there they will be moved by ambulance motor vehicles to a triage unit where proper surgery can be performed and from there to a hospital. Incidentally, as I am sure you are aware, there are several volunteer American ambulance organizations with American drivers. Now, gentlemen, I trust you have the information you came for. Do you have questions?"

"General," the Major asked, "have you been to the front yourself?"

"I have not. I have too much to do here to waste time touring. My staff officers report their observations during planning sessions here. We have phone lines laid to regimental headquarters just behind the front to keep me informed, except of course when enemy artillery or patrols cut the wire. In that case, messenger runners are used. Also, for the moment, there are no phone lines to Army Headquarters in Paris. We use motorcycle couriers to rush important messages there."

"And what of weather? We have experienced heavy rain at times getting here."

"We move to attack on schedule no matter the weather. Too much has been put in motion to cancel because of rain. I know mud can slow down an attack but what can one do when such a huge plan is in motion? By the time of the attack there will have been six days of bombardment. What kind of shape do you expect the enemy to be in after such punishment? The order from General Joffre is to attack as planned."

"Do you have an estimate of the casualties your troops may suffer?"

"We have estimates based upon experience, but I cannot divulge that information to you."

"How about enemy casualties?"

"My answer must be the same. We, of course, are not privileged to the enemy's official count, but we have sources that give us reasonable estimates based, for instance, on the first battle of Artois."

The General indicated the interview was over. "Gentlemen, I have much to do. I hope I have been of help to your mission. You, of course, are welcome to spend the night here. In fact, because of the information you have just received, I insist upon it. My adjutant will assign you quarters. I would offer you dinner in the officers' mess, but I would prefer we kept your visit private. Food will be provided in your quarters. You are free to leave in the morning. I have given you this time and information in a spirit of anticipation of the day when you Americans are no longer just neutral observers, but comrades in arms against the Central Powers."

After the Major thanked the General, the Americans were escorted to their quarters where they were provided a meal of potato soup, wine and *la viande de cheval*, grilled horsemeat, tough but edible. They were happy to sleep in real beds though sleep was slow to come. The familiar rhythm of artillery fire, much closer than the night before, was hardly a serenade to induce sleep.

After a quick breakfast, also in their quarters, the Americans met up once more with Capitaine Paquet and Corporal Mott waiting at the Renault much lightened of its original load of provisions. All three Americans took notice that Paquet and Mott were wearing helmets. They also noted that for the first time, Paquet and Mott both were equipped with holstered Lebel revolvers.

"But Paquet," Ansel stated, "this is a neutral vehicle marked by a white flag."

"But of course, *mon ami*. You are neutral and Corporal Mott is your protector. If we meet the enemy, he will fire his revolver to scare them away."

"And if they don't scare?"

Paquet smiled. "Then, as ordered, I will fire mine to prevent whatever the General told you from getting into enemy hands."

"Some friend you turn out to be."

Paquet shrugged his shoulders, hands displayed palms out. "*C'est la guerre.*"

"You two stop snickering at each other and let's go!" The Major was not amused.

Paquet swept his hand toward the Renault. "You will notice gentlemen that on each of your seats there is a new M-15 Adrian helmet, courtesy of General d'Urbal. At the General's orders, I must insist that you wear them when we arrive at our destination." The helmets were painted light blue and had a flaming grenade badge on their front to denote infantry. Ansel translated the instructions for the Major.

Now closer to the front, their permits and identification papers were closely examined at checkpoints and bridges. They were often delayed until an officer could be summoned to give permission for the group to proceed.

At road forks and intersections they were usually given directions by road guards or signs, but when there was no one to direct them, they chose the road leading in the direction of gun fire. The only maps both they and the French Army in the field had at the time were Michelin road maps that, prior to the war, were given away at tire stores and petrol stations. They were no longer too reliable since the movement of large armies had resulted in many new roads, some trailing off to the heads of communication trenches that fed the main lines. Nor could you always identify railroads depicted on the maps as many new rail lines had been laid to directly supply ammunition dumps and troop assembly areas.

As the sun dimmed into twilight, they were advised by a sergeant at a crossroad checkpoint not to venture further until morning. "You might be mistaken in the dark for a Bosch patrol and fired on." Mott pulled the Renault off the road into the trees.

"Well, Mister Hampton," Major Crosby smiled, "tonight you sleep like a soldier, on the ground."

While Corporal Mott unpacked blankets and waterproof sheets Major Crosby invited the six French soldiers guarding the crossroad to share rations with them. The *poilus* readily accepted. There could be no cook fire at night they said, nor even the use of a Primus stove. "We are within range of the German long guns. Their forward observers will call down fire on any light at night and any smoke during the day."

Still, there were no complaints about the canned ham and beans eaten cold with good wine. It was better, they said, than army issue rations—paper-wrapped biscuits, the canned boiled beef they called "monkey meat," dry salt fish and cheap wine referred to as pinard or plonk.

"Sergeant," Capitaine Paquet said, "my guests are here as neutral observers by permission of the French War Ministry. We were told we should join an artillery observation post on high ground in this area. Can you direct us to the site?"

"Yes, sir. Down the road but a few minutes by car, no more than three kilometers, there should be a road guard who can direct you to an artillery observation post on a hill about a hundred meters off the road toward the front. They have telephone connections to their gun battery and to regiment. That would be the spot. You can see a broad area of the front from there. But I caution you, a stretch of road you must cross runs along a ridge. You want to cross that fast. The Bosch artillery has that ridge registered. They can quickly fire on any movement up there."

"Thank you, Sergeant. We appreciate both the directions and the advice." Hampton, having listened, translated the Sergeant's statements to the Major.

"We need to get moving before dawn. Wouldn't want to come this far and miss—" the Major caught himself. He was going to say miss the attack, but he remembered that Paquet and Mott were not privy to the information of the impending attack. He said instead, "Tell Mott to put the top down; make us a little less a target crossing that ridge in the morning."

All night they heard artillery fire, very close, followed by the sound of the shells passing over them and the thump of their explosions in the distance. From time to time star shells dropping over 'no man's land' reflected off the low clouds sweeping in from the north.

With little sleep they were up by four. Mott packed the gear and they moved out with false dawn leaking dim light onto their path. The poor condition of the road made for slow going. They broke out of cover to realize they were at the beginning of the exposed kilometer of road leading across the ridge, the one they had been advised to cross quickly; advice found difficult to follow. The ridge road was rutted, eroded and in places required crossing poorly patched shell holes. Ten miles an hour was as fast as Mott dared without risking a blowout or worse, a broken wheel or axel.

They had crossed two thirds of the ridge when a round landed to the front right of them, luckily down the forward slope of the ridge. Rough road or not, Mott gave the Renault the gas. From the sound of it, the second shell went directly over the car to hit far down the back side of the ridge. As they bounced and jarred across the exposed terrain, one last shell hit just below the crest of the ridge behind the car. The forward slope absorbed most of the shrapnel, but the car and passengers were showered with clods of dirt before they escaped down into a hollow shielded by trees.

"I think the Bosch were just having fun," Paquet offered.

"Some fun," Andrew Hampton said, brushing dirt from his shoulders and dusting his hat over the side of the open car.

The Major and Lieutenant had quickly exchanged their soft caps for the French helmets.

Hampton, the only civilian, had not thought to do so.

A few minutes later, they reached a guard at the junction of the road and a trailhead. They were directed to pull off the road under trees to hide the motorcar should a German reconnaissance plane fly over.

Sunrise burst blood-red through low clouds to the east while gray clouds filled the western sky. Mott remained with the car while Paquet and the three Americans quickly walked to the observation post. Since the shelling on the ridge, Hampton did not have to be reminded to wear his helmet.

Paquet explained their presence to the forward observation team. From the brush-camouflaged bunker on the forward slope of a hill flanked by scrub trees the view afforded the visitors encompassed some 2,000 meters of trench lines, both French and German. The thud of the guns behind, the eerie sound of the shells overhead and the reverberations of their explosions on the German lines across 'no man's land' continued as it had for the five previous days.

Paquet, after investing the Americans with the French forward artillery observers, begged his leave. He said he knew his companions were there to watch Tenth Army launch an attack, had known it all along. "I have lived through three such attacks and do not need nor care to observe another one." Paquet's hand trembled slightly as he offered cigarettes all around. "With your permission, Major, I will wait at the Renault with Corporal Mott."

The Major nodded. Capitaine Paquet saluted, turned and walked back up the trail using his cane to transit the uneven ground.

Right on schedule, wave upon wave of Frenchmen poured up out of their forward trench, moved through the open lanes of their barbed wire, spread out and began the assault across six hundred yards of open ground; ground that had once been forest and farmland now turned into a moonscape plowed bare by shot and shell, fouled by obliterated flesh and un-retrieved bodies, cratered with water-filled shell holes and punctuated by limbless, charred and splintered tree trunks and stumps.

As the first wave of French infantrymen closed to less than a hundred yards of the German trench, the French forward artillery observers called, "Cessez le feu!" (Cease fire!) over the phone lines linking each with their respective batteries.

The German line, which had been cloaked in the smoke of bursting shells, suddenly cleared. Each of the three Americans had been issued artillery field glasses manufactured by L. Petit Fabt of Paris. Lifting the glasses to their eyes they could clearly see what had appeared moments before to be an abandoned trench, come alive with German soldiers climbing up on their firing steps as the first wave of *poilus* closed to within fifty yards. More ominous, machinegun barrels suddenly poked through concrete and steel shielded emplacements.

"My God," Hampton stated what they all were thinking, "How could they have survived artillery bombardment for six days?"

As if a light switch had been thrown, the entire German line opened fire. Frenchmen began to fall, at first in ones and twos from rifle fire. Then, before the sweeping, overlapping arcs of machinegun fire, they fell by the dozens. As the first wave of *poilus* reached the German barbed wire, strung ten rows deep in places, it was obvious that six days of artillery barrages had done little to cut up the strands of wire. Where the wire had been blown off the ground by heavy shells it had fallen back to earth in tangled cat's cradles even more difficult to cross than the standing wire. The leading French soldiers fell to their knees and began using wire cutters to clear paths through the wire. Some of the charging *poilus* chose not to wait. They struggled over the wire, many only to be cut down in the attempt, their impaled bodies dancing from repeated impacts of sweeping machinegun fire.

In some places, the Germans had set seemingly wide-open gaps in the wire that deliberately beckoned soldiers into the open mouths of inverted 'Vs' ever crowding them together as the open lanes narrowed. Machineguns cut them down in piles. To add to the mayhem, German artillery shells began to fall into 'no man's land' among the advancing second, third and fourth waves of Frenchmen. It was like nothing Ansel and Major Crosby had ever imagined, like nothing taught at West Point. Lee, Grant and Napoleon may have seen men charge into musket and cannon fire, but not through artillery fire into the teeth of machineguns. Within sight of the observers at least twenty machineguns along the defensive German line were delivering a potential combined rate of fire of 10,000 rounds a minute. Quinn and Crosby held their glasses steady, but Hampton lowered his. He had seen more than he wanted of the horrific images the glasses provided. He did not raise them again.

In several places along Vimy Ridge, what was left of the French first and second waves reached the enemy trench, firing down into it, tossing in grenades and jumping in to engage in brutal hand-to-hand combat.

German troops began pouring out of the first trench and retreating to their second trench. The French followed with the third and fourth waves close behind. Though units were thinned by thirty to as much as fifty percent casualties, the French reached their objective on Vimy Ridge, but just like months before, their achievement was short lived.

Large numbers of German reserve troops moved up through the retreating defenders to counterattack. The French reserves rushing to join the depleted first assault troops were cut up by artillery. Once again they were too few and too late. The fierce German counter attack overwhelmed them. Forced to retire, the exhausted *poilus* now struggled under fire to reach their own lines. Heavy rain began to fall as the low, dark clouds overhead spilled their liquid burdens. Retreating Frenchmen began to lose their footing and slide down the forward slope of Vimy Ridge as the Germans regained their trench and fired down on them. German artillery dropped shells among them. Old shell holes were already full of water and new ones began to fill as the rain fell. The withdrawing *poilus* found themselves trying to run in ankle-deep mud, some sinking into the stinking slop almost up to their calves, all the while taking fire. Men tried to help their wounded comrades. Some, using the shoulder of a friend for support, stumbled along. Many stopped to lift a wounded soldier onto their back and struggle toward the safety of the French line. More than a few died trying to help a comrade. The standing order on an attack was for soldiers not to stop to aid the fallen. Stretcher bearers were to collect them. That never worked well in the attack, and not at all in retreat under fire. There were never enough stretcher bearers and in deep mud it took not two but four men to carry a stretcher.

To add to the slaughter, German artillery continued to fall in spite of the French artillery using what ammunition they had left as counter battery fire. Men were blown to pieces, and simply disappeared into black smoke and pink mist. Others were hit by shrapnel or had limbs cut away by razor-sharp hot shards of steel from exploding shells. Still others, not directly hit, were knocked unconscious or killed outright by the concussion of exploding shells. Wounded or whole men sought protection in shell holes hoping to reach their line after dark. As the level of rainwater rose, those not strong enough or conscious enough to hold their heads above the filthy slime would drown.

The exhausted Germans, satisfied to retake their lost trench, did not pursue the French. Instead, they returned to their firing steps and machinegun emplacements to fire at the withdrawing enemy until once again a French artillery barrage drove them into their well-designed and reinforced underground bunkers.

The artillery observers told Ansel that had the Germans known that the French artillery units were almost out of ammunition, they probably could have broken the French line, but both sides had had enough for the day. (*The Entente would not take Vimy Ridge for another three bloody years.*)

Major Crosby, Andrew Hampton and Ansel Quinn, soaked to the bone, returned to the Renault. Mott had put up the top and had a dry blanket waiting for each of the 'voyeurs of battle.' There was no conversation. Mott started the Renault, turned it around and started back the way they had come. Covered by mist and rain, they received no fire when crossing the ridge. The road was more difficult having turned to mud, but Mott was able to navigate the car through slips and slides in muck almost up to the axels. Twice the officers had to get out in mud up to their calves and push to free the bogged down car.

They passed the chateau turnoff without stopping.

"General d'Urbal will be in no mood to receive us," the Major said. He had Lieutenant Quinn inform Capitaine Paquet of his desire to return to Paris as soon as possible. "We will drive sunup to sundown, sleep on the ground wherever darkness catches us, and drive into the night once it is safe to do so without being shot at check points. Tell Corporal Mott we will take turns driving. No stopping for meals. We eat cold rations while we drive."

Andrew Hampton translated the Major's orders to Paquet and Mott, neither of which complained. They stopped only to answer calls of nature, fuel the car from the five gallon tins and fix flat tires, using all but one of the spares they carried. They gave what remained of their rations to the soldiers at the last two check points before reaching the Paris fortifications. Major Crosby called a halt long enough for him to get out and remove the white flag from the bumper. He left the American flag in place and tried to clean enough mud off to make it recognizable.

Reaching Paris midmorning, the mud splattered Renault and its filthy, mud-covered passengers drew stares from the crowded sidewalk cafes along with occasional shouts of "Vive les Américains!" by those who recognized the tattered flag on the bumper.

When they reached the American Chancellery at Number 5 Rue de Chaillot, all of them were bone tired. Major Crosby gave Andrew Hampton and Lieutenant Quinn a week to pour over their journals and present a draft report of their independent observations, findings and comments.

"You are to be accurate in recording your observations and absolutely honest with your findings and comments. Your reports will be kept confidential. The

Ambassador will use your drafts to compose an official report to be sent by courier to President Wilson and the War Department. Any questions?" There were none.

The Major told Lieutenant Quinn to instruct Corporal Mott to drive him and Capitaine Paquet to their respective quarters before returning the car with compliments to Commandant de Montravel of the French Army motorcar service of Paris.

Andrew Hampton and Major Crosby were quartered at the Chancellery. They lifted their gear from the car and nodded goodbye at the curb. Fatigued beyond caring, they drug themselves into the building. The French doorman looked with a degree of shock, or was it contempt, at the mud covered apparitions trudging through the opened door. He could hardly believe it was the always fastidiously dressed American Ambassador's Assistant Second Secretary and the Embassy's Military Attaché. Both men, leaving trails of mud and dirt behind them, were too exhausted to care. The doorman immediately sent for house maids to clean the carpet, elevator and upper floor hallway leading to the men's separate quarters. When they reached his door, Hampton told them to go away. They could clean his room later, much later. The Major never answered his door. Major Crosby wearily bathed, dressed and reported the party's return to Ambassador Sharp. Hampton slept through lunch and dinner. He did not appear in his office until the next morning.

Five days later Ansel turned in his draft report to Major Crosby as ordered. It was titled:

Confidential Report

Observations during travel to and from the front in the vicinity of Artois, France including the Assault upon Vimy Ridge by 10th French Army, May 9, 1915.

Ansel presented detailed observations of the battle. In addition, he included information given by Capitaine Paquet of his time in the trenches, the recollections of Doctor and Madame Arceneau, and the details of the planned attack on Vimy Ridge as given in the briefing by Tenth Army Commander, General d'Urbal. As agreed, he did not name Capitaine Paquet or General d'Urbal as sources in his report, stating he had given his word as an officer and gentleman not to reveal his sources. Aware that the general summary of his report might gain the animosity of high ranking officers in Wilson's War Department, Ansel nonetheless bluntly stated conclusions he had drawn from what he had personally witnessed. The report, marked confidential, consisted of thirty-two pages and was signed:

With respect,
I remain your loyal servant,
1st Lieutenant Ansel Quinn, United States Army

CHAPTER THREE

French War Ministry, August 1915

Nearly three months after the sinking of *Lusitania,* documents began to arrive addressed to Lieutenant J. Ansel Quinn, United States Army, in care of French War Ministry, Rue St. Dominique, Paris, France. Beginning in March, 1915, Ansel was serving a two-year assignment to the French Army as a neutral observer.

The documents were from the law firm of Todd, Cochran and Roberts, Vicksburg, Mississippi, the firm that had for years represented Beverly Bethany Quinn and her various business interests. The cover letter of each document began:

Dear Lieutenant Quinn:

We understand your grief at this time, but our legal and fiduciary duties and responsibilities require us to ensure all proper formalities and legalities according to the laws of Mississippi are carried out in the settlement of your aunt's estate. Although, because of the tragic circumstances of her death, it will be some time before your aunt can be declared legally deceased. We have petitioned the courts, based upon the tragic circumstances, to expedite such legal findings in order that your aunt's interests can have continuity of management and enterprise. Please read the enclosed documents carefully, especially those dealing with appraisals of property, bank accounts, accounting documents of your aunt's business enterprises, tax documents, stock portfolios and personnel files on current management staffs of both the Mississippi and Cuban holdings. If you find them satisfactory, please affix your signature where indicated and return same to us. We, of course, will entertain any questions and any requests for more information which you may have.

Ansel sat down and wrote a letter to Lizzy Culberson, Bethany's long-employed house keeper and cook to assure her that she would, indeed, keep her job; that Bethany had always considered her as a member of the Shamrock family and for her not to worry. Lawyer Todd would be instructed to continue her pay as always. In addition, she should see that her husband Elijah along with Jake, Will, Ben and Essie Mae stay on to care for the farm cottage, gardens outbuildings and town house as always. He signed the letter *Ansel Quinn* and posted it, along with various communications to the law firm of Todd, Cochran and Roberts, with Major Crosby for inclusion in the next diplomatic mail pouch.

Some weeks later, a package of a different sort arrived from the attorneys. Ansel sat at his desk in his cramped, dingy office with its one small, grimy dormer window on the top floor of French Army General Headquarters and opened the well-wrapped package. Inside he found another parcel carefully enclosed in wrapping paper yellowed with age and tied with string. On the paper wrapping, handwritten in pencil, were the words: *For Ansel Quinn: To be delivered upon my death.* It was signed, *B. B. Quinn.* The contents consisted of two diaries and a most unusual gold and lead pendant.

I'll be damned, it's a spent bullet enfolded in gold!

Embossed in gold on the worn leather binding of the first diary was the single name, *Annielise.* The second diary had a soft, cloth cover bearing the hand-inked name, *Bethany.* Pinned inside its front cover was a French Legionnaire's insignia.

The first diary was that of his father's younger sister, who Ansel had been told was his great aunt Annielise, Bethany's mother. It told of the siege and surrender of Vicksburg and the return of the Quinn family to the burned remains of Shamrock Plantation. As a boy, Ansel had spent his summers at Shamrock in a cottage Bethany had built there. He had heard some family stories of that time from his father, Jonathan Hillary Quinn.

He read the written words of his great aunt, Annielise, and those of his great-grandmother, Nannie Keturah Quinn, and at the end, words added by Annielise's godfather, Doctor Theodore Perkins—after Annielise, Nannie and grandfather Quinn were murdered in a shootout melee with three discharged, rogue Yankee soldiers, all but one of which were killed that terrible day. It was the doctor's words that explained the pendent, the lead bullet enfolded in gold.

Ansel was not sure it wasn't a joke or that the doctor had lost his mind. Dr. Theodore Perkins wrote that the bullet was, in effect, his aunt Bethany's father; that it had passed through the testicles of a young Confederate soldier, rumored to be part Choctaw, and thus, slathered in his semen, struck his great aunt, sixteen at the time, in the lower abdomen penetrating her reproductive organs. The result was her pregnancy and the birth of his aunt Bethany.

My God! Could this be true?

Ansel put down the diary. His mind wandered back to Shamrock plantation in Mississippi. He had known that his father, Captain Jonathan Quinn, facing the family's terrible financial losses of the Civil War, saved Shamrock and gained a sugar plantation in Cuba by running guns to the Cuban rebels in their quest for freedom from Spain—first in the Ten Years War and later in The War of Independence that evolved into the Spanish American War. He knew his Aunt Bee Bee, as Bethany was called, had been a spy in Havana for the Cuban rebels during the insurrection prior to the American declaration of war against Spain. As a young boy he was sent from Havana, when fighting threatened the city, to Marion Military Institute in Alabama. He remembered how proud they all were much later when he graduated from West Point, all except for Bethany who never wanted him to follow a military career. She wanted him to join the family enterprises.

A cold thought struck him. *Maybe she was right. With her death, who is left to run the business? Me? Here I sit accumulating military information on a war my country-men don't want to fight.*

Next, he picked up the second journal, the one with the cloth cover. If he was shocked with disbelief in what he read in Annielise Quinn's journal, he was thunderstruck by the revelations contained in Bethany's diary.

It was daybreak the next morning when Ansel finished reading the last page of the last diary. He got up from his desk and walked to the little window to stare out at a gray dawn accompanied by a light drizzle descending morosely upon the soot-stained rooftops of Paris.

I'm not at all who I thought I was. No one was.

Bethany's words had revealed the incredible truth about him and the secret his family had kept from him. Ansel's real mother and father were not Jonathan and Louisette. His real mother was Bethany! She had had an affair with a French officer while she attended school in Paris, an officer ten years her senior, a Captain Henrí Bourget. A man who, like Bethany, had lost his family to civil war; in his case when the Commune of Paris revolted against the new French republic formed after the Franco-Prussian war of 1870–71. Bethany hadn't discovered she was pregnant until her return to Havana and her lover's departure to Cochin China halfway round the world. She determined her child would not grow up without a father and be the victim of mean gossip as she had, and so contrived a plan. Louisette, who was childless, would go from Havana to New Orleans with her. En route they switched identities. Who in Louisiana would know the difference? By assuming the identity of Louisette, Bethany's baby was officially born the son of Jonathan and Louisette Quinn.

No wonder none of them wanted me to know all that is revealed here until they were gone. In her love for me, Bethany gave me a wonderful, legitimate mother and father. How hard it must have been for her to pretend to be just my aunt all these years. They loved me as I loved them. They kept faith with each other for my sake. But now, what in God's name would they have me do?

Of all the disclosures presented in the diaries, one was so stunning as to burden Ansel with a dilemma Bethany could never have envisioned.

What would you have me do? he asked Bethany, and then of himself, *If the roles were reversed what would I want?*

Ansel had never suffered such emotional stress, not even in jungle fighting in the Philippines.

Bethany's secret was now his secret.

I could let it die, do nothing. How the hell could fate play such a trick?

At that moment, Ansel remembered a time at Shamrock Plantation, when he was home just after graduation from West Point. Bethany had gotten a little tipsy on bourbon. He had never seen here that way before. She looked at him and said a very strange thing. "Ansel do you know your Aunt Bethany was born of war and is fortune's whore? Yes. It's true. Your Aunt Bethany, it seems, has always been fortune's play-thing." She paused, and with a sad smile on her pretty face, she continued. "What tales

I could tell of the tricks fate has played on me," she paused again and looked at him. "But I won't. Now be a dear and get me another bourbon and water with a little ice."

Ansel picked up the diary. Looking at Bethany's hand written name on the cover he asked himself, *Has fate played the last trick on you or on me? If I do nothing, I'll be haunted by the secret, but what turmoil will I cause if I act on your belated revelation; what price the consequences? You planned it so I would not know until Jonathan, Louisette and you were dead. In the end you wanted me to know. But Bethany dear, you could not have dreamed the burden it has placed on me.*

Daylight found a sleepless, disheveled lieutenant still at his desk in his cramped little office. He remained there on duty for what seemed an endless work day through which he was unable to accomplish a single task.

At day's end, he hailed a taxi and gave the driver an address. The taxi made its way along the Champs-Elysées to the Place De l'Etoile, past the colossal Arc de Triomphe, on toward the Bois de Boulogne before turning into Villa Saïd in the 16th arrondissement and stopping at house number six. It was Bethany's house, the one she had inherited from Louisette and Jonathan, the one that had been Louisette's home when Jonathan first met her, the one they had kept all through the years to use whenever they ran away together from all the stress of Havana for a romantic visit to Paris.

Tristan and Pauline Babineau, the elderly couple that had cared for the house for years, met Ansel at the front door.

"Oh! Monsieur Quinn," the woman said, "we were so worried when you did not come home last night."

"I had to finish an important report. I should have sent word," Ansel replied as he started up the stairs with the two diaries tucked into his attaché case. "Don't bother with supper. I'm too tired to eat."

"But you must eat something. A little soup, sir?"

"I'll see you in the morning," Ansel said and kept going to his room where he collapsed on the bed without undressing.

Sleep would not come. He turned on the bedside lamp, picked up Bethany's diary to re-read a little, then drifted into memories.

I know now why you were so loving. How hard it must have been for you to play my aunt. You were such fun, and we did such daring things. You taught me to ride almost before I could walk. You taught me to swim and to sail in your own boat at the Havana Yacht Club. No other woman even owned a sail boat in Havana. I remember when you sneaked me off to the cock fights and taught me how to bet. My mother, no my adoptive mother Louisette, always let me go with you whenever you asked. Now I know why.

I remember your little pistol and the story about the time you shot a man that was trying to rape you. As a young boy, I was impressed. Oh, how I complained when you gave me dancing lessons. You said one day the ladies would like me for that, although I wasn't interested in ladies at age thirteen. I am happy to report you were right. And you instilled in me a love for books. Jonathan and Louisette were wonderful parents. Jonathan taught me to be a man, but you were such fun, so daring. You gave me a love of adventure. When I was sent from Havana to school in Alabama, how lonely at times you must have been. I'm glad you found lasting love with my father's, I mean Jonathan's, partner in Cuba. Felipe Alacon was a fine man. He never knew did he? I guess you are all together now . . . but I am here. What in God's name would you have me do?

For more than a week, Ansel agonized over the most difficult moral and personal conflict he had ever faced, a conflict he knew Bethany and his loving, adoptive parents never imagined. He could not concentrate on his work. His reports to the American Embassy suffered. He hardly ate anything and lost weight. He took on a haggard appearance from lack of sleep, drawing glances from those who knew him and those who did not as he walked the halls of the French War Ministry. One staff officer asked if he was feeling well. Ansel replied that he felt fine and asked to be allowed to go to the front again to observe and report on war with Germany first hand. His request was refused, both by the French and by Major Crosby at the American Embassy.

In the end, he reasoned what his mother, his real mother Bethany, would have wanted given the inconceivable circumstances. It was left to him to fit the last piece into the puzzle of Bethany's adventurous life; a task she never intended would fall to him.

CHAPTER FOUR

The previous night, Lieutenant Ansel Quinn had made the hardest decision of his life. Wearing a freshly cleaned and pressed uniform, he left his closet-like office, descended several sets of stairs leading to the main floor and walked down a long hall to stop at a crowded outer office. He spoke to the nearest of several busy French army clerks who directed him to the sergeant in charge.

"Sergeant, I have a pressing need to speak to your commander in private. I won't take but a moment of his time."

"Is it important, Lieutenant? A military matter?"

"It is important, Sergeant. My mother was lost on *Lusitania*."

The soldier looked at the haggard, drawn face of the young American officer, paused a moment, then nodded toward the open door of a spacious inter-office. Ansel knocked on the door casing.

A distinguished looking, gray-bearded officer sitting behind a large desk stacked high with reports spoke without looking up, "Well, what is it?" he said impatiently.

Unable to find the words with which to answer, Ansel walked forward, placed a journal with a plain cloth cover on the desk, saluted and stood at attention.

The officer, agitated by the interruption, picked up the journal and glancing up at the young American lieutenant asked, "*Qu'est ce que c'est*?" Ansel remained silent but cast his eyes down at the diary. Following his gaze, the officer looked at the cover of the journal held in his hand.

He was silent for a long moment before gazing up with a look, it appeared to Ansel, of a man who had recovered a lost piece of his soul. The officer dropped his eyes back to the diary and softly spoke the name written on its cover. "Bethany?" He opened the cover and stared at the French Legionnaire's insignia pinned there. Like a whispered prayer he repeated the name and looked up at Ansel, a trace of moisture forming in the corners of his questioning eyes. "Bethany Quinn?"

Ansel nodded and lowered his eyes to the engraving on a brass plate affixed to a polished wooden block sitting on the officer's desk:

Général Henrí Bourget, Legionnaire
Armée de France

General Bourget glanced through several pages and looked up in silent questioning. "I think she would have wanted you to read it, sir. Bethany was lost with *Lusitania*."

The General looked as though he had been struck a blow, an expression of shock as if the air had been sucked from his lungs, his face white, drained of blood. He tried to stand but sank back into his chair. "Forgive me, but you see, I loved her those many years ago here in Paris . . . I have loved her across all the years."

What have I done? Ansel questioned himself. *I should have kept this all to myself. Oh, Bethany! I know you could not have known he was here or even that he was still alive.*

The General struggled out of his chair. "Who are you, Lieutenant? I have seen you in the hallway once or twice. You are the American assigned here as an observer, are you not?"

"Yes sir. My name is Ansel Quinn. I have read the diary which was sent to me by the attorneys of her estate according to the instructions of her will. She could have had no idea that you would be in Paris, no idea that you would outlive her, certainly no idea that she would die so unexpectedly. Under the circumstances, sir, I believe she would want you to read it."

The General, still trying to contain his emotions ask, "I don't speak English, only a little. Could you translate her writing for me?"

"Sir, I think I cannot. I was shocked by her death and I only received her diary a short time ago. Please, sir, if you have a source, a confidant who can translate her words, I think it would be better. Then, perhaps we two could talk, or not, as you may wish. I will leave the diary with you, but I cherish it and ask that you return it to me. I am sorry I have interrupted your work, but I have done so only after days of soul searching. I think she would want you to read it."

"I don't know what to say to you, Lieutenant Quinn." General Bourget paused. "Yes, I think I know someone I can trust who will agree to translate the diary. You are sure the words are hers?"

"I am sure, sir. They are written in her own hand. I received the diary sealed by her with the instructions that upon her death it was to be given to me. I had never seen it or knew of its existence."

"Whatever it contains regarding me I trust you will keep confident."

"Yes sir." Ansel saluted, did an about face and walked from the room.

The General picked up the diary, opened the cover, touched his Legionnaire's insignia pinned there and whispered, "Dear Bethany, after all the years you have torn open this old soldier's heart once again."

Holding the diary, he picked up his képi and walked from his office telling his sergeant on the way out that he would be absent for the rest of the day. The sergeant who had been with Bourget since he was a major simply answered, "Yes, General." Bourget placed the képi on his head and left the building.

Several junior officers just arriving saluted the General as he walked from the front door. It was a beautiful day with downy clouds lazing in an azure sky. The General didn't notice. It could have been raining and he wouldn't have noticed. A few blocks away he turned into a public square, mostly deserted, and found an unoccupied bench facing a small fountain. He sat there very alone, holding the diary in his hand, staring into a fragment of the past that had arrived with an ebullition of memories.

It must have been, what, nearly thirty years ago when I met you here in Paris? I was twenty-nine, home from Algeria to attend staff school. We met the first time at one of Madame Dagobert de Mudon's grand parties. I saw you from across the room. You were the most beautiful creature I had ever seen, raven hair, green eyes and a smile that lit up the room. You stole the heart of every man there. I already knew your name, Beverly Bethany Quinn, and had been startled to find you were from the Southern United States. I watched you move from one small group to another, as bored by the gossip and shallow conversation as was I. Standing alone, my back against the wall, I saw you glance my way. When I caught your gaze and returned it with a smile, you seemed embarrassed and walked to the refreshment table, your champagne glass empty.

I had no idea you were only nineteen, Bethany. I followed you.

"Mademoiselle Quinn, may I fill your glass?" *I remember the conversation as if it were yesterday.*

"You have me at a disadvantage, sir. You seem to know my name, but I do not know yours, Captain. You are a Captain are you not?"

"You are very observant, Mademoiselle. May I apologize at my rudeness and introduce myself. I am Henri Bourget, a poor soldier at your service."

"Well, Captain Bourget, how is it that you know my name?"

"I would say that every man in this room has asked the name of the lovely young lady with the interesting accent and emerald eyes, even this old soldier."

"I don't see an old soldier. Is there one here?" *You looked about, then back at me and laughed.*

"Perhaps not, if a young lady is willing to grant him the pleasure of her conversation."

"And when did you ask someone my name? Was it when you caught me stealing a glance at you just now?"

"I asked your name two weeks ago."

"Two weeks!"

"Yes, the first time I saw you. It was at the Opera. You were wearing a white dress."

"Well, Captain, I must return to my escort, it is almost time to leave." *Yes, of course. Is your chaperone with you tonight?"*

"I see you know about that also. Does it seem silly to you in this modern age?"

"I think it is charming. If I were your uncle, I'm sure I would insist on such an arrangement for my niece alone in Paris."

"My, you seem to know a lot about me, Captain. Is it just curiosity about a Southern American girl?"

"It is the foolishness of an older man about a beautiful younger woman. I hope I have not offended you."

"The younger woman finds offense only at the reference to an older man. You can't be that much older than me. Look around the room. I see mostly boys here, and I sometimes tire of the company of boys. For instance, take the tall one there."

You indicated to me three young men standing in front of the marble fireplace.

"He claims to be a count or something and is with my boorish young escort, a banker's son who can talk only of money. The serious one, with his back to us, studies music. I *believe his name is Debussy or something. As you can see, they seem uninterested in the company of this lady."*

"I have seen you one other time," I said, "You were riding in the Bois de Boulogne."

"I believe you have been spying on me," you laughed.

"In France, taking notice of a beautiful lady is not spying. It is the national pastime, but I would prefer the role of escort to that of spy. Would you consider riding with me next Sunday? I can provide your chaperone with proper references if you like."

"Why, Captain Bourget, I would love to go riding next Sunday."

"Do you know a stable called Le Cheval du Roi?"

"Yes, I know that stable."

"Would two o'clock be convenient?"

"Two o'clock will be fine."

We rode that Sunday, and the next and often after that. You filled my heart. You fill it now in this joyful, sad, sweet moment. I remember we would dismount and walk along the trail, talking. Sometimes we picnicked in the shade of trees. Your wit and laughter and our conversations veiled the desire that played between us like a butterfly in the wind. I knew better. I was ten years older. I told you that. You looked up at me with those smiling eyes of yours, laughed and called me silly. I told you that I would soon leave for duty in Cochin China, half a world away, and that your duty was to your family and mine was to France. You touched my lips with your fingers and told me, "Enough," then kissed me and told me you wanted to make love before I left; that you, too, soon would be leaving Paris and returning to Cuba, that we should share our love now or a beautiful thing would be lost forever.

I tried many arguments, but none was strong enough. "What you ask, dear Bethany, no man could refuse. In the end, it will be painful for both of us."

You must have known that. It was a love neither of us could keep except in our hearts. This thing you insisted upon, this invitation, this brief affair, I told you would haunt me all my life. It has. You listened quietly to all my arguments. Your answer was always the same—a pleading look, a silent kiss.

I knew your chaperone, that mysterious island woman, would not let this happen. I counted on that, but somehow you won her to your side. How did you do that?

And so I engaged a pied-à-terre, the small one with a view of the Seine you picked out for our weekend rendezvous.

That first time you admitted that you felt a little strange, not embarrassed, just awkward. I wanted to send you away, I felt so guilty. You asked me to hold you for a moment. I told you that I was the one who felt awkward, worse, guilty. I knew you should not be there.

I remember you words, Bethany. You lifted you head from my shoulder and said, "Don't speak of guilt. There will be enough of that later. I was afraid you would not be here. This little apartment, it is all we will ever have, our only time is now."

I told you I was not sure I could make love to you, that I was afraid.

You looked up and asked me, "Afraid?"

"Yes!" I told you. I was afraid of hurting you, afraid of the haunting memories of you that would follow me the rest of my life. They have you know. You are here with me now.

I have never seen anything so desirable as you were that day. Adam's real tragedy was that he knew the consequence of eating the apple and still could not help himself. After that first time, I propped up on one elbow and looked down at you with your hair spilled over the pillow, your dark eyelashes contrasting with the lovely complexion radiating from a face serene in sleep. You, Bethany dear, represented the essence of what men live and die for, whatever other excuses may be written.

I remember being gentlemanly by gathering your clothes from the floor and putting them on the bed when a small silver pistol spilled from them.

I lifted the pistol. "You are even a more dangerous woman than I imagined," I told you. I am sure true surprise was showing on my face.

"Yes, I am," you said smiling, "and don't you forget it." I never have.

I remember that bright day in April of 1883 when we met at Le Cheval du Roi stable. Time now weighed heavily upon my thoughts. The last of your schooling, your reason for being in Paris, would be finished at the end of May. My staff school assignment in Paris was over. My scheduled departure to the Orient was approaching.

You asked me, "Why Cochin China?" You had no idea where it was or how far away. I told you that Napoleon III had invited himself to protect the country back in 1861, that France had built a beautiful city there called Saigon and there was trouble in the countryside. I had been ordered there and, as a soldier, I must go.

I could have asked you, "Why Cuba?" but I didn't. It would have started an argument I could not have won. You knew that, didn't you?

We stopped for a picnic. You set lunch on the cloth and I opened the wine. That is when you asked about my scars. I reminded you that you promised not to ask again. You laughed and told me that you fibbed. I didn't mean to tell you, but once I began to talk about those days I had kept inside so long, I couldn't stop. I had never told anyone. I told you that the first one came from a Prussian rifleman at Sedan where we lost the Franco-Prussian war. When I started to talk about the other wound, you sensed the pent-up torment inside me and tried to stop me, but like an open wound that had festered in my heart and soul, the memories burst from me. I know I told you more than you wanted to hear; that by the time I was released from the German hospital and returned to Paris a group instilled with class hatred by the writings of Karl Marx had gone mad. They called themselves the Commune of Paris and started civil war to overthrow the new Republic. Once more in the uniform of France, I found I had to defend my country against Frenchmen, if I can use the term for those Communard bastards. I told you how they killed my family. You tried again to stop me and I should have, but there was more you needed to know about this soldier. I think you were shocked when I told you all of it. The army was all I had left, my only family, my only home. They offered me garrison duty here, but I could not bear to stay in Paris with such memories. I volunteered for the Legion. I had returned from seven years in Algeria when I met you. I only returned to attend staff school and receive a briefing on my new assignment. If you had not captured me with those green eyes, I would not have stayed so long in Paris. I used all my leave to be with you. That was the cruelest act I have ever committed. I carry the guilt of loving you tempered only by the knowledge that you were far better off free of me. For thirty years, memories of you have haunted me. It was insane of me to allow our love to happen, to hurt you.

I remember your brave words. You said, "Henrí, we agreed. No regrets. Besides, my poor soldier, you could not help yourself. Madame Wombi and I cast a Voodoo spell on you. It was out of your control. Of course, you will miss me terribly." You smiled a brave smile.

You'd asked me to pour you another glass of wine and then take you to the apartment, our apartment, and make love to you as if the world would end that day. You said you would make love to me better than any woman ever had or ever would and you did! Oh! Bethany, you did!

Do you remember the day we planned a picnic and it rained? We spread the picnic over the bed, opened the wine, got naked as the day we were born and fed lunch to each other.

You finally tired of making excuses and told me how your family, too, was murdered. And remember how surprised I was when you told me the fact that your uncle Jonathan's J & Q Shipping sometimes dealt in arms. "My God!" I said, "I thought I held an innocent angel only to discover you are a gunrunner, which I should have suspected when I found your beautiful thigh laced with a pistol."

You gave me joy when I had forgotten the word, much less its meaning. You taught me to notice blue skies, the flight of birds, the laughter of children, the fragrance of flowers, to believe there still was good in the world, to live again.

There was a deadline to our weekend lives together. You said you could not face a goodbye. You made me agree not to tell you the date of my departure; that there would simply come a weekend when I would not be at the rendezvous. It made me feel such a coward, but you were right. I never could have stood before you to say goodbye, for I never could have left you. I think you knew that.

I know you found the note I left you because you have the Legionnaire's insignia I pinned to the note, the note that told you to forget your old soldier, and forgive him if you could.

Your beauty and free spirit would have dried up and died as a Legionnaire officer's wife dragged from outpost to outpost, from desert sands to lands of jungle fevers. I could not ask that of you. A whole world awaited your youth and beauty and spirit, a world I could never give you. In the note I wrote that I would love you until the day I die. That was true, Bethany. That is true.

Now this Lieutenant Quinn has brought me your diary. I am almost afraid to get it translated, afraid of what you will say about me. My hope is that it will tell me you have had a full life, an exciting life, the life you could never have had as a poor soldier's wife in all the drab and dangerous places I have been assigned. I have seen the toll it has taken on other soldiers' wives. I could never have done that to you.

And yes, Bethany, there have been women over the years, some were fun, some wild, some just filled a need. I am ashamed of that, but there were none such as you. And no, I never married, never loved the way I loved you. I am just the way you left me—no wife, no family, except of course, the army, always the army. And now, I am truly an old soldier brought back to duty because of this cursed war that has taken your life. The Germans think they will gain French land, but in the end they will destroy themselves after wasting the lives of untold young men. It is madness.

"Monsieur! Monsieur!"

Henrí, startled back to the present, looked up to see a little girl holding a red balloon on a string staring at him.

"Who are you talking to?" she asked. "Who is Bethany? I am sure I heard you talking to her, but I don't see her."

"Adélaïde!" A woman called. "Come here child and leave that nice man alone."

Henrí stood and touched the brim of his képi. "She was no bother, Madame. Such a pretty little girl. I was just leaving. Enjoy this beautiful day."

"*Oui monsieur, c'est une belle journée.*"

Henrí wondered how many of his thoughts had escaped through his lips while he sat daydreaming of Bethany. *I thought only old men did that.* He smiled at himself, walked to the street and flagged a taxi. "23 Quai de Conti," he told the driver. They arrived at the Bibliothèque Mazarine, the oldest library in France.

He paid the driver, entered the enormous edifice and made his way to the small English auxiliary reading room. There he approached an attractive lady seated behind the desk.

It would be hard for a stranger to judge her age. Her eyes were light blue. Her red hair, cut short in the new "war" fashion, was showing streaks of grey, but her fair skin was smooth without blemish. She was dressed in a dark suit with silk blouse and wore no jewelry save a simple gold English bar pin with seed pearls and garnets. She smiled with recognition when she looked up to see the officer approaching her desk.

"Bonjour, Aileen."

"Bonjour, Henrí. What brings you to the library today? I haven't seen you in ages."

"I've been busy, but today I am on a special quest." He laid the diary on the desk. "I wonder if you would take on a very private task for me. I will pay for your time, of course."

"Why Henrí, what is it? And no, I will not accept any pay from you. Now tell me, what is this you have that makes you act so mysterious?"

"I have been loaned the very personal diary of an American lady I once knew. En route to visit a young American officer, in Paris as a neutral observer, she was lost aboard *Lusitania*. He received her diary among other documents sent by the attorneys for her estate. Strangely, he has loaned it to me saying she would have wanted me to read it. I can't, since it is written in English. And since you are English, dear Aileen, I thought perhaps you would translate it for me."

"But surely you have translators at your headquarters?"

"I've come to you because the lady was and remains very dear to me. I am sure it is the very personal story of her life. You are the only one in Paris who I can trust to keep the contents private. I suspect, if made the object of gossip, the contents would violate the memory and trust of a lovely lady. I don't care about me, but I am not at all sure that the contents won't embarrass you. Now, will you still take on the job?"

"Of course Henrí, how could I refuse? And don't worry, I promise to keep whatever is there a secret. We are, after all, very old friends," she smiled. "We have our own secrets, don't we?"

"We do." Henrí kissed her on the cheek. "Thank you, Aileen. It will mean a great deal to me. And how is Gaetan? He is still teaching history at the Sorbonne I trust."

"Yes, but Henrí, I am so worried about him. He is depressed. So many of his students have left for the army. He keeps a list of the names of those who have been killed in this horrible war. He visits those who have returned wounded. With no children of our own, his students are his children. I think it is breaking his heart. He hardly eats, hardly speaks at home. He sits in the garden with books in his lap, but I don't think he reads them. I try to comfort him. I don't know what to do anymore."

"The war touches so many lives, especially those who, like Gaetan and yourself, must carry on in spite of it all. Perhaps I should not have brought this to you." He reached for the diary.

"No! No! It gives me something new and different to do. The English desk is not so busy these days. With the war, most of the English and Americans have gone home. I really want to do this for you."

"Bless you. Please let me know if I can do anything for Gaetan; maybe take you two to dinner or get him out of the house for a walk."

"Thank you, Henrí. I think he would like that."

Henrí nodded, turned and left for headquarters where he tried unsuccessfully to carry on as usual while waiting for the translation.

It was the same for Ansel.

Two weeks later a knock came on his office door.

"*Entrez!*"

A clerk entered. "Lieutenant, sir, General Bourget asked me to deliver this." He handed Ansel a sealed note and stood discretely out in the hallway.

Ansel opened and read it.

Dear Lieutenant Quinn,

Would you be available and willing to meet me for dinner tonight at the restaurant Champeaux, Place de la Bourse, eight o'clock? If you come, I would request that you dress in mufti, as will I. The clerk will wait for your answer.

Ansel wrote:

Yes Sir. I will be there. Eight o'clock.

He signed his name, refolded the note and handed it to the waiting clerk.

Ansel sat at his desk and tormented himself with questions only time could answer. *How does one, thirty years late, meet a man who is one's father, a man who only just discovered that astonishing fact? Does General Bourget even believe Bethany's words, or that the diary is in fact hers? Would I if I were in his place? And what will he think was my reason for giving the diary to him? To hurt him, make him feel guilty or that I want something from him after all these years? He is sure to ask my reason. What will I answer?*

There was hardly room in his small office to pace, but pace he did, five steps from the back wall to the door and five back.

Bethany, have I done the right thing, what you would have wanted, or have I caused unnecessary suffering to a man who never had to know? The circumstances in which you have put me, put Henrí Bourget would never have entered your mind. I know that. What would you have done if you had arrived here safely and discovered he was here? Would there have been joy between you two or sadness? Rekindled love or recrimination? Would you have even told me and Henrí the truth, or kept silent knowing I would know only upon your death as you planned? I know you did the unselfish kindness of giving me a loving mother and father so I wouldn't grow up fatherless as you did. How hard that must have been for you.

Well, Bethany, I have done what I have done and will have to accept the consequences whatever they may be.

At the end of another worried, stressful, unproductive workday, Ansel took a taxi home, bathed, dressed in a grey-striped, three piece serge suit and, with nothing left to do, sat impatiently watching the clock.

Tristan Babineau entered the parlor to tell Ansel the taxi he had arranged had arrived. Ansel picked up his homburg, walked to the street and gave the driver the address of Champeaux restaurant. He hoped to be early, and was, but upon giving his name to the maître d'hôtel he was directed to an occupied table in a quiet corner. The General stood. Bethany's diary was on the table.

For a few awkward moments, each man stood silently searching the other for physical similarities a father and son might see in one another.

Henrí was about five feet eight inches tall. Ansel was a little taller, five feet ten and a half inches. Ansel's complexion was fair. Henrí had a handsome but weathered face; a man who had seen years of harsh climes. The look reminded Ansel of Jonathan who had been exposed to years at sea. Ansel's dark hair was in contrast to the white hair of the man he faced, but there were similarities in texture, shape and part. Both men had slim builds and similar cheek bones. Ansel noted the faded scar on Henrí's cheek. Ansel's eyes were a greenish hazel color while Henrí had light blue-grey eyes of a color sometimes found in France near the border with Germany. They each noted there was a similar, though not pronounced resemblance.

Ansel was the first to speak. "I hope I have not kept you waiting, sir."

The General, dressed in a dark blue worsted suit, shook his head and motioned for Ansel to sit opposite. "You are quite on time, Lieutenant. Why don't we see if we can work our way through this remarkable revelation. I can only assume that it is as startling to you as it is to me."

Both men took their seats.

"Yes, sir. I have had many sleepless nights trying to decide what Bethany would have wanted me to do, given circumstances she could never have imagined."

Their waiter approached and gave each a menu.

"I think a bottle of wine is in order for this special occasion." He looked at the *garçon.* "Ask your sommelier if he has a bottle of Haut-Brion Bordeaux 1910."

The waiter returned shortly. "*Oui monsieur,* we have it. An excellent choice may I say." Ansel started to speak. The General stopped him with a raised hand. "Let's order and enjoy the meal and wine before we take up the diary. You first, Lieutenant."

Ansel looked at the menu a moment. The waiter stood by with pencil poised over pad.

"Come, Lieutenant, this is not a funeral. Bethany would want this to be a celebration," the General smiled for the first time.

"Yes, sir." Ansel felt a little better about the meeting. "I'll have *Crevettes sauce boursin, soupe à l'oignon*, and *filet de porc sauce Normande*."

"Very good, and you, sir?" the waiter inquired, turning to the General.

"*Champignon portabella aux fromage, salade d'epinards* and *filet de boeuf sauce poivre*." The waiter left as the sommelier arrived with the wine, showed the label to the General,

uncorked the bottle, poured a sample and stood by. Bourget tasted, nodded approval, and the glasses were filled.

"A toast," the General lifted his glass. "To the son I never knew I had." Ansel held his glass and asked, "You have no doubts?"

"None, Lieutenant. Bethany never lied to me and she would not lie to her own diary. All these years I kept a private note she once sent to me by her chaperone, Madame Wombi. The handwriting is a match to the diary."

Ansel lifted his glass to the General's. "To the father I never knew I had."

They both took a sip of the very good wine, and looked each other in the eyes as strong men often do. Neither blinked.

"Tell me about the Bethany I did not know, the business woman, the spy, the manager of estates in Cuba and Mississippi."

"I am sure all the years she was the same Bethany you knew. She grew older, of course, but to the very end she was beautiful, brave, headstrong, smart, adventurous, determined, loving."

"Yes," the General nodded. "That is the Bethany I knew. I wonder if she is watching us."

"She could be, General. You know, when I was very young, I spent summers with her at Shamrock while my mother and fa—while Louisette and Jonathan ran off here to Paris. I used to leave the cabin to roam in the woods pretending I was a great explorer. Once I caught her watching me from behind a tree. She let a little boy think he was very adventurous. She allowed me freedom to learn self-reliance, but she made sure I was never really lost, even at times when I was afraid I was."

"A wise and courageous mother."

"Yes, but I thought she was just my fun-loving aunt."

"She thought that best for you. My first impression is that you have turned out just the way she wanted. You are a man of principle and character. If you were not, we would not be sitting here. There is one thing . . ."

"Yes?"

"She wrote in the diary that she never wanted you to follow a military career. She wanted, and I think needed, you to help with the business."

"I have lately realized that, but with the war, how can I resign now that my country may be drawn into this mess?"

"Only you can answer that, Lieutenant. But as a newly discovered father, if America does enter the war, and you take part and are lucky enough to live through it, I believe you should do just what she wanted. In the meantime, I hope the people managing your family holdings are honest and loyal to her memory."

"Meaning, I somehow have to determine that."

"She kept it all for you. There is no one else. If you don't show an interest, who will? In your absence there should be an accounting."

The General motioned to their waiter who refilled the glasses.

"But let's not waste this extraordinary occasion on such matters. I never had children. Now I find to my complete surprise, and I admit, unexpected joy and pride, that I have a son, the son of a woman I have always loved. I would like to know more about you, and I am sure you would like to know more about me."

The waiter delivered the first course of the meal.

"Let us eat, Lieutenant. We have all night to get to know one another. A full belly and a bottle of wine always makes for a more amiable evening. To begin, when on duty, I am afraid you will have to continue to call me General, but in private at least, would you please call me Henrí?"

"It will be hard for me to do, General. I always addressed Jonathan as Captain, Father or Sir. But I will try, if you will drop the 'Lieutenant' and call me Ansel when we are in private."

"Agreed. Now tell me about yourself, Jonathan Ansel Quinn."

There's not much to tell. I was named after my fa—my adoptive father, Jonathan, and his father, Ansel Quinn, who was killed in the Civil War. I had a wonderful childhood, winters in Havana and summers at Shamrock in Mississippi, until all of that was interrupted by the Cuban War of Independence that culminated in the Spanish-American War. I did not know how involved my father," Ansel looked at Henrí, "and my aunt were," he looked at Henrí again.

"No offense felt here, Ansel. You grew up with wonderful parents and a loving aunt. I am the newcomer here. Now, to get back you."

"When the fighting between Spain and the Cuban rebels came close to Havana, Jonathan couldn't leave and Bethany refused to do so. They were both involved in the rebellion. Louisette would not leave without Jonathan. But I guess all three wanted me out of harm's way. They agreed to send me to Marion Military Institute in Alabama where Jonathan had attended school before the Civil War, and for the same reason. They didn't figure I would like it, but I did. Jonathan had friends in Washington who arranged an appointment to West Point. Upon graduation, I received a commission and orders to the Philippines where I saw a little action and met General Pershing who was appointed governor of Mindanao. I guess that got me here, that and the fact I speak French, thanks to Louisette. I only recently received promotion to First Lieutenant. Promotions come slowly in America's peacetime army."

Bourget smiled and ask, "How about your social life here in Paris?"

"Since you brought that up, I can say there was little opportunity to meet women in the Philippine jungles, but since I arrived here in Paris I have met a lovely American girl with the ambulance service and a couple of charming French ladies who, shall I say, are very entertaining." Ansel grinned. "But that is all I will say about that. My father taught me that a gentleman never kisses and tells. That's about it for me. Kind of boring I guess. Now it is your turn, Gen—I mean Henrí."

General Bourget took a sip of wine and paused a moment before speaking.

"To begin, I suppose you should see me at my worst. In 1870, I was a young, inexperienced lieutenant fresh out of the École Spéciale Militaire de Saint-Cyr, which is the French equivalent of your West Point. I had just married when Napoleon III started war with Prussia. I was wounded and taken prisoner at Sedan, where France lost the war. Napoleon III was exiled and, after the Germans went home, a new French republic was established. By the time I was released from a German hospital and re-turned to Paris, Marxists, filled with class hatred and calling themselves the *Commune of Paris*, had started civil war. I tried to find my family, but couldn't get into the center city because of the Commune's barricades. I heard the Republic was assembling what was left of the army at Versailles. I made my way there to find I had to defend my country against Frenchmen. The Communards committed an orgy of slaughter of defenseless civilians, teachers, doctors, shopkeepers, priests, nuns, anyone considered bourgeois, part of the establishment. They invented new barbarous ways of killing for their own entertainment." Henrí's expression changed from a man telling a story to one reliving it; his facial muscles tightened into a hard mask. "They killed my mother, my father, my sister, and my young bride and burned their bodies with our house. When I learned of what the Commune had done to my family, I went a little mad.

"I later received a medal I do not wear. I don't remember all of it, but enough to know I was not a brave soldier. I was a berserk, vengeful murderer. I rushed into buildings ahead of my troops to kill Communard bastards myself, or perhaps to have them kill me. When they tried to hide, I found and killed them. When they tried to surrender, I killed them. I was later told that my own commander had my troops take me into custody and sent to an institution. Months after the fighting ended, I was pronounced cured, sane I guess, and released from a sanatorium in Normandy.

"The army took me back based on records I don't remember. I was offered staff duty, but I could not stomach Paris, its bloodstained streets and burned out build-ings, including my home where my family was murdered. French officers command Foreign Legion troops; that's the duty I requested. There was trouble in the desert sands of Algeria. I was young and foolish and still a little crazy, a perfect fit for the task. The Legion is made up of foreign nationals, most of whom have run away from their past—from prosecution for crimes, failed revolutions, wives, tragic love affairs, or debt. Some join to escape their failures in life and get a new start. Others simply seek what they mistakenly think a romantic adventure. Legionnaires are not allowed to register under their real names and nationalities. They use what we call "declared identities." The Legion doesn't want to spend time turning a man into a good soldier only to have him tracked down through his real name and nationality, then taken from us for some offense he committed in the past. A Legionnaire has no past. Training and discipline are hard. Those who are accepted become brothers; their loyalty is only to each other; their esprit de corps high. Legionnaires swear allegiance to no country, only to the Legion. Their motto is "The Legion is our country."

"The Legion was created to protect and expand the French colonial empire. From its creation, the Legion was never meant to be brought to France. There was fear in some circles that if brought to France, it could become some sort of Praetorian Guard for an ambitious leader. Units of the Legion have been brought to France only twice: once to fight the revolt of the Commune of Paris of 1871 and today, because of the need for ever more troops to defeat the Boche. I understand from papers that crossed my desk that you were with a party of neutral observers at the second battle of Artois. A unit of Legionnaires was there. The Legionnaires I commanded were the toughest and best soldiers with whom I have had the honor to serve."

The General smiled. "You will have to excuse me. Your interest lies in me, not the Legion. I can get carried away talking about them. They are, after all, a part of me."

The General took another sip of wine. "So, back to Henrí Bourget. After years in Algeria and later in Morocco I obtained the rank of captain and was selected to return to Paris under orders to attend staff school. That is when I met Bethany. You know the rest from her diary. I left for Cochin China with a broken heart, knowing she would be better off with her family than with a soldier in God-forsaken Legion outposts. I didn't know about you, but neither did Bethany at the time. After going mad over losing my family, the way they were killed, I knew I could never live through losing another family. I never married. The Legion became my only family. Bethany knew that, yet I could not help but love her desperately. I still do.

"Four years ago I retired at the rank of colonel, the old man you see before you, a man who had worn out his soldier's hard shell, a soldier that had seen more than enough killing and cruelty on foreign soil. I bought a cottage near Chantilly. In trying to find peace, I attempted gardening, even dabbled in painting, but settled for long walks and reading literary works. What else was an old soldier to do?

"Then, in August a year ago, my search for personal peace was interrupted—the Prussians again. I was recalled, given the rank of general and a desk job I hate. It seems Foreign Legion officers are looked down on by the regulars. We are not given front line commands in this war, even though we have had more experience commanding troops in battle than most.

"So here we two are. Two strangers bound by blood in a world gone mad. You, a neutral on staff duty because you speak French, and me, well I am on staff duty shuffling papers, filing records and assigning duty to young replacement officers. The latter keeps me busy. We are losing so many, so very many. Quite a pair of soldiers, we are, Ansel."

"All that may change, sir."

"In your case, I hope not," Henrí replied. "I have only just been given a son. I don't want to lose him in the endless gristmill this war has become."

Ansel offered, "I think it is safe to say that nothing will change regarding America, at least until after next year's presidential election. President Wilson's big pitch to voters is that he has kept America out of the war. The United States wants no part of it and is not prepared for war.

Besides, it is making money supplying France and England with food and material. I don't think the report our ambassador is compiling will do anything but reinforce President Wilson's stand. Little will change unless Germany sinks more American ships or the Entente appears to be losing all Europe to the Central Powers. Americans are angry about the sinking of *Lusitania*, but not enough to declare war on Germany. At least that is the opinion of this lowly American lieutenant. I hope the General will forgive him for speaking out like this."

"The General reminds the Lieutenant that in private it is Henrí and what is said between you and me stays between us." Henrí smiled. "This city is paranoid on the subject of spies."

It was Ansel's turn to laugh. "What was it Sir Walter Scott wrote? 'Oh what a tangled web we weave, when first we practice to deceive,' or something like that."

"Well, Ansel, keeping our newly found relation reasonably quiet is not an attempt to deceive. The purpose, from my point of view, is to keep you here in Paris so I can enjoy your company, know you better and you me. If powers that be discovered that you are my son, both our countries would wonder what we were up to, just what information we might exchange. I wouldn't blame them. Your country would certainly scrutinize your reports for bias toward aiding France in the war, and certainly reassign you. It is a delicate situation you must admit."

"I had not thought that out," Ansel replied.

The General smiled. "Your mother must be laughing, too. We aren't dancing with the Spanish governor to obtain information for the Cuban rebels as she did, not quite spying, but she has arranged for us to enter into a clandestine agreement to conceal your relationship with me, just as she did to conceal your relationship with her."

Ansel was quiet a moment contemplating what the General had said. "Well, there is at least one other person who knows the whole story." The General looked worried. "You haven't told anyone?"

"Not I, but you must have given the diary to someone to translate."

"Ah! Yes! That person. You must meet her. In fact, she insists on meeting you. She is an old friend and lovely lady whom I trust completely."

"Then here's a toast to the lady." Ansel raised his glass. "Do you suppose they will hang her along with us two rogues when our intrigue is discovered?"

The extraordinary meeting, first looked upon with great anxiety by both parties, ended rather late with a new beginning neither could have anticipated.

Ansel slept restfully for the first time since the day Bethany's diary arrived. He awoke bright and alert in spite of the consumption of a generous portion of wine the night before.

"Madame Babineau!" Ansel shouted down the stairs as he was dressing.

"*Oui, Monsieur*," she answered from below, wiping her hands on her apron.

"Would you be so kind as to fix breakfast? I am starving."

"Oh! *Monsieur*! I am so happy to do it. You are feeling better?"

"Wonderful! I feel like a new man. As a matter of fact, *I am* a new man."

Pauline Babineau cooked and Tristan Babineau served a superb breakfast, American style, as the Lieutenant preferred, and were happy to see him eat it all for the first time in weeks.

Tristan, helping wash the dishes after the Lieutenant had left for the morning, smiled at Pauline. "I bet we see the ladies return and parties, too."

"You are a wicked man, Tristan."

"I am wicked? What about Monsieur Quinn?"

"He is a soldier and young and in Paris."

Tristan started to speak but Pauline interrupted. "And don't you forget, he pays our wages now."

CHAPTER FIVE

It was a Sunday morning. Ansel opened his eyes, blinking at the sunlight beaming through the window of the master bedroom located to the rear of the second floor. He moved ever so slowly, managing to slip from the bed without disturbing the nude young lady sleeping soundly on her belly, her lovely face turned away from the window and her long dark hair tossed across the pillow.

Ansel found his underwear, slipped them on and tiptoed across the room, careful not to step on the dainty undergarments, stockings and silk gown sprinkled across the floor, to the *salle de bains* where he cleaned up before going down to the kitchen. Walking around in his underwear was permissible on Sundays since Pauline and Tristan Babineau always had the day off.

In the kitchen, he put on a pot of coffee, gathered four croissants from a bread box, lit the gas oven and popped them in. He placed two cups and saucers, a sugar bowl, a small pitcher of cream, butter, a jar of peach preserves, two small plates, napkins and butter knives on a tray. After a few minutes, he added the fresh pot of coffee and placed two warm croissants on each plate. He started to lift the tray, stopped, went into the parlor, took a flower from an arrangement there, added it to the tray and took the whole thing upstairs to the bedroom.

"Good morning!"

The lady rolled over, sat up rubbing her eyes, pulled the sheet up to cover her breasts, and seeing the breakfast tray in the Ansel's hands, parted her beautiful lips in a smile. "You are an angel, *mon chéri*. And look! A flower for me?"

Ansel slid onto the bed and placed the breakfast tray between them.

"Just one moment," she said, "close your eyes."

"You didn't ask me to close my eyes last night."

"It was dark in here last night. Now close your eyes while I take my turn."

She slipped out of bed, gathered her undergarments, glided across the floor to the *salle de bains* and closed the door. A few moments later, smelling of soap, she returned to the bed. Her hair was still tussled.

"You didn't keep your eyes closed."

"What man could?

"Oh! Be quiet and pass me the preserves."

He did and scolded, "You're getting crumbs all over the bed."

"That is nothing, J Ansel. Look what you have done to my hair. It is a mess, and I have a matinee this afternoon."

"I think we should have a morning matinee right now." Ansel reached for her but she brushed him away.

"That was last night my *Américain soldat*. Blame it on the champagne."

"I will not. I never use liquor nor lies to win the favors of a lady."

"Well, perhaps it was your charm or the flowers you sent to my dressing room or this little bracelet. She raised her wrist and admired the fashionable bangle. I bet you treat all the girls this way."

"Not all. Just one at Folies Bergère. Now how about dinner next Saturday?"

"You are a naughty boy, J. Ansel. I like you, but I have an engagement with a nice little member of the Chamber of Deputies."

"A nice rich little member of Parliament I bet."

"A girl must do what a girl must do."

"We do have fun, don't we Gisella?"

"Oh! We do my handsome Américain, but now I must dress, go home, get my hair fixed, my makeup on and get to the theater. Why don't you get a motor car? It would be so much easier than arranging a taxi. Speaking of which," she looked at the clock on the mantle, "one should be waiting for me at your door."

Gisella kissed him lightly on the cheek, jumped out of bed before he could embrace her, slipped on her dress, picked up her shoes and stockings, and laughing, ran down the stairs leaving Ansel to find his pants and shirt. Before he could do all of that, he heard the front door open and close.

"What a woman. God! I love Paris."

Every Friday, Lieutenant Quinn reported to Number 5 Rue de Chaillot to have lunch with Major Crosby. The purpose of the meeting was to discuss his weekly report which usually consisted of the French War Ministry's unclassified, and therefore unreliable, summary of the week's military situation. At such meetings, Lieutenant Quinn sometimes received special assignments from the Major, most originating from Ambassador Sharp.

On this particular Friday, Major Crosby selected a table in the corner of the American Chancellery staff dining room. After the waiter had served the main course and retired out of earshot, Major Crosby informed Lieutenant Quinn that Ambassador Sharp had a special request.

"The Ambassador is interested in learning the estimated casualties the French suffered at the second battle of Artois, which as you know was fought from the 9th of May to the 18th of June, and which failed to take the objective. He feels he cannot finish the report we all worked on without an estimate for both French and German casualties."

"I thought surely by now that report would have been finished and in the hands of the War Department."

"The Ambassador is still accumulating data: translations of both French and German newspaper articles, voluntary reports of the French and English delegations, as well as promised reports from the Spanish, Dutch and Italians. He has asked for the casualty figures, but the French closely guard such information. They, of course, do not want the Germans to have it, and dare not allow the true figures to reach the public or, for that matter, the chamber of deputies. Individual casualty notifications are sent out to relatives, but they are never linked to particular campaigns. Would it be possible for you to gain such information? You would have to be very careful for if you openly pressed for classified material, the French War Ministry would very likely kick you out. We would not be pleased if that happened, Lieutenant. We have too much invested in you. We believe that the department headed by a certain General Bourget handles troop records including assignments and unit strengths and, we think, casualty reports. Do you know him or can you cultivate an association with him?"

"Is Ambassador Sharp trying to get me shot as a spy?"

"Don't be droll, Lieutenant. We don't want you to act covertly. That could result in a diplomatic mess."

"Yes, and get me thrown into a French prison."

"Lieutenant, French Headquarters knows you are there as an observer to gain useful information and intelligence, or be fed false intelligence, if it suits their purpose. That is what neutral observers do. They allowed us to observe their offensive at Artois, though I admit they did so expecting to show us a different outcome. Our government has not publicly revealed any information so gained. The Ambassador does not want you to break into a safe or steal documents off desks, but you could perhaps gain this information in casual conversation or simply ask for it. See if you can get to know this General Bourget or one of his staff. That is all we are asking. Do you know the General?"

Ansel hesitated. "I have seen him at the Ministry, passed him in the hall. I think he knows who I am."

"Well then, the game has started. See what you can do, Lieutenant. The country waltzed into the Spanish American War with flags flying and bands playing thinking it would be a piece of cake, a road to glory. We were so unprepared that *Splendid Little War,* as some called it, cost nearly 4,000 men in less than four months. From what you and I have seen, we know the war over here is no road to glory. It is a slaughterhouse. By damn, if our politicians and president get us into this mess, they ought to do it with their eyes wide open. Now what do I tell the Ambassador?"

"Tell him I will do my best."

Lieutenant J. Ansel Quinn walked out of the American Chancellery talking to himself. *Well Bethany, if, as you thought, you were 'Fortune's Whore', it seems with your untimely departure she has adopted me as a new toy. Just look at the mess she's gotten me into.*

That afternoon, Ansel received a sealed note from a clerk who stood outside his office awaiting a reply. The note read:

Lieutenant Quinn,

If convenient, lunch Saturday, 1 PM at the Beauge on Rue Saint-Marc? If yes, dress mufti as before.

Ansel wrote, *Yes, General. Thank you. 1 PM.* on the note, signed his initials, resealed it with mucilage and handed it to the waiting clerk.

CHAPTER SIX

It was half past noon on a warm, late summer day when Ansel arrived at the restaurant on Rue Saint-Marc. Dressed in white flannel trousers, white shirt with a narrow, four-in-hand tie, a navy blue blazer and wearing a boater, he arrived deliberately early and asked for a table toward the back of the room. He tipped the head waiter to make sure he, and not Henrí, would receive the check. The restaurant was tastefully decorated with white tablecloths, linen napkins and a carnation in a small tulip vase on each table.

Being Saturday, the dining room was sparsely occupied. There was a large table of businessmen, lively with talk and fogged by cigar smoke, several tables with older couples silently studying the menu, and a table by the front window occupied by a young couple seemingly enthralled with each other and oblivious to the diners around them. The waiter guided Quinn to a table for four.

"How many in your party, Monsieur?"

"Two," Ansel answered.

He ordered a bottle of wine while the waiter cleared all but two settings. The wine and two glasses were brought to the table. Quinn barely had time to take the first swallow before he saw Henrí and a lady enter the front door.

Ansel stood as the maître d'hôtel showed the couple to the table. The General was dressed in a light three piece suit. The attractive lady wore a sky blue, full-skirted dress that was hemmed above the ankles in the new 'war crinoline' style. Her shoes were sensible-laced style with rounded toes and wedge heels. Her red hair was cut short in the 'war fashion' of the day. She had blue eyes and fair skin. Ansel guessed her age somewhere around late forties to early fifties. She had a lovely smile and offered her hand.

"Lieutenant Quinn, meet Mrs. Gaetan Giard. Mrs. Giard may I present Lieutenant Quinn." Taking her offered hand Ansel remarked, "Mrs. Giard I am guessing you must be the General's trusted and mysterious special translator." The lady smiled.

After Henrí seated the lady the two men joined her at the table. The waiter arrived with a third set up—plate, silver, napkin and wine glass and poured wine for the new arrivals.

"Please, Lieutenant, call me Aileen."

"As you request, Aileen. Please call me Ansel."

"Of course, Ansel. After reading your life's story in Bethany's diary, I feel I have known you since childhood."

Ansel actually blushed. "What can I say, except to ask how do you two know each other, especially with such mutual trust?"

The lady laughed away a slight blush and replied, "Henrí and I met a long time ago in a far off land. He and my husband were childhood friends here in Paris. He is not with us today because of the nature of the secret we three share. We are able to meet today because Gaetan is at a faculty meeting at the university and I . . . well, I was out shopping and just happened to run into Henrí who invited me to lunch with him and a representative from neutral America. That's my story, you see, all on the up-and-up as you Americans say."

"Your French is flawless, not like mine with my Southern American-Cuban accent."

"My mother was English, my father French, a sort of reverse of your upbringing, Ansel."

"Yes, I forget you know practically everything about me. Bethany is still playing a part, isn't she?"

"In your and Henrí's case, I think she always will. She lived a fascinating life."

"She did at that," Ansel replied, "a life that ended too soon. Now, Aileen, you know so much about me I think it only fair that you take a turn. That way we all three share secrets enough to silence this whole matter. For instance, just how did you and Henrí meet 'long ago and far away'?"

Aileen glanced at Henrí who just smiled.

Aileen began in English. "My father was with a French trading company. I was in my mid-twenties, practically an old maid by Paris standards, and dating a man my father said was a scoundrel. Well, he was a scoundrel, but such a nice, if wicked, one. Father decided to get me safely away from all that. His company had interests in rice and rubber plantations in Cochin China, now part of the Union of French Indochina. Anyway, Father scheduled a trip there to inspect and audit the company's holdings. Next thing I knew, I was shanghaied aboard ship bound for Saigon. Goodbye handsome scoundrel.

Saigon is a beautiful city. When we arrived, the military governor gave a dinner party and in walked Major Bourget."

Henrí interrupted, "Did I hear my name? You two back to speaking French!" Aileen laughed, touched Henrí's hand, and continued in English. "Even though he is somewhat of a grump these days," she took another furtive glance at Henrí, "he was a charming man then. During the six weeks Father and I were there, we occasionally saw a little of each other . . . well, maybe more than a little—lunch at the Rotonde sidewalk café, carriage rides down tree shaded Avenue Jacareo and Princess Huyen Road. He looked so handsome in his dress uniform. There were parties and dances. What was a girl to do?

Although there was no proposal, Father felt compelled to once again save his daughter from marrying, of all things, a French officer of the Foreign Legion. As often with girls and soldiers in faraway places, there was a tearful goodbye at the dock. Father and I boarded ship for a miserable 8,000 mile voyage via Suez to France.

"Once back in Paris, I met a sweet, wonderful young college professor who, though poor in my father's eyes, was decent, intelligent, and a respectable member of French academia, and I love him. He teaches at the Sorbonne and I am a librarian at Bibliothèque Mazarine. Now you know all about me. Oh! I forgot to tell you, like your Jonathan and Louisette, we are childless. That's why, now that I have seen you," her eyes sparkled in harmony with a pause and a smile, "I am thinking about adopting a handsome young American lieutenant with a most unusual history."

Ansel blushed again.

Henrí laughed out loud. "I don't want to hear anything the lady said about me. No more English. Now let's order please. I am starving." He raised his hand to signal the waiter.

Menus were quickly brought to the table and glasses refilled. The waiter then stationed himself at a discrete distance while his customers perused the chef's many offerings of the day.

"There may be a war on," Henrí leaned across the table and commented in a conspiratorial manner, "but from reading the menu, the Beauge shows no sign of food shortages. Do you suppose these new prices are a reflection of the rumored rise in black market activities?"

"More talk like that," Aileen admonished, "and we may not get anything to eat."

They did eat. The food was delicious.

"There is one thing," Ansel said.

Aileen and Henrí looked at him.

"I think that we three, the only ones alive who know Bethany's true story and mine, should continue to refer to Bethany as my aunt. That is the way all who knew me and her, and all legal documents concerning her will and estate refer to my relationship to her. I ask that we not change that. To do otherwise would have me going around trying to explain my somewhat complex family tree. I grew up thinking I was the natural son of Louisette and Jonathan Quinn, which is what my birth certificate states. Then with the arrival of the diaries, I discovered that my Aunt Bethany was the daughter of Annielise Quinn and a bullet that passed through the testicles of an unknown Confederate soldier who was part Choctaw, and furthermore that my Aunt Bethany is my real mother and that my real father is a French Legionnaire named Henrí Bourget. I always thought I had an American father and a French mother, but now I find I had an American mother and a French father. I just never want to have to explain all this to anyone else. I absolutely mean no disrespect to my real mother or my real father." He looked at Henrí.

Henrí laughed. "Who would believe you? Who would believe me?"

Aileen said, "I believe you."

The two men looked at her.

"Oh! All right! I will sign the pledge to keep the family secret."

Henrí raised his glass. "Let's toast to keeping the secret. Giving our word to each other is stronger than any written pledge."

Aileen said, "Blackmailing you two would be more fun."

The two men looked at her again.

She laughed and raised her glass.

The three clicked their glasses together and repeated, "To the secret."

To the consternation of Henrí, Ansel got the check as planned.

At curbside, after an exchange of pleasant goodbyes, Henrí helped Aileen into a cab. As he walked to the other side, he asked Ansel if they could drop him off somewhere. Ansel declined, but took the opportunity to quietly say, "I had intended to speak to you privately about something that has come up at my embassy, but considering the pleasure of Aileen's company, today is not the time. Could we meet privately next week?"

Henrí hesitated, noting Ansel's worried expression. "One evening next week?"

Ansel nodded, and as Henrí entered the taxi beside Aileen, he said, "Madame Giard, your company has made this a lovely and memorable Saturday."

"And you, Lieutenant, have made it a most interesting one." She smiled and the taxi pulled away.

The following Wednesday, the two men, dressed mufti as usual, met in the Restaurant Hubin at number 22 Rue Brouot. They gave the waiter their orders including a carafe of *vin ordinaire* red.

"Well, Ansel, what is troubling you?"

"Major Crosby, the military attaché at our embassy, asked me if I knew a certain General Bourget at French Army Headquarters and if not, would I try to get to know him."

Henrí laughed. "And what did you tell him?"

"That I knew who you were and occasionally passed you in the hallway."

"And?"

"I am to get to know you, or someone in your office for the purpose of gaining accurate information on the casualties the French suffered at the second battle of Artois as opposed to what is printed in the news. I asked the Major if he was ordering me to spy, and if so, would he be so kind as to send my body home after I was caught and shot."

"And his answer?"

"He was not amused and said he was asking no such thing. He obviously thinks such information passes over your desk. He said he was not asking me to steal or copy French documents, but thought I simply might gain the knowledge in conversation after I cultivated an acquaintance with the General."

"And the reason? Never mind. We French are aware that your President Wilson is facing an election next year, and that he could use such information as a reason to keep America out of the war. We understand that he is running on such a promise."

"True, but such information could also be used by military planners to estimate the number of troops that would be needed should we decide to enter the war. You know the Major and I visited the front and the Ambassador sent a report based on our observations. Now they want another report of similar nature."

"Your simple-minded major may get us both hanged. Should you get such information, I trust, if made public, will not be traced to me for I can't give it to you."

"I am relieved, sir. I tried and failed in my mission. Now let's enjoy the wine. It's not bad."

"You know, Ansel, you will never make a good spy. You are much too honest, and I drink to that. Of course, if I were you, I might have someone check hospital records, talk with patients, especially unit officers fresh from the front, ambulance drivers, tally what you learn with what the newspapers have written, that sort of thing. Of course, when word that a young American lieutenant is running around asking questions reaches French intelligence, you will probably be expelled rather than hanged. Why don't you just make a guess, for instance, a percentage rate, something like thirty to thirty-five percent when attacking across 'no man's land' and twelve to fifteen percent when defending? Of course France will call those estimates outrageous lies, but at least that won't get you hanged or expelled. I would not like that for I am just beginning to enjoy your company, even beginning to notice a certain resemblance between us."

When they finished the meal, Henrí asked for the check. "You got the last one," he said before Ansel could protest. "Besides," he smiled, "knowing it was my turn, I picked this restaurant. It is much less expensive than the last one."

In spite of the war and its terrible toll on young French soldiers at the front, 1915 Paris carried on as Paris always had, except the "City of Lights" was dark out of fear of night Zeppelin raids. The prime target of Paris was the Eiffel Tower which served as the antenna of the most powerful wireless radio in Europe. Serious shortages of food, coal, clothes and petrol were only just beginning. For a certain young American lieutenant with his army pay augmented with a generous allowance from his family's holdings, weekends were a challenge of sorts. For one thing, Paris was a city of beautiful women in abundance, while somewhat short of young men due to the war. This made Paris, at least for a brief time in 1915, a weekend playground for a group of young American men who often headquartered at Ansel's house. Ansel had met most of them at a watering hole named *The New York Bar* owned by famous American jockey, Todd Sloan. Sloan bought a venerable bar in Manhattan, stripped the wood paneling, furniture, fixtures and memorabilia and had it all shipped to Paris and reassembled in a building at 5, Rue Daunou situated between Avenue de l'Opéra and Rue de la Paix. Opened in 1911, Sloan was successful in capturing business from wealthy Americans taking the Grand Tour of Europe. As the bar's reputation grew, business increased. Too busy enjoying the high life himself, Sloan hired a Scotsman from Dundee named Harry MacElhone to bartend and manage the place. Though there were not too many Americans left in Paris in 1915, those that remained often gathered at *The New York Bar*.

Ansel dropped in every weekend where he joined other adventurous young Americans.

There was Fred Zinn who happened to be visiting France in August 1914 when war began. He immediately joined the Foreign Legion. He was convalescing from a leg wound when he and Ansel met. Like Ansel's French friend, Paquet, Fred walked with the aid of a cane.

Norman Prince was from a wealthy family in Massachusetts who owned an estate in Pau France. After graduating from Harvard, and unknown to his father, he got a flying license in 1911. Prince was in Paris to try to convince the French to start an American flying squadron.

Victor Chapman was another American who had served his time in the French Foreign Legion. Like his friend Prince, Chapman had become interested aviation.

Jasper Crocker, an older American expatriate who claimed to be a reporter for the English language *Paris Herald*, told the group at the bar one Saturday, "You young Americans are crazy. Go home. America will be in this war soon enough. You are going to get yourselves killed about the time your own country needs you."

"Well," Zinn asked him, "if we're crazy for being here what's your excuse?'

"Same as it's been for twenty-five years—women and wine." He laughed at his own story and bought his young friends a round of French 75's, a popular cocktail invented by Harry the bartender. It consisted of gin, simple syrup, lemon juice and champagne, and was said to have the kick of its namesake, the French artillery piece.

"Very generous of you, Mister Crocker." Zinn lifted his glass.

"Oh! Don't thank me young soldier. Mister James Gordon Bennett, Jr. will take care of this. He owns the paper, don't you know, pays my expense account. I get all my war stories from you gents. Only way I can. The French threaten to shoot me if I get caught at the front again. Censorship is serious business over here."

The conversation was interrupted when the front door opened and in walked four young ladies in uniform. A number of independent, young, American women living in Paris, having defied their parents' orders to come home, volunteered for service at the American Ambulance Field Service and the American Ambulance Hospital at Neuilly. They, too, had adopted *The New York Bar* as their unofficial headquarters. Some were nurses, some were drivers. Having defied the protests of their families, they also defied the "rules of polite society" by patronizing the bar unaccompanied by male escorts. They were the vanguard, they said, of the modern woman.

Ansel turned to one he knew, Gloria Gibson, a pretty girl with blonde curls peeping out from under her uniform hat.

"Well, Glo," Ansel offered, "you girls look a little beat this afternoon. May I offer you all a glass of wine?"

"It's not nice to tell a lady she 'looks a little beat,' but we have just had another long debate with the French Medical Service and I guess it shows."

"What sort of debate?"

"While American male volunteers drive our ambulances to the front, they won't allow us women to do it. All we are allowed to do is drive patients between the trains arriving from the front and the hospitals. Do you know they pull the window curtains down so people can't see the trains are loaded with wounded?"

"You don't want to go to the front, Glo; don't want to see all that."

"All that what? The 'front' comes through our door at the hospital every day. I help in the receiving hall. The wounded come in filthy, wounds infected, limbs missing. You think we don't see as much as we would at the front?"

"Glo, you girls could get seriously wounded or killed at the front. It happens to ambulance drivers up there. Artillery shells can't see the red crosses on your trucks."

"We just received twenty-five new Model T Ford ambulances. We could help get the wounded to the hospital faster. In some areas they're using horse drawn ambulances. We could at least drive to the regimental aid stations behind the lines."

"I take it all back, Glo. You don't look beat. You look very pretty when you are angry. Now take a sip of wine and calm down. What are you doing for dinner?"

"Don't you patronize me, Ansel Quinn."

"I wouldn't think of it. You might run me down with an ambulance."

"I might. Now it's your turn. A certain Mister Hampton at the Embassy told me you have been to the front. Tell me about that."

"I can't. The French would put me before a firing squad. In all seriousness, Glo, don't go around telling that. He should not have told you about it."

"He was trying to impress me. He didn't. Now it's your turn to take a sip and calm down, Lieutenant. I'm not a silly gossip."

"Will you have dinner with me tonight?"

"If you will let me go home and change out of this uniform."

"Why? You look charming in brown, that long wool skirt, blouse, tunic, Sam Browne belt, boots and that slight smear of grease on your cheek."

"I do not have grease on my cheek. That only happens when I work on motors."

"You actually work on motors?"

"I can clean carburetors, change spark plugs, belts, hoses, gear bands, tires and anything else to keep our Model T Ford ambulances running. They are marvelous machines. What do you think an ambulance driver would do with a breakdown in the field? We've had the same mechanics courses as the men drivers."

"I am impressed, Miss Gibson. Pick you up at seven?"

"Yes, Major. I have established a friendly relationship with General Bourget. We have dined together a couple of times. Unusual for a general to dine with a lieutenant, but I think he wants to pump me for information about our army. Like all Frenchmen these days, he wants us to join the Entente against the Central Powers."

"That's all very nice, Lieutenant, but your assignment was to obtain accurate casualty numbers, remember?"

"As we discussed, sir, I am a little shy about covert espionage and French firing squads. I just came right out and asked General Bourget. He refused to divulge actual figures but he did give an interesting challenge and a rather startling rule of thumb."

"A challenge and a rule of thumb?"

"Yes sir. He said that the challenge of my assignment would be to calculate a number based upon information gleaned from visiting hospitals, talking to ambulance drivers, hospital supply clerks and medical supply houses to tally orders for bandages, medicines, drugs, and medical implements, that sort of thing. Of course, if French intelligence gets wind of our snooping they might want to know what we are up to."

"How about the 'rule of thumb'?"

"He gave me a rule of thumb that can be applied to either side."

"Either side?"

"The General said, and we cannot divulge him as the source, that even with artillery preparations, an attacking force crossing 'no-man's land' and assaulting trench lines can expect thirty-five percent casualties. And further, that the defending force will sustain fifteen percent casualties, and that is if they have well-engineered bunkers as shields from artillery and hold their line against the attack. If they fail to hold and the attacking force gets into their trench or if they retreat, that number can greatly increase. He added that is a rough rule of thumb for planning purposes."

"My God! If the President sees those kinds of figures he will refuse to increase the budget for the war department; say we won't need to because we aren't going to war. We won't get new weapons or an increase in troops, and you, Lieutenant, will remain a lieutenant until you're an old man."

"General Bourget believes, and said the British believe, that Germany and the Central Powers cannot be defeated unless at some point America enters the war."

"We know what they believe. Ambassador Sharp hears that every day. What our would-be allies can't understand, because we won't tell them, but what the Germans probably know, is that at present the entire American Army stands at just thirty regiments, 175,000 men scattered all over the country. I'm told we have about two machine guns per battalion and there is an ongoing debate about how to deploy them. Curtiss Aéroplane has just started building a training plane, but we don't have a single combat aircraft and damn few Army pilots. Truth is we couldn't go to war today if the President ordered us to do so."

"Major, I was sure the attack on *Lusitania* would have caused some reaction."

"We all were, Lieutenant. There were a few in Congress who tried to persuade Wilson to mobilize. He did threaten to do so if the Germans didn't give up unrestricted submarine attacks and abide by international cruiser rules. They agreed in the hope that would keep us out of the war. Cruiser rules require U-boats to surface and warn merchant ships to get their crews and passengers off before sinking them. I don't think Wilson or Congress will do much unless the Germans return to unrestricted submarine warfare. Wilson is standing by his campaign slogan not to go to war, but keep in mind that politicians will say anything to get elected. By the way, Lieutenant, you repeat anything said in this room and you will face a court-martial."

"Yes sir, I understand. But there is another matter I would ask permission to discuss."

"All right, Lieutenant. What is it? And no, you can't sneak off to the front."

"It may be a bad time to ask, sir, but I have not taken any leave in two years. The attorneys for my mo—aunt's estate are advising me to return home to review details of the settlement of her will and the procedures they are recommending for supervision of the family businesses in Mississippi and Cuba during my absence."

"I can understand your request, Lieutenant. Perhaps now while we remain in the never-never land of neutrality is as good a time as any. If I can arrange leave, the Ambassador may have a request or two for you while you are in the States." Ansel nodded and the Major continued. "The War Department may want to talk to someone who has been on-site here in France—at least I hope they do. They could use a little first-hand knowledge. I will ask the Ambassador to ask the French foreign office for permission to use the undersea cable to transmit your request to the War Department. The French cable runs under the Channel and connects to the British Atlantic cable network to the United States and Canada. It is more secure than the Eiffel wireless. They allow us to send short coded messages, but the cable between France and England is too busy to handle any of our long coded reports. Besides, because messages must go through French telegraphers even the undersea cable is not considered secure. That leaves our diplomatic pouches. They are delivered by courier to a ship's purser who locks them in the ship's safe room. Upon reaching the United States the purser turns the pouch over to a duly authorized courier who delivers it to the State Department in Washington. If your leave is approved, Ambassador Sharp will likely assign you courier duty to deliver a pouch all the way to Washington.

"In a month or so, we should have approval for the trip, or not. If the request is approved, we will cut orders for you that will include travel to and from Washington and any special instructions Ambassador Sharp may request you to carry out. Your leave travel to Mississippi and Cuba will be at your own expense, Lieutenant, and your time will be short."

"Yes sir. Thank you sir."

"Don't thank me yet. We might not get approval. If we do, your orders will include reassignment back here, Lieutenant. I don't want to have to break in a new man. You have been trouble enough." The Major smiled, a rare occurrence.

Ansel requested a meeting with Henrí on the following Saturday afternoon. At Henrí's suggestion they met on the left bank in a small restaurant founded by an Alsatian named Lénard Lipp.

"What is the news my new found son called this meeting to reveal?"

"That information will cost you a beer, Alsatian, not German, I understand."

"Yes, not German. That would be unpatriotic. Some 30,000 French Alsatians immigrated here after the Prussians took Alsace and Lorraine in 1871."

Henrí ordered the beer and turned back to Ansel. "Now what is it?"

"I have asked for leave to go home, as you advised, to check on the management of Bethany's land."

"It's your land now. Need I remind you?"

"I have a hard time accepting that. I suddenly find myself a land owner and an absentee land owner at that. Reminds me of the absentee Yankee carpetbaggers whose agents bought Southern land for pennies on the dollar from widows. You are right about me needing to have a hand in it, but I'm still in the army and there's a war on."

"It's not your war yet."

"That word "yet" is the rope that hangs me between my duty to Bethany and my duty to the army and my country."

"Maybe I could send you to visit the front again and get a friend to shoot you in the leg. That could settle the argument."

"I don't think fathers having their sons shot is according to Queensbury Rules."

"The Marquis of Queensberry was an Englishman, much too prim for us French."

"I'll try to be more careful if I get another chance to visit the front. As a matter of fact, I was threatened by a Frenchman with a pistol on my last visit."

"I don't suppose you will give me the man's name." Henrí smiled. "But you will be back? I'm just getting used to you."

"I'm told my orders will include the return trip. Now, you have heard my news. What about you?"

"I am all right but there is sad news I'm afraid. My childhood friend, Gaetan Giard is so darkly depressed over the deaths and suffering of his former students gone to war that Aileen is afraid of what he may do. When I can, I take him to lunch and on long walks, try to interest him in subjects other than the war, but what can one do when a friend suffers such melancholia? He told me he is afraid to learn the names of his new students, afraid to look at them. He says when he looks out over his lecture hall he sees not young bright faces, but the faces of former students who have fallen. And when I look at Aileen, I can see the toll it is taking on her."

"I am sorry, Henrí. I don't know Gaetan, but Aileen is such a vivacious lady. I wish I could help her in some way."

"So do I."

Henrí took out his pocket watch. "I am afraid I have to go. I promised to visit with our sad friend this afternoon. When you know your schedule for the trip please let me know. Next time, the beer is on you."

When Henrí and Ansel left Lénard's restaurant, the sky had clouded over and was pregnant with moisture. It was the beginning of a fall and winter that would drizzle its way across the battlefields of France and Belgium transforming roads, trenches and shell-pocked 'no-man's-land' into miserable quagmires.

Ansel continued his work at French Army Headquarters while he waited interminably for an answer to his request for leave. Promotion wasn't the only thing that crept ever so slowly through the U.S. Department of the Army. Apparently requests for leave from lieutenants in small, shorthanded, isolated posts overseas were repeatedly shuffled to the bottom of increasing piles of paperwork following the outbreak of war in Europe. This was especially true in the case of requests by military attachés since such requests first went through the State Department and then the War Department in Washington.

CHAPTER SEVEN

Months passed. A snowy, subdued Christmas arrived in wartime Paris. Because of the blackout, there were no gay, festive lights to brighten the nights, but there were other signs of the season. Christmas trees of all sizes for sale. Some were small enough to place on a dining room table. Some were eighteen to twenty feet high. Most of the big ones went to the hospitals where they would be gaily decorated and hospital staffs made sure that every soldier patient would have a package under the tree. Shop windows drew crowds of small children. Little girls were interested in dolls dressed as nurses and there were plenty of toy soldiers, planes, cannons and ships to garner the wishful attention of little boys. On the street and in cafes, one could see ambulatory French, Belgian and English solders on holiday leave from the hospital, some on canes or crutches, others with arms in casts and some with head or face bandages. Many had young French women on their arms.

As a child, Christmas at home with his family had always been a wonderful experience, but now, with Jonathan and Louisette and Bethany all gone, the holiday had a depressingly sad effect on Ansel. Still, he got a little into the spirit by purchasing gifts for his housekeepers, Tristan and Pauline Babineau, and for Henrí and Henrí's friends, Aileen and Gaetan, and of course, several ladies including Gisella and Gloria were included on his shopping list.

There were parties at the American Embassy as well as a ball for staff members of French Army Headquarters to which Lieutenant Quinn received an invitation. Except for talking with Henrí and Aileen and meeting Gaetan for the first time, Ansel found the occasions boring.

He took Gloria Gibson to a new one act opera composed by Xavier Leroux that premiered at the Salle Favart Theatre on Christmas Day. Afterward, Ansel wished he had not gone. The opera was built around the story of four children whose parents had been killed by German soldiers.

The theme was that the children somehow found hope in spite of a bleak Christmas. The opera resonated with the French audience facing their second wartime Christmas.

New Year's celebration at The New York Bar was different. In spite of the cold and snowy night, all the usual crowd was there: the American volunteer nurses and ambulance drivers, Ansel's flying buddies, various expatriate writers and painters and lots of lovely ladies, escorted or not. Harry MacElhone, the manager, and his bartenders did yeoman work keeping the wine, whiskey, gin and rum flowing. It was a rip-roaring, American style New Year's Eve. Ansel was sure it had been a great success as measured by the severity of the hangover he had the next morning. He knew he had brought a lady home from the party by the red silk garter he found on the floor of his room and the displeased look he got from Pauline Babineau when he finally walked downstairs looking for something to eat at three o'clock in the afternoon.

Almost a month later, Ansel received his orders granting leave following official courier duty. The farewell party at Number Six Villa Said was attended by an eclectic crowd. There were girls from the American Ambulance Field Service and hospital. Ansel's friend, Capitaine Paquet, arrived with a very pretty French girl on his arm. Jasper Crocker from the Paris Herald and the crowd from The New York Bar filtered in as the evening progressed.

Norman Prince, Victor Chapman and Fred Zinn managed to bore their dates nearly to death talking about flying. Prince announced he was absolutely sure the New Year would bring French approval for the formation of an all American volunteer flying squadron. Zinn, who photographed almost everyone at the party with his new Autographic Kodak camera, stated he was excited about flying, not so much as a pilot but as a photographer. He expounded that aerial photography would change the war. "They have been using cameras from tethered kites and balloons, but aerial photography from an aéroplane over enemy lines will revolutionize battlefield intelligence."

Such lectures failed to impress the ladies or enhance the love lives of the fliers.

Speaking of the ladies, they contributed a great deal of gaiety to the affair with their laughter, lovely smiles and wit. There was lots of dancing to the latest popular American records played on a hand cranked, spring driven Victrola; such songs as "Down Among the Sheltering Palms,"

"The Little Ford that Rambled,"

"China Town, My China Town,"

"Ragging the Scale" and "Memphis Blues." Although the ladies were willing dancing partners, many, especially the American girls, disappointed their escorts with firm refusals to not-so-subtle invitations whispered in their ears.

For the last night in Paris before his ocean voyage, things were going well between Ansel and the very pretty Gloria Gibson . . . until the door opened and in sauntered Gisella. She took off her long winter coat to reveal a dress of burgundy silk that outlined the graceful movement of her long legs and revealed a breathtaking cleavage. Conversation stopped as every man in the room turned to look at the beautiful late arrival. She glided across the room, arms out, lips parted to embrace the host.

"J Ansel, I hope you will forgive me for coming late and being overdressed. I made some excuse to get away from the opera crowd when I heard you were off to the United States. I couldn't let you leave without giving you a bon voyage kiss and wish you safe return." She put her arms around him and gave a kiss that was no light peck on the cheek. "I would love a glass of champagne while you tell me all about you travel plans."

Gloria, who had been studying French in Paris when the war broke out, understood every word. She smiled prettily and said in English, "Yes, Ansel dear, do sit down and tell us all about your travel plans," and switching to French turned to Gisella. "By the way, I'm Gloria Gibson." She shook Gisella's hand. "And what do you do for the war effort? I drive an ambulance."

Ansel tried but never got a chance to intercede in the barely civil, cutting wit exchanged between the two beauties. From time to time both ladies would turn simultaneously to look at him. They made him feel like a little boy being scolded. The best he could do was refill their champagne flutes and smile like a grinning idiot to the audience gathered gleefully round to watch the ladies spar and Ansel squirm. The end result was that, after seeing all of his guests off, a very sober Lieutenant Quinn went sadly to bed alone on his last night in Paris.

On a bitter cold day, Tristan Babineau carried Ansel's small trunk to the waiting embassy car. His wife Pauline waved from the doorway. "We will take good care of your house, Monsieur Quinn. We pray for your safe return." Ansel waved as the car pulled away and headed for the American Chancellery at Number 5, Rue de Chaillot.

Major Crosby was waiting when Lieutenant Quinn arrived. "Washington is in the process of organizing and training what the State Department calls 'special agents' to act as couriers for diplomatic mail, but for now they are using Army officers. Here are your orders, pay voucher and steamer tickets as discussed, Lieutenant. For the first time since the Civil War, the State Department requires a passport for international travel. Seems with this war, nations have gotten a little fussy as to who comes and goes. Ambassador Sharp said one has been made for you. It's a little late for me to check but I assume you have it."

"Yes sir."

"Fine. Now here is the next order of business."

The Major handed Ansel a shoulder holster with a Colt 1911 forty-five, semi-automatic pistol and loaded clip. "I would keep one round in the chamber just in case you really have to use it to protect the documents you will be carrying. Otherwise, please try not to shoot anyone. You will hand in the pistol when you deliver this." The Major then handed Ansel a large leather-reinforced canvas pouch with the words "U.S. Diplomatic Mail" embossed on both sides. The pouch weighed about thirty pounds and looked somewhat like a mail carrier's bag but was secured with a brass lock and seal.

The Major continued, "The pouch contains documents which, if made public, could cause an international incident. Should they be lost while in your care the Ambassador and the President will not be pleased. You are authorized to protect them by any means at your disposal."

Ansel opened his mouth, but before he could speak the Major went on, "Don't worry, Lieutenant, if you shoot someone in the line of duty, you will probably be given permission to do so after the fact. You should also be aware that if the pouch is found with the seal broken there will be a court-martial. You will sign this receipt for the pouch in triplicate. Take one copy with you. You should obtain a similar receipt from the clerk at the State Department to whom you deliver the pouch. Have you got that, Lieutenant?"

"Yes sir."

"Good. Now take off your overcoat and gloves, step into the toilet and put on the shoulder holster beneath your tunic. The pistol is not the sort of thing we would want the chancellery servants, your driver, the French populace or German spies to see. Neutral military personnel are not to be seen armed."

Ansel stepped toward what polite society termed "the necessary room."

"I think you forgot something, Lieutenant."

Ansel turned, saw the Major's eyes drop to the pouch. "Don't let this pouch out of your sight until the ship's purser, under your supervision, locks it in the ship's safe room. The same goes between the time you retrieve it from the ship and deliver it to the State Department."

Ansel picked up the pouch, took it to the toilet, removed his tunic, fitted the shoulder holster to the left, inserted the clip into the pistol, worked the slide to load a cartridge into the chamber, thumbed on the safety, slid the pistol into the holster and replaced his tunic. He checked himself in the mirror. *How the hell am I expected to draw a pistol from inside a tunic buttoned all the way up to my throat while wearing an overcoat?* He returned to the anteroom.

"Have a good trip, Lieutenant. I'll expect you back here in six weeks at the most."

Ansel saluted, picked up the pouch and walked out of the Chancellery to the Embassy car waiting at curbside. During an hour wait at the train station he sat with his back to the wall, his small trunk at his feet and the diplomatic pouch on the bench beside him covered by his overcoat. Although he took note of anyone who came near, he was more uneasy about the obvious bulge in his tailored uniform which had not been cut to accommodate a pistol in a shoulder holster. When the train arrived, a porter put the lieutenant's trunk aboard, but was not allowed to touch the diplomatic pouch.

Three or so hours later, the near empty train pulled into the new Gare Maritime at Calais. As it slowed to a stop, Ansel could see that the rail yard and sheds adjacent to the station had suffered serious damage and questioned the conductor about it.

"That's from a recent night zeppelin raid that bombed the area for a terrifying twenty-eight minutes. Seven railroad workers were killed. Somehow the fine new station and hotel were spared. They were built to replace the small facilities that had grown inadequate for the booming cross-channel tourist traffic prior to the war. Just as all this was completed in 1914, the continental ferries that plied the twenty-six miles across the Pas-de-Calais, or as the English call it, Dover Strait, discontinued regular civilian service because of the war. The terminal has been given over to the military and is now principally used by the British for ambulance service."

The tide was in when Ansel arrived and the large ferry at dock was being loaded with British wounded having arrived on an earlier train from the nearby front lines in Flanders. Many still had dirty faces and mud from the trenches clinging to their uniforms.

Ansel showed his papers and was allowed to board. He dragged his trunk and the pouch to a seat forward out of the way of the wounded which seemed to be divided into two categories: the sitting and the lying. Most of the attending medical personnel, who helped the wounded to their place aboard, left to return by train to the front in Flanders, while the few who remained for the voyage circulated among the casualties.

The crossing took a little over two and a half hours. The channel was rough, making it an uncomfortable trip for the wounded. Few recognized Quinn's uniform as American and those who did were too uncomfortable, too in pain, too drugged on morphine, or in the case of the attendants, too busy to engage him in curious conversation. Ansel, for his part, tried not to look at the more seriously injured. Many of their wounds were ghastly, missing limbs; faces completely covered in bandages save for holes for mouth and nose. Ansel was struck by the fact that there were almost no cries or moans. The wounded sat or lay suffering stoically as if to do otherwise might disturb their wounded neighbors. The only sound he heard was labored breathing from several men with chest wounds and from those who could manage to speak the words, "Thank you nurse," for the attention given: a cup of water, a kind word, the holding of a dish while the seasick vomited, the injection of morphine to one badly burned patient and to another with multiple shrapnel wounds to face and torso. The odor in the ship's salon was a mixture of disinfectant, urine, sweat, excrement, burned flesh, cigarette smoke, vomit and that of coal fired boilers and hot oil drifting up from the pounding engine room below.

Quinn was offered a sandwich, but a cup of hot tea was all he could handle.

On the British side, the new Dover Marine Station, like the Gare Maritime at Calais, had just been completed when war broke out. It was renamed the Dover Admiralty Pier and taken over for military use only.

A train was waiting. At rail side, medical personnel relieved the boat nurses of their charges which they loaded aboard passenger rail cars that had been modified to handle casualties. Curtains were pulled over the windows, a practice to hide the damaged cargo from citizens who might otherwise look through the windows to see the large number of wounded in transit. Such a sight, it was thought by the government, might depress morale on the home front.

It took until late afternoon for the train to make what normally would be a relatively short trip to London. Hundreds of makeshift hospitals had been established in government requisitioned schools, buildings and even large mansions to care for the ever increasing number of casualties. The train made several stops to detrain wounded assigned to such facilities scattered along the route.

Near dusk, the locomotive, puffing like a pulmonary patient itself, pulled its carloads of casualties slowly to a stop on a siding just outside the covered train concourse at Victoria Station in central London. It was met by a long line of ambulances waiting to transport the wounded to London hospitals.

With little time to linger, Lieutenant Quinn hefted his small trunk onto his shoulder, grabbed the pouch, walked down the track, climbed steps to a loading platform and entered the cavernous station. The interior was crowded with British soldiers disembarking from what Ansel learned was one of the "leave trains" that almost daily brought service men just arrived across the channel for well-earned leave back home.

Some still had grime and mud encrusted on their clothing. Many soldiers were laughing and joking, but Ansel noticed that the expressionless eyes of some belied outward joviality; eyes that seemed focused on distant things others could not see. He had seen that look in his friend Paquet's eyes when they visited the front at Vimy Ridge.

The soldiers moved toward a row of trestle tables set against a wall over which hung a Union Jack and just below it a large banner reading "FREE BUFFET." The tables were covered with piles of sandwiches attended by ladies dressed in dark blue dresses adorned with Red Cross badges. On a separate table sat several large copper urns from which ladies were filling china cups with steaming hot tea. The only decorations were a few jars with bright flowers in them lending a splash of color to otherwise drab surroundings.

As he walked by, Ansel noticed several men trying to pay. He was close enough to hear the ladies tell them, "No, No! Put your money away. This is for you men, all provided by the Free Buffet Society here in London."

"I say, governor, can I give you a hand with the baggage?"

Ansel turned to see a porter with a wheeled baggage dolly. "You may indeed, my man." Ansel gladly gave the station porter his trunk, but did not let go of the pouch. "I'll manage this one, and I need a taxi."

"Good as done! Just follow me. Where to?"

"The Surry docks, the Atlantic Transportation Line berth."

"Crossing the Atlantic are you, governor? I don't know as I'd be doing that, what with all them U-boats we been hearing about."

Ansel followed the porter without comment.

The man questioned, "If you don't mind me asking, what uniform is that you're wearing?

I've seen Belgian and even a few French over here, but not one quite like yours. It's like our Tommie's but of a bit different shade in color."

"I'm an American."

"Bloody good! Haven't heard your country has joined in, but we all have been waiting!"

"I'm afraid we haven't just yet. I'm over here as an observer."

"You been observing over there?" he asked cocking his head to the left.

"I have, but I'm afraid I can't talk about that."

They reached the taxi stand. The porter put Ansel's trunk in beside the driver of a Unic cab, gave him the destination and added, "You take this here American officer straight to his ship. I'm thinking he's got important business."

Ansel paid the porter and climbed into the cab for a ride across drab, wartime London. It was dusk and blackout shades were being pulled down over the windows of houses, shops and government buildings alike. It was cold and there were traces of soot-dirtied snow in the roadside gutters and on sidewalks. The streets were crowded with people intent on getting home by dark.

"This bloody blackout business makes traveling about risky," the cabby complained. "Come night proper you can't see your hand afore your face. A bloke can get lost, fall victim to crime or knock himself silly walking into a lamppost. Seen it all happen. Some blokes get hit by motorcars. All headlamps are painted or taped over, don't you see? Part of the blackout drill. Might as well be driving by candlelight. I nearly hit a fellow just last night. Drunk he was. Still, I guess the blackout throws them Krauts off; them Zeppelins what come over at night dropping bombs. Gives us cabbies a fright I tell you."

The route from Victoria Station eventually took Quinn through Rotherhithe in South East London and to the Surry Docks located on the south bank of the Thames across from Wapping and the Isle of Dogs on the north bank.

It was dark by the time Quinn arrived dockside. The cabby turned his trunk over to a porter who led Quinn to the shipping line's receiving area. Quinn showed his ticket and passport to the gate officer who tagged his trunk. Carrying the diplomatic pouch himself, Ansel crossed the gangway to board the Atlantic Transportation Line's SS *Minnehaha*.

Launched in 1900, the ship was a handsome vessel: black hull, white superstructure, four cargo masts and a single stack amidships painted red with a black ban around the top. Six hundred feet in length with a displacement of 14,000 tons, her twin screws gave her a speed of sixteen knots, fast enough to sail alone rather than in slow convoys. Since going into service she had made some 160 Atlantic crossings between London and New York. She and her sister Atlantic Transportation Line ships were classified as fast freight liners. Just as passenger liners carried mail and cargo to increase profits, fast freight liners carried passengers for the same reason. *Minnehaha* had some eighty-two cabins on her mid-ship superstructure that gave her accommodations for up to 118 passengers, all first class. Prior to the war she was a favorite of Trans-Atlantic travelers offering comfortable quarters, luxury salons and fine dining facilities at attractive prices. In 1914, her sailings to New York had been at full capacity as Americans, Canadians and those non-citizens lucky enough to get visas rushed to cross the Atlantic and escape the war. Now, in early 1916, times had changed.

Ansel witnessed the pouch locked in the ship's safe room by the purser, John Lang. He told Ansel that it would be a somewhat lonely cruise as only fifteen passengers had booked passage.

"We'll be sailing in ballast as there is little cargo being exported from England due to war demands for every kind of item normally exported. On the other hand, the cargo holds on the return voyage will be filled to capacity to meet the ever growing shortages here." Lang looked at his watch. "We'll be sailing with the tide at ten o'clock tonight and transit as much of the war zone as we can before sunrise. Passage at night is a little safer, not that I remind most passengers of that, but you being a military man, I thought you would appreciate the fact."

Ansel nodded.

The Purser continued in confidence, "This will be our last trip from London. We are shifting to Liverpool where we hope there will be less chance of encountering U-boats. They've been pretty busy in the English and Saint George's Channels, not to mention the North Sea. I'm thinking that out of Liverpool we'll be a little safer, clear the war zone a little faster."

(For lack of demand, passenger service would be stopped in early 1916. Though never taken over by the military, Minnehaha was known to carry munitions. In September of 1917 she would be torpedoed and sunk by U-48 twelve miles from Fastnet off the Irish coast with a loss of forty-two lives.)

The purser changed the subject. "Don't worry about the pouch, Lieutenant. I'm the only officer with a key. If you will stand by a moment, I'll fetch a steward to show you to your cabin. Because your embassy made arrangements you have been assigned to one of our best cabins with an adjoining bath. Most cabins share large common bathing facilities located centrally to both starboard and port passageways."

"Thank you, Mister Lang. And Mister Lang, I hope my uniform will suffice for dinner. I didn't bring much luggage aboard. I have neither a dress uniform nor black tie outfit. If that's not acceptable, I can eat in my cabin."

"Your attire will be quite suitable, Lieutenant. We've gone not quite so formal since the war, you know. Dinner is normally at 6:30, but tonight, because of our late sailing, and for the convenience of late arriving passengers, we will dine at 8 o'clock."

A steward led Ansel up a flight of stairs to the promenade deck and down a passageway to cabin number eight on the starboard side. He was given the key and found his small trunk had been placed inside. The cabin was fitted in white paneling with varnished mahogany trim, an iron bed with brass trim, an electric light nicely shaded for reading, and an electric fan. The porthole was painted over black. The steward warned that it was not to be opened at any time after darkness. "To show a light would be a serious breach of safety rules. Sealed portholes make nights a little stuffy in warm weather, but with the ships ventilator fans, and with winter temperatures this time of year, you'll find the cabin comfortable." He knocked lightly on a side door, turned the latch knob and opened it to reveal a bath. "This cabin shares a bath with the adjoining cabin. You will find the bar and library on the upper deck. Dining is below and aft on the salon deck." He removed a life vest from the closet and placed it on the writing table; "Just a precaution, sir. We will sail with the lifeboats swung outboard until we are well clear of what the Kaiser claims as his "war zone." You'll find mineral water in the lavatory and extra blankets on the shelf in the closet. We will have a lifeboat drill at nine-thirty just before sailing. The lifeboat assembly signal is normally seven short blasts followed by one long of the ship's horn, but such a signal here in port would likely send the whole Thames area into a panic. The drill will be announced by cabin stewards. With so few passengers, all will meet at lifeboat station number one, starboard side forward. Is there anything else, sir?"

"No, Steward. I think that covers it, thank you." Ansel closed the door after the steward. On the back of the door there were two notices, each posted in a glass frame. One was a diagram of the route to the lifeboat station from the cabin, and instructions for passengers to assemble with life vests upon hearing the assembly signal. The second notice displayed:

Information for Passengers

TEA and COFFEE at 7 a.m.

BREAKFAST 8.30 a.m.

LUNCH 1 p.m.

DINNER 6.30 p.m.

Meals for Nurses and Children:—BREAKFAST, 8 a.m.; DINNER, 12, TEA, 5 p.m.

Please apply to Second Steward for seating accommodation at Table.

LIGHTS in the Salon are extinguished at 11 p.m.; in the Smoking Room at 11.30 p.m. **BAR** closes at 11 p.m.

SMOKING is not allowed in the Salon, State-rooms or Companion-ways.

THE SALON STEWARD will supply Stamps, Wireless Telegraphy Forms, Books of Reference, and Railway Time Tables of the Principal Companies.

DIVINE SERVICE—Information regarding Divine Service will appear on the Notice Boards every Sunday morning.

VALUABLES—Passengers are enjoined to be very careful in the disposal of small articles of baggage, more especially during Embarkation, when there are always strangers on Board. Money, jewelry and valuables of any kind should always be left securely under lock and key. Passengers may deposit with the Purser any Money, Jewelry, etc. for safe keeping during the voyage, but no responsibility can be accepted for same.

LUGGAGE—Only hand-bags and trunks which will fit underneath the berths are allowed in the State-rooms; all large or heavy luggage must be placed in the Baggage Room, to which access can be gained by applying to the Officer in charge of Baggage. Passengers will greatly expedite the disembarkation if they will have their State-room Baggage packed ready for removal directly on arrival, so that the transfer may at once be proceeded with.

ELECTRIC BELL CALLS—For Steward, one ring; for Stewardess, two rings. **PASSENGERS' ADDRESSES** should be left with the Purser in order that any letters sent to the care of the Company may be forwarded.

LETTERS—Passengers may have their letters forwarded by deposit with the SALON STEWARD.

I should send a telegraph to Charlie Todd in Vicksburg and to Lizzy at Shamrock; let 'em know I'm coming. He paused to think about that. *On second thought I'll send one to Lizzy, but I think it best to surprise Todd, give him no warning I'm coming to inspect the books for Shamrock and for the holdings in Cuba. Sneaky, but that way I'll find out if they're earning their management fee.*

CHAPTER EIGHT

It had been a long day. Ansel checked his watch to find he had a little over an hour to nap before dinner. He took off his overcoat, Sam Browne belt and tunic and hung them on coat hooks mounted on the cabin bulkhead. He removed the shoulder holster and put it with the pistol on the bedside table and stretched out on the bunk. When he woke to the steward playing the dinner chime in the passageway he felt as though he hadn't slept more than five minutes. He considered skipping dinner, but dragged himself out of bed, locked his cabin and made his way along the passageway to a set of stairs leading down to the salon deck.

The dining salon was a large room capable of seating 120. On this night only three tables for six were covered with white linen, set with fine china, silverware, water glasses and wine goblets. Mahogany swivel arm chairs upholstered in tasteful fabric completed the setting. The dining salon had windows along the port and starboard bulkheads with portholes across the aft bulkhead. The windows were fitted with drawn blackout curtains and the portholes were painted black. The room was illuminated with indirect lighting. The dining salon bulkheads soared two decks high beginning with a horizontal border of fine molding to set off the towering walls decorated with panels of raised decorative designs framed in fine millwork, all of it painted a soft ivory color. The ceiling was capped by a beautiful, rectangular stained glass dome, although at present it was covered over by a tarred canvas tarpaulin that would be removed only during daylight hours. This was ocean liner elegance scaled down to a passenger-carrying, fast cargo vessel.

Passengers who had arrived ahead of Lieutenant Quinn filled the first table. Ansel approached a second table and asked the four already seated, "May I join you?"

"Please do, lieutenant. You are a lieutenant are you not?" Before Quinn could answer the gentleman continued, "I'm Frank Drage," He was well-dressed though heavy. He introduced Mrs. Drage stylishly dressed, if rather stout herself.

"I'm Ansel Quinn."

The second couple was introduced as Mister Walter Ferguson and his daughter, Isabel, a strikingly beautiful young woman with a hardly-concealed sad countenance. Ansel guessed her to be in her early twenties. A second single male approached and went through the same introductions. His name was John Rollins.

The conversations at table followed the usual pattern of strangers meeting on shipboard.

Mister Drage was an architect who had just completed a contract on a new office building. "War or no war I had to stay and finish it if I wanted to get paid." He laughed. "There is nothing like a war to encourage a man to complete a commission."

Mister Rollins stated he was a hardware salesman returning home after a successful trip. Mister Ferguson said that he had come over to rescue his daughter from the war and take her home to Memphis. "Like her late mother, Isabel is a bit strong-willed. Against my better judgment, she was in Paris for a year to learn the language and take art courses. When war broke out, my daughter had sense enough to cross over to England, but refused to come home. Instead she volunteered for hospital work. I suspect, although you won't tell me, will you darling?" He looked patronizingly at his daughter. "I suspect a young man may have been in the picture." Ferguson chuckled. Isabel did not.

The others turned questioningly toward Ansel. Mrs. Drage challenged, "Your turn, Lieutenant."

Ansel didn't volunteer much information. "I've been in Paris for some time attached to our Embassy there." Turning to Mister Ferguson he added, "I think, in defense of your daughter, sir, many Americans in Paris and London volunteered in some way when war struck so suddenly. I can assure you that what your daughter witnessed in hospitals was anything but romantic."

Isabel Ferguson glanced at him, her eyes locking momentarily on his.

"Yes. Well, the United States is not part of it and not likely to be. My daughter's place is at home, not on some warfront."

"Perhaps I spoke out of turn, Mister Ferguson. I apologize."

"No need, Lieutenant. I'm just a father worried about a daughter caught up alone in a Europe gone mad." He turned to his daughter and smiled. "I'm just a foolish, old father who loves his daughter." Isabel looked at him, smiled weakly, her beautiful brown eyes expressionless. Without comment she lifted her glass for a sip of wine.

A waiter served what everyone agreed afterward was a fine meal.

"Food shortages may be occurring in Europe, but for a ship that regularly visits America there seems to be no shortage in her galley," offered Mister Rollins. He then addressed Mister Ferguson. "And what do you do in Memphis, may I ask?"

"I'm a commodities broker."

"And how is business?"

"With the demands of this war, business is very good, although cotton has dropped a little. German textiles formerly bought a lot of cotton, but the British blockade of Germany has lessened demand. However, there is increasing demand for food crops and a boon in canning factories to meet overseas' needs."

"Well, Ferguson, I find the same is true of certain types of hardware. But let me offer a toast to what is on all our minds." Rollins lifted his glass. "Here's to a safe voyage home."

They all lifted their glasses, repeating hopefully, "To a safe voyage home." Coffee and dessert followed.

The passengers, all dressed for the cold, assembled for the lifeboat drill at station number one where the respective boat had been swung out on its davits and lowered to the boarding position. The crewman in charge frowned when he discovered that two passengers had arrived without their life vests. He told the pair, "Vests are available in containers located on the boat deck, but in a real emergency, you may not have time to retrieve them." He then demonstrated the proper way to put on and secure a life vest. He went on to explain. "All eight lifeboats aboard, four to each side, will be swung out in position for boarding once we get underway and will remain there until we clear the war zone. In the event of a real emergency you will all assemble where you presently stand here at boat station number one. Each boat can carry twenty passengers and a crew of five consisting of one coxswain and four oarsmen. Since there are only fifteen passengers, one boat will suffice for all of you. The ship's crew will man the other boats as necessary."

The steward then demonstrated the proper way to enter the boat and explained how the craft would be lowered by the crew using a system of blocks and tackle. There was nervous chitchat and labored laughter in an unsuccessful attempt at bravado by a few of the passengers. Most listened intently.

When the assembly was dismissed, John Rollins invited Ansel to join him for a drink in the ship's bar on the upper deck. The two climbed the stairs to find a cozy, mahogany-paneled lounge. There was a large painting of SS *Minnetonka*, one of *Minnehaha's* five sister ships, hanging behind the bar. Other nautical paintings decorated the bar's bulkheads.

The men retired to a table in a corner, pulled off their overcoats, draped them over empty chairs and sat down. Ansel was pleased to find the bar stocked with bourbon, an elixir that was both hard to find and expensive in Paris. Rollins ordered a whiskey.

Both men sat in silence a moment, each taking a sip of his beverage.

"I suspect your job at the American Embassy is as a neutral military observer," Rollins began.

He paused for an answer. Ansel made no comment.

"And I further assume as such you have witnessed action on the front. That is the purpose of military observers, I understand. And if you have been to the front, I further assume you have seen the effectiveness of the machine gun."

"I'm afraid that I am not at liberty to discuss the subject," Ansel answered and took another sip of his iced bourbon.

"Lieutenant, I did not lie when I described myself as a hardware salesman, I just did not describe what kind of hardware. I have been in England negotiating with Vickers Arms in behalf of my company, Colt Arms, for license to manufacture their newly improved machinegun. If, as I suspect, you have been to the front in France or Belgium, then you surely have seen the awesome effect the machinegun has on the battlefield."

He looked for a confirmation from Ansel, but got none.

"I assume you have been ordered not to discuss such matters. I admire your loyalty and ability to follow orders. Because of that, I feel you will keep in confidence information about which you may not be aware."

Ansel nodded in the affirmative.

"The inventor of the modern machinegun, Hiram Maxim was American-born but became a naturalized citizen of Britain. In 1912, he tried to sell his machinegun to the Brits. The British high command was not particularly interested, was still confident in the ability of massed riflemen with bayonets to carry an attack; they disdained a defensive roll for Britain. They believed that any modern war would be one of rapid movement and maneuver. They noted the machinegun is heavy and requires four to six men to carry, man and supply with ammunition, hardly conducive to rapid attack they said. Disappointed, Maxim then took his machinegun to the French. Their attitude was much the same as the Brits. They have a light, magazine fed automatic rifle called a Chauchat. It is a sorry weapon that often jams.

"Anyway, discouraged, Maxim demonstrated his gun with its rapid rate of fire, 500 rounds a minute, to the Germans. It seems the German high command immediately recognized its potential. Germany negotiated a license to build Maxim's gun. As a result, Lieutenant, Germany entered this war with 12,000 machineguns. They are rapidly adding to that number.

"Maxim went into business with Vickers, who improved his gun. Even so, England and France entered the war with less than a thousand machineguns each. It is the machinegun that in less than a year put an end to rapid movement and maneuvers and caused the conflict to stagnate into trench warfare. Our United States, Lieutenant, as of last month had a total of 450 machine guns."

"And just why are you telling me all this, Mister Rollins?"

"Because, Lieutenant, I saw you come aboard carrying a diplomatic pouch. I assume you will deliver it to Washington. And because of your assignment as an observer in France, I further assume you may be requested to report in person to the war department to enlighten them with what you have observed, to confirm or not the reports they have received on the situation."

"Mister Rollins, I doubt the War Department pays much attention to lieutenants."

"Lieutenant, the United States needs machineguns, and Colt Arms is now in a position to manufacture the improved Vickers-Maxim gun, the best available. I want the army to buy it. If, as I believe, you have seen machineguns in action, you will be of the opinion that the army, if called to war, will need machineguns, lots of them. We both know America will go to war. There is no other way to prevent Germany from taking over the whole of Europe. France and England together cannot do it. They are being slowly bled white at about twice the rate of German losses. Perhaps German women have been busy having babies while English and French women have been more interested in the suffrage movement and Paris fashions. In any case, census figures forecast that if the war continues, England and France will run out of replacements before Germany does."

"Are you a philosopher, salesman or patriot Mister Rollins?"

"All three," Rollins smiled.

"I will keep what you have told me under advisement. That is the best I can offer."

"I could offer you much more, Lieutenant."

"It would be in your best interest, and that of Colt, not to, Mister Rollins."

Ansel emptied his drink, put money on the table, stood and retrieved his overcoat. "I've had a long day, Mister Rollins. The conversation has been informative. I think it best we leave it at that."

"As you wish, Lieutenant. I enjoyed the drink. Have a good night."

Ansel made his way down to the promenade deck. He put his overcoat over his shoulders and stepped out on deck to let the crisp air clear his head. He was angry. What Rollins had told him, he already knew; that America was grossly unprepared for war; angry that Rollins had tried to use him; angry that on one hand his family's estate needed him, while on the other he had a sworn duty to his country.

A startling blast from the ship's klaxon interrupted Ansel's thoughts. Looking over the side he watched stevedores onshore free the ship's mooring lines from the dock-side bollards. With the aid of a steam tug, *Minnehaha* maneuvered into midstream and headed down the Thames for the North Sea.

Quinn stepped inside and walked forward up the passageway to his cabin. He dropped his overcoat on a chair, took off his shoes and undressed, put on a robe and knocked on the shared bathroom door. With no response, he unlatched the door, refreshed himself for bed, returned to his cabin, latched the door behind him and put on his pajamas.

He turned off the overhead light, lay down on his bunk, turned on the reading lamp and picked up the book he had purchased at a kiosk at Victoria Station—*The Thirty-nine Steps* by John Buchan. According to a notation provided on the leaf of the book jacket, it was a mystery that takes place just before the war in a Europe filled with spies.

Ansel had just opened the book to "Chapter One, The Man Who Died," when he heard a light tap. He wasn't sure the sound came from the cabin door or the bathroom door. Perplexed, not sure of what he had heard, a second soft, double tap left no doubt. He put down the book, put on his robe, moved to the bathroom door, unlatched and opened it just a crack.

"Lieutenant Quinn, may I come in . . . just to talk?" It was Isabel Ferguson.

Ansel was a little shocked. "It would seem a little improper, Miss Ferguson. What will your father think?"

"My father is asleep in a separate cabin next to mine." She paused. "I need some-one, someone to talk to. From what you said to my father, you seem to be the only one aboard who doesn't think I'm a spoiled, defiant daughter, the only one who might understand. May I please come in?"

Ansel stepped back. Isabel walked in, closed and latched the door behind her. She was dressed in a fashionable flowered silk robe. A blue nightgown with a white lace collar was partly visible beneath the robe. She was barefooted.

"May we sit together? I must talk quietly so as to not be heard through the cabin door." She walked to the bed, sat and patted a place beside her. "I will not injure your reputation, Lieutenant."

Ansel hesitated. "It's not my reputation, but that of a very lovely young woman I'm concerned about."

"Please. My life has been shattered. I don't know how to go on. After dinner I went on deck, told father I needed some air. I thought the chill would clear my mind. I am not a stupid woman, Lieutenant. Standing by the rail I thought how easy it would be to slip over the side into the cold dark, beckoning water. I always thought I was too proud to do something like that, to give up like that, but now . . . If I am not to do that . . . I need . . . what? Human understanding perhaps? Could you, would you just hold me a moment? I am not insane you know, just a little broken."

Ansel thought of the time recently when he desperately needed someone to talk to and there was no one. He sat beside her and put an arm around her. She buried her face in his shoulder. She did not weep, just hid her face for a long moment like an embarrassed child. After a moment or two she sat up and faced him.

"My father was right. There was a man, Lieutenant, a good man, an English officer. His name was Leslie, Lieutenant Leslie Worthington. We were secretly engaged. He said for my sake we should not marry until the war was over. He was very loving and very wise, and too damn brave. You were right, too, Lieutenant Quinn. What I saw at the hospital was not romantic. I learned to be, what . . . blind? No, hardened to the horror while managing to be gentle to the suffering, all without collapsing as I saw some of the women do. And then came a day . . ." Isabel paused and swallowed hard. "The last thing I remember seeing that day in that awful place was Leslie, or what was left of him. I was in receiving when they brought him in. There was still dirt on his face, but I recognized him. He was missing a leg and his bare chest was covered with bandages soaked with blood. I held him in my arms." Big tears appeared and ran down her cheeks, but she did not openly weep. "He knew I was there. I told him the leg didn't matter, because it didn't. He spoke my name and smiled and asked, "How can someone so beautiful look so clownish in that awful uniform you are wearing." He always loved to joke. He tried to laugh, but only blood gurgled up. He tightened his grip on my hand . . . and then was gone."

She dried her eyes on her sleeve. "I'm sorry," she apologized. "I wasn't going to cry. Anyway, as fate would have it, that very afternoon my daddy showed up out of nowhere to take his little girl home to Memphis. He thought it his fatherly duty. He said I was only a volunteer and un-volunteered me with the hospital administrator. And here I am, no time to grieve, no time to decide what to do, no time to explain, not that I ever will to Daddy. So you see I am here with the only man who took up for me at the table, the only man in uniform, the only man I hoped would lend me, as they say, an ear and a shoulder to cry on. I never needed, never knew the value of that before, not even when Mother died. I hope you will forgive me for burdening you this way."

"I'll only forgive you if there is no more talk of 'slipping overboard.' I have lived enough, seen enough to know it will take time for you to heal, but I now know you are strong, Isabel. If you weren't you would not have been able to work day-after-day with war casualties. I know good men who could not stand seeing what you saw and doing what you did to save the treatable and ease the pain and fear of those who could not be saved. You will not forget, but you will heal."

Isabel looked up at him and her beautiful eyes filled once more with tears. "Lieutenant Quinn—"

"Please, my name is Ansel."

"Ansel then, I have a strange request; you will think it strange. Would you lay with me and hold me for a little while, not make love, just hold me. I want—no, I need to know there is still human warmth in this world with its horrible war. If I can be held in kindness for just a little while, then perhaps the sun will come up and I will find there is still a horizon out there and maybe somewhere beyond, something to live for."

Ansel didn't say a word. He crawled onto the bunk, drew Isabel to him spoon-like and held her that way. He could faintly smell perfume and nuzzled his cheek against her hair. That is when she finally let go and wept uncontrollably, her body shaking, her hand at her mouth in an attempt to soften the cries of a lonely and broken heart.

Ansel held her without a word and let the pent up sorrow run its course. Exhausted physically and mentally, the woman in his arms drifted into sleep.

Sometime in the wee hours of the morning, Isabel Ferguson slipped from the bed without awakening the bone tired lieutenant. She kissed his cheek and whispered, "You are a good man, Ansel Quinn."

With the porthole painted over, no sunlight entered the room to announce the arrival of a new day. Ansel slept later than usual. His first dim thought was how lovely Isabel's slim body had felt next to his, and then he felt guilty for thinking such a thing under the circumstances that placed her there. The thought of Isabel snapped him fully awake. Panic squeezed his chest. *Isabel!* He looked at his watch. *Eight fifteen!* He opened his trunk, took out a pair of dark trousers, a white shirt and maroon sweater. *Surely she's too strong to have left in the night to slip over the side.* He wasn't sure he believed it. Skipping his morning routine, he hurriedly dressed and left running for the dining salon one deck down.

Quinn burst through the salon door to startle those seated for breakfast. He saw her and let out the breath he hadn't realized he was holding. Isabel was there, sitting beside her father at the second table. She looked tired and drained of emotion, but when their eyes met, she smiled at him.

She knows I was frightened she would not be here.

Ansel realized everyone was staring at him. He laughed and said "I overslept and was afraid I had missed breakfast. I'm starving and ran all the way."

There were a few chuckles as the diners settled back to their meals and conversation. The salon was a much cheerier place with the blackout curtains rolled up to allow sunlight to brighten the room and penetrate the stained glass dome overhead. A tall gentleman stood at the last table and beckoned him to an empty seat.

"Come join us, by all means. We certainly have room for a starving man at this table." Ansel walked over and shook the man's offered hand. "Ansel Quinn."

The tall man smiled. "Marvin Falkner. Let me introduce you. This fellow to my left is Phillip Sawyer, architect from Boston. Next, Mister and Mrs. Harrison from Baltimore, and this distinguished fellow in the navy blue uniform is Dr. Gatley, Ship's Surgeon."

Each nodded to Ansel as the introductions went round. A waiter brought him coffee. "Would you like to order, sir?"

"Please do. We all already have," Mrs. Harrison offered.

Ansel ordered scrambled eggs, bacon and toast. "And English marmalade, if you have it." The conversation was typical of new acquaintances.

"Just what is it that brings you to join the voyage Mister Quinn?" asked Mrs. Harrison. "My husband and I noticed you in uniform last night. We couldn't imagine what an American officer was doing in England. Was that a diplomatic pouch you brought aboard? We would love to hear just what you were doing over there."

Ansel was taken off guard. "I have been in Paris actually, not England, assigned to our embassy there. I'm going home on leave."

"We would love to hear more about your time in France. Have you been to the front? We would all like to hear about that. I hope the reports in that pouch will be enough to keep our boys out of this war as President Wilson has promised."

Ansel smiled but made no comment. He noticed Mister Harrison give his wife a stern look that seemed to say 'enough.' In any case she asked no more questions.

In an attempt to change the subject, Ansel turned to Mister Sawyer. "You are the second American architect I've met aboard."

"Yes, and I am here under the same circumstance as Frank Drage. I was in Paris when everyone thought the Germans would be putting their flag at the top of the Eiffel Tower. I fled all the way to Vichy, as did the government of France, I might add, before the Kaiser's army was stopped just outside Paris. I went back to Paris, of course, to keep from throwing away three years' worth of work. Just like Frank's, my contract on designing a new department store stated I received nothing over living expenses until I finished my work and it was accepted. I did and it was and I can't tell you how happy I am to be going home."

"How about you, Doctor, how long have you been sailing?" questioned Marvin Falkner. Dr. Gatley answered, "I confess I have had a love for the sea since I was a boy. My father insisted I attend medical school. I did, and as you can see, I found a way to please my father and to go to the sea in ships as I always wanted. I have been with the Atlantic Line for almost twenty years. I alternate between the Atlantic runs and those across the Pacific to the Orient—one long ocean adventure. But on the medical side, I must say that I have experienced nearly every kind of sickness and injury known to man. I might add that I am happy to see such a healthy group of passengers on this trip."

"Do you have a family?" Mrs. Harrison asked.

"Indeed I do, a wife and four children. I am at sea for six months and home for six months. Makes for a rather romantic life. The wife and I are never together long enough at a time to tire of one another, don't you see, and a wonderful homecoming every six months. It's a wonder we don't have a dozen children."

The normally somber Mister Harrison smiled. Mrs. Harrison did not.

CHAPTER NINE

With breakfast ending and guests drifting out of the dining salon, Marvin Falkner asked, "Lieutenant Quinn, would you have another cup of coffee with me? I would like to talk to you if I may."

"I don't see why not. Mister Falkner, isn't it?"

"Splendid!" Falkner ordered coffee and the two sat facing one another while the room cleared of guests and the dishes were removed.

When they found themselves alone, Falkner put down his cup. His initial sunny 'hail fellow well met' countenance faded into a somber expression.

"Lieutenant, I am a major in His Majesty's Army. I thought perhaps in private we might exchange views on, as the poet wrote, 'Shoes and ships and sealing wax and cabbages and kings,' all in mutually agreed confidence, of course."

"I believe that quote came from Louis Carroll's *Through the Looking-glass*. Even as a child I never liked the book; thought it insane."

"Exactly the point, as insane as this bloody war we have."

"True, but back to the quote a moment, Major. When I was about nine or ten, my father, a ship captain, read to me that very part of Carroll's poem. It's from the conversation between the Walrus and the Carpenter. I remember it because my father read it to me again and explained the conversation as one of deceit and treachery whereby the walrus and the carpenter talked gullible young oysters into going with them on a picnic, then ate them. He said it was a lesson I should not forget and I haven't."

"Your father was obviously a perceptive man. Let me assure you my intention is neither deceitful nor treacherous. In fact, I must trust that you are neither, and will keep this conversation in confidence. I suspect that you are on your way to Washington, and if true, that you will be questioned by your War Department or Department of State, perhaps both. It is not every day that they have access to someone fresh from overseas to supplement the written communications and propaganda they receive from all sides including from the German Embassy in Washington. What I want to emphasize is that smug Ole England was caught flat-footed in 1914. Germany used the dust-up between Austria-Hungary and Russia to attack through Belgium in an attempt to outflank and defeat France. We believe their plan was to quickly defeat France before Russia could fully mobilize. Then they could turn on a sluggish Russia without the burden of a two-front war. As you know, they nearly succeeded. Brave little Belgium had declared itself neutral. It refused a request to allow Germany to march its army through to attack France. When Germany violated their neutrality, Belgium tried valiantly to defend its borders. Our treaty with Belgium brought England into it. In our arrogance we thought it would all be over in a year. Here we are into 1916 with no end in sight. With 450 miles of opposing trenches, it is doubtful there will be an out and out victory for either side unless some new means of breaking through the trench defenses can be found. Both sides thought gas would do it, and both sides have tried it, but no significant ground has changed hands. Simply throwing men across 'no man's land' at each other has accomplishing little gain for either side at unsustainable cost. Have you been to the front?"

"I was witness to the second attempt by the French to take Vimy Ridge."

"Then you know what I am talking about. Recently, we and the French tried again. The British part of the attack we called the Battle of Loos, our largest offensive effort to date. We committed six divisions, gave the Germans a taste of gas and used aircraft to direct our artillery fire. The battle lasted twenty-four days and cost us 50,000 casualties. The losses of the German defenders, we calculate, was half that."

"Why tell me? I assume the information must be labeled confidential."

"It is and I could face a court-martial, if you name me as the source, but I am telling you this on the chance that you may be asked such questions when you deliver the diplomatic mail you are carrying. Surely someone in Washington will want to hear first-hand information from someone who has been to the front in France."

"Major, I have been told that the Wilson administration hears an appeal from England and France to join the war every day. I am just a lieutenant delivering a diplomatic pouch before going on leave. I doubt I will be interviewed or asked my opinion on anything. And I think I should tell you that after what I saw at the front, I am no more in favor of sending American troops into such a slaughter mill than our President."

"The purpose of my trip, Lieutenant, is not to persuade your government to go to war. Our Foreign Service meets often with your State Department to ask for more material support. Our navy is blockading Germany and we hear they are rationing food because of it. On the other hand, their U-boats are sinking ships faster than we can replace them. We need food, armaments, ammunition, medicine, trucks, raw materials, anything and everything. It can only reach us by sea. We have begun putting merchant ships in convoys hoping enough will survive to reach England. This very ship and her sister liners secretly carry such supplies on their return voyages—what to the Germans is contraband. This war is bleeding Britain of both men and treasure and will soon be starving our citizens unless such help continues. We don't raise enough food to feed the British Isles even in peace time. Now U-boats are seriously cutting our imports of food. If your country will not send an army, at least, we pray, it will not only continue, but increase material support. We ask that your country at least give us the means to continue fighting. What is at stake is the choice between a free Europe and one ruled by Germanic barbarians. If you don't believe that's what they are, ask the poor Belgian and French villagers who have suffered under the Kaiser's Imperial Army. They have seen their crops stolen, their women abused and their men shipped off to slave labor. It's all part of Germany's strategy to inflict terror. I hope that there are documents in that diplomatic pouch you are delivering that confirm what I'm telling you."

"Major, I have no way of knowing what is in the pouch. What I can say is that I do know how desperate the fighting is from what little of the front I have been allowed to visit."

"When do you plan to return to France, may I ask?"

"My orders say in six weeks including travel. That gives me four weeks to settle my family's estate."

"You mentioned you have visited the French Army on the front. If I can arrange it, would you be interested in visiting our British Expeditionary Force at the front?"

"I would, sir, but I doubt the State Department or my commanding officer at the Paris Embassy will allow it."

"Well, Lieutenant, I'll see what I can do."

"All the attention being paid to a lowly American lieutenant makes me wonder if I am on a ship of spies. You are the second passenger aboard who has bent my ear and asked my aid should I be interviewed by the powers-that-be in Washington, not to mention the inquisitiveness of Mrs. Harrison."

"The second passenger you mentioned would be Mister John Rollins who is looking for support for the Colt-Vickers gun. I hope he gets it. Mister and Mrs. Harrison are a different story. I advise you to be careful of what you say to them."

"Yes. Well, I told Rollins what I'm telling you. There is slim chance of anyone in Washington asking my opinion on anything. I might add, with no offense intended, that in talking to an insignificant American lieutenant on the rather long odds that he can in some small way influence any decision makers, whether military or civilian, gives the impression that England and France are becoming a little desperate. I understand that the German attack on Verdun, that has just started, is sucking in much of the French Army. The news in the West is not good."

"I can't speak for France, but the word 'desperate' is premature for England. We are entering the third year of this war and have little to show for it but shortages of strategic materiel, food and reserve manpower. We need whatever help we can garner from your country and that includes credit. As it stands, our American cousins already have taken in trade a considerable portion of our treasury reserves, but let's put aside the word 'desperate' for the time being."

"Major, some in America wonder why you English entered this war at all. You are isolated by your English Channel and no enemy has successfully invaded since the Normans in 1066 if I remember my history."

"In the first place we had a treaty to protect neutral Belgium. To ignore that agreement would be to forsake our honor and obligations as a nation. That may sound foolish, but the real reason is that if France, Belgium and Russia should fall, and we are worried about Russia as it is, how long do you think we could hold against the whole of a German controlled Europe possessing the modern weapons of today not to mention French ports for their battleships and U-boats just across the channel? If nothing changes on the battle front, if our losses continue, we and France will be hard-put to defeat Germany without your country joining us in this struggle. Germany fears that. It is why they have backed down from unrestricted submarine warfare. It may sound trite, but I believe without America's help, democracy on our side of the Atlantic may not survive. Lieutenant, if no one in your war department takes the time to interview you, they will waste an opportunity I doubt they often get these days.

"One other thing, please. I ask you to remember that no one aboard, with the exception of yourself, knows I am a major in the service of the King. I ask you not to disclose that fact."

"Or, as I suspect, that you are in the King's intelligence service."

"Just remember to call me 'Marvin' whenever we meet on board, Lieutenant. Care for another cup?"

Quinn declined and the two filed out of the dining salon as waiters began resetting the tables in preparation for lunch.

Ansel thought of taking a turn around the promenade deck, but found the North Atlantic, on this late January day, not very conducive to a stroll. The temperature was dropping and the wind picking up. The ship responded with a noticeable increase in pitch and roll. Instead of exercise, Ansel chose a more pleasant way to spend the morning. He fetched his book from his cabin and made his way to the library on the upper deck.

He was not alone in his choice. Half a dozen passengers sat around the room. It was well appointed with plush bench seating against the bulkheads with a few cozy 'U' shaped booths in the corners. At intervals around the room there were mahogany shelves stocked with a wide variety of books and periodicals. John Rollins and Phillip Sawyer were playing gin in one corner. Mister and Mrs. Harrison were seated against the back bulkhead opposite the door. Mister Harrison rose and motioned Ansel over just as his name was called from a corner booth to his right. He recognized the voice as that of Isabel Ferguson. She and her father were sitting with a large atlas spread open between them.

"Do come join us, Lieutenant."

Ansel gave a friendly wave to the Harrisons and joined the Fergusons.

"The Atlantic is beginning to kick up a bit don't you think? We were just looking at this atlas trying to figure out our position," Mister Ferguson said. "We ran into the purser on our way here. He said we have traveled a little under two hundred miles, are still within the Kaiser's War Zone, but by sundown we should be in the clear."

Isabel asked with a slight smile, "How did you sleep last night, Lieutenant?"

"Warm and snug, Miss Ferguson." Ansel tried unsuccessfully not to smile.

"Please call me Isabel. Father said he tossed and turned all night thinking about U-boats, but I slept better than I have since . . . well, in days . . . must be the rocking of this ship." She smiled the first genuine smile Ansel had seen on her pretty face.

Perhaps this morning she's found that new horizon we discussed last night.

"Would you tell me about the commodities business, Mister Ferguson? As you can imagine I am a little tired of people asking me about a war in which I've played no part. I assume you deal in cotton."

"That's right, Lieutenant."

"Please, you all call me Ansel."

"All right, Ansel if you will call me Walter. This war in Europe has been a boon to American farmers I tell you, and to me as well. My business has never been better. Besides fetching Isabel home, I visited in person with London firms with whom I do business. Personal contacts are always the best way to do business. Ferguson and Company buys and sells commodities—in my case mostly cotton—but because of war demand overseas, I'm increasingly dealing in feed crops, mules and lumber. Memphis is considered the cotton, mule and hardwood capital of the country. At first, cotton fell off some due to the blockade of Germany, and the fact that France and England converted many of their textile mills into such things as ammunition factories, but the British Isles and France are ordering huge amounts of cotton, lumber, horses, mules and enormous amounts of feed for them. I'm sure you know that cotton, because of its high content of cellulose, is also used to make munitions. Memphis has the largest cotton warehouse in the country. I'm branching out by putting together consortiums of small farms. That way they can consolidate their crops into large shipments to compete on a level with the big boys. In return, I get a small percentage of the profits."

"Walter, I suddenly find myself responsible for a farm back home. As a result, I am in need of more than a little advice and expertise. Perhaps you can help."

"Tell me about your land? What do you raise?"

"Mostly cotton. I have not been involved, you see. The place is a little over six sections. For a long time it limped along with mostly sharecroppers. That paid the taxes most years, and sometimes the expenses, but never much profit. Then when my Aunt Bethany started living there full time, she put more of it in production. According to the books it's done pretty well the last few seasons. My aunt, who ran things in Mississippi and Cuba, wrote me that she had ordered not one but two new Case gasoline tractors with plow and harrow attachments. That cost a pretty penny, but each one, according to her, can do the work of four or more mule teams at much less cost. I guess they've been delivered by now. As you know a lot of cotton land has played out, but for years most of Shamrock lay idle in clover or grasses cut for hay with just enough maintenance to keep the brush and saplings down. I think when she was living in Cuba, Bethany just didn't want to fool with it."

Ferguson paused to do the figures in his head. "My God! Six sections! That's over thirty-five hundred acres! With this war, fortunes are being made off spreads that large."

"The family has always made good profits on our land in Cuba, most of it in sugar."

"How much land is under cultivation in Cuba, may I ask?"

"We have about three thousand acres under cultivation there; mostly sugar and some tobacco. Aunt Bethany talked about building a rum distillery since all the ingredients are there—sugar, molasses and good water—but I frankly don't know how that's going."

"Your aunt must be quite a business woman. You say you have just been put in charge of your family business. Is your Aunt Bethany ill?"

"My aunt was lost with the *Lusitania*."

"Oh! Ansel, I am so sorry." Isabel's smile disappeared. She reached over to touch his hand in a gesture of sympathy.

"That must have been a terrible shock," Walter Ferguson added.

Ansel was silent a moment, his face grave. "I blame myself. You see she was coming to Paris to visit me. She was so full of life. I was to take leave right in Paris. She loved the city and lived there as a young woman at school, something like what you were doing when the war broke out, Isabel. I had planned to show her a wonderful holiday. Now I'm the last of the Shamrock Quinns and have only a short time to make sure it all is in capable hands until this war is over."

There was a heavy silence for a moment or two. Tears welled in the corners of Isabel's eyes. After a moment, Mister Ferguson spoke, "How do you plan to run all that until your army obligation has ended?"

"Now Daddy, you shouldn't be prying into the Lieutenant's affairs. You just met him and he doesn't know you or your company."

"No, I don't mind Isabel. I'm very interested. As I said, I need your kind of expertise. You see my moth—I mean my Aunt Bethany ran everything even before my father died. I went off to West Point and have been in the army since. She has been after me to resign my commission and learn the business. I have thought about it, my duty to the family, but now with the war, I doubt the army is of a persuasion to discharge any officers at the moment, especially West Pointers. As a result I really never learned much about the business of farming.

"Bethany has a farm manager, a Mister Jedediah Jamison. He goes by Jed. Our family and his go back a long way. The Jamisons lost about everything in the Civil War including two sons, one of which was Jed's father. My father sent Jed to the Agricultural and Mechanical College of Mississippi. Afterward he worked his way up at Shamrock and has been manager for about the last fifteen years. For longer than that, lawyer Todd, audited the books every six months. He was my father's age and now that he's gone, his son, Todd Junior, has the law firm and is handling the estate as called for in Bethany's will.

"Look, I'll only have about thirty days to determine if any management decisions need to be made before I have travel back to France. I know we've just met, but could I talk you into coming down to see the place in Mississippi first hand? It's out of Vicksburg and that's not so far from Memphis. I will pay for your time and advice. As I said, right now it is all in the hands of the family law firm, Todd, Cochran and Roberts. The purpose of my taking leave, while I can get it, is to evaluate the job Jed is doing at Shamrock and the job the law firm is doing or not doing, as the case may be. I could certainly use someone with your experience. Now that Bethany is gone, I need to be sure things are set up right—purchasing, payroll, labor, stock, equipment, buildings, maintenance, banking, bookkeeping—and a way to monitor it all."

"Well Ansel, I've been away from my office so I'll have some catching up to do in Memphis, but your situation does interest me. Let me think about it. We have worked through similar problems for some of our clients."

"Walter, I certainly would like to have your first-hand opinion and advice on organization and management. I think Jed is all right, Bethany thought so, but she was always there to see how he was doing and make the final decision on important matters. Until this war is over, I won't be directly there to make such decisions. I lose sleep over it.

"We have a comfortable place there at Shamrock to put you up for a few days. It's not fancy, but I think you will find it satisfactory. I can promise the food will be good. I think both you and Isabel would enjoy a stay in the country, especially after the brush you've had with the war and this crossing of the Atlantic."

"You call the place Shamrock?"

"Yes. My family came from the Carolinas to the Mississippi territory in 1806 and gradually built Shamrock. There once was a lovely, grand plantation home, but the Yankees burned it. The family would have lost it all to debt and taxes after the war except for the hard and dangerous work my father did as a sea captain and eventually as a ship owner. He made enough money to keep the place going."

"Sounds like a romantic history," Isabel smiled again.

"Not romantic, Isabel," Ansel paused. He looked at neither Walter nor Isabel as he continued. "It's a history of hard times, good times, tragedy, suffering, joy, risk, maybe adventure, all put down in my aunt's and grandmother's diaries. I suppose it's the same as most human stories. Success, as measured in land, a little investment in stocks and a little cash in the bank is the sum result of generations of hard work. Up until now, I realize, I've benefitted without contributing to it. My great grandfather was in the Mexican War; my grandfather was killed in the Civil War, my father served on the raider *CSA Alabama* and later played an important part in the Cuban struggle for independence and the Spanish American War. I suppose, as a boy at military school, I thought my duty was to carry on that tradition of military service. My aunt never wanted me to do that. It looks like she was right. Now, suddenly, the land is my responsibility." Ansel paused as if considering what he had just said. He looked at Walter Ferguson. "That's why I would like your advice." Then, looking a little embarrassed he added, "I don't know why I told you all that. I should not have burdened you with my problems."

"Oh! But we are glad you did. Daddy can help. He really can, can't you daddy?"

"Well, let's not jump too far ahead. Let me get things in Memphis taken care of first."

"Mister Ferguson, I know it would be an imposition, but I would very much appreciate your giving it consideration. If you will give me an address where I can send a telegram from Washington I will let you know when I expect to be at Shamrock. I will include the phone number there." Ansel saw surprise on Ferguson's face. "Yes we have a telephone, but no electricity. A main phone line was laid from Natchez to Vicksburg, generally following the Mississippi River. My aunt paid a good deal to have a line run off of it up to Shamrock. It allowed her to communicate with her shipping agent in Florida and from there telegraphs to Cuba through the underwater cable. That cut her trips to Cuba down to once a quarter or less. The phone is connected to the Vicksburg switchboard. Maybe one day the power plant at Vicksburg will run a line our way. A lot of farms could sure use it. Anyway, if you prefer, I'll have Lizzy, that's Bethany's housekeeper, open the townhouse in Vicksburg. It has all the conveniences. I would very much appreciate it if you all would come down from Memphis. I have such little time. Before my leave runs out, I have to go to Cuba to check on the Alacon-Quinn sugar plantation there. Things there are a little more in hand. The same Cuban family my father selected years ago is still managing the place. Whatever time and duty I am obligated to remain in the army, and that looks like until the war ends, I will sleep better, so to speak, if I know my new responsibilities at home are under control. God knows I'll have enough to worry about in France."

A steward entered the library sounding his three-note chime to announce lunch.

Walter Ferguson handed Ansel a business card. "Here's my address and office telephone number in Memphis. I can't promise anything, but if I can work a week into my schedule, I think I would like to see your place. Would it be all right if Isabel came along? I keep trying to interest her in the business. How about it darling?"

"It might give me a little respite before you drag me back into the dull and silly social whirl of Memphis. Ansel, if you haven't noticed, my father keeps trying to get me into the business; somewhat like your aunt did you. Daddy has no son to train, you see; that just leaves me." Isabel rolled her eyes at her father, but kissed him on the cheek and said, "I just might surprise you."

"Heaven help me! My headstrong daughter has subjected me to surprises all her life." Walter Ferguson laughed. "Let's go to lunch. And no talk on this matter at the table, Isabel. I'm sure Ansel wants to keep it private."

Ansel nodded in agreement and the three left the library for the dining salon two decks below.

Walter Ferguson, Isabel and Ansel were joined at the table by Marvin Falkner and Mister and Mrs. Frank Drage. For the first time, the ship's captain, Frank Garet, joined the passengers for a meal.

The lunch menu listed a choice of lamb's head broth or tomato soup, codfish steaks, corned beef and vegetables or roast beef, baked or mashed potatoes, and for dessert, Gorgonzola and cheddar cheeses, roll jam pudding or rhubarb tart.

The main course had just been served when the ship turned so sharply to starboard that plates slid off the tables, slopping laps and crashing to the deck. Passengers would have followed if the swivel dining chairs in which they were sitting had not been bolted to the deck. Into the hard turn the ship listed over ten degrees. Ladies screamed. Waiters lost their trays and fought to stay on their feet. The clatter of pots and pans colliding about the galley amplified the clamor and dissonance filling the dining salon.

Captain Garet, without a word, swiveled his chair round, got to his feet, charged out of the dining salon and headed for the bridge three decks above.

The ship's claxon sounded four sharp blasts, an international signal for danger. Passengers held on to their seats and tables until the ship rolled level and steadied on a new course.

"That was jolly good fun!" Marvin Falkner bellowed. "What is the helmsman going to do for an encore?" The humor of his statement and his steady voice elicited nervous laughter from the dining crowd, many of whom had laps full of spilled food.

Their ordeal was not over.

Ansel and John Rollins quickly followed the captain out of the salon, up the stairs and out onto the promenade deck. Through the soles of their feet they could feel the vibrations of the ship's two, huge, quadruple compound steam engines straining at full power. No sooner had they arrived at the starboard rail than the ship took another hard turn, this time to port. They heard a distant report coming from somewhere astern of the ship followed a few seconds later by a splash and explosion fifty yards to starboard. There was one more explosion somewhere behind the ship as it steadied course at full speed.

A half hour later, with the ship still at full speed but on steady course, stewards began rounding up the scattered passengers, some of them wearing life vests, herding them back to the dining salon where waiters had done a passable job of cleaning up the mess and resetting the tables. With so much of the prepared main course wasted, the best that could be provided was corned beef and potatoes with choice of desserts and wine, coffee or tea.

As the passengers, at least those who still had an appetite following the extreme evasive maneuvers the ship had taken, were finishing their belated lunch, Captain Garet entered the salon to apprise them of the incident.

"Ladies and gentlemen, the first officer received reports from our lookouts high aloft that a submarine had been sighted surfacing an estimated two miles off our port. The U-boat was too far away and our speed too great for them to have a chance with a torpedo. We think their captain tried to frighten us into stopping by firing his deck gun which missed due to the rapid maneuvering carried out by the first officer. He relays his apologies, along with mine, for upsetting your lunch, but by his decisive action he avoided the gunfire and quickly hauled out of range. Within the hour, we will be out of the war zone and should have smooth sailing to New York. Please enjoy your dessert." Captain Garet paused. "If any of you were thrown about and are bruised or injured, or would like a sedative to calm your nerves, our Dr. Gatley is available in the ship's dispensary. On behalf of The Atlantic Transport Line, I again apologize for your inconvenience and assure you that our greatest concern is your safe arrival at New York."

The captain departed the salon to enthusiastic applause.

Isabel Ferguson was the first to speak at the table. "I think I'll have roll jam pudding and coffee. How about you gentlemen?"

Marvin Falkner responded, "I'll have a brandy, if it's all the same to you, Miss Ferguson." Walter Ferguson and Ansel spoke in unison to the waiter, "Make that three!"

"We are Baptist, but after a U-boat attack, make that four," Mister Drage said.

"No, honey, not four. Make it five. I think the good Lord will understand," Mrs. Drage said. "Why Mary, I never thought I'd see the day."

"Well, Frank, with this ship doing whirligigs and U-boats shooting at us, that day has arrived. Praise Jesus!"

The ship's bar enjoyed a flourishing business early in the afternoon, but excitement has a way of bringing on fatigue once calm is restored. The salons and passageways became deserted as most passengers retired to their cabins for late afternoon naps.

After having lunch slung all over the guests and deck, the galley staff and head chef were determined to make up for the disaster by presenting the very best dinner the ship's stores would allow. The evening menu read as follows:

Little Neck Clams	Anchovies and Tomatoes
Consommé Petite Marmite	Green Turtle Soup
Salmon	Sweetbreads Parisienne
Broiled Squab and Champignons	Tenderloin of Beef, Claret Sauce
Quarters of Spring Lamb	Turkey Financier
String Beans	Egg Plant
Windsor and Puree Potatoes	Salad
Viennoise Pudding	Compote of Fruits
Creamed Rice Florentine	Macedoine Jelly
Vanilla Ice Cream	Welsh Rarebits
Coffee	

In spite of the shock most passengers had sustained, not to mention the outright hysteria exhibited by some during the attack, all had recovered sufficiently to assail the evening meal with voracious appreciation as evidenced by the clatter of silverware and china. Added to that cacophony was the din of chatter about the afternoon's adventure. There is absolutely nothing that will liven up a crowd so much as the avoidance of near disaster. With a starlit sky and calming sea, SS *Minnehaha* sailed west into the chilled Atlantic night.

After the excitement of the U-boat contact, the cruise became rather boring. There were bridge games daily, which Ansel avoided, much preferring to read or do almost anything besides play cards. For group entertainment, games were organized and contests of wit and knowledge were held. A talented quartet made up from the ship's crew performed on piano, drums, saxophone and ukulele. They played what some passengers laughingly claimed was noise while others recognized the sound as a brand new music called Jazz. Selections included such popular pieces as *Araby, Are You from Dixie? Blame it on the Blues* and *Down in Bombay*. Few could dance to the beat, but Lieutenant Quinn and Miss Ferguson, having learned in wartime cabarets, cut quite a sight dancing in the narrow aisles between the tables.

Then there was another night when the quartet played two of the most popular songs of the year: *I Didn't Raise My Boy to Be a Soldier*, by Morton Harvey, and *It's a Long Way to Tipperary*, by John McCormack.

Isabel left the salon.

Ansel, wondering if he had somehow offended her, followed to determine what had happened. He caught up with Isabel standing by the ship's rail. Her evening dress rippled in the icy breeze. Without a wrap, she was trembling. By the moon's light Ansel saw her cheeks wet with tears.

He knew without asking. The last two songs had reminded her of Leslie, the soldier who had died in her arms.

She must have read his thoughts for she said, "Oh! Ansel, it's not just Leslie. It's all the boys who have died and those who will in this horrible, senseless war. I complained about my father coming to get me, but the truth is I could not have stayed in that hospital much longer. I must be a coward."

"You're no coward, Isabel. I couldn't do what you were doing day after day."

She turned and hugged Ansel hard, her face buried in his shoulder. Then she pulled away and asked for his handkerchief. She dried her eyes and looked up at him. "Ansel, I like you very much. You are kind and gentle and brave, but you are a soldier. I cannot lose another. I would die. Could we just be friends, just not take it further? That's selfish of me, I know, but you and America will be drawn into this war. Anyone with any sense, anyone who has seen what is happening in France and Belgium, what is happening to French and English and Belgian boys has to know that. No," she said and put her fingers on Ansel's lips, "don't speak. Just hold me a little longer."

He did and kissed her forehead "I'll be all right in the morning." Isabel pulled away. She tried unsuccessfully to form a smile with her trembling lips "I think we better go back now, I'm freezing."

That night, Ansel lay in his bunk thinking of the unsettling effect the girl he had met only days before was having on him. He had never taken any girl seriously, especially one he had known for so short a time. He had known other beautiful women, but this one was different.

How, he could not answer. He tried to read, but found himself starting the same paragraph over several times. He put the book down, turned out the light and waited for elusive sleep.

The last thing Ansel expected to hear in the night was a tap on the locked door to the adjoining bath, but near midnight such a tap came. He turned on the reading lamp, walked to the door, unlocked and opened it. Isabel Ferguson was standing there, once again barefooted and wearing her silk robe.

"I can't promise I won't confuse you with Leslie. You can send me away if you want, but I need you. You proved you are a decent man that first night you held me and ask for nothing. I can't do that in return—be held and ask for nothing. I'm still fighting for my life. Tonight I need you, Ansel Quinn."

CHAPTER TEN

Breakfast was a little awkward. Mister Ferguson walked into the dining salon, saw Ansel, and joined him anxious to discuss, over eggs and bacon, the possibilities offered by Quinn's Shamrock plantation considering the war demand for foodstuffs and cotton. When Isabel arrived she could hardly avoid sitting beside her father. Quinn was more than a little distracted by her occasional glance across the table. Try as she might, she could not suppress a smile now and then. With a beautiful girl sitting across the breakfast table, a girl he now knew more than casually, Ansel found it difficult to concentrate on the business of Shamrock. Thoughts of their night together were crowding his mind as he tried to carry on a serious conversation with Isabel's father. He could not continue.

"Mister Ferguson, I find your interest in Shamrock very compelling, but I must beg to be excused. Can we take up the discussion later? For some reason," Ansel mustered enough self-control to dampen all but a fleeting look at Isabel, "I did not get much sleep last night and I am dragging a little this morning."

Isabel quickly lowered her gaze to hide the smile on her face.

Later that morning Ansel and Mister Ferguson did sit and discuss the Quinn holdings in Mississippi and Cuba and possible offerings that could be to their mutual benefit.

By lunch time, a force 6 wind had pushed up a moderate sea and lines of rain squalls swept in from the darkened horizon. There were fewer passengers at lunch that day, and even fewer took advantage of the fine dining the following day as an entry in the ship's log stated "Beaufort 7 wind, rough sea, overcast."

Isabel paid only one more midnight visit to Ansel's cabin. While lying nude propped up on one elbow she noticed a pistol resting on the bedside table. With genuine curiosity and laughter she asked Ansel, lying on his back next to her, "Do you always make love with a pistol at the ready? Just what kind of ladies have you had in your bed?"

"That, mademoiselle, is a military secret. I was ordered to protect the diplomatic mail entrusted to me, especially from beautiful spies. To fail will get me hanged."

"How did you discover I am a German spy paid to get such secrets from American lieutenants?"

"*Fräulein*, if you are being paid Deutsche Marks to spy on me, I intend to see that you earn your pay." Ansel kissed her and rolled her upright astraddle his hips.

Later, with Isabel resting close beside him, Ansel confessed, "If you are a spy, I will be hanged with a smile on my face."

"Oh all right! I will not tell the Kaiser you have been a naughty boy. Now let me go. I will be hanged alongside you if Daddy catches me doing my patriotic duty."

She got out of the bunk, put on her nightgown and robe and paused at the door. Her expression was unguardedly solemn. "You have saved my life, you know." She departed the cabin the way she had entered.

Ansel lay a long time before sleep finally came.

Although there were no more rendezvous in Ansel's cabin, Lieutenant Quinn and Miss Ferguson managed to run into each other in the library or while walking on the leeward side of the promenade deck, bundled up against the cold, rain and spray kicked up by the weather, days when hardly any but the hardiest of souls braved the chill of a heaving deck. Drawn together by feelings both tried to suppress, they laughed and spoke of anything but war and love. Occasionally they met in the lounge for drinks but only in the company of Mister Ferguson as was considered proper for a beautiful young woman traveling with her father.

More times than not during the afternoons, Ansel could be seen in the lounge sharing a table with the outwardly jovial, but inwardly mysterious Mister Falkner, known only to Ansel aboard ship as Major Falkner of the British Army Intelligence Service.

"I think your interest in me is misplaced," Ansel said. "I am aboard as a courier of a diplomatic pouch to Washington, which is no secret, and after delivery I will be on leave."

"It's true I had no idea you would be aboard, but it has presented me with the opportunity to invite a neutral American to observe the British Expeditionary Force at the front when you return."

Ansel started to speak but Falkner raised his hand to stop him. "I know, the invitation will have to go through your ambassador and your commanding officer at your embassy, but if you are agreeable, I will make the effort through proper channels."

"I've seen the French in action. The experience was not encouraging as far as my country entering this thing. You must know that."

"No one in the West is encouraged by the failure to break the German defenses, but what choice is there? Surely your country does not wish to see all of Europe under the boot heel of Germany."

"That may be true, but as I understand it President Wilson is the leading proponent of the current isolationist policy. I don't see what advantage Britain can gain from America if they get more firsthand reports like the one our observation team submitted describing the costly and failed attempt the French made against the Germans at Vimy Ridge. Perhaps if you Brits have a successful offensive in the spring, attitudes in America may change."

The Major paused in thought before speaking. "Americans have a stake in this war whether they are ready to admit it or not. First hand American observers are rare. What your country needs is a true picture of the struggle both militarily and politically."

"There are many Americans who believe the war is entirely a European matter. The feeling is that no American should die in a war where both sides are fighting to preserve or expand old European empires be they English, French, Belgian, Russian, German or Italian."

"I can understand that, but Germany, Austro-Hungry, Russia and the Ottoman Empire are all dictatorships. England, France and Belgium are democracies. We have a king, but it is our Parliament and Prime Minister who run England; not too different from your Congress and President. How long do you think England could stand if all Europe is under German domination? Whatever the outcome, this war will change the old world. I doubt the empires of which you speak will last long once it is over. Colonies from Africa to Asia already seek self-rule. After this war ends, some if not many will probably get at least autonomy from a war-broken Europe. Sooner or later what your country will have to decide is what kind of Europe they want—one of democracy or military dictatorship. It is a near thing at the moment. I want you to see that from the front and report what you find first hand to your superiors."

"Well, Major, I'm just a lowly first lieutenant, but if you can get me such an assignment, which I doubt under the present circumstances, I am willing to accept it. And while we are discussing such things, you know the reason for my travel to the United States. I am very curious as what your assignment may be."

"I have spoken somewhat more than I am authorized to do, but my purpose is not so secret that I cannot tell a future ally." The Major smiled. "Your country is in the business of supplying my country with food, raw materials, arms, ammunition, and any number of other items England desperately needs, for which, I might add, your country is paid. The Germans know this. Of course your country, your neutral country, has made the diplomatic gesture to sell to Germany too, but our naval blockade of Germany prevents direct shipments to them, though some material goes through neutral Norway, Sweden, The Netherlands and Denmark. America is not only the food basket but the industrial lifeline of our war effort. My job is twofold. One is to encourage your government to set up an official intelligence agency in the mold of British Intelligence. Your Army doesn't even have an intelligence service. Your Secretary of State is trying to set one up on his own. That will be difficult in that your President Wilson, I am told from reliable sources, disdains the use of spies and is generally suspicious of intelligence. He believes gentlemen don't read other gentlemen's mail. My second assignment is perhaps more urgent. That is to convince your government of the need to set up a coordinated anti-sabotage effort."

"Sabotage in America?"

"Lieutenant, I have news for you. There are over eight million Germans in your country, most fairly recent immigrants. Your major Northeastern and Midwestern cities have German populations of thirty to as high as fifty percent. For example, there is a German language newspaper in New York that prints 75,000 copies a day. Almost all German Americans, according to our information, support the American isolationist movement. Many of your German immigrants are skilled and work in factories. In addition, more than a few industries in America are German owned or tied to German investment. There are already reports of mysterious accidents. There have been six explosions in American factories that produce munitions for Allied powers.

In addition, we are getting artillery shells that are faulty. You are exporting probably 1,000 horses and mules a day. Much transport in this modern war still depends on horses and mules. Anthrax has suddenly appeared on some shiploads. That didn't come from the American stock yards and holding pens. It showed up on the ships. We know of four British ships bound for England that blew up after leaving New York. We believe German spy and sabotage networks in your country are responsible for such occurrences."

"How does a German agent blow up a ship without being on board?"

"Germany has come up with a dandy little device we call a pencil bomb. It consists of a small lead tube about the length of a cigar inside of which are two types of acid. One is in a glass vial separated from the other by a copper disk. When one crushes the end with the glass vial, the acid released takes a predetermined amount of time to eat through the copper disk. When the two acids meet, they explode into an intense fire. If placed in a factory or ship next to flammable material or explosives, the results are not pretty."

"Major, I have heard nothing of any sabotage from the American embassy in Paris."

"We have informed your government of our beliefs and provided what we feel is proof, but your President Wilson, I am told, has a way of rationalizing news of the war in Europe and viewing it with detachment. However quiet it is kept, proof of sabotage is causing concern.

"I am not saying that all German immigrants in your country are spies and sabo- teurs, but we think there are some among them who are. For instance, I had no idea that you would be aboard this ship, but I did know that Mister and Mrs. Harrison would be. They are the couple who have been so interested and inquisitive about a certain American lieutenant they discovered was aboard, and what he has been doing in France. Their name, Harrison, is an Americanized version of the German name Harries. They are second generation German which is why they speak American English with no ac- cent. We believe they have been raised by German immigrants whose loyalties remain with the 'Fatherland.' Now you know why I suggested you avoid them.

A known association with them might not look good on your record should America declare war against Germany. We know Germany's Ambassador in Washington, Johann von Bernstorff, has given his Military Attaché, Franz von Papen, orders to organize spy and sabotage rings in the U.S. Ambassador von Bernstorff speaks English perfectly and his wife is American. He has the reputation of being charming and circulates widely in Washington society. We also know that the 'Harrisons' have surreptitiously met with von Papen and that under pretense of business interests have made two trips to England to meet with known German agents there."

"If British intelligence knows this, why haven't they been picked up?"

"Because they don't know we know. We hope they will lead us to more contacts in America and England. We want to wrap up their whole network. In the meantime, we are having a hard time convincing your government of the danger that exists not only from acts of sabotage but from influence inside unions and industries critical to the war effort, ours and at some time in the future, yours."

"Well, Major, I wish I could help, but I am at the bottom of the totem pole."

"Not as low as you think, Lieutenant. From what I have learned, you are in a position in Paris to at least catch the ear of the American Embassy and French Army Headquarters. Questions concerning such matters from your ambassador in France will help raise flags in America. In any case, it is my job on this trip to try and teach a thing or two about both anti-sabotage and intelligence gathering if your Departments of the Army and State will listen."

"Would you, Major, consider it insulting if I asked to see some proof of your rank and outfit?"

The Major laughed. As he reached in his jacket inside pocket, he said, "You see, you are learning already." The Major took from his wallet his army identification card headed with the words Royal Army Intelligence Corps and complete with photograph, rank and serial number.

"I apologize, sir." Ansel reached for his inside jacket pocket, but the Major raised his hand. "That's not necessary, Lieutenant. With the Captain's permission, I used the ship's wireless to send and receive a coded message concerning your bona fides shortly after leaving port. Otherwise, you would not have received the information I have given you. We have dossiers on personnel at most embassies around the world. I believe the official practice of such clandestine record keeping may have begun with Disraeli during the reign of Queen Victoria. I'm afraid your country may be a little behind in the game. Everything your country knows about the personnel at the German Embassy in Washington came from our Foreign Service, which in turn came from British Intelligence."

It was at that moment that the Harrisons entered the lounge. Immediately, Mrs. Harrison waved to Ansel and approaching the table said, "There you are, Lieutenant. We have been dying to hear all about France and your duties there. In spite of the war I bet you have enjoyed being in Paris."

Both Ansel and Falkner stood as Mrs. Harrison approached. Ansel immediately seated her at the table and motioned Mister Harrison to the fourth chair.

Looking at his watch, Ansel remained standing. "I am terribly sorry Mrs. Harrison, but I have promised a game of gin with Dr. Gatley in the ship's dispensary. I'm sure you will find Marvin Falkner's company as entertaining as I have." With a raised eyebrow, he smiled rather wickedly at Falkner. "Because I have to leave this nice company, the round of refreshments is on me. Now if you will excuse me." Ansel motioned to the waiter to put the next round on his tab and left the lounge.

It wasn't two minutes later that Dr. Gatley walked into the lounge. Falkner was quick. "Dr. Gatley, old sport, Lieutenant Quinn just left to meet you in the dispensary for your game of gin." The doctor looked a little perplexed, but caught Falkner's raised eyebrows in a questioning expression.

"Oh! Yes! I was just coming up to remind him." The doctor wheeled around and left.

"Well, that just leaves the three of us," the Major smiled. "Just what business brings you across the dark and dangerous Atlantic, Mister Harrison?"

CHAPTER ELEVEN

Washington 1916

In spite of the cold temperature and low clouds threatening rain, the passengers gathered on the promenade deck as *Minnehaha* steamed into the Narrows separating Lower New York Bay from the Upper Bay and New York-New Jersey Harbors. The ship slowed and a small boat came alongside to deliver a harbor pilot aboard.

Lieutenant Quinn, wearing his army overcoat, stood forward at the rail with Isabel as the ship continued past the Statue of Liberty. Isabel was wrapped in a long, navy blue wool coat and wore a chapeau adorned with feathers that were teased in the breeze. With light makeup on her perfect complexion and rouged lips she was exquisitely beautiful.

The bay separating New Jersey and New York was busy with both harbor and ocean-going traffic. There were a great deal of signals being exchanged between vessels; a cacophony of shrill whistles and deep throated klaxons making it hard to carry on a conversation. Ansel and Isabel had to stand very close to hear one another.

"Are you one of those kiss-the-girls-goodbye kinds of soldier, Lieutenant Quinn, or do you suppose we may meet again?" Isabel tried hard to be nonchalant about their imminent parting.

"Memphis is a long way from France, but I would hope you and your father will come to Shamrock before I return to duty."

"I will have to think hard about that. You are the kind of man a girl could fall in love with you know, but I intend not to do that.

I can't change the fact that I'm a soldier, at least for a while, and I know how you feel about that. Meeting you has caused me a great deal of consternation. You see falling in love is something I have been able to avoid up to now, although French girls are very nice." He smiled when Isabel gave him a sharp look. "There will be an ocean between us for a while."

"An ocean and perhaps years if Europe continues to tear itself apart."

"You said we could be a little more than just friends. Does that mean lovers?"

"A girl should blush at such a statement, but then I haven't been a girl since I volunteered to care for torn and dying boys."

"And you look at me and think I might become one of them."

"No! Yes! Damn it! I look at you and see a man I could love."

"Come to Shamrock with you father. I may stop off in Memphis to convince you."

A steward with a megaphone called to the passengers on deck, "All passengers please check your cabins for belongings and prepare to disembark. We will be docking in thirty minutes. Thirty minutes, ladies and gentlemen. Please have your papers ready and claim your baggage on the dock for clearance by Customs."

Mister Ferguson approached the two. "I am overjoyed to see America again. Isabel, I think we better get ready to go ashore. Lieutenant Quinn, I hope to hear from you. I'm anxious to explore the possibilities if your invitation is still open."

"It is, sir, and I will let you know when I can be there to receive you for a visit."

"I look forward to that. Come on, Isabel, you have a lot of baggage to look after." As the Fergusons walked away, Major Falkner approached Ansel.

"I doubt we will have a chance to meet in Washington, Quinn, but I hope you will keep in mind our discussions and disseminate their contents should you get the opportunity. I will see if I can put in motion an invitation for you to visit the BEF front in the not too distant future."

"Maj—, I mean, Marvin, I will accept the invitation if offered. I better get to the Purser's office. Good luck to you, sir."

"Same to you, Lieutenant."

Quinn made his way to Purser John Lang's office to retrieve the diplomatic pouch. He carefully checked the lock and seal before signing a receipt in triplicate bearing the crest of the Atlantic Line, the ship's name, the date, time stamp, name and signature of the depositor and the purser. Quinn retained a copy and the Purser retained two remaining copies, one for the Atlantic Line and one for the ship's records.

Ansel longed to speak to Isabel one last time before parting, but he reached the street only to see her and her father leaving in a taxi. As he stood watching them disappear into the bustling automobile and horse drawn traffic of New York, he felt his heart miss a beat and it startled him. He had never experienced such feelings in his happy-go-lucky relations with women.

Standing absently by the curb, he was surprised to hear his name.

"Lieutenant Quinn?" Ansel turned to see a sergeant coming toward him.

"I'm Quinn."

"Sir, I'm Sergeant Murphy of the 69th Regiment here in New York. I've been assigned to escort you to the Pennsylvania Station. There's a train leaving for Washington in an hour and a half. I have your ticket here." He handed the ticket to Ansel. "It includes a meal."

Ansel checked the ticket. The price, New York to Washington, was five dollars and sixty-five cents with an additional charge of one dollar and twenty-five cents for the meal.

"I'll take your trunk, sir." The Sergeant hoisted the trunk to his shoulder. "If you will follow me I have a Ford waiting over at the taxi lot."

Sergeant Murphy didn't offer to carry the pouch. *Guess he knows the drill*, Ansel thought as he followed Murphy to a Model T Ford truck painted army brown with 69th Regimental markings stenciled in white.

"I appreciate this, Sergeant. Please thank your commander for me."

"Lieutenant, the 69th does this for every courier arriving from overseas."

The Sergeant put Quinn's trunk in the truck bed, and pointed the lieutenant to the passenger seat. From the driver's side, he reached to the left of the steering column and adjusted the spark lever, then adjusted the throttle lever on the right side, switched the ignition to the battery position, which made a buzzing sound, walked around to the front, bent down and gave the crank a mighty turn. The Ford came to life with a syncopated tune emanating from the exhaust pipe, a rhythmic tick of the engine and a gentle shaking of the frame. Murphy climbed into the driver's seat, adjusted the spark lever to smooth out the engine, switched the ignition to the magneto and moved the brake lever to the neutral position. With expert skill the Sergeant worked the three pedals on the floor (clutch, reverse and brake), adjusted the throttle on the steering column, and maneuvered into traffic shifting from low to high gear as traffic allowed.

"I'll be taking you to Pennsylvania Station. Have you been there, Lieutenant?"

"No, I haven't."

"It takes up two city blocks. Inside the ceiling is fifteen stories high. Except for the brand new Grand Central Terminal, there ain't nothing like it in the world. It's big enough inside to hold a battle. Wait 'til you get there. You'll see what I mean."

Dodging autos, streetcars, carriages pulled by horses, wagons pulled by mules, pedestrians and bicycles, all crossing traffic willy-nilly, the Sergeant pulled up in front of the huge edifice. Ansel looked up at what was said to be the grandest example of Beaux Arts architecture outside of Paris.

"I'll have to let you out at the curb, sir. Don't get lost in there, Lieutenant."

The Sergeant smiled, retrieved Quinn's trunk, set it on the sidewalk beside him, saluted got back into the truck and drove off.

Before Ansel could pick up his trunk a Negro man wearing a red cap had it on a dolly. "I can take that satchel, too."

"No, I better carry it."

"All right, suh. Which train you catchin'?"

Quinn looked at his ticket. "The 12:45 to Washington."

"That'll be the National Limited on track number four. It'll be leavin' in 'bout twenty minutes. Just follow me."

Ansel followed the Redcap through the huge waiting room and a long distance down the train concourse along track number four. After the Redcap tagged and stacked Ansel's trunk on a railroad baggage wagon he directed Ansel to his assigned coach. Ansel tipped the man, climbed the iron steps onto the car and found his seat about halfway down the aisle.

The National Limited pulled out of the station into a dull, gray afternoon with light rain weeping from the low overcast. The coach was not crowded. Ansel sat the pouch on the seat beside him and covered it with his overcoat. He regretted having packed his book away in the trunk. With nothing to do, he stared out the window, his view blurred by soot streaked rivulets of rain running down the glass. Somewhere along the way, before he fell asleep, or was it after, Ansel was never quite sure, a rather strange thing happened. He was looking out the window when, for a moment it wasn't his own reflection in the glass. It was Isabel's.

At Union Station in Washington, he stepped down from the train to the platform carrying the pouch. He found his trunk among the pile of luggage set out on a baggage wagon. He pointed it out to a Redcap who retrieved it to his dolly. They had hardly begun the long walk down the covered train concourse when they were met by a man dressed in a three-piece, navy-blue suit.

"You must be Lieutenant Quinn."

Quinn nodded.

"I'm Special Agent Winthrop." The man opened his coat to show a badge pinned to his vest. The badge displayed in raised blue letters the words SPECIAL AGENT DIVISION at the top with the words DEPARTMENT OF STATE at the bottom and in the center the letters 'U' and 'S' were artfully intertwined.

"I didn't know the State Department had special agents."

"Officially, it doesn't," Winthrop answered. "Congress and the President are some-what paranoid about maintaining neutrality. They aren't quite ready to openly admit the need for increased security for the ever-growing number of documents the Department of State is receiving from overseas since the war in Europe began. They can't envision gentlemen from one country stealing 'the mail' of gentlemen of another. Secretary of State Lansing is not so naïve, but is keeping his special agent program somewhat close to his vest. For now, the Department doesn't have funds for increasing the number of couriers which is why, when we can, we use military personnel like yourself."

"Well, I don't suppose I should ask any more questions about special agents in the department."

"That's right, Lieutenant, you shouldn't. Now, if you will follow me, I will relieve you of that burden you've carried such a long way."

Ansel still had a long way to carry the pouch. The Redcap followed them with Ansel's trunk.

They walked down the enormous covered train concourse into the mammoth main building.

Winthrop crossed to an unmarked door leading off the huge high-ceilinged wait-ing area.

"Ask your man there if he can wait for us here."

"Oh, yes, suh, I can wait."

Ansel followed Winthrop through the door, up a narrow staircase and down a hall to another unmarked door. The agent unlocked the door and motioned Ansel in. It was a small office furnished with a table, two wooden chairs and one overhead light. Winthrop closed the door, latched it and turned to face Ansel.

"Please put the pouch on the table."

Ansel did.

"Now the pistol and holster."

"Was I really supposed to shoot anyone who tried to grab the pouch?"

"That's why you were given the pistol, Lieutenant."

Ansel took the pistol out of his overcoat pocket and laid it on the table. As an ex-planation he said, "It would be the only way I could get to the thing if I really needed it."

Winthrop nodded his concurrence. Ansel took off his overcoat and tunic to retrieve the shoulder holster and lay it on the table beside the pistol. The agent then
asked for the receipt from the ship's purser. Ansel retrieved it from a tunic pocket. The
agent read it, then closely examined the lock and seal on the pouch. Satisfied, he took
two forms from his jacket pocket and gave them to Ansel to read. Both forms were in
triplicate, with carbon paper behind the first and second pages. One was a receipt for
the pouch; the other, a receipt for the pistol and holster.

Ansel read both, careful to verify that the number stenciled on the pouch and
the number on the seal were the same on the first form, and checked the second
to confirm that the serial number on the pistol was the same as that on the form.
He signed both forms and passed them to Winthrop who added his signature and
handed Quinn the original copy of each.

"The information we have on you is that you are attached to French Army
Headquarters in Paris as a neutral observer, that you speak French and Spanish and
that you were part of a party that visited the front and contributed to the American
Ambassador's report on that subject. Is that correct?"

"You fellows don't miss much."

Winthrop ignored the remark. "Normally a courier would be released at this exchange, but I've been given instructions to deliver you along with the pouch to the
Department of State. Is that trunk all your baggage?

"Yes."

"I have a car waiting."

"Is that an order?"

"I shouldn't think you would want to disappoint the Secretary."

They went down to the main floor. This time Agent Winthrop carried the pouch.
The waiting Redcap with Ansel's trunk followed them to the street where a Dodge
Brothers motorcar and driver were waiting at the curb. The streets were wet but the
rain had stopped. Ansel tipped the Redcap, put his trunk in the back seat and climbed
in beside it. Winthrop got in the front with the pouch. The driver pulled away from
the curb, skirted round the Columbus Memorial in front of the station, passed the
large, landscaped green and turned into the traffic on Massachusetts Avenue.

Ansel's thoughts drifted to the only other time he had been to Washington. He was
about twelve and in the company of his father, Jonathan Quinn. It was just after the
Spanish American War. They had stayed at the Willard Hotel and gone to the Capitol
where Jonathan introduced him to several congressmen. Although he did not mention
it to Agent Winthrop, he had visited the State, War and Navy building on that same trip.
He and his father had lunch with then Secretary of the Navy, John Long. Ansel remembered the meeting well because the Secretary seemed to know Captain Quinn. The two
men talked of the Spanish American War and the part Captain Quinn had played in it.

As they drove down Massachusetts and turned onto New York Avenue, Ansel's
thoughts returned to the present. He noticed many new buildings had been constructed since he last visited the Capital: hotels, commercial enterprises and government offices. The driver turned right onto Pennsylvania Avenue, skirted around piles

of dirt and groups of workers rehabilitating streetcar tracks, continued past the White House and made a left on Seventeenth Street. They stopped at the State, War and Navy Building. (Today it is called the Eisenhower Executive Office Building.) Designed in French Second Empire Architectural style by Alfred Mullett, many critics thought the massive, five story building bizarre because of the extensive exterior baroque-like decorative details. Samuel Clements had pronounced it the ugliest building in America, but Ansel rather liked it. It reminded him of Paris.

"Your trunk will be safe with the driver," Winthrop said as they got out of the Dodge and walked into the Seventeenth Street entrance where Winthrop showed his Identification to a security guard and stated that he was escorting Lieutenant Quinn. The guard wrote a temporary pass for Quinn and reminded him that he must remain in the company of Agent Winthrop at all times.

As they walked away from the watch station, Winthrop explained that recently Secretary Lansing had tightened security. "Before the war there wasn't much public interest in European diplomatic affairs. It used to be that visitors were allowed to roam around marveling at the building, its great halls and reception rooms. After the war began, it was found that unsupervised newspaper reporters looking for story leads wandered into offices and read papers left on desks or found in waste baskets. As a result, indiscreet articles began to appear in their newspapers, some of them harmful to diplomatic relations. Lansing put a stop to that."

Ansel could understand visitors wanting to see the building. He marveled at it himself. The structure, with its great rooms, offices and architectural and decorative details, was designed with fireproofing in mind. The major materials were iron and granite. Ansel followed Agent Winthrop up a gray granite stairway decorated with intricately designed bronze balustrades topped with mahogany hand rails. The only other use of wood Ansel observed in the building was the polished, two inch thick wood doors. Reaching the second floor, they walked down a twelve foot wide hallway paved with alternating squares of black slate and white marble and entered an office marked with a plaque bearing the name William Phillips and below that the title, Third Assistant Secretary of State.

Assistant Secretary Phillips rose from his desk to greet them. He motioned for the visitors to sit on a leather-covered office couch, old, worn and cracked, and took a chair facing them.

"As I am sure Agent Winthrop has informed you, Lieutenant, the United States has been rather lax in matters of security. Prior to this war we considered ourselves merely a regional power and weren't too concerned with the affairs of Europe. Increasingly we find ourselves of interest to the Entente and the Central Powers alike. The Entente wants us in the war, the Central Powers do not. Some in our government are slow to realize that security should be more of a concern to us especially because our industry and agriculture are sources of materials deemed vital to war by all parties. There have been increasing instances of sabotage.

"Secretary Lansing has proposed a diplomatic security force. However, certain established bureaus, the Post Office, the Secret Service and the Justice Department don't want any more competition to their respective bailiwicks and that includes competition not just for power but for funding. They're reluctant to even share information among themselves. As a result, the President has stalled making any decision on the matter of State Department security. As you may have learned, Secretary Lansing has discretely created a small unofficial group of agents to perform certain security and intelligence tasks not undertaken by other bureaus, tasks which I am not at liberty to discuss. We find that covert espionage is occurring here. We hope that our president can be persuaded to authorize and fund a true diplomatic security agency. In the meantime we have no official security agency with international reach. The United States Army is in a similar position to the Department of State as regards intelligence. As a matter of fact, the Army at present has no intelligence service whatsoever. We have discovered that the only man in the Army who has any experience in what can be defined as military intelligence is Major Ralph Van Deman. While at the Bureau of Insurgent Records in Manila, Philippines, Major Van Deman saw the need for counter-intelligence to help stop the attacks by Muslim Moros. Your records indicate you saw action in the Philippines."

"Yes, sir, I saw a little."

"In the Philippine theater, Major Deman tried to expand what is known as the Military Information Division. You may know it as MID. He organized an unofficial counter-intelligence group in the Philippines by recruiting locals as agents. General Pershing told us the intelligence they gathered was instrumental in controlling and limiting the insurrection.

Last July, Major Van Deman was assigned to the War College out at Washington Barracks. What he found there was a general apathy about intelligence-gathering, and that the MID had been downgraded from the second division of the General Staff and merged with the third division, ending its separate identity, making it even less useful.

Van Deman is convinced the Army must have a coordinated intelligence organization, especially in the event we become involved in the war in Europe. He was finally able to get an audience with the Secretary of War to present his case. The War Department was not convinced even after a Colonel Claude Dansey of the British Security Service proposed similar ideas to Colonel Edward M. House, one of President Wilson's closest advisors.

In any case, Van Deman is not giving up. There is at this very moment a Major Falkner of the British Intelligence Corps visiting Major Van Deman at his invitation. I suppose he is here to update Deman on the organization and activities of British Army Intelligence."

"Did you say Major Falkner, Mister Secretary?"

"Do you know him, Lieutenant?"

"I met him on the ship over, sir."

"I guess that brings us up to you, Lieutenant Quinn. Secretary Lansing was impressed by the detail of observation evident in your portion of the report made and transmitted to this office by Ambassador Sharp concerning a visit to the front by Major Crosby, Assistant Second Secretary Andrew Hampton, and yourself during the French assault on Vimy Ridge. I suppose that, plus you language skills and your present assignment in Paris, is the reason your presence has been requested by Major Van Deman. We thank you for performing courier duty. I believe the driver with you baggage is waiting outside, Lieutenant. He will take you out to Washington Barracks."

There was little Ansel could say. "Yes sir. Thank you, sir."

As required, Agent Winthrop escorted the lieutenant out of the building. At the waiting car, he smiled and said, "You're going to love it at Washington Barracks."

"And why is that?" Ansel asked.

"Because the War College is there. You have never seen so many colonels and generals as you will find there at the moment. The war in Europe has cleaned some of the cobwebs out of the place. A lieutenant out there will be quite a novelty. Good luck, Quinn."

It was a long drive.

CHAPTER TWELVE

Ansel reported in, was assigned a billet, squared away his gear and tidied up a bit. Agent Winthrop had been right. Lieutenant Quinn saluted at least twenty superior officers on his way to the office of Major Ralph Van Deman.

"I'm glad you could make it, Captain."

"Sir, I'm just a first lieutenant."

"You were, Quinn," the Major smiled, "but orders were cut this morning promoting you to the rank of captain. I believe you can pick up captain's insignia at the base quartermaster. If not, there are several uniform shops in town."

"Yes sir. Thank you sir."

"Now I know you're anxious to begin your leave, but you will be assigned special additional duties to your current assignment in France. As a result, you will spend a week here with me, Captain. Have a seat and I will explain."

Ansel sat down and tried to hide his disappointment in having a week carved out of his furlough.

The Major began. "Don't worry, your furlough will be extended plus a week for the time you spend here." Ansel was sure the relief he felt was visible to the Major who continued, "I suspect that you were told over at State some of the problems both Secretary Lansing and I have faced in trying to wake certain officials up to the need for intelligence. As for the Army, the Chief of Staff, General Scott, refuses to see a need for an Army department of intelligence and said the Army couldn't afford the funds to create and support one. At our first meeting, he told me that if the British and French already have such good intelligence departments we could simply asked them for information if we get into the war. At our last meeting, he said he was tired of hearing from me. He not only refuses to see me, but ordered me not to contact Secretary of War Baker on the matter. Before you ask, I did not disobey that order exactly. It was through the efforts of a sympathetic general and a certain unnamed lady that Secretary of War Baker approved my assignment here at the War College for the purpose of teaching a little something about military intelligence to the top officer corps. Military intelligence, at the very least should consist of enemy signal interception, code use and code breaking, direct military tactical observation and analysis, counter intelligence, interrogation of prisoners, patrols, raids, secret agents, recruitment of spies and other related activities. Because of a bunch of woodenheaded officials, both politicians and Army paper-pushers, which shall remain unnamed, there is no Military Intelligence Department in the U.S. Army much less the funding to create one.

"It is my opinion, Captain, that we will at some point be drawn into this war. As far as an intelligence organization is concerned, the best that can be done for the present is this. I have talked to Secretary Lansing. He is agreeable to the State Department quietly utilizing the military attachés at our foreign embassies not only as neutral observes, but as intelligence gatherers including tactical analysis. There also may be an opportunity for covert operations should favorable circumstances exist. This is all we can do under the present circumstances.

"You, Captain, with your language skills and your present duty at our Paris Embassy assigned to French Military Headquarters, are in a prime position to be a part of this effort. Only Ambassador Sharp and Major Crosby will know about your intelligence activity assignment.

You will have their permission to accept any Allied invitations for meetings or visitations you may receive. No one, I repeat, no one else should know of your special assignment and activities.

Neither France nor England allows foreign coded messages to be sent by their wireless or Atlantic cable systems. We certainly can't send intelligence reports in the clear. I should caution you also that telephone communication is not secure. It is a simple matter to tap into a line. Your reports will be sent by Ambassador Sharp to Secretary Lansing via diplomatic pouch. Secretary Lansing will share any information of military value with me.

"If you accept this assignment you should know that some in the Army, like Chief of Staff Scott, consider me somewhat of a maverick. If you take this job, association with me might rub off. It could hurt your military career, but your work could save lives in the event we are pulled into the war. At the moment I can't order you to this duty since officially such duty does not exist. I'm asking you to volunteer."

"I so do, Major."

"Fine, Captain. Notice of your additional duties will be sent by the next State Department pouch to Ambassador Sharp in Paris."

"Yes sir."

"Now, I realize you have been traveling hard. Please take the rest of the day off. I will see you in this office tomorrow at eight o'clock to begin a one week crash course in military intelligence based on the British model. You, of course, will tell no one. If asked your cover is that you are here as my aide-de-camp." Deman smiled. "The rumor is that I am so picky I have yet to find a man satisfactory for the job. I have already instructed one officer each assigned to our London, Berlin, Madrid and Rome Embassies. Sadly, you understand, they were all found unsatisfactory as aides-de-camp and were sent back to embassy duty just as you will be.

"By the way, I understand you served briefly under General Pershing while he was governor in the Philippines."

"Yes sir, I did."

Van Deman continued. "He and I attended the War College together, class of '04. We were both promoted to captain about the same time." Deman paused. "I can tell by your expression you're wondering how he got to be a general while I remain a major.

No, No! It's all right. We are still good friends. You see, Teddy Roosevelt wanted to promote him three ranks from captain to colonel for the good job he was doing in the Philippines and the fact that his duty assignment called for at least the rank of colonel. Roosevelt got mad as hell when the Army turned down the promotion. Promotions in the Army are, as a rule, based strictly on seniority not merit. Well Teddy discovered that the only rank a president could bestow, without the approval of the Army, was the rank of Brigadier General if approved by Congress. So that is what he did, promoted Pershing ahead of some 1,200 odd officers on the Army promotion list. That was resented by many, but those of us who knew him knew what he had done on assignment and supported Black Jack. Do you know how he got the sobriquet, Black Jack?"

"I believe he got that name because he commanded Black Buffalo Soldiers out west and during the Spanish-American War."

"He doesn't like it, but the name stuck. Anyway, he and I are still best of friends." Deman smiled. "It never hurts to have a general as a friend."

Ansel left the office wondering if his promotion had come because his name was next on the list, or if Major Deman had played a part in it putting him before those ahead of him. *Was that the reason he told me about Black Jack Pershing's promotion?*

Whatever the case, that afternoon Ansel sent out his shirts and underwear to be laundered, his spare uniform to be cleaned and his overcoat to have a captain's second 'thread knot' added to the single lieutenant's 'thread knot' on the cuffs. He then purchased new captain's bars and put them on his tunic.

After the week of instruction under Major Van Deman, Ansel sent off several telegrams and purchased a small satchel into which he transferred from his trunk a set of clean underwear, shirts, socks, civilian trousers and sweater, night robe, and toilet items. On Sunday morning, February 13th, he caught a ride to Union Station, checked his trunk, and carried his satchel aboard a Southern Railroad Pullman coach bound for Memphis, Tennessee.

CHAPTER THIRTEEN

The next morning, Monday, February 14th, Ansel, wearing his bath robe, carried his uniform and satchel to the men's dressing room at the end of the car while porters began converting the Pullman's curtained sleeping bunks back into day seating. He waited his turn to clean up and shave. He then dressed in civilian trousers, shirt and sweater, folded his uniform into his satchel, placed it in the rack over his seat and went to the dining car. There he shared a table for four complete with white tablecloth, silverware and a tulip vase containing a fresh long stem rose. Ansel enjoyed a fine breakfast of eggs, bacon, grits, pancakes and coffee while a panorama of drab, winter-bound landscape, occasionally brightened by sunlit snow, drifted past the large dining car window.

After returning to his seat he fetched the book he had bought to read on the Atlantic crossing, but never did so due to a lady named Isabel. With nothing to do as the miles slid by, Ansel spent the day reading *The Thirty Nine Steps*, a story full of German spies and murder set in 1914 just before the start of war. It seemed very apropos in light of his new assignment.

Early in the evening, right on time, the big locomotive, with bell clanging, pulled into the huge, new, Beaux-Arts style Union Station in Memphis. Facing Calhoun Street, it was the largest stone building in the city. Ansel draped his military overcoat over his shoulders. It was the only outerwear garment he had to combat the late afternoon chill.

A Redcap took his trunk and satchel. "You need a taxi, suh? They out on South Second Street. Or is somebody meetin' you out front on Calhoun?"

Walking from the platform into the cavernous main building, Ansel was about to direct the Redcap to the taxi stand when he heard his name.

"Lieutenant Quinn!"

He looked up to see Walter Ferguson coming toward him. Walking just behind was his daughter Isabel dressed stylishly in a cashmere coat trimmed with black fur collar and cuffs. Ansel had to fight the urge to rush past Mister Ferguson and hug Isabel to him. Instead, he reached out to shake hands with her father.

"You didn't have to meet me, Mister Ferguson. I didn't expect to see you until tomorrow."

"What sort of Memphis hospitality would that be? We got your telegram and decided you needed company for dinner tonight. Where are you staying?"

"I was told the Chisca was the newest hotel and was near the station."

"That's a good choice. I've heard it's not as fine as the Peabody used to be, but then the Peabody, which is just across from the Chisca, is getting a little seedy. It's rumored it will be torn down and a new Peabody built one of these days."

Isabel caught up to the two men. "Hello, Lieutenant."

"Hello, Isabel. You look charming as ever."

"Daddy says all you soldier boys are the same; always saying nice things to the girls in hope of favors."

"Yes, well, Lieutenant," Walter said, "this cold air makes me hungry. I'll get my car and meet you two out front." He motioned for the Red Cap to follow him with Ansel's luggage and disappeared out the South Second Street exit.

"Hello again, Lieutenant Quinn."

"It's Captain Quinn, Ansel corrected, then laughed. "A very new captain I might add, and one who is very glad to see you again."

"I should tell you that when Daddy got your wire I almost didn't come with him to meet you."

"Tell me why," Ansel said with a slight, closed-lip smile curling into his cheeks.

"You know why. Because I like you . . . a lot, but you are a soldier."

"I'm not dressed like a soldier."

"That overcoat says you are."

"I intend to change that when I can."

"But not while that damn war over there is on."

"You know, I read somewhere that back during the Peloponnesian War, a Greek warrior had to explain that to his lady."

"And what did that soldier of old say?"

"He said to her, 'How could I love you, loved I not honor more?'" Isabel looked up at him. "Who is talking of love?"

Ansel was shocked at his own spontaneous answer. "I am."

Ignoring his answer, Isabel asked, "Did that Greek warrior return home?"

"I don't know."

Isabel stood on her toes and kissed him on the cheek. "I think we should go out front. Daddy should be there by now."

A few minutes later, Mister Ferguson drove up to the curb in a new 1916 Simplex 5 four door touring car complete with button on curtains with isinglass windows for protection from the cold and wet. It was painted yellow with black fenders.

"That's quite an automobile."

"Daddy's business has done well, especially since the war started. He heard that Rockefeller owned one, so he said a Southern farm boy ought to have one, too. It arrived by train from New York two weeks ago. Daddy works hard. This car is the only toy he has ever allowed himself. I think now that he has it, he is a little embarrassed by the extravagance. He came up hard. His family lost everything in that terrible War of Northern Aggression. We don't say Civil War in Memphis. Anyway, that's the reason he is interested in your Shamrock. Your family managed to keep their land when his lost theirs."

Ansel's luggage was in the front seat beside Mister Ferguson. The couple got into the back. "How about a good steak tonight, Lieutenant?"

"He is a captain now, Daddy."

"Congratulations. Are you hungry, Captain?"

"Yes sir. A steak sounds fine."

"We're going to Floyd's; oldest and best restaurant in town."

The couple in the back seat sat primly proper and silent, each holding back a great deal they wanted to say. Ferguson found a parking place a half block from the restaurant. The three got out to find it was cold enough for their warm breath to condense into vapor as they walked toward a large lighted sign reading FLOYD'S hanging out from the two story facade of the restaurant at 279 Main Street. There was a striped awning over the entrance and lace curtains in the large windows on either side of the door. The interior was warm and friendly. The waiters were all dressed in tuxedoes. The maître d' obviously recognized Mister Ferguson and led the party to a table toward the back. It was set with white tablecloth, water and wine glasses and napkins in pyramid folds resting on service plates flanked by silverware. The two men stood while the waiter seated Isabel.

The water glasses were filled from iced pitchers and menus were presented.

"Miss, do you care for a refreshment?"

"Thank you, Billy. I'll have red wine, the house vintage will do."

"And for you, suh?" The waiter asked Ansel.

Ansel turned to Walter Ferguson. "I thought Georgia, Alabama, Mississippi and Tennessee evangelicals got prohibition laws passed back in '10 or '11."

"They did, but here in Memphis, no one pays attention. Although at present, our mayor and sheriff are being sued by our teetotaler Attorney General for not enforcing the damn fool law. An election year is coming up, don't you see?"

Ansel turned back to the waiter. "I'll have bourbon on ice."

"Make that two," Ferguson added.

The waiter left to fetch the 'refreshments.'

"It's about the same in Vicksburg," Ansel offered, "and Natchez doesn't pay much attention to laws in general, especially that one. Of course they can bring it in by riverboat, like I guess you do here in Memphis. It's a little harder to get in some parts of the state. Before I went overseas, I was told drugstores in Jackson and small inland towns were doing big business by mixing a little cherry or peach syrup with brandy and selling it for cough medicine or rheumatism remedy. My Aunt Bethany said it was surprising how many Bible thumpers developed coughs or rheumatism all of a sudden. Plenty of moonshine is being made in the piney woods or down south in the marsh."

"That's enough talk about whiskey" Isabel said. "That's no way to entertain the Memphis Queen."

"Queen?"

"My daughter was Queen of Cotton Carnival years ago and has never gotten over it."

"Years ago! It was just four years ago. I suppose next you are going to call me an old maid."

"Almost five years, young lady. You were nineteen. I should warn you, Captain Quinn, you are in grave danger, as are all men in the company of old maids."

Isabel gave them both a mock stare of disgust before turning to Ansel. "By the way, Captain Quinn, this year's ball is the first of next month, just ten days away. How would you like to escort this old maid to the top social event in Memphis? The gala will be held at the Peabody and anyone who's anyone from the Mississippi Delta will be there. They will probably even allow an army officer to attend."

"Isabel! You're acting like a hussy. That's a shameful way to treat our guest."

"Not a'tall, Walter. If I can find white tie and tails, my escorting your daughter might be just punishment for so bold a lady."

"I'll take that as a 'yes,' Captain. My honor is now in your hands." Isabel raised an eyebrow and gave him a devilish smile. "It would be scandalous for a queen to show up unescorted."

"You can't say I didn't warn you, Ansel," Walter Ferguson stated. "She's been like this since I brought her home."

"Been like what, Daddy?"

"I don't know. Wish I did."

Billy, the waiter, delivered their 'refreshments'. He took out his pad and waited for the trio to order.

"Billy, we are not quite ready to order. Could you give us a few minutes?"

"Yes, suh, Mister Ferguson."

The three sipped their "refreshments" while they perused Floyd's elaborate menu. It listed eleven soups, fifteen cold dishes, twelve fish dishes, several offerings of lobster and shrimp, Biloxi oysters on the half shell, a large selection of chafing dish specials, a wide selection of poultry and game, steaks and chops, twelve desserts, seven cheeses, and ten different ice cream and sherbet choices.

"What an offering. Not even in Paris could you find such a selection, even *before* the war. In fact, when I left, France was beginning to suffer food shortages due to the U-boats, and I understand Germany is suffering badly because of the British blockade."

"Well this country is sending big shipments of cotton, food, materials, finished goods and livestock to England and France on every ship that sails," Walter said.

"At big profits, too." Isabel added.

"Well, my darling, we can't just give it away. Our country would collapse along with them."

"You know, Walter," Ansel said, "I suspect regardless of who wins, the need for food after the war will be terrible, especially for the loser."

Billy showed up to end the conversation. "Your pleasure, Miss Isabel?" he asked, pencil and pad in hand.

"I'll have onion soup au gratin, lobster Newburg, asparagus with Hollandaise sauce, and a little more red wine."

"Very good," and turning to Ansel. "And you, suh?"

I would like a half dozen oysters on the half shell, a sirloin steak, medium rare, a baked potato with sour cream and string beans."

"And you Mister Ferguson?"

"I'll make it easy for you, Billy. Give me exactly what our guest ordered, and," looking at Ansel he added, "I believe two more of those fine bourbons, right Ansel?"

"Sounds good to me, Walter."

Billy responded, "I'll be right back with y'all's refreshments and bread fresh out of the oven." He quickly returned with the goods promised.

"What does your schedule look like, Walter? I hope you still plan to have a look at Shamrock?"

"I need one more day to clear my desk. We can catch the train day after tomorrow. What about you, Ansel?"

"I need to catch the train tomorrow. That will give me a little time to catch up with things at home before you arrive; make sure Lizzy has things in hand at the cottage and give lawyer Todd, Jr. notice I want to look at the books after you arrive. I can pick you all up at the Vicksburg station. Then, I guess I will head for Cuba right after the 'Old Maids Ball' at the Peabody." After the last sentence he cocked his head directly at Isabel.

"If I hear that word one more time out of either of you—well, just remember they have yet to hang a lady in Tennessee for killing a man."

"I regret my sarcasm dear lady. In the future I shall only use superlatives to describe beautiful ladies and what I believe is referred to in these environs as the 'top Memphis social event of the year'."

"You are granted provisional forgiveness, Captain Quinn, provided there is no further breach of conduct unbecoming an officer and a gentleman."

The conversation was interrupted by the serving of dinner.

During the brief ride to the new Chisca Hotel, Ansel asked Isabel, "You are coming to Shamrock with your father aren't you?"

"I don't know. What I do know is that I should not, and don't asked me why because you know."

"I know I have so much I want to say to you and so little time."

"That's exactly why I shouldn't come," she whispered as she glanced at her father in the front seat. "Besides you have only known me maybe at the worst of times. There must be other ladies in your life in Paris, the 'city of love' as they call it."

"There have been ladies in my life, but not one like you."

"What does that mean?"

"It means there is much more to you than a pretty face. It means I can't get you off my mind. It means . . . what do you want it to mean?"

"You know what I don't want it to mean. I'm afraid of you, Ansel Quinn."

"Afraid of me?"

"Yes, afraid. I'm not coming to Shamrock with Father. I can't. I shouldn't even let you take me to the ball."

"But you will."

"Yes. It is ten whole days away, days I'll use to convince myself I don't love you." Ansel kissed her, hard.

"We have arrived at you hotel, Captain," Isabel said and pulled away.

"Here we are, Ansel," Walter Ferguson braked to a stop as he tried not to eavesdrop or look in the backseat. "I'll see you in Vicksburg day after tomorrow."

Ansel stepped out of the car looking at Isabel. There were tears running down her cheeks. "Yes sir. I will pick you up at the station."

"Good. We'll see you there." Ferguson replied.

"Thank you for the fine dinner, and thank you both for a wonderful evening."

"It was our pleasure, wasn't it, Isabel?"

"Yes Daddy. Bye, Ansel."

Walter Ferguson, with Isabel sitting in the shadowed back seat, pulled away from the curb. Ansel stood watching until the car disappeared down the street. A bellboy gathered up his luggage and followed him into the hotel entrance. Even after a large meal with several drinks, sleep came slowly.

The next morning at Union Station, track No. 9, Ansel boarded the Yazoo and Mississippi Valley Railroad (Y&MV) Train No. 15 carrying his book. The spy story occupied his time as the train rumbled south, stopping at Tunica, Clarksdale, Cleveland, Leland, Hollandale, Rolling Fork and finally Vicksburg. It would continue to Baton Rouge then swing east to terminate at New Orleans.

CHAPTER FOURTEEN

"Lordy, it's good to see you Mister Ansel. I knowed you'd find a way to git here from way over yonder." Turning to her husband, Lizzy ordered, "Elijah, take Mister Ansel's belongin's to da' car."

"I have the satchel, Elijah. My trunk is the small one there on the baggage wagon."

"Yes, suh. We mighty glad to have you home."

"I'm glad to be here, glad to see you two again, and anxious to see the place after being away so long."

Ansel followed the couple to the Model T where Elijah put the baggage on one side of the back seat.

"You want to drive, Mister Ansel?"

"No. Y'all sit up front and take me home. I'll sit in back so I can take in the scenery along the way. You learned to drive yet, Elijah?"

"Naw, suh. I can harness a mule and hook 'em up to plow or a double or triple tree wagon rig, but I ain't learned all dem switches, levers, pedals and such in 'dis here automobile. I don't have to crank a mule to git it goin' neither. Course, Lizzy been after me 'bout it. Lizzy do such a good job drivin' on account Miss Bethany taught her. I was worried at first what white folks think 'bout a black woman drivin' a fancy automobile to town and back. Ain't many white folks drivin' round here, but nothin' come up 'bout it. Some think it a might queer, but 'dey don't do nothin' on account they knows she doin' it foe Miss Bethany Quinn."

"Speakin' of Miss Bethany, you should a' seen her teaching Lizzy to drive this thang out in the pasture. I mean it was *funny*. Lizzy wrestlin' 'dis thang, it jumpin' and jerkin' like a young mule, goin' 'dis way and 'dat, both of 'em shoutin' and laughin'."

"You gonna be walkin' home you keep joshin' me 'bout dat. Besides yo' time be comin'. Mister Jed say you gonna have to learn to drive dem gas tractors. Mister Jed and his boy been driving 'em but say he can't be doin' it all the time."

"Well, Lizzy, Miss Bethany wrote me that you drive better than she does, I mean did." There was a long silence. Lizzy turned to Ansel and gave him a sad smile of understanding.

It was the first time he had spoken of Bethany in the past tense.

Lizzy quickly busied herself with setting the controls. She turned the switch to battery and called, "All right, Elijah."

Elijah walked around front, bent down and gave the crank a good turn. The Model T came to life. Elijah got up front with Lizzy. She switched to magneto, adjusted the spark and off they went.

"You want to go by the old townhouse? Miss Bethany only opens it up for her annual Christmas party, but I seen to it that everythin' be dusted and clean. The lights, gas water heater and furnace all workin' and ready foe yo' guests. Essie Mae and her husband Ben are there to look after everythin' and do the cookin."

"Thank you, Lizzy. I expect they will stay there at least the first night. Now before we leave town, I want to make a stop at lawyer Todd's office."

"Yes, suh."

As they left the station and drove through town, Ansel noted that little had changed in the nearly four years since he had last visited. In fact, except for a little new paint here and there it appeared, like most small southern towns he had seen from the train, to still be struggling to recover from a war that ended fifty years ago. Of course it *was* winter. Not much going on. There were few shoppers out braving the cold. Things would soon get busier with spring planting. Some of the warehouses along the river were still holding cotton and lumber for shipment down river. There were more buggies and wagons than automobiles on the streets.

The stop at the law firm was brief. Within twenty minutes, Ansel returned to the waiting car carrying a large ledger and a file box of receipts and reports. Although he had little choice, Todd Jr. had not seemed reluctant to give the Shamrock records to Ansel as requested. Ansel explained to him that there was little time to review them and that everything would be returned within a week. "I don't doubt that you have done a good and honest job, just as your father did," Ansel assured him, "but I need to go over them in the short time I have before returning to duty. I find I am suddenly responsible for it all."

The fact that Todd Jr. did not complain or argue about relinquishing the records was encouraging. On the other hand, Ansel did not reveal that a man of much experience in the business of agriculture and commodity trading would examine them.

They quickly left town and turned south on a road that generally followed the route of the Y&MV Railroad toward Warrenton and eventually on to Natchez. Ansel, wrapped in his overcoat, scarf and gloves enjoyed the crisp air and clear sky, a rarity for February, the wettest month of the year. The road was in fair shape considering it had recently rained. Lizzy sat at the wheel tooting along most stretches at twenty-five miles an hour, skillfully avoiding the deepest potholes, washes and ruts. Ansel assumed that most of the small farms visible from the road were worked by sharecroppers and tenant farmers. The chimneys of the cabins trickled thin swirls of smoke indicating parsimonious use of firewood. Thrift in the rural Southland had been a necessary requirement for survival for fifty years. Bethany had told him in a letter that once she had decided to put Shamrock back into full production, she had done away with sharecropping on the place by hiring her sharecroppers at fair wages while letting them keep their cabins and garden plots and mules at no rent. She said she received complaints from several large land holders who did not agree with the move. But that move ensured her enough permanent hands, mules and plows to work the place. She only had to hire extra hands at cotton picking time.

Ansel noticed there were large stretches of fallow land that lay between farms. Years back all of the flat land that lay at the foot of the hill country just south of Vicksburg where the Delta petered out, had been, like Shamrock, cotton land. Now much of it lay grown into woodlands. Bethany said a lot of it belonged to Northern speculators or was tied up in disputed ownership or family feuds; a sorry legacy of war after more than a half century.

Ansel appreciated the passing scenery. This time of year the deciduous trees, red maple, sweet gum, black cherry and white oak stood winter-naked, their fall multi-colored leaves spread like thick carpets at their feet. All was not a monotonous vista of bare limbs. Scattered evergreens were shimmering verdant in the clear winter sunlight. Holly, magnolia, live oak, cedar and pine all stood proudly defiant of winter's chill. Ansel thought of the stark, treeless 'no man's land' between the trenches in France and Belgium. *It looked much like these fields before the great artillery barrages tore it all into lifeless moonscape.*

"Lizzy," Ansel broke the long silence, "I remember when it was a real undertaking to travel by wagon from town out to Shamrock. What was it, thirteen hours?"

"It be mo' like fo'teen."

"How long in the T-model?"

"Well, if the road's near dry like today, 'bout two hours and a half. If it be real wet, 'bout three and a piece. Now that's if you don't git a flat tire or git stuck in mud or, Lawd help ya', push this thang too fast and go tearin' off the road someplace. Heard tell a drunk fellow in town got a goin' too fast and done clum up a tree with his'en. Kilt him they say. Miss Bethany said the book what come with it allows as how this thang can do forty-five mile an hour. I kind a' believe she tried it on account one day she drove up to da' place, hair all blowed in a tangle, the bonnet she left with gone, and she just a laughin', saying as how I should have been with her. Ask me if I wanted to go out and see how fast this thang would go. I told her my mama didn' raise no fool. I was afraid to get in that thang with her most part of the week. And another thang, you sho' better not run out of gas. Me and Miss Bethany done that once goin' into town; got pretty close. Waited three hours foe a fellow come along in a buggy. He was kind enough to take Miss Bethany on in while I waited with this thang fo' mo' hours 'til a wagon with three gallon jugs of gas come from town. Believe me, we ain't done that since. We keep two welded steel barrels of gas at the farm. One goes empty, we starts usin' the full one and git da' empty one refilled quick as we can. Now, with them new-fangled tractors, we keepin' mo' gas out there."

"How about the old place? Those brick chimneys fallen down yet?"

"Naw, suh. I reckon they built 'em good way back then. Them four blackened chimneys still standin' tall like they guardin' da' place. It must a been one fine place foe them Yankees burned it down. Don't anybody go up there much. Some say there's ghost round there. Considerin' all I been told 'bout what happen up there, I wouldn't be surprised none. In any case, Miss Bethany gets mad she catch curious folks messin' round the old place. She say folks ought to have the decency to respect the place where her mama, her grandmamma and her great granddaddy was kilt that terrible day. She say she catch strangers or poachers round there she liable to shoot 'em. I wouldn't be surprised she do it, too."

"As a boy I used to play up there. She said it pleased her to see a Quinn at the old place; that if there were ghosts it would please them, too. Ghost talk didn't scare me as a child . . . well not much anyway. I played out at night catching lightning bugs, but I didn't go up there in the dark."

After the mention of Shamrock ghosts, there was no more talk for a while.

Lizzy braked for a red fox that ran across the road in front of them and disappeared into the brush only to flush a covey of quail.

"The wild animals seem to be doing well."

"I know the rabbits is. They gittin' in my garden and eatin' my winter greens."

"Speaking of greens, Lizzy, I hope you have laid in enough good groceries to show off your cooking for our guests. They'll be here day after tomorrow."

"Oh, we got plenty, and I made some apple pies. Miss Bethany put in a ice house to keep things fresh. Don't you worry none."

"I'm not worried, Lizzy. I can't wait to have some of your cooking. I ought to take you back to Paris to show those people what real food tastes like."

"No, suh. Ain't gittin' me to cross no ocean."

Lizzy knew when she said it she shouldn't have. Ansel's joking stopped and he grew quiet. She knew it was because she mentioned crossing the ocean; knew he got quiet thinking of Bethany dying trying to cross over to see him.

They passed a wide field where last year's cotton stalks had been harrowed under getting ready for spring plowing and planting. At the corner of the field, Lizzy turned off on a side road familiar to Ansel. He knew he was now on Shamrock land. The ancient fence lines on both sides of the road were grown into thick hedgerows. He could see a few rusty bits of barbed wire and the scars it had left on the trees as they grew to absorb the wire decades ago. Even a rabbit would have a hard time getting through. Where the road crossed a stretch of soft loam soil it had sunken nearly six feet over the years.

"There wasn't near as much cultivated land when I was here four years ago. Bethany really got into putting the place back in production, didn't she?"

"You know Miss Bethany, once she takes a mind to do somethin' there ain't no stoppin' her."

"Yes, that was Bethany. Tell you what. Before we turn off for the cabin, let's go on up to the old place. I know a lot more about it after reading my Grandmother's and Bethany's diaries than I ever learned growing up during the summers I spent here."

"You sure, Mister Ansel? I figure you have time to look it over after you settle in."

"Just take me on up there and drop me off. I'll walk on to the cabin."

"Yes, suh, but you be careful crossin' the creek on that old foot bridge. You fall in the creek today you likely to freeze b'foe you git to the cabin."

Ansel stepped down from the running board of the Model T. He watched Lizzy and Elijah turn around and drive off the way they had come, the sound of the motor fading away as they dipped down into the well-settled road. He turned to look up at the four, tall, blackened chimneys rising nearly forty feet from the ashes of the once beautiful, antebellum home, a ruin undisturbed for over fifty years. The site was softened by vines of ivy and confederate jasmine creeping thickly over the piles of ashes and burned timbers. Curiously, the vines had chosen to climb the heights of only one of the chimneys. He walked through knee high weeds toward what, besides the four chimneys, was all that remained to remind a visitor of the elegant home that once stood there: twin brick stairways that curved gracefully up to meet at a landing leading nowhere. Ansel climbed several moss covered steps before turning and taking a seat. He looked out over what was once, he had been told, a well-kept lawn encompassed by a circular graveled drive and flowering shrubs. Neither he nor Bethany had any memory of the house as it once stood. It had been burned before either of them was born.

He looked over his shoulder at the chimneys. *What grand and tragic times you sentinels have witnessed.*

Sitting there in the stillness he let his imagination conjure up the days of plenty; a driveway lined with fine horses and carriages bringing guests to grand parties. His father, Jonathan, his adoptive father he reminded himself, had told him about those times he remembered as a boy before the war.

Ansel's mind shifted to his grandmother's diary, the stark details of her death added by Dr. Perkins so that one day her daughter Bethany, when she was old enough, would know how her brave mother and the others had died. Sitting there where it all had happened, he thought he could almost hear the echoes of gunshots that killed Shamrock that terrible day.

Ansel had played on these very steps as a boy spending summers with Bethany, but had never really known what happened here until he learned about it in the diaries.

A sudden chill ran down his spine, an involuntary shiver of his whole body. Recovering, he remembered the old wives tale about that sudden feeling. They say it happens because someone in the future walks on you grave.

The silence was broken by the call of a bobwhite quail somewhere across the field. Ansel waited for an answer, but none came.

His thoughts drifted to the long history of the Quinns on this land, land that suddenly, unexpectedly was now his responsibility.

How in hell can I fulfill the debt to this land I owe my family while an ocean away bound by the Army and my oath to my country?

He sat for a long while allowing his mind to wander freely over the years he had spent growing up during summers and winter holidays at Shamrock. That period in his life had been filled with adventure and fun; times when he gained self-reliance and independence all because of Bethany. Now, sitting in the silence of a fading afternoon, a heavy, soul-deep feeling descended upon him. For the first time in his life at Shamrock, he felt sad and lonely.

Jonathon must have felt this way when he returned to find his family, except for a baby girl, gone forever. That baby girl was you, Bethany. You grew to be bright and beautiful and fun. I know now how Jonathan must have felt, never returning here, blaming himself for being absent on the day it all happened. Then on your own you secretly built the cabin and convinced him that the ghosts of his family wanted him to return, wanted Quinns to walk the land once more. Now you have joined them, and I share the blame for that. You sent me the diaries that revealed who I really am. I was bred and raised to take my place among the Quinns of Shamrock. What twists and turns fate has given us Quinns, Bethany, but then you knew that for you told me so in your own written words.

An owl in the distance announced the arrival of dusk, or was it a mournful requiem for a dying day. The sun had dipped below the treetops when Ansel's mind returned to the present. In the chill of the evening he set out on a familiar hard-packed path that led from the ruins down a hollow, up past a flat that was once the site of slave cabins, across a creek and through a stand of hardwoods to the back of Bethany's cabin. The air was lightly scented with wood smoke.

As he approached the back door to the kitchen, it struck him that a house illuminated by oil lamps gives the allusion of welcoming warmth that is not achieved by the harshness of bright electric lights.

The real warmth that welcomed him into the kitchen came from the large stove. The kitchen was filled with the aroma of cornbread in the oven.

"'bout time you got here, Mister Ansel," Lizzy scolded. "I reckon I can put on the pork chops now. By the time you git out'a that overcoat and wash up I'll have supper on the table. Seems like old times. As a boy, you was always late coming in to supper."

"Yes, but most evenings this time of year, I brought in a brace of rabbits or a bag of squirrels or quail."

"If that ain't the truth. But you go on now. Elijah kindled a nice fire in your old room. It's gonna be cold tonight."

After supper, by the light of two lamps atop Bethany's desk, Ansel poured over the ledgers of the last year of Shamrock operations. He verified monthly statements by randomly picking bills from the file box to see if they had been entered by Jed Jamison.

Then he went over the six month audit reports and summaries by the firm of Todd, Cochran and Roberts. Ansel pushed back from the desk and rubbed his weary eyes. The old case clock in the hall struck 1:00 AM. He dragged his tired self to his room, threw a couple of logs on the glowing coals in the fireplace, undressed and crawled into bed under a down feather comforter. For the first time in weeks, sleep came quickly.

Lizzy cracked open the door and poked her head into the bedroom. "You better git yo' self up, Mister Ansel. Mister Jed's here fo' breakfast like you asked."

Ansel threw back the covers and put his bare feet on a floor that was cold as ice. It was six o'clock. Ansel felt as though he had barely fallen asleep. He washed up with the cold water on the wash stand, pulled on his shoes and got a heavy wool robe from the armoire.

Jed was sitting at the breakfast table in the warm kitchen sipping a cup of coffee when Ansel entered trying to smooth his sleep-tussled hair with his fingers.

Jed stood and shook Ansel's outstretched hand. "Good to see you, Mister Ansel."

"Now we are going to stop that 'Mister' stuff right now. You never called me mister in your life."

"That was before we lost Miss Bethany. You're the boss of Shamrock now."

The word 'boss' took Ansel aback. "Jed, I'm not ready nor am I qualified to be boss of Shamrock. I'm still wrestling with the fact that I am suddenly responsible for it, but that is different from being the day-to-day boss of a 3,000-acre plantation. Bethany held you in high regard and depended on you. Now I will depend on you to continue management of Shamrock. You're the only man I know of who has a college degree in agriculture. I went over the books last night and they are well-kept. Lawyer Todd and his firm agree.

I have an experienced business man and friend who I have asked down from Memphis. He's coming down by train, will stay in town tonight and be here tomorrow. I would like for you to take us both around the place, show us the operation, which has changed and grown since I was here last. His name is Walter Ferguson and he is a cotton broker who has a lot of experience in the business end of farms and commodities. I'm not bringing him down to interfere in your management of Shamrock. It's just that I'm obligated to be across an ocean for a while yet. You used to turn to Bethany with both ideas and problems. My hope is that if you and Walter get along, he'll be someone you can pick up the phone and talk over a problem with instead of waiting weeks to get hold of me. That's the idea anyway. I'll want to know what you think of the idea and Walter Ferguson, Jed. We'll talk it all over after Ferguson is gone, before I leave for Cuba and then France. If that seems a good idea to you, fine, but if not, you tell me. You're the boss here."

Jed answered, "If it works out with Mister Ferguson, it might lift a little of the load off both of us considering you'll be an ocean away."

Lizzy served the two men pancakes, eggs, bacon and grits.

Ansel drove into Vicksburg and parked on Levee Street in front of the handsome three story brick station building. Right on time, the Yazoo & Mississippi Valley engine number 77, trailing white steam and black smoke, chugged into the station pulling a mail car and six coaches. Ansel saw Walter Ferguson coming down the iron steps of the coach alone and walked toward him.

She did not come. His heart sank and he hoped the disappointment he felt did not show. A few moments later, his mood changed. The car porter in his white jacket and black cap stepped down carrying a large suitcase and pink hatbox. He put them down and turned to ensure that the lady following him did not stumble on the steps. "Well you sure don't look like a captain in those clothes."

"For this week at least, I'm a farmer, not a soldier." Ansel walked past Walter and kissed Isabel Ferguson lightly on the cheek, then turned to belatedly shake Walter Ferguson's hand.

"Welcome to Vicksburg. The car is out front."

A station porter followed them to the car with the luggage, piling it on one side of the back seat. Ansel helped Isabel in beside it and directed Walter to the front seat.

He then went through the pageant of starting the engine, climbed in and pulled away from the curb with only a slight jerk or two.

"I'm afraid this doesn't compare to your Simplex, Walter, but it sure beats a wagon and mule, although I can probably drive a wagon better than an automobile. I don't have a lot of experience—don't get much of a chance to drive in Paris—but I'll try not to frighten you."

"Oh go ahead and frighten him," Isabel chimed in. "He's getting a little cocky in that new car of his."

"A father doesn't stand a chance with a spoiled, modern daughter; no proper respect at all."

"Poor Daddy. Where are we going, may I ask?"

"Well, things are still a little primitive at the farm. I thought you could spend at least tonight at our old townhouse. It has more conveniences like hot and cold running water, a central furnace and electric lights. It once belonged to Dr. Perkins who helped raise Bethany and gave it to her in his will. In times past, you needed a place to stay when you came in town from Shamrock by horse and buggy. It was about a fourteen hour trip then. Today it takes about two hours by auto."

"I look forward to a hot bath after that train ride. It got too hot in the coach, but if you opened a window you got cinders. I feel gritty."

"You don't look gritty, but you do have a little soot on your cheeks."

"I do not!" Isabel retrieved a silver, *guilloché*-patterned compact from her purse and checked her face in its mirror just to make sure.

"Careful, Ansel," Walter said. "I haven't won an argument with her since she turned fifteen."

"My father told me it was a waste of time to argue with a woman."

"Now you are both in trouble."

Ansel left the depot, turned north on Washington and then east on Grove Street. After a few blocks he parked in front of a large, raised cottage.

"Here we are. The ground floor used to be Dr. Perkins office and servants quarters." Ansel helped Isabel down and led her and her father up the steps to a broad porch. Essie Mae, wearing a freshly laundered bib apron, and her husband Ben dressed in a white waiter's jacket, greeted them at the front door.

Essie Mae instructed, "Ben, you git the bags in while I show these folks to their rooms. It's sure good to see you again, Mister Ansel."

"Essie Mae this is Miss Isabel and her father Mister Ferguson. They've come from Memphis for a visit."

"I be pleased to meet you folks. If you will follow me, I b'lieve everythin's ready."

They entered into a wide hallway that continued through the house past open-pocket doors to the left revealing the parlor and dining room and beyond them, the kitchen. The house was warm from a coal-fired furnace that had been installed on the ground floor. It fed heat into four floor grates on the first floor. The second floor was not heated, but warm air from the first floor rose up the stairway. The old fireplaces in the bedrooms were still used on particularly cold nights. The back door of the hallway opened onto a wide gallery like the one in front. On the right of the hall was a study, and just past a stairway was a large room that had been Dr. Perkins' bedroom. Part of the back porch off his bedroom had been enclosed to provide a bathtub, lavatory and gas water heater. The hall stairway led up to an identical large central hallway on the second floor with two bedrooms off either side. The door at either end of the hallway opened onto front and rear galleries. Just as on the first floor back porch, a part of the second floor back gallery had been enclosed to provide another bathtub, lavatory and gas water heater.

The house had fourteen foot ceilings throughout and full length French windows to provide cooling in the summer. The heart pine floors were brightly polished, the oriental rugs cleaned and the furniture dusted. Much of the furniture was antebellum, original to the house.

"Where does you want this luggage?" Ben asked.

"Walter, you can have Dr. Perkins' room if you like. I'll put Isabel upstairs in the back bedroom closest to the bath."

Ben put the smaller bag in Dr. Perkins' old room and went up the stairs carrying the larger case and hatbox.

"I thought I would go on out to Shamrock and pick you all up about mid-morning. We can repeat that schedule while you are here so you can spend the nights here in town."

Walter responded, "No need for you to go back tonight."

"Well I thought—"

Walter broke in. "Look, I don't know what is between you two, but you are both grown and too old for me to supervise like children. We'll all get an early start for Shamrock in the morning. Now, what's for supper?"

Neither Ansel nor Isabel knew quite what to say. After a pause, neither looking at the other, Ansel said, "Fine. Let's get out of these overcoats. Just put them on the settee in the hall. I believe the sun is setting. I think it's time for us to retire to the study and have, as they say in Memphis, a refreshment."

The room contained a large desk with padded swivel chair, a leather couch, several arm chairs arranged around the fireplace and a library table and chairs by the front window. One wall was covered in book shelves except for a large double door mahogany cabinet that protruded about eighteen inches into the room.

Ben appeared, walked to the mahogany cabinet and opened the double doors to reveal a well-stocked bar complete with whiskey and wine glasses, a water pitcher and a dry sink holding a full bucket of ice.

"Ben, how did you know we'd be in here?" Walter Ferguson asked.

"Well, suh," Ben smiled, "the sun be settin'. Miss Bethany always had a little toddy 'bout this time o' day. I figured Mister Ansel, being a Quinn, do the same. Now what be yoe' pleasure, Miss Isabel?"

"I'll have bourbon on ice with a splash of water."

"Yes'm. And you, Mister Ferguson?"

"I'll have the same."

"I b'lieve that make three don't it, Mister Ansel?"

"You have it exactly right, Ben."

After Ben filled the orders, he said, "Essie Mae will have supper ready in 'bout an hour."

"Thank you, Ben. You go help Essie Mae. I'll do the bar tending now."

"Yes, suh. You need moe' ice, just call." Ben left the room.

The three sat silently for a while savoring the smooth, ten-year old Tennessee bourbon.

"How do the Quinns get this fine elixir in the dry state of Mississippi?" Walter asked.

"Until a deacon got elected sheriff, no one paid much attention. He made a show of busting up a few stills and a few shipments of whiskey coming in on the river. Then, rumor has it, he started collecting an unofficial and lucrative 'sin' tax to overlook a certain trade in bottled goods, provided the bootleggers exercised discretion and did not do business on Sundays or Election Days. You'd be surprised at the number of people who now run for sheriff in this county. We get our medicinal prescriptions from a druggist in town who receives rather large quantities of cases marked castor oil, Epsom salts and various patent medicine labels shipped on the railroad. Nobody is fooled, but politicians and citizens alike can say that the law is being followed in Vicksburg. As some wag in Jackson said, Baptists and bootleggers in Mississippi continue to stagger to the poles and vote dry."

Walter chuckled. "Well, in honor of such pious folk, I think we should have another round of refreshments."

Conversation at supper mostly consisted of Ansel presenting a picture of the operation of Shamrock as he understood it, including his review of the ledgers and a history of Shamrock's manager, Jed Jamison.

"What I would like for you to do in the short time you have to spend here is to review the records, the operation, and give me your opinions and suggestions. And please, let me pay you for your time and expertise."

Isabel ate her supper mostly listening without comment. When it was time to retire, Ansel and Isabel stood together in the hallway at the top of the stairs for an awkward moment.

Ansel broke the silence. "I was afraid you would not come. I am so very glad did."

"I should not have come. I knew that before we left and I know it now."

"Then why did you come."

"You know the answer to that. I came because of you, but there will be no knock on your door from a barefoot lady."

"I know," Ansel replied, his eyes dropping to the floor like a disappointed little boy. "Goodnight soldier."

Ansel kissed her on the cheek. She looked up at him and he kissed her fully on the lips and held her tightly for a long moment.

"See you in the morning," he said at last.

Isabel walked to the doorway of her room, turned as if to say something, thought better of it and went in, closing the door behind her.

It rained that night.

CHAPTER FIFTEEN

The chilly ride to Shamrock was an adventure drawing shrieks, howls and laughter due to Ansel's slipping and sliding on the rain-slick road. Somehow Quinn managed to keep the Model T out of the ditches on both sides of the road and avoided getting stuck in the low, muddy bottoms by getting up enough speed downhill to carry them through.

When they pulled up at Bethany's cabin, Jed Jamison, Lizzy and Elijah came out on the front porch to greet them.

Ansel introduced them to his guests. "This is the real boss of Shamrock, Mister Jedediah Jamison."

Jamison shook hands with Isabel and Mister Ferguson. "Please call me Jed."

Lizzy and Elijah nodded their heads. Elijah laughed and said, "Looks like Mister Ansel gave you folks quite a ride. I ain't never seen so much mud on an automobile."

"For that observation, Elijah, you have won the privilege of washing this fine piece of machinery."

Lizzy invited, "Won't you folks please come in. Elijah will fetch yoe' bags in right after he gits the mud off 'em. And if you'll let me have yoe' raincoats, I'll see if I can git the mud off dem, too. Mister Ansel, I b'lieve you take first place in the Shamrock road race. Not even Miss Bethany ever got that much mud on that thing, and she got stuck twice and ran in and out of a ditch."

"All right, that's enough talk about my driving in front of my guests. You Fergusons will have to realize that all three of these people you just met helped raise me and no matter what I do, they have yet to notice that I've grown up."

Lizzy countered with, "We'll notice when you quit playin' soldier and come home like Miss Bethany told you to." She crossed her arms and shook her head down once to make her point.

"You tell him, Lizzy!" Isabel clapped her hands.

Ansel took off his hat and took a mock swing with it at Lizzy, who laughed and ran to open the cabin door.

Ansel, Jed and Walter Ferguson followed Isabel up four steps to a wide veranda and into a broad central hallway that ran from the front to the back porch.

Isabel turned to Ansel. "When you said Bethany had built a cabin, I expected to see a little farm house. This place is lovely."

It truly was. The simple yet practical architecture common in the deep south, whether a sharecropper's cabin or antebellum mansion, was the traditional proven plan of the earliest pioneer cabins having wide, open 'dog trots' running through the middle, front to back, to provide summer cooling to the rooms off either side.

Shamrock's verandas in the front and rear were wide and shaded by the overhanging roof. One side of the front and rear verandas had been screened in and furnished with comfortable wicker furniture. The side of the rear veranda behind the kitchen was enclosed and contained a copper bathtub and also served as a large pantry and linen closet. It was adjacent to the kitchen where hot water for bathing was almost always available on the stove. All the flooring throughout the house, including the enclosed hallway, was polished heart pine with a scattering of oriental rugs. In the central hallway, a tall case clock stood against one wall just down from a 'telephone table' complete with a black candlestick telephone and built-in seat. Toward the front there were opposing settees, and toward the back near the kitchen, a mahogany dining table and chairs. The center piece on the table was a large silver punchbowl with a band of green cloisonné shamrocks around the lip. Lighting was provided at each end by a matching pair of brass oil chandeliers with beautiful, hand painted flowered shades and matching oil reservoirs.

Isabel explored the cabin. On one side of the 'dog trot' there was a large room, which served as a combination parlor and study furnished with comfortable overstuffed chairs, two couches and a large desk. Bookshelves lined the wall on both sides of the fireplace, a beautiful oriental rug covered a large portion of the floor and original French impressionist paintings hung on the walls. The next room was a large kitchen complete with a very big stove, work table, butcher block, huge pot rack overhead, china breakfront, a marble counter that held a flour bin and jars for sugar, coffee, tea, and spices. Cabinets filled all the remaining wall spaces. The floor to ceiling windows brightened the whole room. As Bethany had specified, large cisterns were built at the house and stable to store rain water. It was piped into the house. The kitchen had been built over a well so that a hand pump was mounted right beside the large kitchen sink. It acted as a backup to the cisterns in times of drought. The pump water was always cold and had a slight taste of iron.

While the three men retired to the main room to discuss the Shamrock operation, Isabel wandered down the other side of the hallway and into the front bedroom. She could tell by the curtains, flowered wall paper and dresser with mirror that it was Bethany's room. There was a single canopy bed with mosquito netting furled up to the canopy. She noticed her suitcase and fresh towels had been placed on the bed. Instead of an armoire, there were built-in clothes closets across one wall. She opened one to reveal a row of expensive gowns. She did not open any of the others, feeling that it was an invasion of privacy of what must have been a lovely and formidable lady.

What caught her eye were the photographs on one wall. Most of them were of Ansel from the time he was a baby. The last was of him in uniform. There was also a picture of a petite, pretty woman and a man who was handsome in spite of an eye patch and faded scar on his forehead.

Ansel's parents.

Isabel returned to the hallway to enter the middle bedroom. It was equal in size to the front room but had a big canopied double bed also with mosquito netting furled for the winter. Her father's case was on the bed. There was a razor and shaving mug with brush on a double washstand. A walnut dressing table with mirror displayed a silver comb, hairbrush and hand mirror neatly arranged to one side. Each piece of the set was engraved with the initials L Q. There were two very large armoires and two matching walnut Queen Ann highboy chests of drawers. She was sure this bedroom had belonged to Ansel's parents, Louisette and Jonathan. On the wall were several photographs of Ansel, one showing him as a boy on the deck of a sailboat, another of him on horseback. Then there was a photograph of an exceptionally beautiful young lady with dark hair.

This must be Bethany.

Isabel looked closely at the photo. Something about the picture reminded her of Ansel . . . *Maybe the eyes or the mouth?*

Isabel wandered down the hall to the last bedroom. It was smaller than the other two. There was nothing feminine about the room. The furniture was all rather heavy. The chest of drawers was oak and not so tall. There was a mirror on top. She slid out a drawer. It was full of men's clothing. There was a shaving mug, brush and razor on the washstand with a razor strop hanging on the wall beside it. Isabel opened the large armoire. It was full of men's clothing including a tuxedo. She remembered that Ansel had carried no suitcase in the car.

Of course. This is his place. He keeps clothes here in his old room for visits.

The few pictures in the room were of his parents and Bethany. A rack on one wall held two shotguns. She then spied a large chest sitting on the floor in one corner. She walked over, bent down and opened the lid. Inside were blocks, toy trains, boats, farm animals and tin soldiers.

A little boy's toy chest. Ansel's toy chest.

Lizzy called from the hallway just outside the kitchen door. "Dinner be ready shortly, Mister Ansel. Y'all just got time to wash up."

After dinner Ansel and Jed decided it would be best to take Walter Ferguson on a tour the next morning. Jed suggested that if Walter could ride a horse they could take the short way to a couple of the fields that would otherwise require a long drive by car. Walter said it had been a while but he could manage. Jed left saying he would meet them for breakfast with three saddle horses. He apologized to Isabel saying they would love to have her accompany them, but at the moment he only had three saddle horses.

After Jed left, Ansel suggested Walter might use the afternoon to review the Shamrock ledger and the Todd law firm's audit reports. Walter agreed.

Ansel asked Isabel, "Would you like to ride with me this afternoon? I have something to show you."

Isabel answered, "I will have to borrow a pair of pants. I don't know how to ride sidesaddle in a dress."

"We don't have any sidesaddles." Ansel turned to Lizzy.

She told Isabel, "I'll git you a pair of Miss Bethany's riding britches. I b'lieve they fit you. She always ride wearin' pants. You come on with me."

Ansel left for the barn to saddle two of the horses.

Isabel followed Lizzy into Bethany's bedroom. Lizzy rummaged around in the cedar chest at the foot of the bed. She came out with a pair of pants, long johns, socks, a wool jacket, pair of gloves and scarf and laid them out on the bed.

"I b'lieve these will fit you close enough. Be better than tryin' to wear a pair of Mister Ansel's. You wrap up good now, Miss Isabel. It be cold out there and ain't no tellin' where Mister Ansel gonna take you. You can pick out a hat from the rack at the back door."

"Lizzy, Mister Ansel is Captain Ansel now."

"He ain't no captain 'round here. He be Mister Ansel like always, be the last Quinn. That beats being a captain or even a general here at Shamrock. Miss Bethany was goin' over there to tell him that. We all depending on him now."

"Do you think Miss Bethany would mind me wearing her clothes like this?"

"Miss Isabel, I b'lieve she be happy for you to wear 'em. I'll tell you somethin' else, too. I seen the way Mister Ansel look at you. I think Miss Bethany be happy you are here. You pretty like she was and I b'lieve you smart the way she was. That boy needs someone to come home to from that army duty he done got into way over yonder. Miss Bethany told me that befoe' she left, bless her soul."

"Can you keep a secret, Lizzy?"

"I keepin' moe' secrets right now than I can count. What you want to tell me, honey?"

"I think I love him . . . but I'm afraid. I've already lost one love in that war. I just couldn't stand to lose another. I was a nurse. I've seen the hurt and death of boys over there. He's in the army, Lizzy, and I'm afraid for him . . . and for me."

"All you's got is today, Miss Isabel. That's all any of us got. That's all he gots. You might lose him, but if you did, never bein' with him like I think you want to be, never havin' time together . . . I b'lieve that be worse than never havin' him at all."

The two women looked at one another. Isabel hugged Lizzy.

Lizzy pulled away and smiled. "You put them clothes on. I got work to do. Mister Ansel be back here with them horses any minute. I speck you gonna want a bath when you git back. I'll have plenty of hot water on the stove."

Ansel laughed when he saw Isabel.

"What's so funny?"

"I thought I was taking a lady riding. Now I see it's a farmhand. Where did you get that hat?"

"And I thought I was going riding with a gentleman planter, but now I see a stable boy with a smart mouth that's gonna get him in trouble. Are you gonna stand there grinning like an idiot, or give me a boost up on this horse?"

"Give me your left knee."

Isabel placed her left knee into Ansel's joined hands. As he lifted her up, she swung her right leg over the horse, settled into the saddle, took the reins and slid her boots into the stirrups.

"Did I get the stirrups the right length?"

"They're fine. Now who is going to help you up, Captain?" she smiled.

Ansel took hold of his horse's mane and swung himself easily up into the saddle. "Just follow me, my lady."

"Am I going to have trouble with this animal?"

"Not at all, he's woods-broke."

It was chilly, but there was no wind. Ansel led off through the trees. A half mile later they came to a path leading along a creek. He carefully moved his horse down the bank and across the water running swiftly from the recent rains. From the far bank he called, "Careful. This is no day to fall into a creek."

Isabel and her horse crossed with no problem. She was careful to lift her legs high out of the stirrups to keep her boots dry. Midstream, the water reached the horse's belly. Once across they followed a worn path that gradually rose to a flat. Off one side there was a stretch of ground so hard packed that nothing grew on it. She guessed it had been a road because there were remains of cabins along each side. A few crumbling chimneys and, scattered across the ground, rotting lumber and the remnants of wood shingle roofs was all that remained of them.

They continued on up the path. About a quarter of a mile further they broke into a clearing grown up in weeds. There, across the field, Isabel saw a startling sight. Graceful twin brick stairways bearing badly rusted remnants of once beautiful wrought iron banisters curved up to meet at each side of a landing high above the ground. Behind the landing stood four tall blackened chimneys rising out of a huge square of ashes somewhat softened by scattered vegetation, much of it evergreen ivy; the rest some kind of crawling plant nipped brown by winter's chill. A crow cawed at them from atop one of the chimneys and flew off. Except for the soft fall of horses' hooves, there was silence of the kind that comes in winter stillness.

At the base of the steps, Ansel dismounted and dropped the reins on the ground.

Isabel slid off the left side of the saddle into his arms. He kissed her before setting her on her feet.

"Won't the horses head for the barn if you don't tie them?"

"No. They have good manners. They'll graze here and wait for us."

"I know a certain captain who could learn from them, learn not to laugh at ladies in funny clothes."

"Come up and sit on the steps with me, lady in funny clothes." They picked a step near the top and sat down beside one another. Isabel chuckled and said, "I found your toy chest in your old room."

"You have been sneaking."

"Yes, and I found you do have a tuxedo in your closet. Now you have no excuse not to take me to the ball in Memphis. Why did you keep the toy chest?"

"The last time I wore that tux was at Bethany's Christmas Party four years ago. It may not fit any longer, and I've kept the toy chest hoping there may be another little boy to play with it someday."

"Ansel, why did you really bring me out here this chilly afternoon?"

"To tell you a story, one you may not have expected, one perhaps you will not want to hear."

"That sounds like a mystery."

"Perhaps, but the story is fact not fiction."

Ansel was silent for a while as if trying to decide whether or not to proceed. Isabel looked at him. "Well?"

"After the fall of Vicksburg, my great-great grandfather, Daniel Quinn, his daughter-in-law, great grandmother, Nannie, her daughter, Annielise and two freed servants all managed to get here from Vicksburg where they had been trapped by Grant's siege. Barely seventeen, Annielise gave birth to Bethany. Don't ask about the father. You wouldn't believe me if I told you." Ansel continued before Isabel could ask. "Eventually, Jonathan, Annielise's older brother and later my father, returned a scarred, one-eyed survivor of the Confederate Navy. Bethany was his niece, but for some reason I was raised calling her Aunt Bethany. Everything at Shamrock had been burned except a brick cottage that used to stand in the far corner of that field, a repaired kitchen back behind the ruins here, and a row of abandoned slave cabins up on that flat you passed on the way here. That's where they all lived, in the former slave cabins, while struggling to survive. They had nothing really but a few tools, dishes, pots and pans and such, raked from the ashes, a cow and two laying hens the Yankee scavengers missed, and finally a mule, a wagon and a plow brought out to them from Vicksburg by a family friend, Dr. Perkins. Nannie's husband Ansel, my great-grandfather and namesake, had been killed in the war.

"Jonathan stayed long enough to help with spring planting, then left at the invitation of his mentor, an old sea captain named Jones, a blockade runner who had somehow gotten his ship out of Mobile to the Bahamas. He was old and turned his ship over to Jonathan to carry out the dangerous, but very profitable, business of running guns to the Cubans in their struggle to gain freedom from Spain. Captain Jones later made Jonathan a partner and they formed the J & Q Shipping Line. Jonathan sent the money he made to Shamrock, saving it from foreclosure by paying the taxes, the considerable debt and paying for food, seed and temporary labor to help in the fields.

"After the fall of Vicksburg, it was occupied by Union troops. Until well after the war, their job was to enforce the rules of Reconstruction. Then gradually the troops were discharged and headed home. Among them were three pieces of scum. It's thought they rode together with a plan to rob whatever they found worth taking on their way north. I guess they figured that families would be digging up treasure they hid from Union Troops during the war.

"Because of arthritis, Grandfather Daniel couldn't walk without crutches. It was too painful for him get up on a horse or wagon. Dr. Perkins rigged up a goat cart for him that he could easily get into and out of to use for overseeing the work in the fields. Daniel carried a shotgun in the cart with him on the chance he might run up on game he could shoot and add to the cook pot. I think they were always hungry. On any free afternoon, he liked to come up here and dream of rebuilding Shamrock. What I am about to tell you came from the writings of Dr. Perkins. He was Annielise's Godfather. Dr. Perkins put together what happened that day, mostly from what the servants told him and what was found during an investigation.

"Daniel was right there," Ansel pointed to a spot a few yards in front of where they were sitting. "Nannie was reading a book in the old kitchen behind us. Annielise and her baby Bethany were napping in the cottage that used to stand over there." He pointed.

The thought of Bethany caused him to pause.

Why am I telling Isabel all of this? How much should I tell her? Henrí Bourget and Aileen Giard are the only people alive who know of my real mother and father. He glanced at Isabel. *I think it best I leave it that way for now.*

"Well don't stop," Isabel urged.

"You may not want to hear the rest. Maybe I should let it go."

"Do you know you can be infuriating? Why did you bring me out here and start the story?"

"Because I thought you should know."

"Why?"

"Because I've fallen in love with you and I want you to understand this place."

Isabel's heart jumped; her pulse raced. For a moment, she no longer felt the chill in the air. She tried hard to ignore the impact of his statement. "I'll think about that later. Go on with the story."

Ansel looked questioningly at her a moment, turned to look out across the field, took a deep breath and began again. "It was a rare lazy summer afternoon for the folks here at Shamrock. The servants, Arabella and old Nicodemus, were down at the creek—Arabella doing the washing and Nicodemus fishing for bream. They heard shots. It scared them. Still they got up here as fast as their old legs would carry them. By the time they reached the brick cottage over there, a single horseman, a big Yankee soldier, was riding fast toward the main road trailing a spare horse behind him. Arabella found Bethany just outside the cottage with blood on her little feet and hands. She looked up and said, "Momma hurt, Bella." Arabella rushed into the cabin and found Annielise on the bed, violated and with her throat slit. The child had walked through the blood on the floor and gotten it on her hands trying to wake up her dead mother."

"Oh, Ansel!" Isabel looked up with tears forming in the corners of her eyes.

Ansel didn't see her. He was concentrating on the scene as it appeared in his mind from what Dr. Perkins had written. He swallowed hard and continued.

"Old Nicodemus found Daniel half hanging out of the goat cart with a fatal bullet wound. His shotgun lay across the cart. Strangely, the big Billy goat was grazing as if nothing had happened. As the goat nibbled at the grass, he dragged Daniel's face across the ground. A few yards away, one of the soldiers lay blown nearly in half, his body and entrails entangled in the midst of a dead horse with a foreleg severed at the shoulder. Nicodemus figured Daniel had shot the soldier with both barrels at once also hitting the horse behind him, which, from the torn-up ground, must have struggled on top of the man while they both bled to death. Another soldier was found lying on his back, several yards to the side toward the kitchen. He had been shot in his right thigh and frontally through the throat. His face was fixed in a startled expression. Nicodemus figured he had shot Daniel and Nannie had shot him, first in the thigh and then when he turned toward her, shot him again, hitting him in the throat. Nicodemus found Nannie lying on her back still holding a pistol, one that had been kept on the mantel in the kitchen. Nicodemus believed the third soldier, the one that got away, had killed her and then found Annielise, who we figure had probably hidden the baby and run out of the cottage when she saw Daniel and Nannie shot. That last Yankee left with the silver Shamrock bowl he found in the kitchen, the same one you see on the dining table at the cabin. That was the day Shamrock was killed right here where we sit."

"But," Isabel said, "As tragic and horrible as what you have told me, it isn't the end of the story is it? How did the bowl get back to Shamrock?"

"Little Bethany was taken in by Dr. Perkins until she was old enough, eighteen, to go with Jonathan who was building a shipping business out of Nassau. Jonathan taught her to sail and navigate a J & Q schooner on the way there from New Orleans. Then Jonathan decided to send her with an island woman as chaperon to Paris to an exclusive girls' school sort of like your father sent you. Jonathan always laughed and said there was no fine girls' school in the South at the time and he was not going to send her to a Yankee school up North. It was a good choice. Paris is where Jonathan met and married my mother Louisette."

"But what about the bowl?"

"To get to Paris, they first steamed from Nassau on a J & Q ship bound with cargo as far as Philadelphia. From there they planned to go by train to New York and board a new ocean liner to France. Bethany, in her diary, said she knew something horrible happened in Philadelphia. She described strolling on the Philadelphia waterfront with Jonathan when they came upon a saloon. Out front there was a large sign that read *Silver Bowl Saloon*. Above the lettering there was painted a large picture of a silver bowl identical to the Shamrock punch bowl. That bowl had been ordered from a silversmith in London by Daniel as a wedding present to Nannie. He had designed it himself with the band of green cloisonné shamrocks around the lip. It was the only one like it in the world. Bethany wrote that when Jonathan saw the sign his face changed to an expression she had never seen, an expression that frightened her. He sent her to the hotel in a carriage. Jonathan never told Bethany what took place in the saloon that day. When he got back to the hotel suite he walked into the parlor with his hands in his pockets. He told them, 'It was the Shamrock bowl. The big man who owned the saloon confessed he had gotten it in Vicksburg. Bragged it was given to him by a young woman who appreciated him.' Jonathan got the bowl and shipped it home to Nassau. Bethany's diary said he never spoke another word about it. She wrote that when he took his right hand out of his pocket to close the door to the hall, both she and her chaperon saw that the cuff of his shirt was soaked in blood. He retired to his bedroom and didn't come out until the next morning except once to take a bottle of bourbon from a table in the parlor. He never revealed what happened and refused to let them see any newspaper the next day as he rushed them to catch a train for New York. Bethany wrote in her diary that Jonathan hardly spoke at all on the voyage to France and that he avoided leaving their stateroom, taking his meals in his room. Whatever he did that day at the saloon, however he killed the third man, and I'm sure that is what he did, Bethany wrote that she believed he had unleashed uncontrollable violence against the third killer of Shamrock and the realization of what he had done drove him to self-imposed silence and isolation. She could have been right. I saw that happen to a soldier in the Philippines. There was a Moro ambush, one in which our captain was hacked to death. Though wounded, the soldier went berserk and killed a dozen Moros, left not one standing."

"But the bowl was not yet back here at Shamrock was it?" Isabel asked.

"No. Bethany finished school and returned to enter the business with Jonathan after he moved his headquarters to Havana. She had read Dr. Perkins' account of that terrible day and she is the one who returned here to Shamrock to face what happened to her mother, grandmother and great grandfather. Her diary explains how she made peace with their ghosts. She ordered lawyer Todd, Sr. to have the brick cottage where her mother was so brutally killed torn down completely and all the materials taken far off Shamrock property. She had the ground it had stood on plowed and planted with grass. Then, without telling Jonathan, she used her own money secretly to build the cabin. Only after it was built and furnished, including a toy box for a little boy, did she tell Jonathan what she had done. She then convinced him that his family would want him to return; that it was Quinn land they had died defending; that they wanted a Quinn to walk the land again and he should let me grow up there with her in the summers and Christmas holidays. Now you know most of it."

"Most of it! What on earth could be the rest?"

"I'm not quite ready to tell you that."

"You scare me, Ansel. You know I am in love with you, but I'm afraid you will turn out to be some ephemeral being floating into and out of my life, leaving me to disappear across an ocean to do God knows what, to return or not return as fate plays with us. It is all so sudden, so crazy."

"Marry me."

Isabel couldn't breathe for a moment, refused to look at him, tried to make light of the proposal. "What about all those girls in Paris?"

Ansel grinned. "I believe you are jealous. What about all those ballroom dandies in Memphis?"

She did turn to look at him then. "This is insane. There's no time for a wedding. You're leaving for Cuba and from there to France and you won't let me follow you."

"Come with me to Cuba. We can wed in Havana."

"My daddy will want a wedding in Memphis for his little girl. I'm all he has. You talked about ghosts. He will say Mother's ghost wouldn't forgive him if he didn't give her daughter a proper wedding at home. I can't run off. It would break his heart."

"Then let's have a wedding in Memphis instead of going to the ball. Y'all are going home day after tomorrow. Set up a wedding."

"Everyone will think I've lost my mind. I think I've lost my mind. People will think it's a rushed wedding because I'm pregnant."

"I wish you were."

"This is crazy. You are crazy. We had a shipboard romance, if that. You just think you love me."

"I know I love you."

"You can't know that. You don't know me. How could you in so short a time? How many women, Ansel? Why me so suddenly?"

"You are beautiful and smart and courageous and strong. You proved that as a nurse in an army hospital, strong enough to overcome tragedy. In my life there will never be another you. I know that. Don't ask me how, but I know. Bethany would approve of you. You are like her. And I'll tell you something else."

"What?"

"I love you too much not to come back to you."

"What an insane proposal. You tell me of violence and blood on this very spot and in the same breath ask me to marry you in the ruins of Shamrock."

"Say yes."

"The whole world is at war. You'll make me a widow."

"You would be a wealthy one, but I won't let that happen because I wouldn't want my money spent supporting a beautiful, merry widow, the toast of Memphis with all those dandies hanging around you."

"That's not funny." Isabel was crying and holding tight to Ansel.

"You still haven't said yes."

With tears running down her cheeks she looked up at Ansel. "You laughed at my clothes and said I looked like a farmhand."

"Are you ever going to say yes?"

Very quietly, almost shyly she whispered, "Yes," then kissed him like he had never been kissed—a kiss filled with passion, fear, joy, foreboding, a kiss of desperation and doubt, a kiss from some deep place in the heart meant to last a lifetime.

"I believe that kiss made the earth tremble. You did say yes?"

Isabel dried her eyes on the sleeve of her jacket. Her nose was red from the tears and from the cold. "I said yes. Now take me back. I'm freezing."

"I would rather keep you from freezing by building a fire right here and making love to you."

"You are crazy! I'm beginning to think all the Quinns were crazy."

"Say yes again, loud enough for all the ghosts of Shamrock to hear you. Say it and I will take you back."

"Yes!" she yelled for the whole world to hear. It startled the horses.

"Well go catch them! I have a warm bath waiting."

He lifted her to the saddle. "Don't fall into the creek on the way back."

"Would you jump in that icy water to save me?"

"I might laugh a little, but I would jump in."

"You will learn it is a very dangerous thing to laugh at Isabel Ferguson, and it will be even more dangerous to laugh at Isabel Ferguson Quinn. I know how to shoot, you know."

CHAPTER SIXTEEN

Ansel promised her he would ask her father's permission to wed as tradition demanded.

"What if he refuses?" she asked.

"Then I will tie you in a cotton-picking sack, throw you over the back of a horse, race up to the hill country and find a marrying preacher in the wilds of the piney woods."

She had laughed then, but at breakfast the next morning Isabel was unusually quiet. She took furtive glances at Ansel and her father, but said nothing. A storm of emotions swirled inside her head. She thought she might lose her breakfast. Then with not so much as a goodbye, the men, in a hurry to tour the farm, excused themselves, put on their jackets and hats and went out the door to the horses, leaving Isabel sitting alone, brittle with anxiety.

Shamrock was indeed a large operation. The men toured the barns, stables, the new implement shed built to hold the two Case tractors and attachments, a large open-sided shed for temporary storage of cotton, a cotton gin that not only ginned and baled Shamrock's cotton, but made money ginning and bailing the cotton of all the smaller farmers for several miles around who found it cheaper than hauling lose cotton all the way to the gin in Vicksburg. Jed led them to the field where he had set the two new tractors to work pulling plow attachments six rows wide. Jed explained that each tractor could out-plow four double mule teams.

"How will you keep them running?" Walter Ferguson asked.

Jed answered, "There's an automobile mechanic at the garage in Vicksburg that takes care of our four trucks and Miss Bethany's car. Case will supply spare parts. Miss Bethany and I checked all of that out before we settled on Case tractors. They got a lot of 'em working out in the wheat growing country. They pull rakes and mechanical bundlers up there. I wish there was a mechanical cotton picker, but no one's designed one that works."

Later, back at the cabin, the three men talked a while about the operations. Finally, Jed said, "If you two don't have any more questions, I can still get in a little work done before the sun goes down."

When he left, Ansel suggested that he and Walter sit in the parlor.

"Lizzy," Ansel called, "Would you bring Mister Walter and me a little bourbon on ice?" The two men settled into chairs in front of the fireplace.

Walter Ferguson told Ansel, "I reviewed the legers, and after seeing the barns, sheds, stock, gin, fences and equipment and getting to know Jed Jamison and the way he has organized operations here, I'm impressed. The only recommendations I would make is to hire a good accountant to audit the books twice a year in the place of that law firm. You don't need to be paying them for looking after the operation. I think I would increase Jed's bonus instead. You have a good man there. I may be able to get you a few cents a pound more for your cotton through my contacts in England. They're willing to pay a little more than the domestic market, and I can get you good railroad shipping rates from here to New Orleans. Last season the Port of New Orleans was shipping out some 24,000 bales a week. You get your money when the cotton is delivered to the dock or warehouse there. The buyer pays for and owns the cotton before it's shipped. It's his worry after that."

"I really appreciate your coming down here. Your opinion and suggestions put to rest a lot of the worry I have been carrying since all this fell to me. What do I owe you?"

"Not a thing. I would like to broker your cotton for a standard fee that's based on the price I can get for you, the same as I do for clients in Memphis."

"Consider that done. Now Walter, I have another serious matter to discuss with you." Walter looked at Ansel with a questioning expression. "Another matter?"

Ansel took a deep breath. "Mister Ferguson I ask you for your daughter's hand in marriage. You've seen that I can take care of her and she will share all I have. I love her, sir."

Walter Ferguson sat silent for a long moment . . . then he smiled. "I've been waiting for something like this from you two. I assume you have asked her?"

"Yes, sir."

"And she said yes?"

Isabel walked into the room. She had been sitting on a settee in the hall listening to every word. "Yes I did, Daddy. I know it's a little sudden, but I love him." She walked over and sat on the arm of Ansel's chair.

"Are you sure, Darlin'? He has to go back overseas. You may not see him for a long time."

"I love him, Daddy. That's the only thing I am sure of."

"Your mother, God rests her soul, always planned for you to have a big Memphis wedding. There's not time for that. We'll do the best we can. Where will you stay while Ansel is gone?"

"We'll go to Cuba after the wedding. He will send me back before he leaves for France. I might stay here Daddy. Lizzy will look after me. Or I could stay with you, or I could spend time in both places."

"Well, Darlin', watchin' you two, I've kind of seen this comin'. Ansel has proved himself an honorable young man and he has the means to take care of you." Walter stood and offered his hand. "Ansel, you have my permission."

Ansel jumped to his feet and shook his future father-in-law's hand.

Walter grinned. "I'm not losing a daughter, you understand. I'm gaining a plantation for my grandchildren, which you two better give me. I don't suppose we have any champagne?"

Ansel shook his head. "Bourbon will have to do."

Lizzy, who had been listening at the doorway shouted, "Halleluiah!"

If the wedding they had ten days later was considered small by Memphis standards, Ansel was not at all sure he could have survived a big one. Both Walter and Isabel had teary eyes when it came time to give the bride away. Everyone agreed that the bride was gorgeous and the groom looked very handsome in his uniform. Their wedding photo made the society page of the *Commercial Appeal*. The article stated:

The couple will honeymoon in Cuba, traveling by railroad from Memphis to Jacksonville, Florida where they will transfer to the Florida East Coast Railroad aboard the Havana Special to Key West. From Key West they will travel by ferry to Havana. While in Cuba the couple will inspect the groom's family sugar plantation.

The newlyweds spent two wonderful days and nights at the Plaza Hotel situated on the Malecón Promenade in Havana overlooking the harbor. Isabel was fascinated by the stories Ansel told of his childhood in Cuba and how he had been sent away to Jonathan's old school, Marion Military Institute in Alabama, when the fighting between the Cuban rebels and Spanish forces reached the outskirts of Havana. He told her how Jonathan, under the very noses of the Spaniards, directed clandestine shipments of rifles, ammunition and medicine to the Cubans. Isabel was even more enthralled by the stories of how Bethany had been a spy, and of her lover, Felipe de Alacon, Jonathan's partner in the sugar plantation, who had been a colonel in the rebel cavalry.

The couple walked through Old Havana, La Habana Vieja, Ansel called it, where he showed Isabel the house in which he grew up. He told her funny stories of their Chinese cook. He said the home had been sold when Jonathan and Louisette retired to Shamrock after the Spanish-American War. The couple had late afternoon cocktails at Jonathan's and Bethany's favorite bar, La Piña de Plata. (The name would be changed to El Florida and later still to El Floridita to attract American tourists after the Great War.)

The third day the couple boarded the train for a long trip east-southeastward across the plains toward the Sierra del Escambray Mountains. Their first-class coach was that in name only, seeing as it was old and worn. It rattled and swayed along behind two coaches crowded with farm laborers, including a scattering of wives, children, goats and chickens. Ahead of the passenger coaches were several freight cars. The acrid odor of smoke and cinders from the locomotive wafted in through the open windows.

Much of the view was of endless fields of sugarcane shimmering under the tropical Cuban sun. They frequently stopped in the middle of nowhere to let off passengers or pick up little groups of field workers for passage to the next village down the line. The trip seemed endless, but the lovers didn't complain. They wanted to savor every minute they had together before Ansel had to depart for France, a subject they did not discuss.

The sun was low on the horizon when they reached the station at Cienfuegos, a town beside a great natural harbor of the same name on the southern coast of Cuba. The breeze coming off the Caribbean was a relief.

"How nice," Isabel said as they stepped off the train into the pleasant seventy-eight degree temperature.

"Wait until you make the trip in summer when it's ninety-eight. Even then you'll find the plantation cooler. It's at a higher elevation at the foot of the Escambray Mountains," Ansel replied.

A man waved at them. Dressed in riding britches and boots, a white, open collar shirt and a wide brimmed straw hat, he was standing in front of a 1914 Hispano-Suiza touring car.

"Is that your man there in front of that pretty car?"

"Yes. That's Cayo Galano, the manager of Alacon-Quinn plantation." Ansel waved back. While they were waiting for their luggage to be unloaded and gathered, Ansel told Isabel about Cayo.

"He is the grandson of Alonzo Galano, who was Felipe de Alacon's most trusted man, though a humble servant in charge of the stables. Felipe suffered greatly during the war. He had been wounded and captured by the Spanish. They imprisoned him at Moro Castle in Havana and were very hard on him. He would have died had Bethany not found a way to get aid to him. The Spaniards burned the old Alacon plantation. Besides Bethany, Felipe loved his prized Spanish Barb horses, an Arabian cross breed. When Bethany brought him home, he discovered that Alonzo had saved the horses, hidden them in the mountains from the Spaniards. Felipe, that brave man, cried when he saw them. When he found what Alonzo had done, he made him a partner in breeding the finest horses in the Caribbean. As he and Bethany rebuilt the plantation, Felipe paid to send Alonzo's grandson Cayo to school and college just as Jonathan did for Jed. Cayo was and is loyal to the Quinn family. He is not a servant. He is a gentleman and boss of Alacon-Quinn's Cuban holdings of which he now owns twenty percent."

"What are we standing here waiting for?" Isabel asked.

"For our *mozo de equipajes*," Ansel replied.

"There you go again, talking Spanish to me."

"Well, you asked. A little Spanish to go with your French won't hurt. I said we are waiting for the porter coming with the truckload of bags you packed."

"I thought you would want your wife dressed nicely for the honeymoon."

Although Ansel thought ten women could dress nicely in all the clothes his new wife had brought on the trip, he was smart enough not to say anything. A man with a pile of luggage on a cart asked, "*Senior, es su equipajes?*"

"*Si. Por ese automóvile alli.*"

"Show off," Isabel said as they followed the man with their luggage to the car. "Cayo! I believe you've grown younger since I last saw you."

The two men shook hands and then hugged.

"Senior Cayo Galano, may I introduce Mrs. Ansel Quinn."

Cayo smiled, took off his hat, and instead of shaking Isabel's offered hand, he bowed and kissed it.

Cayo was a thickly built man with a beard, mustache, dark brown, sparkling eyes and a beautiful smile. "We welcome you with great joy, Señora Quinn." He spoke in perfect English.

"How nice to meet you, Señor Galano. I've heard a lot of good things about you. Thank you for speaking English. This rude man I married insists I learn Spanish but I'm afraid I know only a little . . . but I will learn." She smiled.

"We have not had such a beautiful lady to grace the plantation since Señorita Bethany's last visit." Cayo immediately realized the remark was painful to Ansel. "We miss her greatly, Ansel, as I know you do."

"What a nice thing to say, Cayo. May I call you Cayo? Please call me Isabel." Her bright smile broke the awkward moment.

It will be an honor, Señora Isabel. That is a beautiful Spanish name. Shall we go?"

Isabel and Ansel rode in the back, Cayo with the driver up front. The baggage was lashed to the boot.

"This is quite a car."

"Yes! Señorita Quinn saw one in Havana and ordered one just like it. She could really drive it, too. I was the only one brave enough to ride with her."

Ansel laughed. "That sounds like her."

"Do you know, Señora Isabel, the first time she arrived at Cienfuegos, my grandfather and Señor Alacon met her in a carriage? There wasn't an automobile in all of Cuba."

"I have heard what a good and brave man your grandfather was."

"You are kind to say so."

They gradually climbed to a flat plain spreading out from the mountains and turned off through a whitewashed arch that had the name ALACON-QUINN painted across the top. After a mile along the road bordered by fields of sugarcane, they turned onto a drive lined with white fences on both sides bordered by flowering shrubs and lined with trees covered in flaming red blooms.

"Those are beautiful. What are they called?"

Cayo answered, "In English they are called 'flame trees'; in Spanish, *flamboyanes*. And Señora, just ahead you will see the finest horses in all the Caribbean, the Alacon-Galano Spanish Barbs."

They drove past a dozen beautiful horses with distinctly Arabian characteristics grazing in a pasture. A few hundred yards further, the car pulled around a curved driveway and stopped in front of a lovely ranch house. It was plainly built, but with round columns on all sides setting off wide, shaded verandas. The roof was covered by terracotta shingles and the exterior had the look of whitewashed adobe. The house was larger than the one at Shamrock, but like Shamrock it had been built as a practical replacement for a once grand plantation home, the victim of war.

A line of six people, two men and four women, was waiting for them to get out of the car.

"What are all these people doing here?" Isabel asked.

"They are house servants, cooks and gardeners come to meet the new mistress of the plantation at her house."

"My God, Ansel, you never said anything about this place. I imagined a plain rural farmhouse in the middle of Cuba with probably goats and chickens running around the yard. This is beautiful."

Isabel smiled as she shook hands with all six people before they walked into the home followed by Cayo. It took two men to carry Isabel's luggage to their room. The maids set to unpacking and putting things away while Ansel and Cayo showed her the house.

"Señora," Cayo said. "You may find the house lovely, but it is a working plantation that is not so pretty in places. You haven't seen our old sugar mill and Bethany's new rum distillery which is only three-years-old, or the wagons, mules, sheds and barns and our own smoky little narrow-gauge railroad . . . and you haven't been here when they burn the fields before harvesting the cane."

"Rum distillery?" Isabel said.

"I haven't seen it either," Ansel answered.

Cayo replied, "Señorita Bethany said we already produce all the ingredients, sugar, blackstrap molasses and good mountain water. You add a little yeast, maybe a touch of vanilla and like magic you have rum. It might even be drinkable provided you have a good distiller and plant. We use pot stills. They make the best rum. We bought about 1,000 charred barrels from a bourbon distillery in Tennessee that we plan to use to age our rum. But for the time being, while we are still perfecting the process, we are selling most of the product to another rum maker to blend with his product. The market is big right now because of war demand. You would be surprised how much rum the British Army and Navy is buying from all over the Caribbean."

"Well, Cayo, according to the books, we have a way to go before the profits will pay for the new distillery."

"You sound like your aunt. It was my idea and she said the same thing when she borrowed the money from the Bank of Havana. I believe it will be a good investment for Alacon-Quinn."

"Enough business you two. Can a girl get a bath around here? I'm all gritty from that train ride."

Like Shamrock, water at the main house was piped in from rain collecting cisterns with well water for backup during periods of drought. While Ansel and Cayo talked business, Isabel soaked in a hot tub until time to dress for dinner.

The newlyweds had a wonderful time. They rode magnificent Alacon horses into the mountains for picnics and made love in fields of wildflowers. They sometimes went swimming nude in a deep, still bowl on a flat where a cold mountain stream slowed to rest prior to tumbling further down the hills, then meandering across sugarcane fields before reaching the Bahia de Jagua, the bay that made such a fine harbor for the Port of Cienfuegos . Ansel drove them in the Hispano-Suiza into Cienfuegos to tour the beautiful and prosperous city with its lovely buildings, parks, shops, theater and fine restaurants. They parked the car and rode all over town on the streetcars, talking and laughing like the young lovers they were.

In the seasonally cool Cuban nights they enjoyed conjugal pleasures in a big tester bed draped in mosquito netting, sleeping late before enjoying breakfast served on the veranda out back overlooking fields of sugarcane glistening greenish-silver in the morning sunlight.

And then . . . it was time.

CHAPTER SEVENTEEN

Paris, 1916

After sending a telegram via the transatlantic cable to Major Crosby in care of the American Embassy, Paris, Captain Ansel Quinn departed New York aboard SS *California* of the Anchor Line bound for Glasgow, Scotland. As he lay on his bunk, his thoughts were with Isabel. They had ridden the *Havana Special* from Key West to Jacksonville during which Isabel argued that she should cross the Atlantic with him and live in Paris, threatening to get to France on her own if she had to by volunteering again as a nurse. Ansel held her in his arms and argued in his turn that her duty to their marriage was the same as his: to stay safe, and more, to learn the business of business so she could keep an eye on the Quinn holdings until he returned. He made the mistake of saying another Atlantic crossing was dangerous, that she had survived one crossing threatened by a U-boat attack and he didn't want her risking another.

"Well, you are risking another," Isabel shouted at him.

"I have to go, but you don't. Bethany was lost on a crossing. Don't you see? I cannot risk losing you too."

There were tears and argument and kisses and more tears.

"Do you already regret that you married me?" Ansel asked.

"No! Yes! No! I love you, Ansel Quinn. Don't you get yourself killed! I could not live if something happened to you."

"Please don't hate me for loving you."

"Damnit, Ansel, it's not you, it's the Army and this war I hate."

Their parting at Jacksonville was brutal in terms of heart rending agony as is always the case when lovers part not knowing when or if they will meet again.

Ansel had notified Walter Ferguson, and so he was there at the station in Jacksonville to meet the train and take his daughter back to Memphis while Ansel continued up the East Coast by train to New York.

Ocean bound, Ansel skipped dinner on the first night out of New York and took what little comfort he could find from a bottle of bourbon, sipping the golden liquid neat while his mind tortured him with questions. *Are you just a selfish, cruel bastard? You knew you would have to leave her and return to duty. By marrying and then shipping out you have hurt the person you love most. How many soldiers have done the same thing in this insane world?* The last conscious thought before sleep shutting down the turmoil in his mind was, *God! I miss you Isabel.*

* * *

Ansel disembarked in Glasgow. SS *California* had escaped a U-boat encounter on this crossing, but her luck would not hold. Both she and Atlantic Line's SS *Minnehaha*, the two ships aboard which Ansel had crossed the Atlantic, would be torpedoed and sunk in less than a year. Ansel would read about their loss among the hundreds of others posted in war dispatches. The reported sinkings bolstered his steady refusal to allow Isabel to risk joining him in wartime France.

From Glasgow, Ansel traveled by rail to London where he changed trains for Southampton. There he boarded a channel ferry to Cherbourg without incident. U-boats were a threat in the Channel, but they were more interested in preventing coal colliers and troop transports from reaching France than wasting torpedoes on small, lumbering, ancient side-wheel ferries like the one he crossed aboard. From Cherbourg he traveled by train to Paris, arriving early evening at Gare du Nord station where he saw two girls in the uniform of the American Ambulance Service handing out cigarettes to *poilus* in full gear with rifles loading on a troop train.

They must be headed for Verdun, poor bastards.

It was too late to report to the embassy. Ansel hailed a taxi to take him to number six, Villa Said in the 16th arrondissement. Upon arrival and before he could get his trunk out of the taxi, the front door flew open and out came Tristan and Pauline Babineau.

"Oh! Monsieur Ansel! How happy we are to see you return to us." Pauline threw her arms around him and kissed him on both cheeks.

"Here, let me take you luggage." Tristan picked up the trunk. "Pauline," he corrected his wife, "How many times have I told you? It is not *monsieur* but *Capitaine* Quinn. You see? He left a lieutenant and has come home a captain."

"Well, I remember him as a young boy here with Mademoiselle Bethany and I am old enough to call him Monsieur Ansel if I want to. And if you want supper, Tristan, I won't hear any more about it." Pauline turned in a huff and marched into the house.

"Just wait until you are married, Captain," Tristan said as he followed Captain Quinn to the door, "and you will see what a husband has to put up with."

Ansel laughed. "But Tristan, I am a newly married man."

Tristan nearly dropped the trunk. "Pauline! Pauline! Our Ansel is married!" he shouted as he entered the house.

Pauline came running down the hall, tying an apron around her waist. "Married!? Our Ansel is married? That is wonderful. Is she coming to live here? What is Madam Quinn's name?"

"Her name is Isabel Ferguson Quinn and she is beautiful and I love her dearly."

"When will she arrive?"

"I would not let her come. Too many ships are being sunk by Fritz's U-boats. She is very angry with me."

"You have done the right thing," Tristan said.

"I am not so sure about that. She is a headstrong woman. I think I am in trouble. But what can I do with this war? Anyway, I am hungry. Hey, do I still have a bottle of bourbon in the house?"

"You will have supper in an hour and you have two bottles of bourbon in the cabinet." Pauline started toward the kitchen but turned, and wagged her finger at Ansel. "And there will be no more women in this house," she said with the authority of a married woman who had known Ansel since he was a boy.

"Yes, ma'am," Ansel replied with a smile. He turned to Tristan. "You are right, Tristan, things certainly change when a man gets married."

Two bourbons, a plain provincial supper, and travel-worn Ansel slept like a log.

Major Crosby looked up from his desk. "You're only five days late Quinn. You owe me for not reporting you absent without leave, but I figured only five days was not bad considering all you got yourself into. And never mind that I had to occasionally fill in for you at French Headquarters. It's hard to believe, but for some reason they like you over there. Now, concerning your telegram . . . you informed us that in a mere forty-five, correction, fifty days, you crossed the Atlantic, settled your late aunt's estate, was promoted, somehow wrangled a special intelligence assignment, got married, visited Cuba and crossed the Atlantic once again. I'd say that may be a record of sorts, Lieutenant, I mean, Captain. We'll have to get used to that around here. I suppose congratulations are in order." The Major smiled, got up from his desk and shook Ansel's hand.

"Thank you, sir."

"I also assume, since you are now a married man, there will be no more wild parties at you place."

"You knew about that?"

"Everybody knew about that. Now, let's go see Ambassador Sharp. He wanted to see you the minute you arrived."

The two walked to the ambassador's office where his secretary ushered them in without delay.

The ambassador walked from behind his desk to greet the two officers. "We are glad to have you back, Captain Quinn. Much has happened over here in your absence, none of it good." Sharp directed them to sit in armchairs arranged for ease of informal conversation. "Would you gentlemen care for coffee or cigars?"

The offer was declined.

"In that case let's get down to business. Everything said in this room this morning is classified. Understood?"

The two officers nodded affirmatively.

"I suppose, Captain Quinn that you were at the right place at the right time to be informed of and included in Secretary of State Lansing's rather covert decision to use embassy military attaché personnel for special assignment in the absence of any official military intelligence organization. I was, of course, informed of this via diplomatic pouch which is the only secure means of official communication available to us. Lansing understands neither the President nor the Secretary of War see the need for a separate department of army intelligence. Incidentally, certain confidential sources have informed me that both England and France have established code breaking offices. The Germans also have a code breaking section. We have none at present.

"I also understand that you were given a crash course in military intelligence by Major Van Deman at the War College: things an observer should be mindful of, questions to ask, what to include in detailed reports and how to safeguard such reports; namely that they be given only to me for transfer to Secretary Lansing. In the event of the need to transmit information of an urgent nature, we do have a sort of code comprised of normal sentences with special meaning we can send via wireless or Atlantic Cable, but that is for use only in emergencies. That simple and limited code is kept locked in my safe. One other thing, Captain, from the attitude of the Secretary of War, you can understand that Major Van Deman is considered somewhat of a maverick and agitator in certain higher military echelons. Army Chief of Staff, General Scott, won't even allow him in his office. Association with him could tar his chosen neophytes with the same brush. I trust you are aware of that."

"Yes, sir, Major Van Deman made that clear before his class began."

"Fine. Now, to get to matters at hand. First, Secretary Lansing's end run around the current official attitude toward establishing and funding a department of military intelligence could get us all in trouble. I suspect that funding for a new department is the most serious sticking point. Existing Army departments are jealously competing for what little money Congress has allocated, never mind that a million men or more have already become casualties over here while the entire American Army stands at 125,000 men.

"In spite of Lansing's orders to keep this matter under the table, word has somehow mysteriously gotten to certain departments of intelligence over here. As a result we have very recently received an invitation for a certain Captain Quinn, presently assigned to French Military Headquarters, to accompany a small party to visit, as near to as practical, meaning as near as it is reasonably safe, the desperate battle for Verdun.

"I want you to understand, Captain, that you are under no obligation to accept any such invitation."

"I understand, Mister Ambassador. What I don't understand is that they have to know I will report what I witness. News of Verdun is already on the front pages of papers at home. News of French losses can hardly encourage America to send troops into what appears to be a slaughterhouse."

Sharp answered, "I think the French are willing to risk that in order to show the great need they have for more ammunition, arms, food, cloth, shoes, all the things they need to continue fighting, and the loans to pay for it."

"When do I go and to whom do I report?"

"I can't answer the question. As for now, you will return to you duties at French Military Headquarters. I've been told that such matters concerning American neutral observers will be handled through their department of personnel rather than through this embassy as was done earlier. The French thinking is that the department of personnel is the least obvious department to handle such matters and therefore easier to conceal. I believe the commander of that department is a General Bourget. Do you know him?"

Ansel wondered if he looked as startled at the news as he felt.

"I have met him at French Headquarters."

If Ambassador Sharp noticed any change in Ansel's demeanor he ignored it.

"Good. Now, Captain, remember that you are an American neutral observer. You are not, repeat, not to embarrass your government by getting yourself injured or killed. We are not at war with Germany. They have an embassy in Washington. Secretary Lansing would be hard pressed to explain how an American in uniform became a casualty in combat. And Captain, please don't get taken prisoner. How the hell would we explain that to an isolationist Congress and President?"

Ansel left the embassy thinking, *Explain it to the President! How about explaining it to my wife! And the whole assignment is going to be under the authority of my newly discovered father.*

It was lunchtime but Ansel had no appetite.

Ansel reported to French Army Headquarters to assume his usual duties. He found a tall stack of papers, all in French, waiting on his desk. They mainly consisted of situation reports mildly veiled to encourage American aid, but there were useful evaluations of the latest German tactics and weapons. Mid-afternoon a clerk delivered a sealed note to him. It suggested dinner that evening with General Bourget at La Closerie des Lilas, a café on the left bank in Montparnasse, the 14th arrondissement. Dress as usual was to be mufti.

"Well, Henrí, this is a charming place." Ansel smiled.

"Yes, isn't it?" Henrí smiled. "It is a hangout for poor writers and artists who not only eat cheap, but can rent a table to while away days and nights with fellow poor writers and artists. The wine is not the best, the bread is better and a meal of onion soup is perhaps the best they have to offer. It is hardly the place where government officials including generals, inquisitive journalists or German agents are likely to spend their evenings. Does that address your curiosity over why I picked this place?"

"German agents?"

"You have been gone almost two months. Things have changed somewhat, and I don't just mean the German offensive at Verdun. Food, electricity, gas, and coal are growing scarce. Paris has become paranoid. German spies are thought to be everywhere and are blamed not only for failures at the front, but also shortages of ammunition, food and everything else. Then there are your and my situations."

"Our situations?"

"Yes, your situation as an intelligence agent for the American Army and the sensitive matter of our relationship. If it were known that I am you father, I could be accused of leaking state secrets and you of being a foreign agent taking advantage of your poor old lost father. As silly as that may sound, powers that be are looking in all directions to place blame for a growing panic over losses at the front and the threat of another

German offensive like the one in 1914 that nearly reached Paris. So, you and I should be careful. The good news is that we now have an official reason to meet occasionally since I am assigned to make arrangements for a certain neutral American observer to visit various areas of our army activities for the obvious purpose of enhancing your country's knowledge of modern warfare, while providing proof of the urgent need for its participation in the defeat of Germany."

"You're right," Ansel said. "The wine at this place is not the best. And I do understand and shall take under advisement all you have just made clear."

"By the way, it will take me a couple of weeks to work out details for your visit to Verdun. Plan on sometime in May. You will only be allowed near but not at the front. Things are too fluid up there. I also want to make clear that you are not to get your head blown-off. Now tell me more about this new bride of yours, who is unofficially my daughter-in-law is she not? I would hope that she is more intelligent than her acceptance of your proposal of marriage would indicate." Henrí smiled.

"To begin with, you, Aileen Giard and I are the only people on Earth that know you are my real father and that Aunt Bethany is my real mother. I have not disclosed those facts even to my wife. I think we should leave it at that for the duration."

"I agree, and our relationship is safe with Aileen."

"Isabel, my wife, was for a while a nurse at a receiving station in England. She saw firsthand what the war is doing to flesh and blood. She almost did not marry me because I am a soldier and she knows Americans will be drawn into the fighting over here. She is beautiful, smart, headstrong, and I love her. Would you like to see?" Ansel took a photo from the inside pocket of his jacket and handed it to Henrí.

"*Quelle beauté!* Poor girl, she has married beneath herself." Henrí returned the photo with a smile.

"She would agree. Now no more talk about my marriage. Let's eat."

CHAPTER EIGHTEEN

My darling Isabel,

I received a bundle of your letters yesterday. I am so glad you are spending some time at Shamrock, and I understand that you, in the company of your father, are planning to visit the sugar plantation in Cuba. I suspect that by the time I get home for good, you will have taken over and there will be nothing for me to do but make love to you. I have always wanted to be a kept man by a beautiful, rich woman. I miss you terribly.

Paris has changed much since you were here at school. There are shortages of everything. Eggs and butter have doubled in price. There is a shortage of coal which is driving the price up when you can get it. Some laundries can't get enough to heat their water and are closing. Those that are open have raised their prices. The coal shortage has resulted in the rationing of electricity. Stores lose their lights at six in the evening and have to use candles. The same is true at my house and at the embassy. This has driven up the price of candles and they are becoming hard to find. Gas has been rationed. At the house we are allowed only one cubic meter of gas a day, barely enough for hot water and to cook two meals on the stove. If we use more, our gas meter will be shut off. I am glad spring is arriving. If the shortage of coal continues, everyone will be very cold next winter.

Don't worry about me. Embassy duty is safe . . . and boring.

I miss you terribly, Mrs. Quinn.

Much love,

Ansel

The letter writing between the separated lovers continued on a weekly basis, but letters accumulated while waiting shipment by sea. On two occasions that were disturbing to both, no mail arrived for weeks. Ansel, through his Embassy, discovered that U.S. mail on two ships had been lost, one attributed to a U-boat in the Atlantic and the other to a mine in St. George's Channel.

Distressing to Ansel were subtle hints from Isabel that indicated she still considered volunteering for duty in Paris with the American Ambulance Service.

To discourage her, Ansel enclosed in his letters newspaper clippings of the increasing number of ships being sunk. He continued to omit any reference to his upcoming assignments to visit the front as a neutral observer.

He did mention dangers she would face if she were in Paris.

Darling,

As much as I miss you, I am glad you are not here in Paris as the Germans are still occasionally sending over their Zeppelins and bombers at night, although London is getting the brunt of such attacks. The first we know of a raid is when the motor trucks of the Fire Department roar down the streets honking their horns ordering all lights turned out, even demanding that smokers on the street put out their cigarettes. Military and police posts all over Paris sound "Garde à vous" on bugles, and Telephone Central sets off some kind of buzzer on all the wires. The powerful search lights come on and swing their sword-like beams all over the sky in a spectacular display, especially when the beams illuminate clouds. After the threat is gone, the bugles play "Cessez le feu" to announce all clear. Little real damage has been done, only a few houses and shops crushed or set on fire. But still, the other night twenty-four people were killed and even more injured. I rest much easier knowing you are safe at home.

Don't worry about me. I'm doing fine. I have been befriended by General Bourget at French Headquarters who has sort of taken me under his wing. It makes things easier at my post there and seems to have the blessing of our ambassador at the embassy. Being the lowest ranking American officer in Paris, it is nice to feel welcome at both places.

As I've written before, food is scarce, except on the black market, but the wine is still good and plentiful.

I'm behaving and I love you dearly,

Ansel

Quinn was behaving. For the first time since his return, he ventured to number 5, Rue Daunou and walked into *The New York Bar* where Harry MacElhone roared at him from behind the bar, "Look here! Our Mississippi friend has returned to us a captain no less."

The bar was not crowded, but one patron sitting alone at a table stood up and offered Ansel his hand. "Good to see an old friend," he said. It was Fred Zinn who had been a member of the wild and jolly trio of American flyers that Ansel had befriended and with whom he shared good times including parties he had thrown at number six Villa Said. Zinn was the pilot that preferred to serve as an observer pioneering aerial photography which had quickly become so critical to war planning.

"Zinn!" Ansel laughed and walked over to grab his hand. "I haven't seen you and your flying buddies since y'all drank up all my wine the night before I left for home. Where are those rogues Prince and Chapman?"

The smile left Fred Zinn's face. "Prince and Chapman got their all-American squadron. It's called *Escadrille Américaine*, although the Germans are complaining about the name."

"Then where are those two; out wooing the country girls near their air field?"

"They did plenty of that, Quinn," Fred paused looking for soft words, but there were none. "They're both dead."

Ansel opened his mouth to speak, but not a word was issued. He sat down in silence.

"I know," Zinn said looking at him. "There's nothing to say. They're gone. It's war and friends die in war."

The latest letter from Isabel opened with the words:

I hate you, I love you, I miss you terribly. Business is good. I'm learning. I plan to spend July in Cuba and August at a business school in Memphis. It is just for four weeks. I enrolled as I. F. Quinn. They will be shocked when they find they have accepted a woman, but they cashed the check written on the Shamrock account and Daddy says to sue them if they don't let me attend. I expect all the boys in the class will fall in love with me, and the professor, too. Just joking, but I am not joking about you staying away from those French girls. I try to keep my spirits up by staying busy, but some nights I can't sleep and some days don't eat worrying about you. Other nights I cry, and then get mad at you for making me cry. Look up at the moon tonight and think of me for I will be looking at the same moon thinking of you. I was insane to marry you. Damn soldiering and the Army! Don't you dare get hurt!

I ache for you, my darling.

Love,

Isabel

"When the Embassy gave me orders to accept any invitation I might receive to visit the front, I didn't realize you would be with me. Isn't it unusual for a neutral American captain to be escorted by a French general?"

Captain Quinn and General Henrí Bourget were riding on a supply train racing through the night toward the town of Bar-le-Duc, the closest rail depot to besieged Verdun, a historic fortress city once described as a dumpy little town in the wooded hills of the Meuse Valley. The train carried food, medical supplies and replacement troops. Several other trains, following at safe intervals that night, carried tons of artillery shells.

"I thought it easier to escort you myself than to wade through all the bureaucratic paperwork and arrangements for an escort party to get you to Verdun and back. Traveling in the company of a general avoids all that. Besides I needed to get out from behind that desk and see for myself what is happening. Our huge losses may be just numbers, a mere balance sheet of battles, to Generals Petain and Neville, but they are not numbers to me. They are individual soldiers whose names come across my desk for assignments, and . . ." Henrí paused.

"And what Henrí, I mean General?"

"I don't intend to turn one Captain Quinn loose to get himself killed or be accused of spying. That would be embarrassing to France and America . . . and Bethany would be very angry with me."

"Now we have the truth. The General has taken it upon himself to babysit me."

"Perhaps for good reason. Your experiences fighting in the jungles of the Philippines and mine in Cochin China and the Algerian Desert are of little use in trench warfare where machineguns and artillery rule between fixed trenches across ground blown bare of vegetation. You are headstrong like your mother. I've seen proof of that. I'm not about to see you set off on your own at the front if I can help it. Now try and get some sleep. It will still be dark when we arrive and we'll have a way to go to reach General Neville's headquarters, if we can get that far."

When they disembarked at Bar-le-Duc, each carried personal travel gear in canvas shoulder bags. What Ansel saw rail-side was a cadre of transportation officers and supply sergeants noisily, frantically, directing labor battalions transferring cargo from rail cars to long lines of trucks; more trucks than Ansel had ever seen. What he was witnessing was a great, if discordant, attempt to create order out of the chaos of what, at the moment, was the largest single supply depot in France. Its desperate purpose was to keep Verdun alive. The date was June 10.

A sergeant approached the pair. "General Bourget, sir, your automobile is waiting. His offer to carry the officers' satchels was declined. Please follow me." The Sergeant was equipped with a holstered Lebel revolver, a canteen and a bandage packet hung on a cartridge belt, an Adrian helmet and the latest French gasmask copied from the German model that covered the entire face and employed an activated charcoal filter.

The pair followed the Sergeant down the narrow space between a waiting outbound line of loaded trucks pointed toward Verdun and a parallel line of inbound ambulances, mostly Model T Fords and Renaults, being unloaded by stretcher bearers who moved what appeared to be an endless line of casualties toward the railhead for transport to hospital. Ansel noticed that most of the casualties carried past them, though painfully wounded, were silent, stoic, even those missing limbs. Their clean white bandages, though stained with blood, were a contrast to their trench-filthy uniforms. There would not be time to clean them up until they reached the hospital. Some of the wounded had their eyes bandaged and wheezed at every breath, victims of gas attack. Several stretchers moved past bearing horribly burned men with blackened faces, reeking of burned flesh, who moaned with every breath. Each had been marked with a tag showing they had received the maximum dose of morphine allowed at the last dressing station. Ansel had to look away.

The General's assigned automobile was found in a line of loaded, outbound trucks. A corporal was waiting beside the car. He handed the General and the American Captain each a blanket roll with waterproof sheet, a cartridge belt with a water canteen and bandage packet attached, an Adrian helmet and a canvas bag with neck strap containing a gasmask.

"The blankets are in case we have to camp roadside in the event we have a break-down or enemy shells block off a section of the road and we find ourselves stuck until repair crews fix it. You will want to hang the gasmask across your chest at all times. At places along the road, we will be within range of the Germans' big guns and they sometimes mix in gas shells."

"Thank you, Corporal," General Bourget replied. He fastened on the cartridge belt and hung the gasmask bag around his neck. Ansel followed suit.

The Sergeant opened the rear door to allow the General and American Captain to enter. They took their seats, piled their satchels and blanket rolls on the floorboard between them, stowed their field caps in their satchels and donned the metal helmets. Satisfied, the corporal got behind the wheel. The Sergeant climbed in beside him and turned in his seat to give them the rules of march.

"This convoy is scheduled to move out in fifteen minutes. We will cover a road distance of sixty-five kilometers. It can take up to four hours depending on weather, breakdowns, accidents, road repairs and enemy shelling. Once we begin, there will be no stopping. The vehicles will be spaced only fourteen seconds apart. This road had to be widened to twenty feet to accommodate constant two-way traffic. There is not enough room to pass a stalled vehicle. If we break down anywhere along the route, we will have to push this vehicle off the road. There are repair motor trucks at the end of every convoy with mechanics and parts. Do either of you have questions?"

General Bourget had none. The Sergeant looked at Ansel.

"Sergeant," he said, "how did those poor men back there get so badly burned?"

"*Lance-flammes*," he answered.

"Flame throwers?" The weapon was new to Ansel.

"Yes sir, another devilish invention by the Boche. The operator carries a tank of pressurized oil on his back with an igniter nozzle at the end of a hose. When he presses the trigger he can squirt a flame of burning oil nearly twenty meters. It sets everything it touches aflame; a terrible weapon. We try to shoot the operators before they can get close enough to use the weapon, but until they light up it's hard to distinguish them at night, just before dawn or in the smoke from artillery fire covering the field. The Germans put them in with what they call *sturmtruppen*, groups of heavily armed, fearless, mad men. Unlike battalions of men spread out walking or running across 'no man's land' in a wide frontal attack, the *sturmtruppen* maneuver in small groups, moving in short sprints from shell hole to shell hole while covering one another. Using automatic weapons, sacks full of hand grenades and often flame throwers, they are very good at opening holes in the line for the main body of German troops following them to exploit and widen. It is an effective tactic."

Ansel took a note pad and pencil from his satchel. Without being asked, Henrí took an electric torch from his and held it so Ansel could write down all the Sergeant had told him.

"I've never seen so many trucks."

Henrí responded. "When the war started two years ago we had only 400 trucks.

Since then we have purchased all the factory output of Berliet, Renault, and other factories and requisitioned every truck in the country for the army. There are now 6,000 working this road day and night and more being put into service as fast as they are rolled out of the factories. As long as the labor battalions and engineers can keep the road open, more than 2,000 tons of ammunition food and other supplies are delivered to the front every twenty-four hours. Tons of crushed rocks are brought from nearby quarries daily to patch the roadway. The crushed stone saves the roadbed, but the sharp rocks gouge chunks out of the solid rubber truck tires requiring them to be changed often. Between rain, snow, heavy traffic and shell fire, keeping this road passable is touch and go. Verdun forms a salient surrounded on three sides by the Germans. A few short stretches of the road that might be visible to the enemy are camouflaged with cloth screens painted to blend in with hills behind them. They're hung from cables strung from poles like theatre curtains. This road and the narrow gauge railroad lying parallel to it constitute the only supply route. It's Verdun's lifeline."

"You seem to know a great deal about it, General."

"It's my job to know about it, and I have been given permission to inform one American observer some, but not all, of what I know in the hope that his reports will both urge and prepare the American Army to join the fight. The one advantage we have over the Germans since Petain took command is that he rotates his units to the rear for rest and replenishment with new conscripts. The Germans don't do that. Their units are reinforced by replacements, but never get rotated to rest areas. We admit that although they have larger caliber, longer range guns than we do, their heavy guns are harder to move up when the line changes. The result is that the German infantry has at times moved out from under their artillery protection while moving into the range of ours. We believe they are losing as many troops as we are, and with no rotation, no relief, we believe they are being worn down."

"If the road is so vital why don't the Germans cut it?"

"They have cut all other routes to Verdun including two main railroads. The hills help protect this road and the current distance to their line prevents all but the largest of their guns from reaching it, which they do from time to time when the guns are not otherwise in demand for shelling our lines or protecting their own lines from counter attack. Let's hope tonight they are otherwise engaged."

"Why don't they send their bombers to attack this road? Paris is sometimes bombed at night."

"They try, but we have four squadrons of fighters based at four new fields along the road. Their only job is to keep the bombers away. On the other hand, large numbers of German fighters are keeping our reconnaissance aircraft from crossing the German lines. It's a serious problem. We can't adjust our artillery from the air or see what they are doing behind the lines. We know they have laid a dozen narrow gauge railroads to supply their needs."

Ansel, with the aid of the General's electric torch wrote in his journal all the General had told him.

A few minutes later a cacophony of coughs, backfires, and rumblings shattered the night air as two hundred motor trucks were brought to life. The convoy began to move. The Sergeant cautioned, "Please put away the torch, General."

Each driver strained to see by the dim "blackout headlights" which barely illuminated a few yards of the road ahead. The ride was bone jarring as they moved steadily along the rough, patched road as it wound its way northeast by east through hills and glens toward Verdun. The constant 'crump' of artillery grew steadily louder. They passed through several villages along the way: Naives, Rumont, Chaumont-sur-Aire, all darkened and shuttered. As they progressed, Ansel counted five trucks and three ambulances off the side of the road. Drivers and repair crews were working in the dark to fix them. Two trucks were pushed well off the road and completely abandoned.

Suddenly there was a Frenchman standing in the road. In the dark he was barely discernible in the dim headlights of the staff car.

"*Merde! Que se passe-t-il?*" The corporal hit the brakes and swerved to miss the ghostly figure. His actions slowed the vehicle just enough for the man to jump on the running board and cling to the door beside Ansel.

"How about a lift? They'll need me up ahead."

Ansel grabbed the interloper who was in danger of slipping off his precarious perch as the car bumped along ruts and potholes. "That was a crazy stunt. You'll have to ask the General. It's his car." Ansel jerked his head to indicate the man sitting next to him.

Leaning across Ansel, Henrí asked, "Just what do you do that's so important?"

"Sir, I'm a truck driver. I lost mine back there; broken rear axle. There's always a shortage of drivers to return trucks from the front."

"Captain Quinn, invite the man to join us."

Ansel helped the man climb over the side. Not wanting to sit in the middle himself, he guided the man over his knees to the middle seat. "You'll have to rest your feet on our gear." The man, thin as a rail and just over five feet tall, did as he was told without complaint.

"General Bourget is on your left and I am Captain Quinn," Ansel offered.

"Thank you for the ride, General. I am Maurice Ravel."

"There is a famous composer by that name," Henrí said.

"I'm afraid I'm the same." The small man answered. "I tried to get into pilot training but they wouldn't take me. Neither would the Infantry. Said I wasn't healthy enough. France is not so choosy when it comes to truck drivers."

"My God!" Henrí exclaimed. "You composed the beautiful score for Daighilev's ballet *Daphnis et Chloé.*"

"You are very kind to remember, General. That was back in '09."

"You shouldn't be up here. You are a French treasure."

"I believe all of France's treasure is at risk here, General; a whole generation; France itself. My music cannot stop the Boche, but the artillery shells I carry can help. I am told that since this battle began over five months ago, we have fired more than 16,000,000 shells. I have carried my share of them and shall continue to do so."

Ansel scribbled a note on his pad. Henrí reminded Ravel, "That is classified information, Corporal. I would advise you keep such knowledge to yourself."

"Yes, sir," Ravel said. "Sorry, but I thought with you officers it would be safe."

"One never knows. The officer beside you speaks French, but he is American. I realize you cannot see his uniform in the dark, but be more careful in the future."

"American! But that is wonderful!"

"I'm only here as a neutral observer," Ansel replied.

"Ah! But you are here. It is a beginning like the first note of a symphony."

More than twenty miles out from Verdun, the sound of artillery overrode the roar and rattle of the trucks and grew louder with every mile traveled. The horizon was continuously illuminated by red-orange flare-ups of exploding shells mimicking an angry sunrise. Real dawn was still an hour away. Ravel ignored the distant rumbling. "This road can receive artillery fire from remote German batteries, but with no spotters to direct their fire they are not so accurate. Then again, sometimes they get a few rounds right. A large shell can make a hole big enough to swallow a truck. We have 8,000 men who do nothing but repair the road. I'm told they opened nearby quarries and lay down more than 50,000 tons of rock a month to keep the road passable; a little rough, eh, but passable. We are fortunate tonight. As you can see on the horizon, the Boche are busy with another attack. I don't think they will waste shells on us."

They drove through a dying night violated by manmade thunder and lightning. Trepidation ruled the silence of the five men in the motor car.

As dawn melted away the darkness, the convoy entered the town of Soúilly on its way to Brûlé and various supply yards just south of Verdun itself. The corporal turned the staff car out of line and stopped in front of a three-story, stone building the General called *la Mairie de Soúilly* (The town hall of Soúilly).

"I'm afraid this is as far as we go, Corporal Ravel," General Bourget said. "You will have to catch another ride the rest of the way."

"Ah! You must be here at General Neville's headquarters to brief the American on the new German attack."

General Bourget did not respond to the comment. "*Bonne Chance*, Maurice Ravel. May we meet at your first concert after the war."

"Thank you, General. I hope we are both lucky enough to make that meeting." Ravel stepped down from the car, saluted and set out on foot toward Verdun. Ansel watched as the famous composer-come-soldier faded into the swirling dust roiled up by the endless passage of trucks.

(Maurice Ravel would survive the war and return to his music to write the ever popular, Spanish-flavored ballet score, "Boléro," for his friend, Ida Rubinstein, the beautiful and famous Russian dancer and actress.)

Ansel followed Henrí up the stone steps and into the Soúilly town hall that served as Neville's headquarters, and before him, as that of Petain. General Bourget presented identification papers to a sergeant in the entrance hall and stated they had an appointment with General Neville. The Sergeant spoke into a telephone. A few minutes later, an officer descended the stairway from the second floor and introduced himself as Colonel Dubois.

"General Bourget, General Neville sends his regrets. As you must know from the enemy artillery preparation throughout the night, the Germans have launched another attack on the left side of the Meuse. The General is below in the communication center. He has assigned me in his place to brief you and our American guest on the situation here."

"I understand completely, Colonel."

"If you will follow me, gentlemen."

The colonel led them down the hall into a large room, the walls of which were covered with maps and montages of aerial photographs.

The colonel stated, "Twenty-eight forts were built around Verdun after the Franco-Prussian War. Later, we modernized them with steel reinforced concrete and some with steel gun turrets. But then our General Staff asked, 'Why would the Germans attack Verdun?' They didn't see it as having any strategic value. The result was that we stripped some of the twenty-eight forts of their larger guns for use elsewhere and reduced the size of the garrison. The remaining troops looked upon duty here as rather easy and relaxed.

"We had little air reconnaissance in this sector and were totally surprised when the Germans attacked . . . and completely unprepared. Some wanted to let the Germans have it. Verdun forms a salient accessible to artillery fire and attack from three sides. From a military standpoint, some thought it made sense to straighten the line by falling back to prepared defenses. However, the politicians of Paris and the people of France demanded we defend Verdun because of its place in French History. Attila the Hun had been stopped here. When the empire of Charlemagne was divided under the Treaty of Verdun in 843, the town became part of the Holy Roman Empire. More recently, in the Franco-Prussian War, Verdun held out longer than Paris. We now think that General Falkenhayn and the German staff believed that French pride was anchored at Verdun and that we would bleed ourselves white to keep it. Unfortunately, they are proven right."

The colonel moved to the large map on the wall. Using a pointer to trace across the map he explained, "You can see the current lines on both sides of the Meuse marked across this fifteen mile front. The Germans opened battle on the 21st of February by firing 100,000 shells a day on Verdun and the surrounding defenses. Fort Douamont fell on the 25th of February. It is the largest fort, but was lightly defended and bereft of its larger guns, as I explained. Still, its loss was played up in the Paris press as a terrific blow. But in May, the Germans paid a very heavy price to take hill 304, and again on May 29th when they assaulted the highest hill, *Le Mort-homme*. Our French 75s cut them to pieces, but they kept pouring in reserves until they took it. *Le Mort-homme* (the Dead Man) was aptly named. Hundreds, perhaps thousands of dead men lie across no man's land still, theirs and ours, rotting to the bone, for there is no way for either side to collect them. Artillery shells of both sides have churned up every square centimeter of 'no man's land.' Both Frenchmen and Germans were buried alive by the upheaval of earth caused by large shells. Our engineers told us that the height of the hill has been reduced twenty meters by shell fire. The Germans have huge 420 millimeter naval guns on railroad mounts that can fire twenty kilometers. Our largest guns cannot reach them with counter-battery fire.

"Now this month, on June 7th, they took Fort Vaux after seven days of terrible close fighting inside the fort. Major Sylvain-Eugene Raynal, the commander, gave up only after they had run out of drinkable water, ammunition, medical supplies and food. The Germans introduced flame throwers and used them against the men in the fort."

Ansel asked, "What has been the price for, as you stated, French pride?"

The Colonel looked at General Bourget who shook his head from side to side.

"I cannot give you the figures, Captain, but I can say the price for both sides has been very high. We think the Germans are bleeding as much as we are."

"Can you continue to hold?"

"It will be a close thing, but we have no choice. Because this battle has absorbed a large number of our reserves, if Verdun should fall and the Germans break through in force, Paris will be in danger. We are holding, gentlemen. The Germans have been unable to cut the road you traveled, or to enter what's left of Verdun itself. As long as the road to Bar-le-Duc stays open, we will hold."

Ansel asked, "What can change between such costly German attacks and equally costly French counter attacks? I deduce from what you have told me that you cannot continue to take such heavy losses."

Again the colonel looked at General Bourget, who nodded his head up and down.

"An Allied attack is planned along a twenty-mile front on the Somme by British forces supported by French on the left flank. The purpose is to take pressure off Verdun. It is scheduled for August but we need and are urging the schedule to be moved up. We believe to meet the Allied Somme offensive the Germans will have to shift several divisions from the Verdun sector to the Somme. If that relief comes soon enough, we will prevail."

"Now, Captain," Colonel Dubois said, "you of course know that everything you have learned today must be held in utmost confidentiality by you and your government's highest authority. You have been given this information in the belief that it will be of value in preparing your military for entry into this war, hopefully in the near future. The information is not to be disclosed publicly by you or your superiors. You must emphasize to them that should there be a leak to the press, the lives of thousands of British and French troops could result. If a leak occurs, the French government will name you as the source and request your expulsion from France. Should your knowledge, for instance in the form of a report, fall into the hands of German agents here or in America, and we will know if that happens, it is possible you could be arrested as a spy. You see the Deuxieme Bureau de l'Ètat-Major Général, our military intelligence agency, is fully aware that you are a member of your Secretary Lansing's newly formed intelligence organization. I might add that France was astounded to learn that the American Army has no stand-alone intelligence bureau.

"Now, before you request it, Captain, we cannot allow you to proceed any further toward the front. Your assignment, as I understand it, was to observe the organization, operation and importance of logistics to the defense of Verdun. We have allowed you to do that. Do you understand the consequences of betraying the confidence France has placed in you?"

Captain Quinn answered, "I do, sir. And on behalf of my country, I thank you."

"Very well, Gentlemen, I must now leave you. We had planned to treat you to lunch with General Neville, but circumstances regrettably have forced cancellation. On behalf of the General please accept our apology. A picnic lunch of bread, cheese and wine has been delivered to your motor car. Your driver and sergeant were fed at our headquarters field kitchen. I suggest you forthwith insert you motor car into the next passing convoy for Bar-le-Duc. I suspect that the Germans, as part of their attack, will try to interdict the flow of supplies on the road using any long range guns they can spare from their main objective, which we believe to be Fleury on the left bank of the Meuse. *Bonne chance* gentlemen."

The corporal managed to pull into a convoy moving south. Most of the trucks were empty, but a number carried wounded. With the thunder of German artillery in support of the attack on Fleury, no one had to remind the four men in the open staff car to wear their helmets.

(The little town of Fleury-devant-Douaumont was to change hands sixteen times. It was obliterated and made uninhabitable to such an extent that it was never rebuilt. The land around it was never again farmed because of shell holes, unrecovered bodies, and unexploded ordnance. The site would be officially designated the "Village that Died for France," parts of which are still to this day considered too dangerous to walk through.)

Although the returning convoy, of which they were now part, carried nothing lethal, the convoys that continuously passed in the opposite direction were loaded with ammunition, including artillery shells. Where possible, trucks loaded with food, medical supplies, barbed wire or bales of sandbags were interspersed between ammunition loads in an attempt to prevent a chain reaction should an ammunition truck be hit. The lethality of such cargo was made abundantly clear when shells, large shells, began falling a few hundred yards behind the staff car.

"Son-of-a-bitch!" was all Ansel could manage.

Everyone in the motor car bent down reflexively as though making oneself smaller would somehow reduce the effect of large caliber shells hitting close by. The corporal scrunched low looking ahead through the spokes of the steering wheel. Neither the Sergeant nor General Bourget issued a word.

Several hundred yards behind their motor car, two screaming shells straddled the road falling some seventy yards to either side. Even so, the large shells had a shrapnel range that caused casualties and damaged trucks. A third shell hit close enough to one of the ammunition trucks to set off its cargo. The resulting spectacular explosion completely obliterated the truck and destroyed the one in front and the one behind it. In addition, two trucks passing in the opposite direction were blown to smithereens. Both had been loaded with wounded. Several other trucks and their crews were cut to pieces by shrapnel. A number of inert shells were blown into the air without exploding. They rained down within a radius of one hundred yards of the initial explosion severely damaging several trucks. The concussions of the explosions were felt by those in the staff car some five hundred yards away. Road dust was kicked up in a cloud around them as falling chips of crushed stone and spent shrapnel fell, clinking off their helmets like hail. Something heavier bounced off the front left fender leaving a fist-sized dent.

Behind the car in the direction of Verdun, both north- and south-bound convoys were unable to continue due to wreckage and shell craters, one nearly twenty feet across and six feet deep, making the road impassable. Drivers wisely left their vehicles and took cover where they could find it. Although enemy artillery rounds continued to fall in the vicinity of the road, it was obvious that the German battery was firing by map coordinates without benefit of an observer.

As random shells continued to fall, the speed of the mostly empty south-bound convoy increased noticeably, even dangerously, considering the general condition of the road and the endless line of halted north-bound trucks in the opposite lane. No one in the General's car complained.

Dearest Isabel,

I understand your hatred of being married to a soldier far away. This soldier hates it, too. I miss you terribly. I have thought about deserting and swimming home to be with you, but they shoot deserters, at least the French do over here. I also have to be careful about reports I write on all I'm allowed to officially observe, and of course, things I might chance to unofficially observe. The French shoot spies as well as deserters.

Quit worrying about me getting hurt. I am a lowly American staff officer and am not allowed to go to the front. For instance, yesterday I accompanied General Bourget to the headquarters of General Neville who commands the forces at Verdun. His headquarters are in the town of Souilly which is miles from Verdun. We were there for a briefing and were not allowed to get near the front. So you see, I am perfectly safe and you are not to worry.

What I worry about are all those dancing dandies of Memphis who are broken-hearted because I stole you away from them. As for the ladies of Paris, they mean nothing since you stole the heart of this simple Mississippi boy.

Speaking of Paris, everything here is growing scarce; food, coal, gas, and prices keep climbing. The information we get is that things are much worse in Germany due to the British Blockade. It must be working, for the German fleet came out of hiding for the first time and engaged in what was called the Battle of Jutland. Both navies claimed victory, but it was pretty much a draw.

Speaking of shortages, could you send over a big sack of sugar and one of flour, and a case of bourbon? My housekeeper would much appreciate the groceries and a certain soldier would welcome the medicinal alcohol. Also a sack of grits. The French have never heard of them. Your letters seem to be getting through lately in spite of the U-boats taking a toll on shipping. Crossing the Atlantic has gotten more dangerous. That's the main reason I don't want you trying to get over here, that and the fact that someone, meaning you, has to keep an eye on things at home.

Which reminds me, how are you doing now that you are in command of all the Quinn holdings? I bet by the time I get home you will be both the Queen of Shamrock and the Condesa of Cuba.

All my love Your Highness,

Ansel

My Dearest,

Your letters mean the world to me. If any time goes by without receiving a letter from you I panic, worrying if something has happened. Your letters have been getting through in batches every few weeks. I am told the diplomatic mail is shipped on the fast liners that U-Boats rarely have a chance to catch. Of course your letters go to Washington and from there are mailed on to me. I understand all that takes time but it tortures me to wait so long to hear from you.

Have you heard what your former boss, General Pershing, is doing? A Mexican bandit, Poncho something, crossed the border and raided a New Mexico town, burned it down and killed some Americans. President Wilson may not want to send troops to France, but he has sent General Pershing with an expeditionary force across into Mexico. They have been chasing all over the place, but so far have not caught the bandit. They say the Mexican people resent the American force and won't help Pershing.

I am busy. I never knew there was so much to check on here at Shamrock and in Cuba. I get mountains of reports. At first, Daddy helped explain them, but I now have a handle on things. As long as you are away, I like being busy. I have gotten to Memphis only twice to shop since you left. By the way, I'm spending your money now instead of Daddy's. What fun, huh? I have learned to drive and Daddy says I'm good at it.

Lizzy is wonderful and is teaching me how to cook so I won't poison you when you return home.

I wanted to write your commanding officer to see if you were really staying safe and away from any fighting like you tell me you are doing, but Daddy said that would be a bad thing to do and could get you in trouble with the Army. I guess soldiers shouldn't have wives, mothers and, as Daddy said, nannies bothering commanding officers. So you see, I am relying on you, my love, to tell me the truth. God, I miss you. Please, please take care of yourself. You hold my heart.

Isabel

CHAPTER NINETEEN

The Ambassador nodded to Quinn. "I want to commend you on your last report concerning logistics, Captain."

Ansel was seated at a conference table at the American Embassy in the company of Ambassador Sharp, Assistant Second Secretary Andrew Hampton and Military Attaché Major Spenser Crosby.

"We were surprised and pleased that General Bourget felt your invitation to visit General Neville's headquarters near Verdun was important enough to accompany you. We are also sure his purpose was to ensure that you were given no classified information.

"As you reported, the stunning amount of logistical support required for the ongoing battle of Verdun has not been seen by the U.S. Army since the Civil War. I believe it will open the eyes of both the President and the Army General Staff as to the great tasks of logistics that awaits them should the United States enter this war. They have some idea, of course, based on the amount of food stuffs, ammunition, motor vehicles, mules and such being exported to both England and France, but your report of the supply demands for just a fifteen mile battle front, especially your estimation of the artillery shells being used is jaw dropping. Without access to actual casualty reports, we can assume, based on ammunition expended and your observation of reserve or replacement troops moving toward Verdun, that the number is substantial. "However, before the report is forwarded to Secretary Lansing, I have taken the liberty of removing one or two sentences which could be taken as criticism of the Army as regards the example of poor organization of logistics in preparation and transport of materiel prior to and during the Spanish American War. I realize your late father was a witness and recorded firsthand the mistakes and omissions made at the time, but the purpose of the report is to educate and prepare the general staff on the enormous logistical demands that will be made should the U.S. join the Allies in this war and not to criticize the General Staff for its past failings. Likewise I removed your, not so subtle and somewhat indiscrete, suggestion that the present standing army is undermanned, inadequately trained and ill equipped for the type of modern warfare you have witnessed in France. I removed these statements, though I believe them to be true, because it reflects on the General Staff, President Wilson and Congress, none of whom are likely to take kindly to criticism from a captain in the Army regardless of the fact that he has based his findings on firsthand observations at some risk to himself."

Ansel noticed that Major Crosby was smiling while shaking his head from side-to-side in an amused 'I told you so' gesture.

With the three senior men looking at him, Ansel responded, "Thank you, Mister Ambassador. You have saved me embarrassment and no small amount of unpleasant fallout from my indiscretions. I shall omit criticism from future reports, that is, if I am assigned to write any."

"See that you do take such note, Captain. Now, since you brought up the subject of future reports, do you know a certain Major Marvin Falkner of the British Army?"

"Yes sir, I met him on shipboard on the way home on leave."

"What do you know about him?"

"What I know beyond the fact that he is an officer in the British Army, I gave my word not to reveal."

"Very good, Captain. It seems Major Van Deman at Washington Barracks trained you well. We know that you know that Major Falkner is in the British Intelligence Service and that he was on his way to America to encourage and help organize a similar service in America and that he had better results with Secretary of State Lansing than with the Army. You must have impressed Major Falkner for he has issued an invitation through Secretary Lansing for you to visit the British Expeditionary Force holding the line in the area of Flanders. He said he had mentioned that possibility to you."

"Yes, sir, he did although the offer was made in general rather than any specific area."

"I have approved your visit. We are working out the arrangements. Major Crosby will notify you of the details in the near future. Those details and instructions will not, and I repeat, *not* include a visit to the trenches. Our British friends will be so informed. A dead observer will be of no use to us. An American officer found dead or captured at the battle front could cause an international incident. We are not at war with Germany. Do I make myself clear on that point, Captain?"

"Yes sir."

"Major Crosby will temporarily fill in for you at French Army Headquarters. Both the Major and I have met most of the General Staff officers at meetings and social functions, but prior to your departure, would you please show Major Crosby around, including the do's and don'ts. It will be a bit awkward for Crosby, for as you know he does not speak French. Please arrange for an interpreter. Also, I would like for you to introduce him to General Bourget. I feel certain the two will want to compare notes on a certain Lieutenant lately become Captain."

"Yes sir."

"Very well, gentlemen, that about covers it."

"So my secret son is going on another secret mission, this time to observe the British?" Henrí and Ansel were having omelets at Ciro's, a small but popular Italian restaurant located on Rue Daunou.

"If you know that, I guess it's not so secret after all."

"I received word from your embassy that you would be absent for perhaps a week and that Major Crosby, your commanding officer, would pay our headquarters a visit or two in your absence. As an interpreter has been requested, I assume your major does not speak French."

"That's correct."

"Nonetheless, I look forward to having a conversation with the Major."

"That's funny. He expressed the same thing. Since he accompanied me on one trip to the front and you on another, I get the feeling my personnel file may suffer when you two compare notes."

"I think you have a very suspicious mind."

"You both act like nannies—you for fear I might foolishly get myself hurt, and the Major that I might foolishly cause an international incident that would embarrass neutral America."

"Yes, but to change the subject, how is your pretty wife?"

"Isabel is doing well. In fact she is managing my aunt's, I mean my mother's estate better than I could. She would also approve of you and the Major looking out for me. Between the three of you, I rarely get a week free of advice."

"Sounds like a fine woman. I do believe you have married above your station in life."

"Now, on that I can agree."

The waiter brought the check. Ansel looked at it and handed it to the General.

"*Mon pére*, I do believe it is your turn to pay."

"*Mon fils*, do be careful not to get shot," Henrí smiled, "or caught as a spy."

"Since you brought up that subject, I don't suppose you know the casualty figures so far at Verdun."

"You *do* want to get caught as a spy."

"How long will that battle continue?"

"Until the Germans give up and go elsewhere. Verdun will not fall."

The two men, dressed in civilian clothes as usual when they met on weekends, walked out of Ciro's into a sunny, warm June day. Paris smelled of flowers and street apples. Horse drawn carriages, taxis and wagons far outnumbered motorized vehicles.

As they walked toward the taxi stand in front of the Hotel Daunou, Ansel asked, "How is Aileen doing? Gaetan's death was so sad."

"She's coping as well as can be expected. He was very depressed over the loss of so many of his former students. He considered them his children. We should have seen it coming, his suicide I mean. In war, perhaps the worst of suffering is not confined to battle. Those who sit and wait at home suffer, too; those who jump at the ring of the telephone or an unexpected knock on the door; those who read the newspaper with trembling hands as they turn to the latest casualty lists; those who must live with the terrible loss of a loved one. You keep that in mind as you go off on your sightseeing jaunts to the front. Think of your Isabel."

"I do. She doesn't know about the trips. I complain to her in my letters of being stuck in Paris bored out of my mind."

"My young friend, women, be they lovers or wives, always know when their men are lying. I don't know how, but they do. Remember that, and take care of yourself. I'll wait and watch for your return, too, you know."

* * *

Toward the end of June, Ansel informed Tristan and Pauline Babineau that he would be away from the house on Villa Said toward the middle of July.

Pauline asked, "Monsieur Quinn, will you have a going away party like before? Since you returned a married man you have not had one party. Your friends sometimes drop by to say they are worried about you, but I think they just miss your parties."

Tristan added, "I think you disappointed several ladies. They don't call anymore."

"Now Tristan," Pauline scolded, "Monsieur Quinn is a married man. I think it is you, you wicked old man, who misses seeing those pretty young women."

"Well," Tristan answered, "I am a Frenchman."

Pauline took a swipe at him with a dish towel.

"You two cut that out and quit picking on me. What my friends miss, those who are still alive and in Paris, is my wine and whiskey. As for the pretty women, I married the prettiest. Now may I have my supper?"

By two in the afternoon on July 2nd, news of the failure of the British opening offensive to break through on the Somme was filtering in to both French Army Headquarters and the American Embassy. Ansel was briefed on the disaster and received notice that on the 12th of July he was to meet his British escort who was to shepherd him to the Somme area for what was expected to be a second attempt to break the German line.

The Renault taxi pulled to the curb at the Gare du Nord, one of several large train stations in Paris. It was here that trains departed to Northern France and Belgium, and before the war, to Germany and the Netherlands. Ansel stepped down from the taxi carrying a small duffel filled with clothes and gear for the trip. The station was crowded with French troops and a smattering of British troops returning from leave in Paris. Ansel overheard a *poilu* mention Verdun while another group was talking about some village in Belgium. The younger troops were joking and laughing. The older hands, smoking cigarettes or pipes, stood silent, glum. Some of them were complaining bitterly that life in Paris carried on as if there was no war. Ansel surmised the young ones were new replacements while the silent ones were returning to duty from leave or perhaps from a stay in hospital. He figured they knew what awaited them at the front while the young had yet to learn.

Because of his uniform, Quinn garnered curious looks as he passed small groups of *poilus*. They didn't know to what army he belonged. He heard whispers of "Canadian" and "Scotts." Others thought he might be British. As he was trying to make sense of the large schedule board in the cavernous waiting area, a British sergeant approached.

"You must be Captain Quinn, sir. I see no other American officer."

"I'm Quinn, Sergeant."

"Right sir. Major Ravensdale has commandeered a compartment, if you will follow me, Captain."

The Sergeant led Quinn down the platform toward a train made up mostly of forty-or-eights, boxcars designed to carry forty soldiers or eight horses. Attached on the end were two, old, first-class coaches marked "Officers Only." French soldiers, some kissing tearful women goodbye, were loading onto all of the forty-or-eights but two set aside for British troops returning to Flanders from Paris leave.

Ansel followed the Sergeant onto one of the coaches set aside for officers. They stopped at a compartment mid-coach. The Sergeant knocked, opened the door and announced, "Captain Quinn, Major."

Major Ravensdale—a ruddy cheeked, broad shouldered, redheaded man with a stiff, waxed mustache, wearing the uniform of a British officer complete with jodhpurs, riding boots, spurs and Sam Browne belt—rose from the compartment's bench seat.

"Thank you, Sergeant. That will be all."

The Sergeant saluted. "Sir!" He did a smart right face and marched off down the passageway. The Major shook Ansel's hand. "Come in, Captain Quinn. Throw your satchel up in the rack and have a seat. I'm happy to have drawn an American to squire around as opposed to my fellow staff members who drew the Spanish and Romanian observers. It seems all they want to do is look at maps, drink and dine in the officer's mess at General Haig's headquarters at Château de Beaurepaire outside of Montreuil. Damn little they will learn there. I understand you observed actual attacks by the French at Vimy Ridge; a bad show that. I'm afraid we did no better. And you visited Verdun, is that correct?"

"Yes sir."

"Jolly good. You already know a thing or two about this bloody business. I'll see what I can do to make your trip worthwhile. Verdun is what this Somme business is all about; all the idea of the French. The expectation is that our Somme campaign will pull a number of German divisions from Verdun; give the French time to catch their breath. I suppose you've learned of the casualties they have taken; at least 200,000 so far. Don't know how long they can continue to hold at that rate. If they break, there are few French reserves left to stop the Germans from reaching Paris."

Ansel nodded agreement, although he hadn't been informed of the latest number of French casualties and made a mental note of it.

The Major continued, "Anyway, our Somme offensive has bloody well pulled in the Germans." Ravensdale changed the subject. "I hope you've had lunch. The rations for the trip aren't much, but I did manage to bring aboard a few bottles of claret that should do. Normally it wouldn't be too long a trip, but with the constant sequence of supply trains running hardly twenty minutes apart, the going will be slow. It takes as a minimum of three thousand tons of supplies a day to keep the Somme front going. The French depend on 12,000 trucks and a narrow-gauge railroad running along a single-open route to keep Verdun alive. For the British Expeditionary Force on the Somme, it's all railroads from the Channel ports with newly constructed branches and marshaling yards to handle the volume of materiel and troops."

It was at that moment that they heard a shrill whistle announcing their departure was imminent.

The Major doffed his belt and tunic. "We might as well get comfortable, Captain. It will be about a five hour trip to Amiens. We'll arrive after dark, so I've planned for us to overnight at what's left of a hotel there. A car will take us on to Albert. Going on that short distance by train can take hours because of the shuffling of loaded and empty cars in and out of all the newly laid yards and sidings. Oh, and pack away your hat. I've brought along a helmet for you. Yours is the one on the left on the shelf there. You might want to adjust the liner to fit; makes wearing the bloody thing a little more bearable. We'll be wearing them full-time once we get to Amiens."

The train lurched forward into a grey afternoon and made its way through a dingy part of Paris. The smoke billowing from the engine added to the accumulation of cinder and soot coating the buildings and houses along the tracks. Leaving Paris behind, rain began to fall intermittently from the low overcast. Water dribbling dirty streaks down the window blurred Ansel's view of the countryside. For a while, fields appeared lush with summer's greenery. But as they progressed, the destruction of war was evident. They passed small villages still struggling to repair the damage from the German push deep into France in 1914. Later, as the sun began to set, they passed villages that were little more than heaps of rubble. And there was something else, the rumble of distant artillery.

The two drank their first glass of wine mainly in silence. After Major Ravensdale refilled their glasses, he looked at Ansel sitting on the opposite bench, its padding uncomfortably crushed and the upholstery threadbare.

"Tell me, Captain, what will it take to get America into this rotten war?"

"Major, my information is that you are in the King's intelligence service."

"And my information is that you are a member of Secretary Lansing's intelligence service. I suggest that we agree to exchange information as gentlemen. No written notes. Afterward we report as we like without revealing the source. Otherwise, I cannot speak frankly and I suspect neither can you. Are we in agreement on that?"

"Agreed."

"Good. Our mutual friend, Major Martin Falkner, said you could be trusted. Now to my question."

"Nothing will happen until the presidential election in November. Wilson has run on a promise of neutrality. The majority of voters are anti-war, not to mention some nine million immigrants of recent German descent who don't want their new country fighting their old."

"And if he is re-elected?"

"I honestly don't know."

"We had hopes Haig's Somme offensive beginning July 1st would shake the Germans, but the opposite has happened. It will come out sooner than later. The opening attack was a disaster. Roll call at day's end showed no fewer than 57,000 casualties, 19,000 of them killed with no gain to speak of."

"My God!"

"Yes, the British Army's worst day in history."

"Will Haig be canned?"

"I think he should be shot. But no, he will continue as commander of the BEF."

"What went wrong?"

"You repeat what I tell you and I will be shot."

"I will keep our agreement."

"I don't think the bastard has ever gotten beyond Napoleon in military theory. He is a cavalry officer from the old school. He brought up two or three divisions of cavalry and expected to rush them through the big hole he was going to tear into the German line, a line the Germans have been preparing and reinforcing, since late 1914, with deep concrete bunkers and machinegun emplacements and belts of barbed wire ten yards thick with second and third trenches behind the front. Haig is either stupid or incapable of grasping modern industrial warfare. We are in an age where the brave soldier with rifle and bayonet and the courageous cavalryman with saber and lance, no matter the tactics or formations, have little to do with victory. What counts today is the weight in numbers and effectiveness of modern killing machines. Whether in trenches or charging across open fields, the infantryman can be cut down by high intensity fire from distant machineguns and accurate, rapid-fire artillery. The day of the bayonet charge is over. That is something Haig has not learned or refuses to accept. He intends to repeat the same attack all over again. He sets these grandiose objectives miles behind the German front trenches when gaining even 800 yards has rarely been achieved. The high command must believe the answer to trench warfare is attrition—the army that bleeds the most will lose to the army that bleeds the least, and usually it's the attacking army that bleeds the most. Haig has been quoted as calling the losses of July 1st as "not unreasonable in light of the numbers sent forward." Not unreasonable? And how did he send them forward? He sent them forward with sixty-pound packs in straight lines, wave after wave walking across shell-pocked, ankle-deep, muddy terrain. He says men advancing in line are easier to control. The sixty-pound packs were to carry what the troops would need when they advanced several miles on the first day. The man has no ability to think of any other tactics. I believe instead of planning for realistic objectives, Haig dreams of grand, decisive battles, war-winning battles, and he blames the fighting men instead of his plans when they cannot reach the distant objectives he sets. The man still believes deep cavalry charges can be made if only his infantry will open the German lines. Then there are the reports that the artillery barrage did not cut the German wire in most places. My God! Cavalry charges across shell-pocked ground, against machine guns, artillery and belts of barbed wire ten yards deep."

"I heard our Civil War is studied at your military academy."

"It is."

"Then Haig must have skipped the battle at Cold Harbor. Grant sent his army against the entrenched Confederates who cut down 7,000 Union troops in twenty minutes, and they had no machineguns, just muzzle loading rifles. Hell, before it was over Grant lost more men at Cold Harbor than Lee had defending his trenches.

"I learned from Paris headquarters that the French learned from their tactics at Vimy Ridge. They now employ their artillery in a rolling barrage moving the shells forward just ahead of the infantry, shielding them by keeping the Germans in their deep bunkers until the French are upon them. They have had some success with that. I know they committed fewer men than the British on the first day of the Somme, but using the new tactics they reached their objectives and lost less than 2,000 men."

"Yes, Captain, I am aware of that. The French have had some success using a tactic they call 'bite and hold' in which, Unlike Haig, they don't plan great offensives with objectives six miles deep. I also have to admit the French artillery is better than ours, more experienced and more accurate. As for keeping the Germans in their bunkers, I heard that Haig's artillery shifted from the first German trench to the second ten minutes early for fear of hitting their own men. Those ten minutes gave the Germans plenty of time to come up from their deep bunkers and set up their machine guns. The troops who got to the German trench found the wire had not been cut as promised—not cut after seven days of artillery fire, after a million shells. Can you believe it? Do you know why? Eighty percent of our ammunition was shrapnel shells. Shrapnel kills men but does not cut wire and does not destroy bunkers and trenches. High-explosive shells cut wire and blow up trenches. In addition, I have learned that Haig did not put emphasis on counter-battery fire, preferring to concentrate all his guns on the German first and second trenches and even deeper. As a result, the German artillery was untouched and had a field day cutting down our retreating men." The Major was red-faced and his hands were shaking with anger as he finished.

"Is Haig going to be relieved?"

"He is commander of the whole British Expeditionary Force. Who's going to fire him at the beginning of a new offensive, the prime minister?" The Major paused, "Captain you are in intelligence for your country. I've given you information. You may repeat what I've told you, but if you credit me we'll both be shot. I'm telling you all this because I believe your country must and will come to our aid. We are already worried about Russia. It may collapse. If it does, the Germans will have a million men to move from the Eastern Front to throw against the West. If that happens, and your country is not here to help stop them, all Europe will be in German hands.

"Now that being said, pay attention to this advice. Your army must learn from our mistakes. And even more important, when America comes over here your forces must fight as a separate army under American and *only* American command. Not under some arrogant butcher like Haig, or Joffre for that matter. The Germans fear a fresh American army willing to fight. Haig will want to simply use your troops as replacements to be fed willy-nilly into the bloody British frontline. The French will try the same thing. By Jove, don't let them!"

The Major opened a new bottle of wine, refilled their glasses and grew silent. The train rumbled into the night.

When they disembarked at *Amiens*, Ansel followed the Major's lead and donned his steel helmet. It was painted matte khaki and weighed about a pound and a half. The dull, persistent rumble of artillery had grown sharper, much closer.

"That's normal harassment fire exchanged by both sides most nights," the Major explained. "Unless a target has been registered in daylight, it's not too effective since it cannot be accurately adjusted in the dark, but it deprives men of sleep and over time depresses morale."

"Well it's working as far as I'm concerned. I can't imagine what it must be like for men living night after night under bombardment."

"Most get used to it. Some go stark raving mad," the Major replied in a dispassionate manner that closed the subject. Ansel and Ravensdale, wearing helmets and carrying their own kits, stepped down from the train, walked across the platform, through the bomb-damaged Amiens station and to the Belfort Hotel situated barely a hundred yards distance.

The hotel clerk, a small man with gray hair and goatee, had a nice smile but bad teeth. Both he and his black suit smelled of cigarette smoke and garlic. His wrinkled forehead gave him an enduring expression of worry. He told the Major he had saved two rooms for him on the upper floor.

"Don't you have anything lower?" Ravensdale asked.

"I am sorry Sir. I had a difficult time saving even those rooms for you. A new Australian battalion arrived a few hours ago. The colonel commanding ordered me to billet all thirty officers here. With eleven rooms unusable due to damage, I managed to save the only two undamaged rooms on the top floor for you, Sir."

The Major turned to Ansel. "Well, Captain, it's the fourth floor for us." The two officers walked toward the stairs.

"What's wrong with the top floor besides the walk up?" Ansel asked.

"Occasionally on moonlit nights the Kaiser's airmen come over to bomb the rail yard. It's easy for them to miss by more than a hundred yards, which puts the hotel in their circle of error. They've dropped short a few times, and that's why there are only two undamaged rooms left on the top floor and no glass in the windows on the back side of the building. Welcome to Flanders, Captain. If the air raid bell goes off, don't get in my way in the dash for the basement."

There were no air raids during the night, but the hotel dining room was overwhelmed the next morning. Even the little desk clerk and the room maids were drafted for duty serving breakfast to the thirty officers, all short on time and anxious to move their battalion out.

Ravensdale, eager to locate their car and driver and get on the road for Albert, hurried Ansel through breakfast. He wanted to get ahead of the infantry battalion moving on foot, followed by its horse-drawn baggage, ammunition, supply and field kitchen carts and wagons.

It took about an hour and a half to travel the fifteen miles to Albert due to traffic and muddy condition of the road. Just before reaching the town, they passed by an artillery park located some hundred yards off the road. The guns were dug in and well hidden under camouflage.

"That battery is a problem for poor Albert. German shells, hunting blindly for the battery, sometimes fall in the town."

The battery fired a salvo as the staff car passed. Both Ansel and the Major ducked down in the back seat.

The corporal driving them chuckled, "You gentlemen will get used to such after a day or two living up here."

There was no comment from the back seat.

The town had been ravaged by artillery, first by Germans in 1914 and later by the British and French in retaking the town. Whole blocks had been reduced to rubble and charred timbers. The buildings and houses left standing had not survived undamaged. The railroad station was completely destroyed, though the rail yard had been repaired and enlarged. It was full of boxcars being unloaded by labor battalions and busy with locomotives shuffling empty cars to make up returning trains while loaded trains arrived, all in a never ending cycle. Ansel was surprised to see citizens moving about a few patched-up shops, restaurants and markets and generally getting on with their lives in spite of the fact that Albert was only three miles from the front lines. The town was famous for the Basilica of Notre-Dame de Brebières with a golden stature of the Virgin Mary holding the baby Jesus atop its massive square tower. In 1915, believing artillery spotters were using the tower, German guns had partially destroyed the basilica and holed the tower knocking over the famous statue but not destroying it. The Golden Virgin, as it was called, lay suspended horizontally out from the crown of the tower.

Passing the basilica, Major Ravensdale pointed up to it. "The superstition among the soldiers is that the statue won't fall until the war ends."

"It looks as if it will fall any minute. What's holding it up there?"

"Somehow the base remained anchored. I've heard a couple of engineers went up there to reinforce the attachment in an attempt to keep it from falling and killing someone, but who knows? Maybe the soldiers are right and she's not coming down 'til it's over."

"Where to now, Major?"

"We are going underground to give you a look at one of our largest telephone communication centers set up in a basement. It's connected to every unit along five miles of the front. The lines are often cut by artillery or raiding parties. That keeps the repair crews busy. Theirs is dangerous work, often tracing wires out in the open to find the breaks and splice them back together. We'll spend the night in an officers' bunker next to the center. The best we can do for food will be fare from the field kitchen."

More wires than Ansel had ever seen snaked into a basement filled with operators seated at switchboards labeled by sectors and units, all of them busy. In addition there were radio operators bent over sets with glowing dials. "How on earth do you sort all this out and keep track of which wires lead where?" Over the cacophony of voices, a sergeant showed Ansel a map and talked of how the system was built. At the end of the lecture Ansel told his guide, "I understand a company running phone lines to battalion and so forth, this is way over my head, Sergeant. I'd hate to think what an enemy heavy shell could do to all this."

"Jesus, Mary and Joseph preserve us, Sir. Let's not be tempting the Devil with such a thought."

After the tour of the center, Major Ravensdale and Quinn took supper at the nearest field kitchen and retired to the officers' bunker. There they were welcomed by a Captain Rawles.

"Welcome gentlemen. Throw your kits on those bunks in the corner and join me for a beer." The bunker was large enough to accommodate eight officers in four double-deck bunks. It was illuminated by a lantern suspended from a low ceiling made of heavy timbers. The bunker had bare dirt walls. It smelled of sweat, kerosene, candle wax, soiled bedding, damp wool, gun oil, tobacco smoke, and the musty odor common to dirt caves.

Rawles motioned to a small field table set in the center of the underground room. "Grab a cup off the shelf over there."

Ravensdale and Ansel picked cups off a wood shelf set into the wall and sat down on ammunition crates that served as benches around the table. Rawles removed the top from a 'dixie', British slang for a metal container used for soup, coffee, food, or in this case, beer. It was large enough to serve several men. "Dip a cup full and tell me what brings an American officer to this lovely part of the world."

"I'm here as a neutral observer and Major Ravensdale is my nanny."

"Well, cheers, Gents. Here's to the next man to die."

The three took a long draft of beer.

Ravensdale grimaced, "French beer is enough to make a drinking man pro-German." Captain Rawles laughed. "Beats horse piss, but not by much." Looking at Ansel he offered, "It won't be betraying the secrets act by giving you a tip this late in the day. There is a show on for tomorrow you might want to observe."

Major Ravensdale spoke up. "I've been told to keep our American friend away from the trenches."

"I understand, Major, but I have in mind a bit of woods a little over 1,800 yards behind our front parapets. An Australian battalion acting as reserve support will be moving in among the trees there about midnight. Their job will be to saunter down the slope and fill the trenches vacated by the troops going over on the attack. We wouldn't want to leave the front trenches vacant in case of counter attack. The edge of the woods should be a reasonably safe observation point. We'll borrow an artillery spotter's scope for you, if you are game."

"That's what I'm here for, Captain. How about it Major?"

"Eighteen hundred yards is just over a mile. That seems reasonable."

"Then I suggest we turn in gentlemen," Captain Rawles said. "Call will be at 03:30 to get you to the observation post before dawn. We don't want any movement in daylight up there before the show starts in case one of their spotter planes gets through. I'll have my corporal guide you there. He has to check on the communication line to an artillery observation post in the same area."

The date was 13 July 1916.

CHAPTER TWENTY

Major Ravensdale and Captain Quinn arrived at the wood before dawn and were introduced to the commanding officer of the Australian Battalion, Lieutenant Colonel Lionel Westfield. He called on First Sergeant Taylor to guide them to a spot at the forward left edge of the wood.

The Sergeant led them to the position and addressed the Major. "Here you won't be in the way of the troops when we jump off. From this observation point, I believe you will have a view from right to left of about 2,000 yards of the front and with your scope you should be able to follow the attack across 'no man's land' to the German first trench. You'll want to keep the sun shades extended on the lenses of your scope there. You wouldn't want the sun's reflection on the lens to give away your position, sir. They surely would suspect you were spotting for the artillery."

"Thank you, Sergeant."

"We will leave a few mates up here at battalion headquarters set about a hundred yards behind you. They will have water and rations if you need any. Can you find your way back to Albert when you've seen enough?"

"We'll be fine, Sergeant," the Major replied. "Thank you and give our compliments to your colonel."

"Yes sir. And may I say, we are glad to see an American here, Captain. Hope you'll tell your mates back home how much we need them."

Sergeant Taylor saluted and returned to his company.

Shortly after dawn, Ansel heard the drone of engines in the sky and looked up to see five airplanes. He assumed the four smaller ones were fighters escorting the larger one he thought must be an observation plane. They were too high to see the insignia, but they were crossing over from the German lines. It was 06:30 and the sun had broken over the horizon. Quinn returned to adjusting his scope when he heard a distant rat-tat-tat of machines guns above. Ansel looked up to see six fighter planes swooping down on the observation flight. Two planes immediately broke away trailing smoke. The observation plane fled toward the German lines as two more of the fighters in the aerial melee broke away, one descending for the German lines and the other for the British.

Ravensdale said, "Quinn, if you are set, I'm going up to battalion headquarters. These Australians were at Gallipoli before being shipped all the way here; that's why they're under strength and held in reserve. They lost some three hundred men to the Turks over there and have received no replacements yet. I want to talk to Colonel

Westfield and learn first-hand how the fighting on both sides was conducted over there. I'll join you back here when the show starts."

"I'm set here, Major. No need to hurry back."

Under cover of the trees, Major Ravensdale walked off toward Westfield's head-quarters. The general offensive was to begin at 0730. Right on time, Quinn, looking through his scope,

saw the British troops in the first trench go "over the top" in two staggered lines, moving out across the cratered, muddy 'no man's land.' By the time the second wave went over, the first was receiving machinegun fire while artillery shells began to drop in on them. Troops from the third trench had moved forward and were going over the top to form the third wave.

Behind Ansel the Australian troops broke past him to the right and out of the woods at a run, one line after another streaming down the slope toward the empty trenches. Two men carrying a large drum suspended between them reeled off tele-phone wire as they went. Ansel assumed they would open telephone communication back to their battalion headquarters in the woods. Just before the lead Australians reached the reserve trench, artillery shells began to rain down on the first trench line and began to walk steadily up the slope catching the advancing Australians in the open with horrific effect.

As the bombardment continued its lethal walk toward him, Ansel quickly turned to move into the trees. There was no other place to seek shelter. He saw Ravensdale moving toward him shouting his name, waving Ansel toward him. A second later another shell exploded fifty yards to Ansel's right front. His optic nerve registered a bright flash, his body was hit by a shrapnel-filled, crushing, concussive wave that lifted him off his feet . . . and then . . . nothing.

CHAPTER TWENTY-ONE

HMHS (His Majesty's Hospital Ship) *Western Australia* had the most unusual history of any hospital ship in the British Navy. Originally built in Trieste as a hospital ship for Russia named *Mongolia*, she was captured by the Japanese during the Russo-Japanese War of 1904–05. She was later sold to Austria. After the start of the Great War, she was captured by the Australians in the Pacific and turned over to the British who brought her home via Suez. In a shipyard on the River Clyde, the old girl was refurbished and put into service as a cross-channel hospital ship. Her stacks were painted yellow, her hull and superstructure white except for a huge red cross painted on both her sides amidships. Last, she was given her new name honoring her bene-factor Australia.

At the port of Rouen, *Western Australia* was loaded with the seriously wounded delivered by hospital train from casualty clearing stations and field hospitals behind the British Somme and Ypres fronts. All the patients aboard had sustained what their fellow soldiers called 'Blighty' wounds; the term 'Blighty' being army slang for a wound that would get you sent to Blighty, meaning England, rather than a wound that would get you rehabbed at one of the field hospitals and sent back to duty. In actuality, most recipients of 'Blighty' wounds did not consider themselves as lucky as talk in the trenches made them out to be. Somewhere along the way all the patients had exchanged their filthy uniforms for hospital pajamas. They all wore small brown envelops hung by string lanyards around their necks that held identification listing name, rank, number and outfit.

On 21 July, *Western Australia* sailed down the Seine past Le Havre into the English Channel where she was met by a Royal Navy escort comprised of two 'P' class patrol boats, converted mine sweepers redesigned to hunt submarines.

Once the patients were settled in, the four doctors aboard began making rounds while two surgeons worked in the ship's operating room repairing bleeding wounds, removing newly discovered gangrenous flesh or operating to try and mend shattered bones to save amputation where they could.

Ward nurse, Miss Gordon, accompanied a Doctor Evans into the large ward on the main deck. Together they worked their way down the beds on the starboard side, the doctor reading patients' charts, asking questions of the nurse and those patients able to respond, and repeating the process down the port side. There were many ghastly wounds: amputees, double amputees, broken and shattered bones, shrapnel and bullet wounds, damaged internal organs, head, facial and eye wounds. (The badly burned and men with terrible facial wounds were isolated in smaller wards.) The doctor tried not to disturb those sleeping or under sedation unless there was indication of bleeding or problems of breathing, the latter often due to exposure to poison gas.

They stopped at a bed about midway down the port side of the ward. The patient's forehead was bandaged and there was a sutured cut that ran from the lower jaw on the right side almost to his right ear. A small amount of dried blood was evident in the ear. The patient's upper chest was wrapped and some bleeding evident on the upper left side. The nurse pulled down the bed sheet to allow the doctor to examine a large bandage held in place by a wrapping around the thigh almost at the hip. A fist-sized indentation in the contour of the thigh indicated a loss of flesh and muscle.

Doctor Evans looked at the patient's chart. "The wound on the anterior of the thigh was deep, but luckily did not break the femur. The wound had been irrigated with sodium hypochlorite and debrided, a lot of dead tissue excised. Some nerve damage is expected. He will have quite a large scar, but they saved the leg and prevented infection." The doctor continued interpreting the scribbling on the chart to the nurse. "The chest wound must have been caused by a bullet or small piece of shrapnel. Whatever it was managed to go straight through without hitting bone and missed the lung. The six inch cut on the right cheek is deep, touched the jawbone slightly as well as the cheekbone, but did not fracture either. It was well irrigated and stitched. There seems to be no infection. He will have a nice scar, but he still has all his teeth. There was bleeding from his right ear indicating a perforated ear drum. The bleeding was not severe. The ear may heal itself . . . or not. He took a blow to the head, but the hospital X-Ray did not reveal a fracture. Still, he's obviously suffered a brain concussion. Has he been unconscious like this since he was wounded?"

"He has been like this since he was brought aboard. We have had to feed him through a rubber tube. He mumbles sometimes and we can see his eyes moving under the lids, but he has not responded to us yet."

The doctor referred back to the chart. "All in all, Miss Gordon, this young man is lucky to have made it this far." Doctor Evans turned to move to the next bed, but the nurse stopped him.

She whispered, "This one is special, Doctor."

"Special?"

The nurse went to the bedside stand, opened the drawer and removed a small brown envelope on a string lanyard. It was the patient's casualty tag.

"You need to see what's inside, Doctor."

Doctor Evans opened the envelope and emptied it into his hand. There was a round metal disk about one and a quarter inch in diameter with a name, rank and the letters U.S.A. stamped into the metal and a hole for a string lanyard. The doctor examined it closely. "My word! I believe this is a U.S. Army dog tag. What in the world was American Army Captain Jonathan A. Quinn doing at the Somme?"

"I have no idea, Doctor."

"Why are we whispering?"

"I just thought the fact that an American soldier was wounded at the Somme best be kept quiet until the authorities sort it out, don't you agree. Everyone wants the

Americans to join in the fight and we wouldn't want to do anything to discourage that, now would we? Yet here we've somehow gone and got an American soldier wounded."

The doctor replaced the tag in the envelope and returned it to the bed stand drawer. He hung the chart on the hook at the foot of the bed. "Do you suppose the authorities have been notified, the Americans I mean, perhaps their embassy?"

"I don't know, Doctor. You are the first officer to see him since we received him aboard."

"Surely someone at the casualty dressing station or the field hospital must have done so; they put this dog tag in the envelope."

"I doubt they noticed. I have served in those places and they get hectic after a battle with hundreds of wounded arriving. There's hardly time to worry about anything but the poor men coming through."

"You are quite right, Miss Gordon. I'll follow up on this one."

American Embassy, Paris, 21 July 1916

The telephone on Major Crosby's desk rang.

"Major Crosby," he answered.

"This is General Bourget, Major. Can you tell me if Captain Quinn has returned from his tour of the English front? We expected him to report back to us two days ago."

"General, he has not returned. Ambassador Sharp is checking with the British Embassy. I suspect he stayed over to analyze the battle of the fourteenth which he may have observed. I will let you know as soon as we have information on him."

"Thank you Major."

The line went dead.

American Embassy, Paris, 22 July 1916

Major Crosby stood in front of Ambassador Sharp's desk. Sharp, with a deeply disturbed look on his face announced, "Major, I have just received a coded message over the channel cable from Walter Page, our ambassador in England. He has received word that American Captain Jonathan A. Quinn is aboard a hospital ship transporting wounded from the Somme to England. At the moment, the ship is anchored in the fog off the Isle of Wight but is expected to dock later today at Southampton. Ambassador Page is doing everything possible to keep that fact from the British press. We don't know his condition but Page has made arrangements for Quinn to receive the best treatment available. British intelligence will meet the ship and provide cover for him. He will be admitted under an assumed name to the Royal National Orthopedic Hospital at 234 Great Portland Street, London, W. Arrangements are being made to give him a private room that will be marked 'quarantine' to hopefully keep away the curious."

"Do you want me to go there, Ambassador?"

"That would be awkward. Questions would be asked about an American Major visiting a British officer in hospital."

"What about Major Ravensdale? He was Quinn's escort. Have you been able to reach him?"

"Ambassador Page is using his contacts in England to trace Major Ravensdale. Page has sent a query through the British Foreign Office to General Rawlinson at British Fourth Army Headquarters at Querrieu near Amiens. To date he has not received a reply. As you know, Ravensdale was with British Army Intelligence. I get the impression they are very closemouthed about their operations and personnel.

"In the meantime I have received a request from General Bourget to meet with me this afternoon. The General indicated he has information he feels he should share with us. I expect it may concern Quinn. He requested to meet alone with me."

General Henrí Bourget was ushered into Ambassador Sharp's office and invited to be seated on a worn, leather couch. Sharp sat in a dark blue wingchair facing him. Speaking French, Ambassador Sharp offered, "Would you care for coffee, General?" When the offer was declined, the Ambassador dismissed his secretary. Once alone the Ambassador asked, "*Vous avez des informations pour nous, Général?*"

Bourget answered, "First I must ask you to understand that my identity as the source of this information must be kept confidential."

"Agreed General, you have my word."

General Bourget began. "We at French Army Headquarters not only respect the professionalism of Captain Quinn, but have grown to like him on a personal basis. When he did not report to his post with us, and I learned from Major Crosby that you had not been able to reach him or know of his whereabouts, I feared the worst. We knew, of course, that the British offensive on the Somme continued with a new attack on the fourteenth. I have contacts in the British Army including British Intelligence. I called in favors owed me. Captain Quinn was invited to visit as a neutral observer on the British front in the vicinity of Albert. This is true?"

The Ambassador acknowledged that he had approved the mission.

Bourget continued, "We know that he was with a Major Ravensdale and that the schedule included a firsthand look at the enormous problems of supply and a visit to the army telephone communication center at Albert. I have also learned that Ravensdale obtained permission for him and Quinn to set up an observation post to monitor the Fourth Army attack on the morning of 14 July. I have reliable information that the location approved was at the edge of a wood over a mile behind the British front line. Those involved in that decision considered a location that far behind the front line to be reasonably safe. The observation post was set up in darkness and under the cover of a small cove of trees, one of the few left standing. That same night an Australian battalion moved under the cover of the same wood to act as reserve with orders to move into the trenches at their immediate front vacated by the attacking forces. It was reported that a German reconnaissance plane was seen over the area just after sunrise on the 14th. We do not know if the reserve battalion in the woods was spotted. What we do know is that at 07:30 the Australian battalion moved out of the woods down the mile long open slope to fill the trenches being vacated by the first, second and third attacking waves going over the top. Almost simultaneously, the trenches received a massive concentration of artillery fire that rapidly walked up the open ground and onto the advancing Australians. Trees were pollarded down to bare trunks standing like splintered poles, some cut clear to the ground. The Australian battalion never reached the front trench. The battalion's original strength of twenty officers and 650 men was reduced to four officers and 115 men. When the barrage lifted, stretcher bearers searched among the bodies for the wounded. Out of more than 550 Australian casualties, only 120 were found alive. We pray that Captain Quinn was among the wounded so retrieved. We do know that neither his name nor Major Ravensdale's were listed among the dead. However, I must report that some eleven Australians are listed as missing. Since none could have been taken prisoner, it can only be assumed that the missing were blown to unidentifiable pieces. Of course the Major and Captain Quinn were not on the battalion's roll.

"If Captain Quinn was recovered along with the Australian wounded, he would have arrived at the 36th Casualty Clearing Station at Heilly. No record of a Ravensdale or Quinn was listed at the clearing station, but that is not unusual when several hundred wounded arrive from the front at one time. It could have been there that Quinn's uniform was hastily removed to initially clean and dress any wounds and his identification quickly put into a casualty tag envelope without anyone taking special notice due to the large number of casualties arriving after the battle. From there, the more seriously wounded were sent to the hospital at Amiens, either the one set up for officers in the Lycee Sainte Famille Girls School or the larger nearby hospital in the Sainte Famille Convent. At these hospitals men receive more extensive care: re-examination of wounds, X-Rays, further surgery, and fresh bandages. In any case, as quickly as possible the badly wounded, the ones that cannot be returned to duty, were sent by hospital train to Rouen and loaded on a hospital ship bound for Southampton. We can hope that Captain Quinn is among them. In any case, there is no Captain Quinn or Major Ravensdale listed among recent burials at the Clearing Station cemetery or the cemeteries at the hospitals in Amiens. That is all I have, Ambassador. You are in a position to learn more than I can from this point on. I would very much appreciate your keeping me informed of any information concerning Captain Quinn."

Ambassador Sharp took a moment to contemplate the information the General had given him and whether or not to reveal the information he had received from Ambassador Page that morning.

"General, you seem to have more than professional interest in Captain Quinn."

"That is true Ambassador. I have grown fond of him. We sometimes have dinner together."

"You have been straightforward in presenting confidential information to us. I will now return the courtesy. General, we can only surmise that Captain Quinn must be seriously wounded, but we do know that he is alive."

In spite of long practiced self-control under stress, Henrí Bourget let out a breath in what was almost a sob, but quickly regained the somber expression of an interested listener.

Ambassador Sharp caught the incident, but continued seamlessly. "I received a coded message from the American Ambassador in London that confirmed that Captain Quinn is on board a hospital ship, but we have no details of his condition. The English are cooperating in trying to keep the incident under wraps. You can imagine what the diplomatic consequences would be if it was reported that an American soldier was wounded in battle at the Somme. The German embassy in Washington would unleash protests along with a propaganda extravaganza. You can envision the fallout President Wilson would have to contend with politically with the presidential election only four months away. He has campaigned on the fact that he has kept American boys out of the war. Then there is Ambassador James Gerard at the American Embassy in Berlin. If this matter can be kept secret, Ambassador Gerard will not be informed of this situation. We have reason to believe that telephone lines in Berlin are not secure and we suspect that security at the American Embassy in Wilhelm Platz may have been breached. Then there is British Army Intelligence to consider. They arranged Quinn's visit. As you know, he was escorted by their man, a Major Ravensdale, whom we have not been able to locate. Until your visit this afternoon, we had no knowledge as to Captain Quinn's movements from the time he left Paris. We knew nothing of the circumstances you have revealed and we are deeply grateful.

"General, our information is that Captain Quinn will be taken from a hospital ship that will dock this afternoon at Southampton and be admitted to the Royal National Orthopedic Hospital in London. To hide his identity, he will be isolated in a private room under an assumed name and the rank of Captain in the British Army. That is all we know at present. I can tell you General that we have grown fond of the young captain ourselves. According to Secretary Lansing, his detailed reports and analyses have been invaluable."

Bourget responded, "Ambassador, when you receive positive information of his condition, do you plan to inform his wife? I am sure that to know something, anything would be better than not hearing from him at all over an extended period. He also has a house here in Paris that has long belonged to his family. Friends are sometimes allowed to use it. It would be best if some explanation of his absence could be established. I have visited there and know his housekeepers. I can contact them when you inform me it is permissible to do so."

Ambassador Sharp replied, "I suppose for the moment we could inform his housekeepers that he is on an extended assignment to England. That should dampen any calls by friends or queries by the house keepers. I agree that you are the best man to handle that. For the time being, we will inform his wife with a similar story until we know his condition and prognosis and what to do with him. He may be fit to return to duty, or not. We will have to determine how and when to explain the situation to her." Ambassador Sharp nodded and stood, indicating the meeting was over. "Please accept my sincere thanks for your information and cooperation. We will reciprocate with any further information we receive. The situation now is in the hands of our ambassador in London."

The General left the embassy wondering if he had revealed just how much he cared about Ansel and how terribly worried he was.

Nurse Gordon, checking on the American patient, noticed his eyes moving under the lids. They occasionally lifted partially only to close quickly. She had seen it many times; live eyes, unconscious patients. She always wondered what they were seeing, especially those who moaned or mumbled. Were they fighting their way back, simply having dreams, or reliving traumatic experiences? She put her ear close to Ansel's mouth but could not make anything of the mumbling. *What is this boy seeing?* She moved away to tend other patients.

Isabel, why are you just standing there? Are you angry? Talk to me! You are fading away. Don't go Isabel! Don't go!

Shamrock is burning! Bethany you are too close to the fire.

Henrí how did you get here to Shamrock?

There they go over the top.

Machineguns! Machineguns are cutting them down.

Don't fall in the creek, Isabel! The water is so cold.

Artillery! It's walking toward us. Get down!

Light! Blinding Light!

Are there voices? Screaming voices?

Am I dying Isabel?

Ringing . . . what is that ringing?

Ansel Quinn's eyelids fluttered open for an instant, closed, opened again.

Ansel's vision encompassed a near-blinding, bright white world. He shut his eyes. He could hear nothing. He had a splitting headache.

Where the hell am I?

He opened his eyes again and slowly comprehended a white ceiling above him. His vision was blurred. He looked down and could see white bed covers and the foot of an iron bed. Through the brightness he could barely make out beds and windows against a white wall across the way. He became sharply aware of pain. He turned his head to the left and saw a man lying covered in white sheets looking at him.

The man called out, "Nurse," then louder, "Nurse!" *Footsteps coming?*

"He's awake, Nurse. He looked at me."

God I hurt! Can't move my right leg!

A woman dressed in white with a red cross on the front of her bib apron took his wrist in her hand and spoke to him.

"Well, Captain, welcome back to the world. We are so happy to see you with us finally." She called to a second nurse tending a patient across the way. "Get Doctor Evans. This patient has finally come around."

Damn! I'm in a hospital!

He saw a face looking down and speaking but barely picked up a word or two with his left ear. He couldn't hear anything but ringing in his right ear.

"Ma'am, I can't hear you. Could you speak a little louder?"

The face, speaking much louder, "I know you must be in pain. The doctor is on his way and will give you something to help that. You are going to be just fine, Captain, but it will take a while to get you fit again."

"Do you feel it, Nurse?"

"Feel what, Captain?"

"The room is moving, rocking. Are we having an earthquake?"

"No." She smiled. "There is no earthquake. This is a hospital ship, Captain. We will be docking at Southampton in just a little while."

"Ship? But I'm expected back in Paris tomorrow night on the 15th."

"Captain, today is the 22nd. You are going to a hospital in London as soon as we dock."

"Is Major Ravensdale here? I was with Ravensdale near Albert just a moment ago."

"I don't know of a Major Ravensdale. And you couldn't have been with him a moment ago. Your chart shows you left a clearing station in the Albert area for a hospital in Amiens on the 15th and then by hospital train to Rouen and this ship on the 20th."

"I'm a little confused. I don't remember much about Albert; a bent gold stature. Things are a bit jumbled. A little while ago, I thought I was talking to my wife."

"You have been through a lot. Give yourself a little time. Things will come into focus. You'll see. Here comes the doctor."

Doctor Evans, followed by a nurse carrying a tray, approached the bed.

"Good to see you awake, Captain." The doctor checked Ansel's vitals.

Nurse Gordon said, "You need to speak up a little, doctor. He cannot hear well."

"How do you feel?" The doctor asked in a louder voice.

Ansel licked his lips and tried to lift his head, but pain shot through his brain. "I hurt all over, Doctor, but my head feels like it's splitting."

"I can understand that. You took a blow to the head. We're going to give you a sedative that will ease your pain a little, but not too much at first. I know you are in a lot of pain, but we want you to stay awake a little while. You have been unconscious for days. I know it's uncomfortable for you, but stay with us for a while. We don't want you to slip back into a coma. The nurse will bring you a little real food, soup and hot tea. Then later, if you are doing all right, we will give you something stronger for the pain."

The doctor took a syringe from a tray the assistant nurse was holding and injected a measured amount of morphine into Ansel's arm.

"I can't remember. I'm trying to remember what happened. We got to Albert. I remember that."

"Now don't aggravate your memory. There will be plenty of time to remember later. What is important now is for you to get better."

"Doctor, I need to contact my commander in Paris and get word to my wife. She will be worried. She hates me being in the Army, you know."

"Captain, you will have to take that up with American officials in England. I am sure they will help you."

"They will probably shoot me for getting into this mess." Although Ansel smiled, he was sure they would like to do so for the trouble he had caused.

The doctor chuckled, wrote something on Quinn's chart and, with his attending nurse, moved on to other patients. Nurse Gordon left to fetch soup and tea.

Ansel was in a state of confusion over what had happened and where he found himself. The injection of morphine eased the pain a little, but made it hard to think. He turned his head to the left and was shocked to see a sleeping patient missing an arm. Ansel immediately began to survey the origins of his pain. He was almost afraid to look.

He felt the bandage on the side of his face and the one that circled his head. He had to strain to look down enough to see a compress high on the left side of his chest held in place by gauze strapped completely around his upper body. He thought he felt the bulge of another compress held in place on his back by the same wrapping. His right leg was throbbing near his hip. He couldn't feel the leg below the knee. He used his right hand and arm to throw the covers back far enough to see a large bandage wrapped from above his knee all the way up his thigh where it joined the hip. It was blood stained. *Why can't I feel my foot?* He could see a lump under the covers where his foot should be. Near panic, he commanded his big toe to wiggle. The sheet moved. *Halleluiah!* With relief he realized his right leg, though numb, was still there. That thought suddenly brought on another moment of panic. He reached between his legs, close beside the bandage wrapped around his thigh, and was greatly relieved to find he had all the parts that belonged there.

Ansel pulled the sheet back in place and rested his head on his pillow. *I seem to be all here.*

That thought helped his pain almost as much as the shot of morphine.

Nurse Gordon returned carrying a tray upon which was a bowl of broth with rice, a cup of hot tea, a soup spoon, a teaspoon, a small pitcher of cream, sugar bowl and a napkin.

"Sugar and cream in your tea Captain?"

"Yes ma'am. Thank you."

"If I help, do you think you can sit up a bit?"

He made the effort and it caused him to cry out, but once propped up on pillows an initial sharp pain to his left side subsided. He still had a throbbing headache.

"I guess I'm a little weak."

"Of course you are, Captain. You lost a lot of blood. You'll get stronger day-by-day, but you have to eat. Now if I set the tray in your lap can you manage the soup and tea with your right hand? We don't want you moving that left shoulder and arm; don't want to start that chest wound bleeding again."

"Yes, ma'am, I can manage."

The nurse set the tray on his lap, put a napkin under his chin and smiled. "You gave us quite a fright, you know, but you are going to be just fine."

Ansel lifted a spoonful of rice and broth to his lips. Nothing had ever tasted so good.

CHAPTER TWENTY-TWO

At Southampton, patients who were ambulatory were guided down *Western Austra-lia's* gangway. About two dozen of them with bandaged eyes were led off the ship in a line, each man with an arm on the shoulder of the man in front. Some patients assigned to nearby hospitals were loaded into motor ambulances while others assigned to hospitals scattered further across England boarded hospital trains waiting dockside.

Once the ambulatory patients were off the ship, bed patients were loaded onto stretchers one ward at a time and carried off the ship to similar transport. Before it was Ansel's turn, a familiar British Army officer appeared at the foot of his bed.

"I'm glad to see you getting good care, Captain."

"You'll have to talk up a little and on my left side. I can't hear out of my right ear yet."

"I know you feel rotten. I've been given a copy of your medical report and I want you to know how very sorry I am to have gotten you in to this mess."

"No apology necessary, Major Falkner. Wait . . . my mistake. I see it is now Lieutenant Colonel Falkner. Congratulations."

"It may be Corporal Falkner, if your story gets out. We are going to wait here until the crowd is gone. You and I will be transported by ambulance to your assigned hospital in London. One of my men will drive. I hope you can appreciate the consequences should the newspapers get a hold of a story of an American soldier wounded at the Somme. Very high officials of your government and mine have their wind up over it."

"I haven't thought of that. In fact, I haven't been able to think clearly at all. I can't remember much."

"That might be a blessing. If the story gets out, I think we both may be shot—me by the Prime Minister and you by President Wilson's campaign manager. If the Kaiser's propaganda minister gets hold of it, it could lose the election for your President Wilson. You, Captain Quinn, are going to be the best kept secret in England, France and the United States."

"Just how will that work, Colonel."

"Until we get you on your feet in shape to travel, you will be known as Captain J. A. Williams of the British Army. You hardly have a British accent so your story will be this: You had a British father and an American mother; just like our Churchill, don't you know. Your father had an import-export business in Cuba exporting sugar and importing British manufactured goods. Thus you have a peculiar mixed accent, British, American English and the influence of Spanish. Since that is not too farfetched from the way you grew up and with your firsthand *knowledge* of Cuba, we should get away with it.

In addition, once we reach the hospital in London you will be placed in a private room marked 'quarantine' to keep you isolated from the curious, especially the press. I know you feel rotten and have had a little morphine, so I pray you will remember all this. I will go over it again at the hospital in the morning to make sure you have it all down."

"And here I thought I would be a star with my picture on the front of every newspaper with the headline: *First American Soldier Wounded in the Great War.*"

"If that happens we both will be shot."

"Colonel Falkner—"

The colonel raised his hand. "We started out aboard ship as Ansel and Marvin. I'd like to keep it that way."

"All right Marvin, who is going to tell my wife? She probably hasn't gotten a letter from me in more than a month. She is going to be worried, and very well may shoot me before anyone else gets the chance. She almost didn't marry me because of the Army."

"I rather think that is something your Secretary Lansing will have to figure out. I suspect someone from his office will personally deliver the message."

"If some government officer drives up at Shamrock, she will think I'm dead before they can convince her otherwise. How about if I just write a letter telling her I'm all right?"

"You are hardly 'all right', but something like that may work if it's done right."

Falkner walked around the room a few laps. "How about this? A letter that explains you are on an extended assignment at an isolated secret base in Scotland to observe a special British unit training in new infantry tactics. It could go out in a diplomatic pouch from the American Ambassador in London."

"Is there such a training base? Secretary Lansing might check on that especially at the urging of my wife. Her father is a close friend with a Senator from Tennessee."

There is such a base exactly as I described it.

"Marvin, you intelligence people are sneaky."

"As one intelligence officer to another, you are spot on. Now tell me how you feel."

"As you Brits like to say, hunky dory."

"I think that is the morphine talking. You look like hell. They will soon take you off that heavenly panacea and start you on a rehabilitation regime. Then, my brave Captain Williams, we will see how hunky dory you are."

"Marvin, you are *so* encouraging. I'll have to get used to being one Captain Williams. And where is Major Ravensdale? No one here seems to know. I still don't remember much, but I am told I will probably regain some memory of just what the hell happened."

Before Falkner could make up an answer, a stretcher team arrived and lifted Ansel off the bed as gently as they could. He tried but could not stifle a cry of pain.

"Sorry about that," he said to no one in particular. "I can't even grit my teeth due to the damn cut across my jaw and cheek."

Ansel was placed in the back of a Rover-Sunbeam Ambulance. Major Falkner climbed in beside him. The doors were shut and they were on their way to London some eighty miles away.

"I know you feel rotten, Captain Williams, but before that last injection of morphine puts you to sleep, all warm and fuzzy, we have to program a couple of things into that concussed brain of yours. Are you with me, Captain Williams?"

"I don't know for how long, but go ahead."

"You must not forget your name is now Captain J. A. Williams. Your dog tag and medical record will show that name."

"I am Captain Williams."

"We don't know what you might say in your sleep or under the influence of morphine so there will be three nurses especially briefed on the situation. They have been formerly sworn to secrecy. You will not be left alone for even a minute. None of your doctors are aware of the situation. We don't think you will need any additional surgery so we are not worried about you talking while under anesthesia. Just remember to answer to your new name and tell anyone who asks that you don't remember anything."

"That won't be hard because I don't."

"That will change as your brain heals."

"I'm a little afraid of that."

"Except for the nurses and me, you will have no company. You are in quarantine, remember. I will come every other day or so and will fetch you what you want: books, newspapers, cookies, but no alcohol."

"Can I call you 'Mother'?"

"Ah! A sense of humor. I do believe you are feeling better already."

"I feel like hell, but that last shot of morphine is beginning to work. I'm sinking into never-never land."

"Good night, Captain Williams."

"Miss Isabel, I'm sure Captain Quinn is working on some assignment and just hasn't been able to post any letters. You know how slow mail is from over yonder. You told me one time a bunch of his letters didn't get here because the mail ship got sunk. If anything was wrong you'd hear from the Army."

"Well, Jed, I'm not so sure. I know his letters come weeks after he writes, but it has never been this long without hearing something. I think he's been fibbing me about never going near the fighting. I know that stubborn man and he's been fibbing. Ansel is not the kind to sit week-after-week in a tiny office. He's been up to something. I just feel it. I could write Washington, but my daddy said that would get him in trouble. Heck, I don't even know *who* to write. Jed, I know you have a lot to do here, but would you go into town and check the post office again this afternoon, please. It's been nearly six weeks since a letter has arrived. You can bring back a couple of more barrels of gasoline to make the trip worthwhile. And as long as you're in town, bring back a couple of bottles of bourbon."

"Ma'am?"

"Oh don't act so innocent, Jed Jamison. Just go to the back door of Caleb Brown's drugstore and get two bottles of good bonded Tennessee bourbon. I know all about that. People even go in there and sit at the soda fountain to get a little 'prescription' in their Coca Cola, including that whole courthouse bunch. Now go on!"

"Yes ma'am."

Late that evening when Jedediah Jamison returned, the mail he brought consisted of bills, advertisements for seed, farm equipment . . . and one telegram from Captain Quinn, American Embassy, Paris France.

Without a word Jed handed the mail to Isabel and the two bottles of bourbon to Lizzy who took them to the kitchen.

"Thank you for going, Jed."

Jamison left without a word hoping the wire he put at the bottom of the pile was good news. Isabel went out to the veranda to go through the mail. In the kitchen Lizzy heard Isabel cry out. She nearly dropped the bottles of bourbon and ran to find Isabel sitting out on the veranda in a cushioned wicker chair reading a long telegram.

"Whachu' yellin' out like that foe, Miss Isabel? You scared me so I nearly dropped dem bottles of bourbon."

"It's a wire from Ansel, and I'm gonna kill him. He says he has been assigned to some kind of secret training camp in the mountains of Scotland and won't be allowed to write for a month or more. Said he's got to write a training book for the Army based on what the British are doing up there. Well, at least he can't get shot in Scotland."

"Well, we glad ta hear that. Maybe now you be a little less cross since you finally got a letter and know Mister Ansel be all right."

"Cross? Have I been cross with anybody?"

"You been 'bout cross as a snake 'cause you all worried 'bout yo' husband. But we all understand. We be worried, too, so I reckon now we all be almost as relieved as you to know he's all right. We jes wish he would come on home."

"I pray for that every night, Lizzy."

"Yes, Ma'am. I do too." Lizzy turned to leave.

"I know it's a bit early to celebrate this letter, Lizzy, but bring me a tea glass of bourbon and water over ice."

A few minutes later, carrying a tall glass of iced bourbon and water, Lizzy came through the screen door onto the veranda where Isabel sat.

"You actin' moe like Miss Bethany every day."

"Don't fuss at me, Lizzy. It's all I can do not to break down and cry. I don't believe him; what this telegram says. I know something has happened to Ansel, I can't explain it but I feel it." Tears began to run down her cheeks. "He works in Paris. Why on earth would they send him to Scotland? This wire doesn't even sound like Ansel."

"Now Honey, don't you go frettin' yo'self. If somethin' bad done happen to Mister Ansel, you would've heard by now. It's jus' army doings got him runnin' round over yonder. You'll see."

"Thank you, Lizzy. I'm too big to cry to my daddy, and Ansel is depending on me to keep up with things here and in Cuba, but I don't know what I would do without you and Mister Jed. I've just been going through the same routine day-after-day waiting for his letters, and now I'm not going to get any for months. I need a change, Lizzy. I'm going to Cuba next week. I'm due there next month anyway."

"I'll start packin' your trunk. It gonna be hot dis time of year."

"Thank you, Lizzy." Isabel held up the glass and rattled the ice. "You might as well bring me another. I'm too upset to get any bookwork done this afternoon."

Lizzy shook her head but fetched the bourbon.

Ain't gonna let on to Miss Isabel, but I's just as worried 'bout Mister Ansel as she be. What has that boy gone and done now?

Rehabilitation began. The morphine was taken away, which left him with headaches, itchy skin, stomach cramps and a runny nose. The healing wounds were not without pain, but he was determined not to complain—then it was time to begin exercising the damaged leg.

The first day two nurses and an aide carrying a pair of crutches came into the room. Ansel said, "Thank you very much, but I won't need those sticks." In spite of the nurses' warnings to stop, he swung his legs out of the bed, stood proudly, smiled at them, took one step on the injured leg and fell on his face. Sheepishly, he was helped to his feet, examined to determine if he had hurt himself, and put back to bed. The nurses left shortly to be led back into the room by a doctor who, Ansel found, had no sense of humor whatsoever.

"Captain Williams," he began, "You just might have broken an arm or leg not to mention your head with your juvenile bravado. I personally wouldn't give a damn, except with a hospital understaffed and full of wounded, we don't need extra work from patients foolishly injuring themselves. For whatever reason you are being kept in hiding, privileged to occupy a private room, you will not, repeat, *will not* put extra burdens of time and effort on our nursing staff. You will do exactly what you are told and cooperate fully in your own rehabilitation. Do you clearly understand?"

Ansel did as he was told and began to walk, first with the use of crutches and, much later, with the aid of a cane. With practice, both he and his right leg grew stronger.

As the days turned to weeks, Ansel's headaches tapered off, he regained partial hearing in his right ear and the stitches were removed from his chest, back, cheek, thigh and forehead. Ansel looked in the mirror at the long scar on his cheek and decided it would amuse his father Jonathan, if he were alive. *We could compare scars, but at least I have my whole right ear.* The scar on his chest was about the size of a silver dollar. He couldn't tell what the scar on his back looked like. Ansel sat on the bed and looked down at his right leg. *That's damn ugly, but I have my leg.* The flesh and muscle ripped off his thigh by a shell fragment and the amount of dead tissue that had to be surgically excised left a long, tapered indentation in the leg large enough at the deepest part to cup a baseball. There was also nerve damage and, with so much loss of muscle and tendon, the leg was permanently weakened.

As days passed and the effects of concussion faded, Ansel was introduced to the dark side of trauma recovery. The 14th of July bubbled to the surfaced of his memory. Ansel wished it hadn't.

In early dreams, he saw only a great burst of light and shapeless shadows flung about helter-skelter. Then his memory began to form recognizable visions, flashes, sounds and smells. Gradually scraps and pieces of memory formed into clear, horrific moments that tore through his mind like shards of shrapnel . . .

Ravensdale saying, "I'm going up to their battalion headquarters. I'll be back for the show." Clearly, through the powerful lenses of the artillery scope, he saw men of the 4th British Army cut to pieces by machinegun and artillery while trying to cross 'no man's land.' Around him Australians moved out from the wood down the slope.

His flickering memory began to focus.

He saw the artillery barrage rolling over the front trenches and marching up the slope among the Australians directly toward him.

The screech and scream of shells ending in ear splitting thunder, tearing holes in air and earth and men.

Invisible concussive waves rending the air.

No cover, no trench, no hole to hide in, no place to run.

Where's Ravensdale?

Turn to see him running toward me.

Hard to breathe, air fouled by acrid, choking smoke.

Scream. Ravensdale! Get down!

Ravensdale, silhouetted by a shell close behind him, disintegrates into blood blackened air. Run!

Trees exploding; their limbs flying about.

Tripped.

Look down. A tree limb? No! God! A human spine with stubs of ribs and bits of pink lung and flesh.

Get up! Get up! Run!

Face! Something hit my face. Run!

Knocked down. Shoulder burns. Get up! Move!

A flash of light. Darkness. Silence. Nothing! Nothing! Nothing. . . !

"Wake up! Wake up, Captain!"

"Run! You'll die if you stay here. Run!"

"It's all right, Captain Williams. You're here with us. It's all right."

"What? Oh, it's you, Nurse. Was I doing it again?"

"You were screaming and calling a name, Ravensdale. You were having another bad dream. I think you must have been trying to run. Look what you have done to your bed covers."

"I'm sorry, Nurse. I'm sorry."

"Nonsense, Captain. You had another bad dream. They will go away in time. Right now we are going to change your bed sheets, bathe you and put you in fresh pajamas. You have sweated them all through. Then we will bring you a nice cup of tea. How will that be?"

CHAPTER TWENTY-THREE

Lieutenant Colonel Marvin Falkner walked into the room with a large package under his arm. "You look awful, which is an improvement over last time I was here. Then you looked terrible."

"Marvin, you know just how to uplift a man's morale. You should go into the ministry."

"Speaking of which, I bring you good tidings of great joy, Captain Williams. You are getting out of here."

"Hallelujah! When?"

"Just as soon as you can change into this British uniform. You'll find it complete with insignia, three pips on each epaulet for captain, a Sam Browne belt, hat and shoes." Falkner put the package on the bed. "Isn't that right, Nurse?"

"It certainly is, Colonel. We are always proud to see one of our patients walk out of here on his own."

Ansel had a little trouble getting his right leg into the trousers, but was soon dressed and ready.

"Let's see you walk to the door and back, Captain."

Ansel took up his cane and proudly demonstrated his ambulatory skill.

Before leaving he asked for pen and paper and wrote a letter to the hospital staff thanking them for all they had done for him. He handed it to the duty nurse. She smiled, kissed him on the cheek and gave him a bottle of pills. "These are to be taken *only* when absolutely necessary for pain. Now you take care of yourself, Captain. We've grown fond of you, but we don't want to see you back here."

"Yes ma'am. Thank you."

With Colonel Falkner following, Ansel thumped his cane rhythmically on the well-polished hall floor and out the front door into bright sunshine.

"Where to Colonel?"

"First we are going to meet a couple of friends of yours for lunch."

"Friends of mine?"

"No questions, Captain. And by the way, you are doing pretty well with that cane. You want to race me to the car?"

"Maybe tomorrow."

A brown Army staff car and driver were waiting at the curb.

"I'm impressed. You rate a staff car these days?"

"I'm afraid not, Captain. The car was sent for you. The mysterious Captain Williams is considered an international security risk. You are not allowed to be on your own. For instance, if you were to step off the curb and get hit by a car, and there was no one there to clean up the mess, how would it look in the papers if the headlines read: WOUNDED AMERICAN SOLDIER IN BRITISH UNIFORM CARRYING FALSE PAPERS FOUND ON LONDON STREET?"

"Well who do I thank for such sympathetic concern for my personal well-being?"

"I would say Britain, France and the United States. I'm quite sure some or all have thought it might be simpler if you just disappeared."

They drove quite a long distance from the hospital. After passing Hyde Park and turning into the Soho district, they stopped at 29 Romilly Street, a Georgian townhouse converted into a restaurant. The name over the entrance said *Kettner's*.

They entered and were led by the maître d' to a small dining room. Bench seats with tufted, biscuit-backed, velvet upholstery were set against burgundy walls hung with large, white-framed mirrors and electric sconces with beige shades. A row of small, marble-topped tables sat before the bench seats with white, cane-bottomed chairs on the opposing sides. Altogether, it gave the room a warm cozy atmosphere.

As the maître d' directed Falkner and Quinn toward two of the tables drawn together to make a seating for four, Ansel was stopped by the sight of a lady sitting on the bench side and a man in uniform standing in the aisle. He nearly fell hurrying to give an unembarrassed hug to the man dressed in the uniform of a French general. Both men drew back with watery eyes, each trying not to let a loose a tear run down his cheek.

Ansel turned his head toward the lady. "Aileen, how lovely you look." He quickly wiped away a tear that had escaped.

"Oh, for heaven's sake, you gentlemen please sit," Aileen laughed.

General Henrí Bourget pulled out a chair for Ansel and motioned Colonel Falkner to the other. He then slipped around the table to sit beside Aileen.

Ansel managed to get out a one word question. "How?"

"Perhaps I should answer that," Falkner stated. "In the first place, the French by nature are both inquisitive and great worriers. This is especially true of French Army Headquarters. It seems they are deeply concerned that one American Captain somehow managed to get himself wounded in battle, or at least that is the way it would be played by international journalists. They are as convinced, as we are that if the story got out, President Wilson might very well lose his election and an even more intractable pacifist politician would be elected to reduce the odds of Americans ever coming to the aid of the allies. Therefore, upon learning the plans of British Intelligence to keep a lid on the matter, French Headquarters insisted that a representative with knowledge of the subject in question be on hand for the next phase of the plan. Thus they sent General Henrí Bourget to witness the closing stage of the great cover-up. As for this charming lady, the General needed a translator and was allowed to choose the one he most trusted."

"What do you mean by the next phase of the plan?"

Marvin signaled the waiter standing by. "First, on this auspicious occasion, I think we should all enjoy a glass of fine champagne, for which this restaurant is famous, and have lunch before business. Please note that in honor of our French guests, I chose the best French restaurant in London. It was opened in 1867 by Auguste Kettner who claimed to be Napoleon III's chef. The food is excellent, so take your time perusing the menu."

The sommelier delivered the bottle of wine, poured a little into Henrí's glass as directed by Falkner.

Henrí's verdict, "Excellent!"

All glasses were filled.

Ansel, ignoring both the champagne and the menu, repeated his question about 'the next phase of the plan.'

"Ansel, I'm afraid you are outranked here. As a matter of fact, you are *not* even here. Captain Williams is here. We will all order and then, while the food is being prepared, we will discuss the matter. Cheers!" Marvin Falkner lifted his glass.

"*À votre santé,*" replied Henrí.

Ansel opened his mouth, but Falkner spoke first. "Later, Captain."

Aileen laughed again. "You two have completely confused our young guest."

Ansel tried a different tack. Looking at Henrí and switching to French he said, "Tell me about you two. At least that's not a military secret."

Henrí smiled. "We are just two old friends who find ourselves alone—me for a long time, Aileen for the first time in many years. We are congenial with each other's company when there is time between Aileen's work at the library and mine at Army Headquarters." He looked at Aileen.

Aileen added, "When Gaetan died I thought I faced the lonely widow's life, but Henrí said he wouldn't let that happen. We are not the youngsters we were when we met in Saigon those many years ago, but we are comfortable together, aren't we my old General?"

Henrí smiled and nodded his head in agreement.

The food arrived and, as promised, it was delicious. The chef had prepared wonderful fish entrees. As a sign of the growing food shortages in England, no beef had been listed on the day's menu.

After coffee and *crème brûlée* were served, Ansel could wait no longer. "Colonel Falkner, I have been patient as ordered. Now could you tell me why I am 'not' here and what you mean by 'the next phase of the plan'?"

With Aileen translating for Henrí, Colonel Falkner began.

"To start with your first question, you are 'not' here because you are 'where you have been' for the past two and a half months. Isn't that correct, General?"

Ansel looked at the Colonel and then Henrí.

"And where might that be and what have I been doing there?"

"You have been at a secret British training base in Scotland writing a training manual to deliver to your Army, all hush-hush. The base is sealed; no communications to the outside allowed. At least that is what your wife, your housekeepers and any inquisitive friends have been informed."

"My wife? You forged a letter to my wife?"

"Of course not. We were worried about matching your handwriting. You sent your wife a telegram explaining you mission in Scotland .You ended by saying *all my love, Ansel*. That was very thoughtful of you."

"And is there such a training base?"

"Certainly. We are developing special trench-raiding teams, but that is all I can say about that."

"I'm afraid to ask about 'the next phase of the plan'. I'm guessing that the first phase was to hide a dumb American who got himself wounded, which if known would embarrass his neutral country and its president."

"Well put! You are not so dumb after all."

"I thank you for not letting my wife know the truth. But now what?"

"The French and British governments are about to be rid of you. Because General Bourget seemed to take an interest in you and took you to Verdun, which the French reminded me resulted in no embarrassing incident, he was chosen to represent France in confirming that the problem, meaning you, Captain, has vanished."

"Vanished?"

"We are not going to shoot you, though some have probably thought of that on both sides of the Atlantic."

"So how do I vanish?"

"You are not going to vanish. Captain Williams is going to vanish. We are going to escort you to the American Embassy and place you in the hands of Ambassador Page whom you have caused considerable worry. Waiting for you there is a trunk containing shirts, socks, shoes, underwear, toiletries and two new American uniforms, like the one you so carelessly lost, the cost of which will be deducted from you pay. You are not authorized to open the trunk and wear the uniforms until you are on U.S. soil. You will continue to be Captain Williams aboard ship, which, purely by chance, will deliver you to Halifax, Nova Scotia. From there you will travel by train to Washington where you will arrive in uniform as Captain Quinn, a little battered from a traffic accident in Paris while on your way to work as a neutral observer. The traffic accident report, by the way, is on file at the Paris Prefecture of Police. When you reach Washington, you will report to Secretary Lansing who is expecting you. After that you will be his responsibility. General Bourget has been kind enough to clear out your office and put your official papers and personal effects in the briefcase he brought with him. You will turn in your official papers in Washington. Also, in the briefcase are rather glowing letters of commendation on your achievements given by Ambassador Sharp and Major Crosby. They also asked me to convey to you their wish for a safe trip and full recovery."

"But why to Halifax and not New York or some other American port?"

"Because that is where the first available fast ship leaving England is going."

"I guess that takes care of all but two things."

"And what are they, Captain."

"First, I ask that you not inform my wife I am coming home. She might ask questions and I will take care of all that in due course. Second, I'm not sure what to do about my house in Paris."

Henrí answered. "Suppose I rent it from you. I'm tired of living in the officer's quarters and my cottage in Chantilly is too far from work."

"That is perfect. I will rent it to you on the condition that my house servants remain. I could never abandon them. I will supplement their wages and let you decide on a fair rental. One day, when this war is over, I will bring my wife to Paris, if you can spare us a room, General."

"I can't wait to meet her. There is so much I want to tell her about the rogue she married." Aileen patted the General's hand, "And I will tell her all about you, my General."

Henrí laughed. "I think if the lovely Mrs. Quinn comes to Paris, you, Captain, and I could find ourselves in trouble."

"How about the Colonel here," Ansel remarked. "He is the one who got me into all this in the first place."

"I think it is time to go before this brash young captain breaches protocol."

There was a heartfelt goodbye between Ansel and Henrí, one only Aileen understood. The recently discovered father and son shook hands looking each other in the eyes as men sometimes do knowing they may not meet again. Then they hugged, kissed on each cheek in the French fashion, stood back and saluted.

The jaw muscles beneath the scar on his cheek proved painfully sensitive as Ansel clamped down hard in an attempt to stop the tears from streaming down his face.

CHAPTER TWENTY-FOUR

The Ansel Quinn case, as his file with the American Embassy in London was labeled, was stamped "Confidential" and "Sensitive." From the time he was located in hospital with combat wounds, he had been under Embassy surveillance. Now on his last day in England, he was escorted from London to Liverpool's Lime Street Station by train and from there by taxi to the docks by none other than Boylston A. Beal, Special Attaché of the American Embassy in London. Beal had timed their arrival deliberately early. He wanted to get Quinn quietly settled-in before the homebound Canadian troops arrived.

Special Attaché Beal carried the charade to the letter. "Captain Williams, we were lucky to get you private accommodations aboard. This ship brought a cargo of munitions and four hundred troops over from Canada. She will be sailing back to Halifax with Canadian ambulatory wounded and will return with another load of war materiel. You should fit in with no trouble. Your accent is little different from the Canadians, except for those from the French speaking provinces, and you are not to let on you speak French."

Ansel looked up at the ship bearing the name SS *Morvada*. She had a black hull, white superstructure and a single stack painted black circled with two narrow white stripes, the company's identifying insignia.

Beal repeated again the instructions he had been given for Ansel. "If questioned on what unit you belonged to and where you were wounded, tell them that you were a member of a special Canadian Army Intelligence project that is still ongoing and aren't at liberty to talk about it." Beal saw that Captain Williams' small trunk and suitcase were tagged with his name and stateroom number and turned it over to the steamship baggage handlers. "Captain, here is your Canadian passport and your sailing papers. I wish you a safe voyage." Ansel noticed that Beal waited for him to cross over the gangway to SS *Morvada* before turning to leave.

What did they think I was going to do, sell my story to the London Times?

The purser checked Captain Williams' boarding papers and directed him to first-class stateroom number forty-three.

"You are fortunate, sir. All but a handful of officers will have to share a cabin, while some of the enlisted gentlemen will be four to the room. When trooping larger numbers, bunks are fitted below in the aft hole, but that won't be necessary on this trip. We will have a doctor and half a dozen male assistants on board to aid you and the rest of the wounded as may be needed for medical care or other assistance such as getting in or out of bed, dressing, negotiating the stairs, fresh bandages and such. All together we'll have about 390 passengers this trip." The purser handed Ansel an information folder and directed him two levels above the weather deck.

Following the diagrams in the folder, Ansel located his assigned cabin on the third deck. He took pride in negotiating the stairs, albeit one step at a time, leading up from the weather deck. Waiting for his luggage to be delivered, there was little to do but look over the ship's pamphlet.

He read that *Morvada* had been built only two years before in 1914 for the British India Steam Navigation Company, specifically to transport war materiel and Indian troops from India to England.

She is small, only 450 feet in length, but she's armed with a 7.5 inch gun on the bow. I wonder if she's had a chance to use that? Odd that she was taken off the India run to make several trips between Canada and England.

Ansel occupied one of sixty-six first class state rooms. The cabin was sparse, not nearly as nice as the one he had aboard Atlantic Transportation Line's SS *Minnehaha*.

A short time later his luggage was delivered by an East Indian dressed in what to Ansel resembled a white sheet tied around his waist. After transferring the contents of his suitcase to the cabin's dresser and putting the small locked trunk under the lower bunk, Ansel walked out on the promenade deck to stand at the rail and watch as a convoy of familiar London type-B, red and white, double-deck buses filled with wounded arrived. All manner of the injured were assisted off the buses; men with crutches, many missing a leg, struggled aboard, most refusing aid. Those with canes walked aboard, some smartly, some limping, some dragging a foot. Most of those missing an arm walked aboard with little effort. A chain of blind men were led aboard without incident. They seemed practiced in the drill.

A hell of a way to qualify for an ocean voyage. I can hear them now. What did that glorious ocean cruise cost you mate? Oh not much . . . just an arm or a leg. On the other hand, I guess it beats lying under the red poppies of Flanders.

Morvada's departure was timed for late afternoon to ensure the first 100 miles of transiting the German-declared two-hundred mile war zone would be under cover of darkness. Normally, aboard troop ships, the rule was to require troops to wear life jackets at all times transiting the danger zone. For this outbound voyage, the wounded were given the choice of wearing or carrying them. All were told to sleep fully-dressed and given canteens of water to carry with them in case they had to take to the lifeboats or go overboard. Every man was assigned a lifeboat station at which to assemble at the sound of seven short and one long blasts of the ship's klaxon. All the lifeboats were swung out on their davits ready to be lowered and would remain so until the ship cleared the danger zone.

As the ship moved out from Liverpool into the Irish Sea, she was joined by two British naval vessels of the Flower class, HMS *Primrose* and HMS *Ormonde*. Originally designed as mine sweepers, they had been converted to convoy escorts carrying the new anti-U-boat depth bombs. Both were painted with what was called 'dazzle schemes,' bands of grey, black and white paint applied at various angles and curves designed to confuse U-boats as to size, type and distance of ships and thereby confound their torpedo solutions. Whether such paint patterns were effective was debatable, but they certainly made the ships floating works of modern art. Some troop ships were painted in the same fashion, though *Morvada* remained in her company's standard livery.

The two escorts would remain with *Morvada* down the Irish Sea, through Saint George's Channel and out into the North Atlantic to the limit of the danger zone.

A short time after getting underway, the call to officer's mess was sounded. The enlisted men had their own galley and dining facility aft, while the officers assembled in the ship's dining salon. Traditionally, officer's evening mess in the British and Canadian armies was a dress affair, but under the circumstances, service uniforms would have to do. At dinner Ansel discovered the food shortages England was suffering as a result of the U-boat campaign was evident as well aboard British ships. The best that could be said was that meals aboard *Morvada* would keep one from starving to death. It was easy to identify the ship as being registered to the British India Company. Except for the ship's officers, the crew was entirely East Indian, including the cooks. The most often served dish was curried rice.

Morvada had been stripped for trooping. There was no entertainment, no music, no ship's library or reading room. One thing shipboard that did amuse the special passengers was the lifeboat drill. Standing at his assigned station, Ansel overheard one soldier who had lost a leg speaking to another who had lost an arm. "It will be jolly good fun, mate, to see this bloody lot try to scramble over the side into one of them bloody little boats."

"Right you are, mate, and not one bloody bottle of beer aboard to cheer us on."

To pass the time, Ansel participated in poker games in the evenings after dinner. He generally did not take part in the conversation at table, pretending to concentrate on the cards and thereby avoiding questions. He had made it clear that he could not talk about where and how he was wounded.

The third evening at the poker table he took notice of a discussion between a captain and a lieutenant from the Second Division of the Canadian Expeditionary Force. They obviously had taken part in the British attack on the 14th of July, the day Ansel was wounded.

The lieutenant, who was missing a leg below the knee, said, "We were hurt pretty badly, but I heard the Gordon Highlanders received over fifty-five percent casualties taking some woodland from Fritz and then couldn't hold it."

The captain who was missing his right arm just above the elbow, and his right eye, commented, "Did you hear about that Australian battalion?"

Ansel's ears perked up The captain continued, "They survived that Gallipoli cockup only to be shipped all the way from Turkey to the Somme to back-up Butcher Haig's attack on the 14th. They drew what should have been a cushy hand. All the Aussies had to do was act as reserves and move from the rear down to man a vacated trench after the attack jumped off. Those poor bloody bastards suffered over seventy percent casualties during an artillery barrage. They never even made it to the front line."

Ansel folded his cards and stood up. "You fellows are too good and my cards too bad. I need some air."

He took up his cane, left the table and stepped out on the promenade deck to stand alone in the North Atlantic chill of an October night. He had never heard the classified figures for the losses of the Australian battalion the day he went down with them.

My God! Seven out of ten fell that day, and Ravensdale, God rest his soul, and me along with them. And my job now is to go to Washington where I'm supposed to tell them what to expect if and when America gets into the war. Hell is what they can expect. Wilson and Congress with their pacifist heads in the sand have waited too long to prepare for what everyone with any sense knows is coming. The Army is not trained or equipped for the kind of war they'll find waiting for them.

He made his way to his cabin, laid down on the bunk and tried to sleep. Every time he closed his eyes, he could see men and trees being blown apart in the woods, and the men on the open ground below being flung in the air like rag dolls. It had all happened so fast, his being knocked unconscious, but not fast enough to prevent the horror taking place around him from imprinting in his memory. Lying in the dark he could hear the scream and explosion of artillery shells and smell the acrid odor of spent gunpowder. He wished for a bottle of bourbon.

With little sleep, he was groggy the next morning when he was startled wide awake by all manner of whistle and klaxon signals being exchanged between *Morvada* and her two escorts. A few minutes later a muffled explosion clanged against *Morvada*'s hull like a giant hammer followed a few seconds later by another, each reverberating throughout the ship. Thinking the ship had been hit, Ansel grabbed his cane, life jacket and water canteen and made for his lifeboat station.

Just as he reached the promenade deck, he could see one of the escorts racing at full speed a half mile away. A moment later, he felt another solid clang and saw the sea rupture into a huge geyser a hundred feet high behind the escort.

One of the ship's officers standing at the rail next to Ansel informed him, "They're dropping 300 pound barrels of TNT, our new depth bombs, trying to bag a U-boat. They spotted a periscope about eight hundred yards out there." Another depth bomb detonated. "That ought to keep the buggers too busy to put a fish in us."

The deck had quickly filled with passengers, some shaking a crutch or cane or the stump of an arm in the air encouraging the escort vessels while cursing the enemy below with imaginative obscenities. The show went on until all the depth bombs had been dropped. Each escort carried only four. *Morvada* steamed ahead putting distance between herself and the last sighting of the periscope. HMS *Primrose*, her deck guns manned, continued to circle the area while HMS *Ormonde* raced to catch up and protect *Morvada*. No official word on the U-boat was received aboard *Morvada*. For most of the passengers, the bit of excitement served as a break in the monotony of the voyage. But for some, the explosions ripped open vivid memories of the war. Their hands trembled and their brows beaded with sweat. The explosions transported their minds to places and moments they were trying hard to forget. Some screamed in their sleep that night. Ansel dreamed of the bloody human spine he had tripped over and woke up wondering if he was among the screamers.

Quinn spent much of his time aboard at the small desk in his cabin organizing his copious notes into a formal journal he would present to Secretary Lansing for transcription and delivery to the War Department. He wrote carefully to make it easy for his work to be accurately transcribed by typists.

After lunch, he sat at the desk with a blank sheet of stationary in front of him puzzling over what to write in a long-overdue letter to Isabel. He did not want to tell her of his injuries. She didn't need more to worry her. He would tell her everything in time, but he decided, none of it in writing. Instead, he composed a letter to be mailed from the State Department in Washington. Isabel would recognize that as the routine by which all his letters sent over in the Paris Embassy diplomatic pouch was handled.

My Darling Isabel,

I have finished the hush-hush business in Scotland and have been given fur-lough to come home after I make a short stopover in Washington to report on my mission. I should reach you at Shamrock within a couple of weeks or less of your receiving this letter. My heart is so full of love for you. I can't wait to hold you in my arms once more.

All my love,

Ansel

There came a morning under cloudy skies on the rolling Atlantic when the two escorts turned back for England. With a celebratory exchange of whistle and klaxon, *Morvada* raised a signal flag hoist that read, WELL DONE NAVY.

There was great relief felt by all. It meant *Morvada* was passing out of the danger zone and sailing in neutral international waters.

(That would all change within a few months when Germany, desperate to win the war prior to America's entry, would revert to unrestricted submarine warfare with more than 300 submarines in an all-out attempt to prevent badly needed food and war materiel from reaching France and England. They knew the resumption of unrestricted U-boat rules would probably bring America into the war, but hoped to strangle and starve England into suing for peace before the United States could raise, equip, train and transport an army to Europe.)

For two days and nights *Morvada* had to slow to six knots in thick fog, sounding one long blast of her horn every two minutes as required by international navigation rules. At first it nearly drove Ansel and everyone else onboard insane.

Strange how the mind can adjust to almost anything in time. No one slept the first night, but by the second day, normal activity and sleep was carried on in spite of the mournful signal and seemingly endless dreary shroud of gray mist.

Just past noon on the third morning since encountering thick fog, *Morvada* emerged from the bank of dank vapor into sunlight revealing the green and rocky shore of Nova Scotia on the horizon. The Canadians on deck let out a cheer. Home! The deck was soon crowded with bright faces, some smiling for the first time since the day of their horror. *Morvada* made her way past McNabs Island and its lighthouse perched on the outer reach of Hangman's Beach. They continued into Halifax Harbor to find it crowded with anchored ships assembled for the next convoy bound for England.

Morvada, with the aid of a tug, docked at three in the afternoon on October 15, 1916. A military band was playing and a crowd had gathered. Ansel noticed that the initial joy seemed to fade from the faces of many of the men gathered on deck. He thought he knew why.

They're wondering if their mothers or fathers or wives or sweethearts are waiting down there on the dock, and what their reaction will be when they see their soldier come down the gangplank missing an arm or leg or sightless led down by a guide. Some are holding back; afraid to go down; afraid they will see shock in the eyes of their loved ones; afraid they will, for the first time since they were wounded, break down and cry. I wonder if my reaction when I face Isabel will be the same. By some miracle I'm in better shape than most men on this ship, but I'm afraid, too; afraid Isabel won't forgive me for lying to her about what I've been doing and for getting myself hurt when I told her over and over there was no danger of that happening. I promised I would come back to her but not with a lame leg and scarred face. If I write about my injuries, Isabel will worry herself sick, but if I don't she is liable to shoot me. I think my plan is the best bet; just show up unannounced and let the hide go with the hair.

Ansel was not in a hurry to leave the ship and mix among the Canadians on the dock. He figured there would be reporters and photographers waiting down there. He wasn't about to blow the whole charade at the last moment. He had instructed the purser to wire ahead and make reservations for his trip to Washington beginning with the next Pullman sleeper train on the Grand Trunk Railway. The purser informed Captain Williams that his train wasn't scheduled to depart Halifax until eight that evening.

Ansel thanked him, ate supper in his cabin brought up from the ship's galley, and followed by an East Indian crewman carrying his luggage, walked off the ship with no one on the dock but stevedores. He got into the taxi the ship's purser had ordered, paid the man for carrying his baggage and headed for Grand Trunk's Bonaventure Station. He arrived to discover that the preceding March the grand old station, built 1847, had been heavily damaged by fire. A cost-conscious railroad had not restored the building to its former Victorian splendor, opting instead for a flat roof in place of the grand tower and dormered, pitched roof that had lent the structure its grandness. Nonetheless it served the Grand Trunk's purpose at a time when passenger train travel, and therefore revenue, had fallen off due to the war.

By the time Ansel boarded the train, he was dead tired and his injured leg hurt like hell as it often did when he walked at lot. The purser had managed to reserve one of the single staterooms at the rear of the coach. It was a Pullman business coach. A number of standard Pullman sleepers had recently been converted to provide a more plush arrangement hopefully to attract higher paying customers. Their converted coaches were decorated in rich mahogany paneling and plush, green upholstered seats. The regular oil lamps had been replaced with brighter Pintsch gas lamps and each coach had a single stateroom available at one end. Besides his suitcase, Ansel had his small trunk placed in the stateroom rather than checking it through. The route was long and required changing trains before reaching Boston and again from there to Washington. He was not going to chance losing his American uniform and papers due to mishandled baggage.

The train had hardly departed Bonaventure Station before Ansel undressed and fell into bed. The gentle rocking of the coach and the rhythmic click-clack of the steel wheels rolling over rail joints lulled him to sleep. For the first time since regaining consciousness in the hospital, he did not dream of the Somme or wake in the wee hours to lay sleepless until dawn.

Prior to changing trains the next day, Ansel took a French bath and shaved using the stateroom's lavatory. Although aching from his injuries, he felt clean and renewed. It was time. He opened the trunk and laid out its contents on the bunk: one attaché case and a new set of clothes. He happily slipped into fresh underwear, shirt, socks, trousers, shoes, jacket, belt, insignia and cap. 'Captain Williams of the British Army' disappeared, uniform, Canadian passport and all, into the trunk as Ansel refastened the lock.

Captain J. Ansel Quinn, U.S. Army, looked at himself in the dressing mirror.

Not too bad. The scar on my face is a little less red, more of a pale pink I would say, and the stitch marks are almost gone. They say the scar will turn white in time. I guess this is the best I can do for now.

There was no one to notice the difference except perhaps the waiter who delivered meals to his stateroom and he would not be around when Ansel disembarked.

Damn if I wouldn't make a good spy.

CHAPTER TWENTY-FIVE

After an overnight run from Boston, Captain Quinn stepped down from the coach, hired a Red Cap to carry his luggage and walked down the long passenger concourse and into the cavernous main waiting area of Washington's Union Station.

There, standing at the passenger entrance, was a man whose face he recognized from the last time he arrived.

"Special Agent Winthrop, I hope you are not here to arrest me."

"I'm here to escort you like last time, Captain. We wouldn't want you getting lost again. We hear you disappeared for a while." Winthrop was wearing the same uniform as before: a three-piece, dark blue suit.

They began walking toward the front entrance. Winthrop stopped at a telephone booth and made a call. Ansel overheard him state, "Yes, sir, he is here and we will be at your office shortly." Winthrop hung up and the two continued toward the front exit with the Red Cap following.

"We are certainly glad you weren't killed in that terrible car wreck in Paris."

"What? Oh yes, of course, the car wreck that did all this to me The French are such terrible drivers."

Ansel and the Red Cap carrying his luggage were led to a black Dodge Brothers sedan. Ansel paid the Red Cap and got in back with Winthrop. The driver started out on the same route they had followed before to the ornate State, War and Navy Building.

"Captain, we have heard the strangest thing. Would you believe there is a rumor circulating at the German Embassy that an American officer may have been wounded in battle on the Somme? They are turning the taps on every covert contact they have on both sides of the Atlantic to track down the origin of such a rumor. We heard that Ambassador Johann von Bernstorff is salivating at the thought of revealing an American soldier in combat on the Allied front. He told his Military Attaché, Franz von Papen, that such news would disgrace Wilson as a liar about not sending American boys to war. He is sure proof would rile the isolationists to the point of demanding America stay out of the war, not to mention upset Wilson in his tight race with Republican Justice Hughes, if they can break the story before the election on the seventh of next month."

"Now where would they get such an idea, Agent Winthrop?"

"We would like to know that ourselves."

"And just how do you know what rumors circulate inside the German Embassy?" Agent Winthrop didn't reply.

They arrived at the Seventeenth Street entrance.

"The driver will take your luggage to the Willard Hotel where there is a room reserved in your name."

"You fellows think of everything."

Agent Winthrop signed Ansel in at the guard desk at the entrance to the south wing and started toward one of the building's nine elevators.

"Agent Winthrop, I use every opportunity to strengthen this leg. I think I would prefer to take the stairs just as we did the last time I was here."

"Suit yourself, Captain. I can carry you case."

"Thank you, but I can manage." With his cane in his right hand and the briefcase in his left, he negotiated the wide marble stairs, sometimes resting a bit against the bronze balustrades supporting the mahogany hand rails. When he reached the second floor his injured leg ached, but he was pleased with the accomplishment. As they walked down the wide hall to Secretary Lansing's office, Winthrop noticed Ansel limping on his right leg. The agent opened the Secretary's office door, but did not enter. "I will meet you here when the conference is over to escort you out of the building and take you to the hotel." Agent Winthrop nodded at the Secretary and left.

Secretary Lansing, Colonel Ralph Van Deman of the unofficial Military Intelligence School at Washington Barracks and two stenographers all stood when Ansel entered the office.

"Good to see you again, Quinn." Secretary Lansing came from around his desk to shake Ansel's hand. Shaking with his right hand, Ansel had learned, was a bit awkward as he had to quickly shift his cane to his left hand. He noticed that former Major Van Deman was now Colonel Van Deman.

"Congratulations, Colonel."

Van Deman nodded a thank you and added, "Glad to see you all in one piece, Captain. You've done a crackerjack job."

"Let's all take a seat." Lansing gestured Ansel toward a comfortable chair by the desk. "As you can see we have prepared for a private conference with you as the main attraction. I know you are in a hurry to get home so let's get started." The stenographers poised with pens and pads ready, which made Ansel a little uncomfortable.

"First let me say, Mister Secretary, I am sorry to have caused so much trouble. I never dreamed my duty would risk creating an international incident. It was purely by accident I hope you realize. I was told if it got out, President Wilson might put me before a firing squad."

"You have a fine sense of humor there, Captain. We have read your previous reports and consider you somewhat of a hero for the risks you have taken to get us first hand intelligence from the war front, though we certainly can't tell anyone about that."

"The word hero is misplaced, sir. I was just an onlooker." Ansel reached into his briefcase and withdrew a thick journal. "I have tried to put all my notes and reports in order along with comments I thought appropriate in this notebook. I hope my handwriting is clear enough so your typists can transcribe it." He handed the book to Secretary Lansing who took several minutes to scan through it.

There followed a long session of questions including what Quinn's opinions were concerning the current status and battle strategies of France and England on the Western Front, and his opinions of such wide subjects as leadership, training, weapons, logistics, and the politics that might surface if and when the United States entered the war on the side of the Allies.

Several times Ansel repeated, "Gentlemen, I am not qualified to answer such questions. I was simply an observer."

His protests were ignored principally because his detailed observations and comments as reflected in his carefully written individual reports spoke otherwise.

The stenographers were kept busy writing every word that was said. There were two, so their individually transcribed notes could be compared to detect any errors or omissions prior to the final, official transcript.

Lansing looked at his watch. "Gentlemen, let's break for lunch. It should be ready in my private dining room. They all followed Lansing into a small room; small compared to the rather large office suite they had just left. The walls were a pale yellow set off with white trim. There was a mahogany table that could seat eight, a matching sideboard and a combination linen and china cabinet. The chairs were straight-backed with upholstered seats. A gas chandelier that had been converted to electricity hung over the table. It was unlit as the drapes were drawn back and sunlight, softened by light window curtains, reflected off the yellow walls to provide a warm, pleasant setting.

"Gentlemen, until we resume business in my office, everything at lunch will be off the record so our stenographers can enjoy their meal. Captain, tell us how Paris was when you were last there."

"It is still a beautiful city with handsome buildings, wide boulevards and lovely parks. I am a married man, but I can say that fashionable ladies are as evident as always. Soldiers on leave have little trouble gaining a companion for dinner and dancing for there are so few men in Paris due to the war. In contrast, some soldiers I talked with complained that Paris life seems unchanged. They leave the hell of the front to find Parisians living as if there is no war. That is not quite true. The hospitals are full of wounded, the casualties have been heavy and you see a great many women dressed in mourning black. Food is scarce, but wine is plentiful. The black market is flourishing, coal and gas are rationed and the City of Lights is blacked out at night because of the threat of air raids. The Eifel Tower is a favorite target because it is the antenna for the most powerful wireless in France. The sidewalk cafes are filled during the day and the bars and clubs are crowded at night. The tango is all the rage. Paris is Paris."

"Speaking of being married, Captain, how is your wife?" Major Van Deman asked.

"She has been burdened with the management of two plantations, one in Mississippi and one in Cuba. She is magnificent, sir, and deserves much more than this soldier. She, of course, knows nothing of my recent duty or my present condition. I suspect she may shoot me for not telling her when I return. If she does, I want you gentlemen to know it will be justifiable homicide. She is a beautiful lady that should not have been burdened with so much work; although I'm sure she is much better at it than I could ever be. I have missed her terribly as all soldiers must miss the women they leave behind."

"Well said, Captain. We are happy to say that she will soon have you back, that is if she doesn't shoot you."

There was laughter around the table at the Secretary's remark. Ansel wasn't so sure it was a laughing matter. He reached in his case and withdrew the letter he had written at sea. "Would you mail this letter to her the usual way for me? I hope it will reach her before I do."

After lunch, they returned to Lansing's office and continued the meeting.

Ansel looked at the Secretary. "May I ask a question?"

"Of course, you may. This conference is for the purpose of asking questions."

"What is the strength of the Army at present?" The Secretary looked toward Colonel Van Deman.

"That's a bit of a sore subject," the Colonel began. "Our present strength is about 100,000 regulars augmented by 112,000 National Guardsmen. This past June President Wilson finally signed what is called The National Defense Act to expand the National Guard and put it under federal control in times of war. It will also increase the Army, but over a period of five years. It also creates a Reserve Officers Training Corps on college campuses. However, if you add it all together, the German Army, with four million troops outnumbers our Army over twenty-to-one. Even at that, the President had a lot of opposition from the liberal wing of his own Progressive Party, especially vocalized by Ivy League university professors and labor unions. To ease their concerns a bit, the President appointed Newton Baker, former Democratic Mayor of Cleveland as the new Secretary of War. He is one of them, an outspoken opponent of increased military preparedness."

Ansel replied, "The French are worried that Russia may collapse. If that happens, they say it will free up a million German soldiers to move to the Western Front. That's in my notes. If that happens, the French and English don't know if they can hold without our help, but they speak of the need for a million or more Americans not a few hundred thousand."

The colonel replied, "Reliable sources in Germany report that Berlin thinks America is so weak it can be ignored. For example, earlier this month on the seventh, German U-53, after wending its way beneath our navy ships off shore, surfaced inside our three mile limit, entered Newport, Rhode Island Harbor and anchored. The skipper, a Lieutenant Commander Rose, said he had come in to mail a letter to German Ambassador Bernstorff. He then was rowed over in a skiff to pay his respects to Newport Naval District commander Adm. Knight and the commander of the destroyer flotilla, Adm. Gleaves. Less than three hours after arrival, without asking for food or fuel, Rose weighed anchor, waved to the gathered spectators, sailed past the harbor lighthouse and slid beneath the waves.

"His purpose was not to mail a letter to Bernstorff. It was to show that if America got in the war, German U-boats could operate against our shipping and navy off our own shore. So much for the Atlantic Ocean protecting the U.S."

Ansel was dumbstruck. "I suppose that was in every paper in the country?" Secretary Lansing answered, "It was and with photographs. You can imagine what a firestorm that is causing among the pacifists. Former Secretary of State William Jennings Bryan stated that the only road to peace is disarmament."

Colonel Van Deman got back to business at hand. "Captain Quinn, we had hoped to have General Pershing sit in on this conference, but beginning March 15th President Wilson has him chasing Poncho Villa all over Mexico. I'm afraid that gives but another example of how woefully unprepared the Army is. That's no reflection on the General, but he doesn't have enough men or equipment and can't get the supplies he needs to do the job. In addition, the Mexican population is all on Villa's side. Although we can't yet prove it, there are indications that Germany is supplying Villa with arms and money. But to wind up our discussion for today, what do you think are the most critical things for us to consider?"

"Sir, the first thing is if and when we do send troops to France, they must be kept together under American command. The British and French will want them integrated into their commands to use as replacements for their horrific losses. If that happens, our troops will be wasted. Let me give you an example, one you will find in my journal. On one attack, the British gained a salient of almost a mile. That mile cost them two casualties for every foot gained. That's right gentlemen, nearly 11,000 men. American troops must fight in American units under American command with well-planned and realistic objectives, not some grand, war-ending breakthrough at any cost. Second, if we raise a volunteer army, is there an existing plan to equip and train a large number of them? As far as I know, we don't have modern heavy artillery and this is a war dictated by artillery. We don't have a single modern aéroplane capable of fighting in the skies over Europe. Our factories are making ammunition for the Allies, but are we turning out rifles and machine guns fast enough to equip and resupply an army of a million or more men? Do we have an existing plan for supplying an American army overseas, and do we have the merchant and navy ships to do the job? Last, before any American commanders send troops into battle, they need to see the terrain and conditions over which they will fight. I've seen plans made by generals upwards of twenty miles or more behind the lines using maps only to send troops out over open ground knee deep in mud to be slaughtered because of ignorance and arrogance."

Ansel realized he was speaking somewhat emotionally and far above his rank. "Gentlemen, I apologize for speaking out of turn. I have gotten a little carried away. I am just a captain reporting on what I have seen. I hope you are not offended."

"Not at all, Captain," Secretary Lansing said. "We brought you here to gain knowledge of what you have observed and experienced firsthand. That was your assigned duty and you have done it well.

"Now for your status with the Army, we have arranged for you to be put on reserve duty. You are certainly not qualified for combat under any circumstances, but you may be called on a temporary basis in an advisory capacity. You are down the list a bit for promotion, but in your reserve status we may be able to work you up to major. You also deserve a medal or two, but under the somewhat sensitive circumstances, they will have to wait. The Colonel and I will both write letters of commendation for a job well done. In the meantime, you are free to go home and take care of your wife and business."

The Secretary picked up his phone, spoke a few words and hung up. "Agent Winthrop is waiting and will deliver you to your hotel. Take care of yourself, Captain."

Lansing and Van Deman rose from their chairs. Ansel did so a little awkwardly. He had to use his left leg and the cane in his right hand to rise as his right leg was too weak to be much help.

"Good luck, Captain, and thank you."

The Secretary and Colonel shook Ansel's hand. He gathered up his attaché case and found Agent Winthrop waiting in the hall. Ansel felt a great weight had been lifted from his shoulders.

"Let's go, Agent Winthrop. They didn't hang me after all."

CHAPTER TWENTY-SIX

With the Washington meeting over Ansel should have felt relieved, but the thought of going home to Isabel weighed heavily on his conscience. He had kept the truth from her. Now he was returning scarred with a permanently damaged leg. As for his plan of just showing up with no warning . . . maybe that was wrong, too.

Here I talked her into marrying me, and then after a month left her with the responsibility of learning to oversee the management of two plantations and nearly got myself killed. Who would blame her if she never forgave me? God I love her, but look what I have done. And I have to tell her they may call me back. I feel like a little boy lost, begging to be found and forgiven.

By the time Agent Winthrop dropped Ansel and his luggage at the Willard Hotel, he was unduly tired from the full day's grilling at Secretary Lansing's office. At the hotel desk he inquired if overnight laundry and cleaning service was available. He was told if a bellman could pick the clothes up from his room by six in the afternoon, it would be delivered by eight the next morning. Ansel then asked if the hotel could make railway reservations. He was directed to a travel office down a hallway off the main lobby.

After stating his destination as Vicksburg, Mississippi, Ansel discovered that getting home was not going to be easy.

"On July 14th," the agent began. The mention of the day he was wounded startled Ansel. The agent noticed and began again. "On July 14th, what will go down in history as The Great Carolina Flood hit and caused immense destruction across North and South Carolina and into Georgia. Not one, but two hurricanes, one from the Gulf through Mississippi and one from the Atlantic through Charleston, combined to produce record rainfalls. Why, one station in North Carolina measured twenty-two inches of rainfall in twenty-four hours. The Swannanoa, Lineville, French Broad and Catawba Rivers reached record flood levels and destroyed miles of rail lines passing through North and South Carolina, flooded towns, washed away houses, ruined factories and drowned we don't know how many people. Southern Railway and other lines have set an army of men to rebuilding rails, trestles and bridges. In three and a half months, they have performed miracles, but there are still sections that are out on the southern routes. Your best bet is to take the Baltimore and Ohio Railway west all the way to Louisville, Kentucky and transfer there to the Illinois Central, which will get you to Memphis where you can transfer to the Yazoo and Mississippi Valley Railway for Vicksburg. I've had to send a lot people that way to New Orleans."

The agent got on the telephone for about five minutes. He hung up and looked at Ansel.

"Captain, I can book you on a sleeper out of Union Station tomorrow and on another sleeper out of Louisville the following day for Memphis, arriving in time to make the train for Vicksburg. I know the route will take much longer than normal, but it's the surest way to get through. Do you want me to go ahead and book your tickets?"

Ansel did not want to spend a night in Memphis where he might be recognized and have word reach Isabel's father, or worse, someone might telephone Isabel.

"Are you sure I won't have to spend the night in Memphis?"

"You arrive there in the early morning. There should be plenty of time to make the connection for Vicksburg."

"How much do I owe you?"

Reservations made, Captain Quinn went up to his room and called for a bellboy. While he waited, he emptied his suitcase and trunk of soiled undergarments and shirts, bundled them into the room's laundry bag and gave it, his spare uniform and a tip to the bellboy.

After washing up a bit and brushing his hair, Ansel took the elevator down to the lobby, walked through Peacock Alley past the Palm Court to the Hotel's fine dining room where he was given a small table to the side near the entrance. He was the only patron in uniform. The menu was large and fancy, but Ansel was too tired to read it. He skipped the wine list, settled for a steak with potatoes and had a tall bourbon and water before, during and after the meal. An elderly matron, and what Ansel guessed where her two grown daughters, arrived and were seated near him. During the course of the meal, Ansel couldn't help but notice the young women glanced at him and smiled more than once. Their view was of the good side of his face. He smiled politely but paid no further attention to them except to think, *I wonder how many men smile at Isabel when she is in town or visiting Memphis; how many Cuban dons for that matter? At least I don't have to worry about Jed and Cayo. They are a little old and have very jealous wives.*

Even after having consumed three bourbons, sleep did not come easy.

Two and a half days of train travel was exhausting. On the last leg from Memphis, on the Y&MV, the train passed Riverside Junction. The conductor, following Ansel's request, told him they were less than an hour out of Vicksburg. Ansel left his seat and went to the men's smoker compartment. There he used the toilet facilities, washed up, brushed his teeth, combed his hair and changed from his travel clothes into clean underwear, shirt and uniform. He stood, braced with his cane against the rocking coach, and checked himself in the mirror. He thought the scar on the side of his face was still pretty ugly.

Well my uniform and I are clean. I guess that's the best I can do.

There was a five minute stop at Kelso.

"About twenty-five more miles to go," the conductor told him.

I hope old Luke Quagg still runs his depot hack and I can get him to take me all the way out to Shamrock. I've never been scared of getting to Shamrock before, but I sure as hell am this trip.

Bell clanging, cylinders puffing steam, Y&MV engine 690 pulled into the Vicksburg station. Ansel and a family with children were the only passengers to get off. One older couple and several young people laughing and talking about New Orleans were waiting to board.

The porter set Ansel's luggage on the platform. "Good luck to you, Captain."

Ansel thanked him and put a dollar bill in his hand. "Thank you, sir." He tipped his cap and turned to help the old couple board.

"Well, I'll be. Is that you, Ansel Quinn?"

Ansel turned to see Luke Quagg who had known Ansel since he was a boy.

"I'm glad to see you, Luke. I'm looking for a ride out to Shamrock. I'll pay you fair price for taking me."

"That's a fer piece." He took out his pocket watch and looked up at the schedule board fastened to the brick wall of the station. "Last train is due in here at seven this evening. I figure I can git there and back by then. It'll cost you 'bout six dollars I reckon, but first I got to take these folks to their home on Cherry Street. I'll be back directly." Luke put the family's luggage in the back of the depot hack, helped two children and their mother into the second seat and the husband up front before climbing up beside him and collecting his fee. "That'll be ten cents apiece for the younger children and twenty-five each for the grown-ups." The man paid, and Luke drove off. Twenty minutes later he returned to pick up Ansel.

Luke Quagg usually wasn't much of a talker, a trait for which Ansel was grateful, but the return of Captain Ansel Quinn sparked him up a little. "We ain't seen you round here since a piece after Miss Bethany was lost. That was a real shame; them Germans sinking ships like that and we ain't even in the war. They say you been in the army overseas someplace 'cept when you come back to git married and set up things on the place 'foe the Army send you back over yonder."

Ansel nodded his head without speaking.

"Folks in town say your wife is mighty pretty and smart, too. Say she take up business jes' like Miss Bethany used to do."

Ansel nodded his head again, this time with a slight smile.

"Folks real proud you an officer and all. Vicksburg ain't had one since the War. I b'lieve you be a captain, is that right? I don't mean to pry none, but dang if you don't look like you been in the fightin'."

Ansel spoke up to address that remark. "It was an auto accident, Luke. They have lots of them in the big cities."

"I reckon so. Heck, you should see how some folks 'round here drive. Old man Watkins like to run me off the street last week in that big Franklin he just got, and me with five folks in this thing. That old man ought to go back to mules . . . and he ain't the only one. You home for good this time?"

"I hope so, Luke."

Luke seemed satisfied and turned his attention to driving, skillfully avoiding pot holes and navigating deep ruts and mud holes.

An hour or so later, when at last they turned up the road to the Shamrock cottage, Ansel paid Luke. "When we get to the gate just put my luggage by the gate post and turn around quiet as you can. I'll walk up to the house."

"You sure, Captain? I mean with that bum leg and all, I can take you right up to the front porch."

"Just let me off at the gate, Luke."

"Lizzy, I thought I heard a truck. Go see if that's Jed with the mail."

Isabel and Lizzy were back in the kitchen canning field peas. Lizzy dried her hands on her apron and walked to the front of the house and out on the veranda. She looked toward the gate to see the depot hack turning around. That's when she saw a soldier walking toward her with the aid of a cane. She caught her breath with her hand to her chest. The man raised his hand and put a finger to his lips, motioning her to him. Lizzy shaded her eyes and looked again.

God bless him, it's Mister Ansel. She ran to him. "Oh! Lord! Mister Ansel, you home!"

"Lizzy, where is she? Don't let on. I want to surprise her."

"She in da' kitchen. She sent me out thinkin' that truck she heard was Mister Jed maybe bringin' the mail. She jes' gonna die when you walk in."

"When we get close why don't you go back in and tell her a visitor is on the veranda."

Just before Lizzy got to the door, Isabel came out. "Lizzy, was that Jed?" The afternoon sun was shining in her face. She could only make out the figure of a man with a cane. She put her hand up to shade her eyes. That's when she saw a uniformed officer walking across the grass toward her. Her hand went to her mouth to muffle a cry.

"Ansel! Oh! Ansel is it really you?" she shouted.

Ansel raised the cane and waved it at her.

She ran to him, tears streaming down her cheeks, and threw her arms around him. He stumbled and but for her strong embrace might have pulled them both down to the grass.

They kissed and hugged and kissed again.

"How?" she asked.

"Later. I'll tell you everything later. Right now just let me look at you."

Clinging arm and arm they walked up on the veranda and into the house. A fire was burning low in the fireplace. The room was warm and welcoming.

Isabel's mood suddenly changed. "Look at me. My hair is a mess, I'm a mess. I've been working in the kitchen. Why didn't you let me know you were coming? Send me a letter? Something! J. Ansel this was a mean trick showing up with no warning. I wanted to look so pretty for you when you arrived."

"You are pretty. I wish I could look pretty for you, too, but I'm afraid I don't."

That's when she really looked at him. She put her hand to his chin and turned his head to expose the long scare on the right side of his face that ran from the lower jaw almost to the ear.

Now anger flared up and flashed in her eyes. "You lied to me Ansel Quinn. You told me you sat in Paris all the time, *but look at you*. You've been in the fighting." She began to beat him on his chest with her fists. "You lied to me and nearly got yourself killed didn't you? You just had to go up on the front and play soldier. Damn it! I ought to shoot you myself."

"Do you know how beautiful you are when you're angry?" She hit him again.

"Please don't hit me on the left side of my chest. I'm afraid I've got a scar there, too."

She started crying again. "J. Ansel Quinn, if the army calls you back I will surely shoot you."

"Well, Lizzy was glad to see me and she didn't beat me. What's for supper?"

"You ought not get any supper. Don't you ever leave me again!"

It was then that they heard a truck in the front. A moment later, walking across the veranda, Jedediah Jamison yelled out, "Miss Isabel, there's a letter from," he burst through the door and was stopped dead in his tracks at the sight of Ansel. "It's from him, Miss Isabel. Nice to have you home, Captain Quinn."

"Ha!" Isabel said. "Saved by the mail! Is that what you think, Captain Quinn? Let me see it please, Jed."

She ripped open the letter and read it silently.

"Now Isabel, you know the mail is kind'a slow from Paris," Ansel said sheepishly.

"I'll say, two weeks slower than wounded soldiers? It says here, everybody, which our gallant captain will be home to us two weeks after I receive this letter."

"I promise I'll explain everything. I just need a little food, a little bourbon and you, Darlin' Isabel."

"Don't you darlin' me. You don't deserve a single thing you asked for."

Jed took two steps backward, said, "I better go," turned around and practically ran out the door.

"Lizzy, you see that! All men are cowards."

"They is when a woman throws a hissy fit."

"You always take his side. Go fix us some supper and get out that bottle of bourbon."

"Yes ma'am." Lizzy walked toward the kitchen with a big grin on her face.

In the front bedroom, the fire had burned down to embers. Isabel lay naked with her head on Ansel's bare chest. "You may have an injured leg, Captain, but everything else works just fine." Ansel stroked her hair. "You being in my arms is a better pain remedy than all the medicine in the world. I love you, Isabel Ferguson Quinn." She sat up and lit the lamp on the bedside table. "What are you doing?"

"You be still and don't you say a word."

She threw off the covers and for the first time examined Ansel head to toe.

"I said I would explain all of this tomorrow."

Isabel didn't answer. She looked at the terrible hollow scar in his leg—almost half of his thigh was gone. Then she examined the puckered scar on the left side of his chest. She kissed it and the scar on his cheek. Then she pulled the covers over them both and blew out the lamp. "I'm sorry I fussed at you. I'm going to thank the good Lord every night that you came home to me."

They made love again in the early light of dawn.

A little while later Lizzy talked to them through the bedroom door. "Y'all ever gonna come to breakfast? I got mo' to do 'round here than fix breakfast for two love birds."

"Go away, Lizzy," Isabel said. "We got mo to do in here than worry about breakfast."

"This younga generation ain't got no shame," Lizzy said and laughed as she walked off down the hall.

Isabel left Ansel in bed and unpacked his bag and trunk that Jed had found at the gate and brought up to the veranda. She stormed back into the bedroom.

"J. Ansel, just what were you doing with a British uniform? You better tell me everything you've been doing or you can sleep in the barn. You lied, lied, lied to me. And what do you mean you could be called back in an advisory capacity?"

Ansel told her what he had been doing, how he had been wounded, why he had to carry on the British officer charade, and how it all must remain secret.

After she calmed down Ansel said it was her turn to bring him up to date on her activities. She went over the books, said she was worried about a bug called the boll weevil that was said to be coming in from Mexico and was ruining cotton crops in West Texas. "We're doing pretty good here and in Cuba. The rum distillery is finally beginning to make a little money."

Ansel grabbed her and fell into a chair with his wife in his lap. He kissed her and said, "You are magnificent. Let's go to New Orleans and buy you a new dress."

"I'm married to a crazy man."

"Yes. I'm crazy in love with you. I'm tired of being the last Quinn. Let's make some new Quinns."

And so they did, and all went well . . . for a while.

EPILOGUE

The Quinns worked hard and lived well. America did go to war and Ansel was called to put his uniform on and go to Washington, first for a command performance before General John Joseph "Black Jack" Pershing and then to serve under Army Chief of Staff, General Peyton C. March. Isabel went with him. Major Quinn was the only one in the Capital who had actually seen the slaughter of trench warfare. Although President Wilson declared war in April 1917, American troops did not see combat until May of 1918. Even though the United States was engaged in combat for only six months, Ansel agonized over American losses—116,016 killed which worked out to a little over 19,000 a month. There were 204,002 Americans wounded and 3,350 listed as missing. That may have been small in comparison to the 10,000,000 men lost by the Allies and the Central powers combined, but there was hardly a city or town in America that didn't lose young men.

Ansel and Isabel saw the prices of their crops fall after the war, and worse they suffered some crop failures, but as a result of the passage of Prohibition in 1919, the rum distillery in Cuba saved them. They danced during the Roaring Twenties in Paris. Ansel almost got into trouble in the rum business. Then came the Great Depression.

The couple did produce new Quinns, two boys. Just twenty years after the Armistice of 1918 ended World War I, a new world war was begun. By 1943, once again young Quinn men were in uniform.

ABOUT THE AUTHOR

Thomas E. Simmons grew up in Gulfport, Mississippi, and attended Marion Military Institute, the US Naval Academy, the University of Southern Mississippi, and the University of Alabama. He has been a pilot since the age of sixteen and has participated in air shows, flying aerobatics in open-cockpit biplanes. In the late 1950s, Simmons served as an artillery officer in Korea. He is the author of *The Man Called Brown Condor*, *Forgotten Heroes of World War II*, *Escape from Archangel*, and the Quinn Saga. Simmons has also written numerous magazine articles and has been published in *The Oxford American*.

THE QUINN SAGA

FROM OPEN ROAD MEDIA

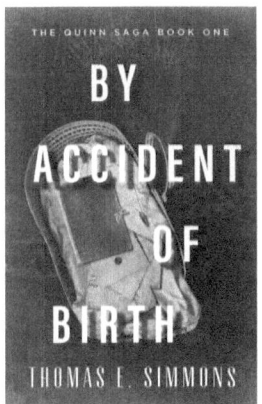

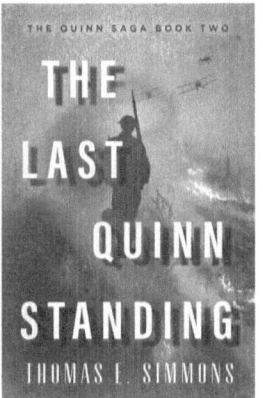

INTEGRATED MEDIA

www.ingramcontent.com/pod-product-compliance
Lightning Source LLC
Chambersburg PA
CBHW031949010726
47493CB00007B/2135